EAGLE Dancer

THE CRYSTAL LEGACY SERIES

SHARON SILVA

EAGLE DANCER
THE CRYSTAL LEGACY SERIES
BOOK TWO

A novel of Romantic Suspense with Paranormal Elements

Copyright© 2014 by Sharon Silva

ISBN 978-0-9906196-2-8 electronic format
ISBN 978-0-9906196-3-5 Print format

Cover and Book Design by THE KILLION GROUP
www.thekilliongroupinc.com

This book is a work of fiction. All names, characters, places and incidents are either products of the author's imagination or used fictitiously. Any resemblance to actual events, locales or persons, living or dead, are entirely coincidental.

DEDICATION

This book is dedicated to my family, my husband, Dan, the love of my life, my son, Jeremy and my daughter, Lizz. Thank you for always believing in me. Even when life pulled me in too many directions and I was unsure of myself, you and your love were always there for me.

This book series is purely a creation of my heart and mind. It is product of my imagination and the pictures that exist only in my mind's eye. It is not intended to precisely depict historic facts or to specifically replicate in any way the beliefs or actions of any ethnic group or sector of the population. It was written solely for the purpose of entertainment and for those who enjoy the adventure of exploring the depths of possibility. And it is to you, too, that I dedicate this book.

The Crystal Legacy Series

The Crystal Legacy began a thousand years ago in the canyons and on the mesas of the desert Southwest, when an ancient secret was passed to a peaceful people destined to become the messengers that will help save the Earth Mother and all mankind.

For the unsuspecting members of a modern day family, the fulfillment of that legacy began with a mysterious letter written by their grandfather's shaky hand.

To my grandchildren,

Expect a package in the coming days. Each of you is about to receive a piece of your heritage, a gift from my brother in the form of family heirloom. Forgive my hesitation in passing these on to you. I am not a superstitious man, but your great uncle's writings give me cause for concern.

A secret, long kept, is somehow associated with these gifts, and I fear my brother left us before it could be passed along. I am unclear on their significance but I do not believe it was a coincidence that he passed from this world on December 21, 2012, the very day of the ending of the Mayan calendar. Though it did not bring the end of the world as many thought, more than one indigenous people believed in the ending of an era, and I for one believe that passage into the next one will not come without an upheaval in the spirit world of monumental proportion.

Go forward with care.

Grandfather Nakai

PROLOGUE

1285 A.D.

Lone Eagle pressed his hand hard against the rock formation. It spoke to him. The stone cried out with the pain of his ancestry, a cry that only he could hear. Not a scream heard with the ears, but one that seared his heart.

Blood Rock. Legend said it was stained red by the gods as a symbol of the bloodshed of recent years. He recalled the story of the old Medicine Chief. To show her anger over the killing, the Earth Mother had vomited the blood of her children and hardened it to stone.

Lone Eagle traced his finger along the deep red lines in the rock's crevices and felt the moisture on his hand as he cast his eyes to the dark cloudless sky. Tonight the stone wept, just as it had the night his mother died. His chest tightened and his throat burned. Grief still haunted his heart.

Tears from the rock were always an omen, an omen of heartache to come. It had always meant that for him. Lone Eagle slumped to the ground and listened to the sounds of the night. Wind whistled through the pine trees and cedars. They whispered his name. It was the spirit voices that called him here. Awakened him in the dead of night. Voices he must keep secret from all living souls.

"Who, who," called a distant owl as if asking the spirits to identify themselves. The screech of a nighthawk joined the shrill cries coupled with the mournful howl of a coyote somewhere on the canyon rim.

A twig snapped in the darkness. Fear caught in Lone Eagle's throat. *Raven.* The mere mention of his murderous uncle's name turned the blood in his veins to ice. He hunkered into a depression in the rock and waited.

The soft sound of approaching footsteps crunched on the gravel embankment. Lone Eagle fingered his hunting knife and tried to still his hammering heart. A shadow darkened the earth in front of him as it stepped between him and the light of the full moon.

A whisper broke the silence. "Lone Eagle, is that you?"

Relief flooded his being. The small figure moved closer. "Mourning Dove." He breathed a heavy sigh. "What are you doing out here?" he scolded, reaching for her as relief filled him.

"You must come," she answered quickly, slipping from his grasp. "Your father wants you in the kiva."

"My father," he huffed. "We should all be asleep this time of night." He pulled her to him.

Her deep brown eyes reflected the light of the moon; beautiful, seductive and full of fire even by the dark of night. At the sight of her, passion flooded his heavy heart. The temptation was too great. He brushed the softness of her cheek as he sought the comfort of her kiss, but she turned away.

"Now is not the time," she whispered, tossing aside her long black hair before she scurried off into the darkness.

He paused to cast a pinch of corn pollen from the pouch at his waist to the four directions. He must show reverence to those who had called him to the rock, and to the spirit of his dead mother.

The chill of the night ran through his body, naked except for a breach cloth covering his man parts. Those too were chilled now, both by the night and Mourning Dove's rejection.

Cool mountain air and his eerie encounter with the ancients caused his flesh to prickle with tiny goose bumps. He was breathless when he reached the hand and footholds in the canyon wall. Above, Mourning Dove disappeared into the alcove just ahead of him. With the strength and agility of a wild cat, he climbed the wall with ease.

His sandals snapped softly on the stone beneath his feet as he hurried back through the dwellings. Striking a large pebble with his foot, it skittered across the plaza. The sound magnified in the silence of the sleeping village.

Light glowed up ahead through the square opening where a rough pine ladder protruded. Descending the ladder into the kiva, the mingled scents of wood smoke and smoldering herbs burned his eyes and singed his nose with its acrid odor. As he neared the last step, the warmth of the fire washed over his chilled body.

"Eagle." Chief Crow Feather sat by the fire. "Come. Sit. We will talk." The older man seemed in a jovial mood for such a late hour. The flames crackled and sparks flew upward into the black night sky. Firelight danced in eerie shadows on the kiva walls.

Lone Eagle eyed him suspiciously. An unexplained feeling of foreboding nagged at him. "The spirits of the night still cover us. What is so important?" he asked hesitantly.

"I am your father. When I command, you obey. I have no need to explain my reasons."

"Obey?" The words struck old wounds; internal scars left by the years Eagle and his mother had lived at the mercy of the oppressive man. The dormant anger fueled new courage. "Why do you speak to me like a child?"

The chief's eyes ran the full length of Eagle's height. "You are surely not a child. Though it seems by your attitude that you have somewhere else you can go," he huffed arrogantly.

Eagle glowered at his father. "I am a grown man and a warrior."

The chief nodded, a discerning look upon his face. "And who then will fill your empty belly and give you shelter from the icy white blankets of winter?"

"I can provide for myself," Eagle retorted.

"I have no doubt. You are a good hunter and you might even survive in the shelter of abandoned villages." Crow Feather pushed at the logs in the fire with a branch, sending sparks scurrying like fireflies. He turned his dark riveting eyes on Eagle. "But tell me, who will protect you from Raven and the others?"

"I think you exaggerate Raven's threat." Eagle stared into the fire, remembering his earlier fear, but avoiding his father's gaze.

"Fool. If Raven knew about your mother, if he knew of your ancestry, you would be as cold and dead as the one who pushed you from her womb." The old man spat into the fire. "Even so, Raven needs no reason to kill these days. If not for me, you would have been fair game for Raven's spear long ago. Now sit by the fire and stop this ridiculous talk."

Eagle glared at his father as he considered the chief's words, then sat on the chilly clay floor across the fire from him. Resentment still boiled in his core. "It was not my mother's fault that she was the sister of the spirit leader, Song of the Eagle. But still you blame her—and me." With the death of Song of the Eagle, it had become a curse.

The chief's brow was furrowed. "Nor was it my fault that my brother Raven turned to evil and changed the lives and the ways of the people. But still *you* blame me."

Lone Eagle shook his head. "The people have little to do with anything any more. What once was exists no more. There is no unity, no peace among them. Years of fear and turmoil have changed the face of all that used to be." The people had divided and hidden away. Many clans had formed and spread across the expanse of the mesa. New villages had sprung up and built their defenses hoping to keep out Raven's wrath. "Death is the only thing certain among the people now."

Crow Feather's lips curled in a menacing grin. "You talk too much to those who lived when things were under the old rule. You did not live here in those times. What do you know of such things?"

Lone Eagle looked down and rubbed his fingers in the dust on the hardened clay floor, the place where many elders once gathered for ceremonies. No matter what his father said, the heart and soul of his history was here. He brought his gaze back to his father. "Peace and freedom were never part of my past, but that does not mean I do not hunger for them."

"Erase such nonsense from your mind. It is because of me that you do not know what real hunger means." His eyes narrowed and his lips rolled over yellowed teeth. "You need to remember that I am the chief of this clan and in my mind the past is dead."

"Dead. Just like my mother?"

"Your mother is dead by her own choice, not mine." Crow Feather hissed.

Lone Eagle's jaw tightened as he choked back his anger. "She may not have died by your choice, but it was because of your actions she did not want to live."

"What would you know of my actions?"

"My mother told me of them—of how you took her by force." Eagle spat into the fire.

Crow Feather's eyes grew dark and a shadow seemed to cross his face. "You may think you understand, but that is only because you do not know the truth. At least you knew your mother. My mother died giving me life. For more than ten years my father and I wandered with a clan of nomads before we came to live among the Spirit leaders. It was here on this mesa that Raven was born to our father's second wife."

Crow Feather's lips drew into a thin line as he continued in a low voice. "What you do not know is that Raven was not the first to hate the Spirit leaders and what they stood for. He was just the one who was successful in destroying them. When I was seventeen and still living in the village, Song's father humiliated my father before the elders of the clan and banished him from the village."

Shadows danced on the wall forming grotesque images as Crow Feather continued his eerie story. "My father's anger was fierce and fueled even stronger when Raven and his mother were allowed to remain. I was offered the choice, too, and I left with my father and returned to the nomads. But revenge festered in my father's soul for three long years, and one night when the band had returned to the area, he stole away the Spirit leader's eldest daughter and took her captive. That girl was your mother, she was only sixteen years old at the time."

He poked the logs of the fire again with the branch he still held and ground the tip of it into the floor. His eyes reflected the flames. "My father took her intending to kill her, and had I not begged for her life, and made her my own, she would have died that night."

Lone Eagle's gut tightened with each of Crow Feather's revelations. "I see, you saved her out of the kindness of your heart. Why then did you not let her return to her family?"

"Because that was never possible again. Can't you see she was better off that I took her than left her to my father's wrath. Even life with me as a nomad was better than no life at all."

"I'm not sure she felt that way."

The older man's eyes narrowed. "Did I do so wrong by her? I gave her a son."

"She was not the only woman you gave sons." Lone Eagle snorted.

"Yes, I became a man much like my father—more than I'd like to be in many ways. But, nonetheless, I gave her a child."

"And took her pride."

"I gave her sanctuary," Crow Feather retorted.

"In exchange for her self-respect."

Anger reddened Crow Feather's face. "I let her live."

"And stole her soul." Lone Eagle shook his head sadly.

"My father would have killed her," Crow Feather hissed between his teeth.

"Then tell me why *you* wanted her?"

Memories clouded Crow Feather's face and his eyes softened. "She was a beautiful woman. I had long admired her from afar."

"So it was just her flesh you wanted?" Eagle's mocking words were filled with contempt.

"That I cannot deny." Crow Feather paused. "But there is still much you do not understand. I loved her in the beginning. Then it became a challenge for me. No matter what I did to her, she did not yield to me. She was the one thing I could never totally possess. The one woman I could not break. She always held fast to some unexplainable peace in her soul that I could not conquer. You have that peace within you, too." His eyes narrowed and his glare was chilling.

Eagle's mouth went dry. The truth made for dangerous conversation with Crow Feather. His were not casual threats. But the pain of his mother's death made Eagle careless tonight. His anger boiled and he pushed for answers. "I still do not understand why she stayed with you."

"Fool. She stayed because of you. Love kept her with me, but it was her love for you, not me. When she was first captured, we were days from here before we stopped. She was very young and very frightened.

Later, she knew she would never survive with a child on such a long journey. When eventually we returned, she wanted no one to know who she was."

"Because she knew Raven would kill us both."

"Yes." Crow Feather hissed. "Finally you understand."

"But why did you bring our family back here when you heard of Raven's take over?" Lone Eagle ran his hand across his face. His father's reasons still escaped him.

The old man studied him. "If not for my relationship with your mother, all of what once existed would now be gone." His voice was calm, but his eyes were troubled. "What if Raven, and the new ways, cannot survive?"

Eagle snorted softly as the realization came to him. "Then you realized that my mother and I were *your* safety, *your* protection, no matter what happened." He shook his head sadly. "If the new structure failed, you had a part of the old leadership to use to your advantage."

"Your mother is gone."

"And your hatred and your challenge is now centered on me." Eagle cast his eyes to the floor, not wanting Crow Feather to see into his soul. "And as long as I live, you have the last of Song of the Eagle's descendants. And you have your tie to Raven. You have protection from both clans and the security that somehow you will always be among its leaders."

"Remember this, young Eagle. Do not take this knowledge for granted. Your mother gave you life. Now I am the one who has the power to decide if you keep it." The old chief shot an evil look from beneath his furrowed brow.

"But why did Raven allow you to come back?"

"Because I am his only living family. The older brother he idolized as a child. And Raven never knew what happened. No one here ever knew. He was too young to remember your mother."

"And you no doubt are his kindred spirit. Unless he knew you were deceiving him."

"Silence. Enough." Crow Feather snapped the stick he held in two and cast it into the fire.

Eagle crossed his arms. His father was indeed the chief, the chief in control of Eagle's life and destiny. And since his mother's death, Eagle carried the dark secrets of her soul. Secrets he now realized he, too, must take to his grave. Silence was indeed his only option.

"And now you will honor my wishes." Crow Feather's expression was deadly serious. Their eyes locked across the fire pit.

The words caught in Lone Eagle's throat, as he knew he must swallow his anger. He nodded. "For now."

Eagle's brave arrogance on this night surprised him. At Crow Feather's order, members of the clan were banished from the camp. And the old man was right. None ever returned. Crow Feather's protection from his brother Raven's wrath was the key to survival, the only chance any one living possessed.

Eagle purposely avoided his father's dark, piercing eyes. There was no love there for him, nor had there ever been. His resemblance to his mother and her inherent fiery spirit had always been a plague to him. Crow Feather loathed him and his existence. And not until tonight did he know why his father kept him in his protective circle.

He'd often thought of lashing out at the chief and his demeaning orders. Eighteen summers had passed since his birth. But for as long as the old man lived, so did the clan, and so did Eagle. In case, some day Eagle might be of use. He swallowed hard. It was an arrangement of survival—for everyone.

Lone Eagle stared into the fire, silently awaiting his father's orders. Waiting to hear the reason he'd been summoned in the middle of the night.

"Tomorrow you will go to the far side of the mesa where the winter snows are melting."

"As you ask, Father." Lone Eagle nodded.

"Bring me back a black bear, the largest one you can find."

Eagle's eyes darted to Crow Feather and the old man responded with a yellowed grin.

"Is it fear that I see in your eyes?" The chief cackled softly.

"No. But I want to know why you ask me to do this."

"I'll get to that. You needn't worry. The bear is just waking from the long sleep. It will be hungry, but still weak and easier for you to find and kill."

Killing a bear was a daunting and dangerous task for the most skillful hunter, but that was not what bothered Lone Eagle. "The bear is sacred to us. He has always been a symbol to our people. We were always taught by the elders that we do not kill the bear for food, for he cries out with a human voice."

"We do not take the bear for food. We are not hungry. We still have venison from the last hunt. That is not my concern or yours."

"Then why kill the bear?"

"I want the teeth and claws. If I were still young, I would kill the bear myself. But I am not and you are youthful and strong. Far better that you do this than I."

Lone Eagle raised his eyebrows. "It is not our way to kill for such things alone. We take only what we need from the land."

"You are your mother's child, not mine," Crow Feather said in disgust. "But I have always known that."

A chill ran through Eagle. If the old man knew the real truth in his words, Eagle would be cold and dead beneath the rock slabs next to his mother.

Crow Feather threw a handful of dried leaves into the fire and smoke swirled in the chamber. "How quickly you forget that we are a new people now. The old ways are not our ways."

"The old ways are still part of some of us."

"And for some, it is time for change." Crow Feather stared into the fire. The flames flared high, lighting the chamber as bright as daylight. "The meat of the bear will not be wasted. The women will see to that. Your job is only to kill it and bring it back to camp."

"I will do as you say. I will bring you the bear." Experience had taught Lone Eagle to choose his battles. There were many others left to fight. He rose to his feet.

The shadows of the fire danced on the chief's face. A crooked smile twisted his mouth. Crow Feather raised his voice and motioned for Lone Eagle to sit. "We are not finished. You agree to violate the old beliefs and kill the animal, but you have not asked for what I would use such spoils."

"The reason seems of little concern." Lone Eagle glared at the old man. "You speak. I honor your wishes. That is as it has always been."

"Indeed it is." The old man acknowledged him with gleaming eyes. "The bear's claws and teeth are to become part of a special gift for your brother, Black Hawk."

"Why am I not surprised?" Lone Eagle scoffed. "I am to put myself in danger and take the life of a sacred animal for a new ornament for my brother. Some things will never change."

"This isn't an ordinary gift. I said it was special." Crow Feather's lips curled as he spoke.

"What does it matter? He has always been the favored son. He may look much as I do, but the blackness of his heart and spirit are undeniably yours."

"He is truly my son in spirit, and I'll not tolerate your insults."

Eagle rose. "I must go now. Dawn will be here soon and I have a hard and thankless task ahead of me."

Crow Feather's eyes narrowed and the smile returned. "The breast plate will be given as a gift for your brother in celebration of his choosing a mate."

"A fine gift indeed. And what unfortunate maiden has agreed to be his wife?" He tired of Crow Feather's constant gloating about Black Hawk.

"Why the most beautiful maiden in the camp." The old man sneered. "Mourning Dove."

Lone Eagle's heart fell to the pit of his stomach. His body wavered momentarily. Blood rushed to his head and pounded in his temples. He clenched his teeth and hissed at the chief. "You are lying. She would never agree to this."

"She doesn't have to agree. It will be done by my command."

Choking back the mass that formed in his throat, Lone Eagle whirled and started up the ladder. "I will die before I allow this to happen and you know it."

"That would be your choice, not mine." Crow Feather gazed into the fire with a look of contentment on his face.

Lone Eagle climbed the ladder, dizzied by anger so fierce it shot pain to the top of his head. The old chief had finally found the key to destroying Eagle's soul. But Eagle meant what he said. He would die before he allowed it to happen. He'd take his chances with Raven before he'd allow Black Hawk to touch the woman he loved.

A rustle in the darkness made him stop. Was it Black Hawk, hiding close to enjoy Eagle's torment along with their father? Lone Eagle whirled, ready to take on his nemesis. Instead Mourning Dove stood trembling in the shadows.

"I cannot believe what I have heard." Her voice was strained with anguish.

Lone Eagle set his jaw. "Believe. He lives only for the sake of evil. He derives joy only from other's pain. And mine pleases him most of all."

She shook her head. "This cannot happen. I will not be the mate of Black Hawk."

Lone Eagle placed his hand on her arm. "Go now. I need time to think."

Mourning Dove stepped away and Lone Eagle stood in the moonlight. He stared up at the full moon. If only the gods would intervene and stop this insanity and pain. It had gone too far.

He turned his head and listened. Music from a distant flute carried on the stiff breeze. Something in his soul stirred. Perhaps the gods had answered.

— ·—

Mourning Dove hunkered low in the shadows watching the warrior she loved dearly. Surely, he would find a way to stop this. She bit her lower lip. And he had the power to do just that. She had seen him use it as a child, but she dared not tell him, dared not speak of it.

He seemed unaware of the powers he possessed, powers that came to him from the great spirit leaders of old. All her life she'd feared to make him aware, feared he would use them openly, and no doubt Crow Feather would kill him. Now they both desperately needed that gift from the gods.

If they could not stop Crow Feather, her destiny was set. She would be the mate of Black Hawk, the man she despised. While the one she truly loved was destined to sit by and watch. Could what lie on the outside be worse than the future that lay ahead if they stayed?

Crow Feather cackled to himself as he sat by the fire. That had gone quite well. The look in Eagle's eyes was worth all the turquoise in Chaco. The pain on his face had brought the old chief great pleasure.

"Now you see that I am the one with power," he shook his fist skyward. Lone Eagle's mother must surely be watching this victory.

Crow Feather huffed in pleasure. Even after eighteen summers, Lone Eagle knew nothing of the real power he possessed. This was good. Each day the chances grew better that he would never know of his gifts. Gifts that threatened to bring the rage of Raven upon them, if word got out. Gifts that Crow Feather himself would keep secret, unless one day he needed to use them to his advantage.

He'd watched the boy playing as a child and knew then that he was not like others. His mother's blood had brought the gifts of the old spirit leaders to him. But fear had kept his mother's tongue silent. His son did not realize what he possessed. And that is, as it would stay.

His cruelty to the boy had kept things just as Crow Feather wanted them. Lone Eagle must live in constant fear of his father and fear for his life. It was how things must remain.

He smiled smugly. Indeed he had been wise to take Eagle's mother and force his seed upon her. Now, he had a secret defense if things went sour with his own brother's murderous rampage. And Eagle was still tightly in Crow Feather's control.

He had failed to revolt against his father even on this night. Lone Eagle would go against his own beliefs and kill the sacred bear for him. And even when Crow

Feather had taken the one thing from him that meant the most, his beloved Mourning Dove, still his son did not raise his hand against him. Crow Feather chuckled contentedly and lay back on his sleeping mat. His world was secure beyond his own imaginings.

CHAPTER ONE

Present Day

The girl's shoes clattered on the brick-lined path that wove through the tall trees in the city park. The sound echoed. She slowed her steps, glanced around and listened. A dark eerie feeling crept over her and held fast like the smattering of damp leaves clung to the stones under her feet. It was broad daylight, mid-afternoon in high summer, and no logical reason existed for the foreboding possessing her soul.

She would be late getting home and no doubt she'd be in trouble—again. It was a stupid choice to listen to her friends. At fifteen she should be more responsible, but those were her mother's words, not her own.

Shaking off the sensation, she picked up her pace. Crossing at the signal, she made her way down the quiet street. Distant flute music from the plaza drifted on a breeze that swept hair across her eyes. She tucked the long strands behind her ear. The music was high pitched and surreal. Normally, it made her feel wild and free, stirred something in her soul. Today it ran a chill down her spine. A heavy feeling carried on the wind and hung in her chest unlike anything she'd ever experienced.

Her feet seemed weighted, protesting their movement as if they didn't want to go this way. But some other force drew her down the street. A whispering voice seemed to call her name. An invisible hand pushed her forward, onward, ever closer—.

A large black and white magpie pecked at the brick sidewalk a few yards ahead. As she neared, it turned a dark eye in her direction. The bird sized her up then hopped into the shadowy space between two adobe buildings. Suddenly, a boy clad in black stepped from the alley and into her path. A black hat, pulled low, hovered over his eyes, blocking them from clear view. A black and white feather hung from the hat's brim partially covering one side of his face. He folded his arms and turned in her direction. She watched from the corner of her eye and attempted to sidestep him. As she did, she glanced up.

"Oh, it's you," she uttered, relief flooding her at the sight of a familiar face. The boy didn't answer. His gaze met hers, but the strange eyes that peered from under the hat's brim were like those of a wild cat watching its prey. Their odd light stopped her heart in mid-beat.

Fear grabbed at her throat, and robbed her voice. Something about those eyes filled her with terror. She must get past him. She hurried ahead. His hand caught her arm, stopping her short.

"Let go," she squeaked in protest. A flash of white passed through her field of vision. He spun her around, her head whipped back. Piercing pain and intense pressure seared her neck. It took away her breath, stole her voice before she could scream.

She grabbed at her throat. Her fingers grasped a taut cord. Fighting for air, her lungs racked with pain. The cord tightened. Spots exploded behind her eyes. Her knees buckled. The weight of her body drove the cord deeper. She struggled to her feet. Her throat seized and she fell to the ground. A sensation of slow motion masked her senses. Blackness engulfed her. She fought it at first then at last gave way to it.

In the midst of the blackness, a distant white light burned then came closer. Bright, warm, soothing. It beckoned her weary body to its comfort. A drifting feeling pulled at her. She allowed herself to move toward it, away from the agony in her throat and lungs. The pain eased.

Into the light stepped a shadow. An image emerged from the bright glow as if it had stepped through a cloud. The silhouette became a dark-haired man, broad at the shoulders and narrow at the hips. Floating around him in the light were feathers, brown and white feathers. His face cleared. Soft brown eyes greeted her. Hands reached for her, offering help. A breeze tousled his hair, as a slightly crooked smile deepened a scar on his upper lip. The intensity of the light overshadowed his face, the image faded and the pain was gone.

The icy lash of a crashing wave jarred Nathan Nakai back to reality. He shifted his feet and steadied himself on the San Francisco pier. The haunting picture of the dark-haired girl with the rope tight around her neck vanished as quickly as it had overtaken him. He loosened his tie. The pain in his throat eased and he wiped beads of cold perspiration mingled with ocean mist from his face.

Breathing in the cool salty air, his head began to clear. The girl's face was ingrained in his mind. He shook his head trying to push it away. Maybe he needed a sabbatical from this fast-paced life worse than he thought. Or maybe this was the sign he was seeking here in the darkness and solitude of a foggy night, as his discontent churned like the white-capped waves that pounded the wooden pillars and planks beneath his feet.

The unsettling emotion lingered as Nate stared into the heavy fog that rolled into the bay. He pulled the overcoat up around his ears. He glanced over his shoulder at the towering buildings and city lights of downtown behind him then looked out across the rolling ocean waters that disappeared into fog and darkness. He thought of the vast horizon beyond where sea met sky and appeared to become one and he knew without doubt—his purpose here had been served.

Gathering focus back to his purpose and his future, he reread the job offer he grasped in his hand by the light of a nearby street lamp dimmed by the mist. The letterhead read, "Public Defenders Department, Staff Attorneys District Office, Santa Fe, New Mexico."

Why the hell had he even considered leaving his successful law practice in San Francisco? He'd asked himself that question a million times and still he didn't have a clue. Some voice deep inside was calling him, something he couldn't identify, something he couldn't name and stronger tonight than it had ever been.

The cold wind that blew in from the bay suddenly shifted, and ran a chill down the back of his neck. He pulled the coat collar tighter. He only knew one thing. He had to go.

Flipping aside the job offer, he eyed the envelope he clutched behind it, the letter from his grandfather. He'd received it along with a package two days earlier. The chilling words of the strange letter haunted him and now he regretted not taking the time to open the box. He was curious, but the package was in a moving van in route to Santa Fe. Undeniably, his grandfather's words had invoked thoughts of his family, and kindled a curiosity about his own heritage.

Nate reflected on his last conversation with his brother Alex. He'd wondered at times if Alex had slipped a cog somewhere between California and Southwestern Colorado. After all the time his archaeologist brother had spent poking around old ruins in Mexico and South America, maybe something had gone wrong with his thinking.

But it was Alex's words that had started a fire in Nate's soul—a need for change that had become insatiable. An emptiness he'd never realized existed had opened up like a gaping pit in the core of his being. He sighed. *Gee thanks little brother.*

Nate rubbed his temples. He was tired, yet he couldn't put his finger on why. Worse yet, he was sickened by his own existence. Maybe it was the big city, the people, or the rat race—

Or maybe he was simply sick of what his practice had become. A parade of rich people and their kids who failed to find happiness in their wealth. And who tried to buy their way out of drug charges, abusive behavior and sometimes worse. He wasn't proud of the course his life had taken, a criminal lawyer, whose clientele and lonely life left him cold as the foggy mist surrounding him.

Alex had found something that brought him peace in what he referred to as his "ancestral past." It was Nate's past, too, Native American in origin—Navajo and Hopi according to Alex's research. Nate wasn't sure how to find that kind of peace. Heritage was something they'd been distanced from all their lives. Alex could dig it out of the earth and hold it in his hands. Nate would have to find it in his own way.

He clutched the letters as the stiff ocean breeze tugged at them. "Oh no," he whispered as he tucked them into the inner pocket of his overcoat and again looked out over the bay. "I'm not giving you any more."

A spray of salty ocean water blew over him as another wave crashed against the pier. A cleansing, he thought, symbolic of the cleansing of his life and spirit. Tomorrow he'd board a plane and within the week he'd begin a new life. A fresh start in a new land lay ahead of him—on a path paved with questions he'd never dared ask.

CHAPTER TWO

If Satan himself, complete with a pitchfork, had walked through the door, Nate doubted the boy would have looked more surprised. When Nate entered, the boy's jaw dropped. His face went pale as the gray walls of the stark interrogation room of the Santa Fe County Jail. It seemed an odd reaction to a total stranger, even for a fifteen-year-old kid who'd suddenly found himself accused of attempted murder.

Nate met the wide-eyed stare of the boy's dark deep-set eyes. He looked like a hoot owl caught in a flashlight beam, but the look immediately fell to the gray table top in front of him.

A young Hispanic deputy punched the boy's arm. "You better wake up, kid. This guy's your lawyer." Nearly frozen in his chair, the kid glanced up as if he half-expected Nate to be gone.

The deputy shook his head and turned to Nate as he crossed the room. "Knock on the door when you're done."

"Thanks." Nate turned his attention to the figure seated at the table. The boy looked up as the door closed, dark shadows haunted his eyes. They followed Nate across the room as he seated himself in a chair on the opposite side of the table. The boy leaned cautiously closer, frowning as he took in the details of Nate's face

"What are you doing?" Nate asked quietly, then feeling self-conscious ran his hand over his face.

Damn. Was half his lunch stuck to his chin or something?

At Nate's question, the boy pulled back. His shoulders drawn back like a soldier at attention.

What the hell was that all about? Nate shook off the strange greeting and studied his new client. In the stark gray room, the boy looked small and out of place. Nate's gut wrenched. *Kids and crime.* It was one thing he'd hoped he'd left behind in the big city. Obviously, he had not.

Hoping the strangeness of that first encounter would pass, Nate attempted an introduction. "Nathan Nakai." He reached out a hand to the boy then drew it back, feeling a little perturbed by the boy's lack of response. He shook his head. This could end up as murder one. *Kid, you better get your act together.*

The boy stared at his hands. Nate detected a quiver. The boy was scared shitless. He was clad in a black T-shirt and blue jeans. His dark eyes were set in a narrow bronze face and his straight black hair touched his shoulders. A piece of rawhide encircled his head. Nate stifled a grimace. Give or take a headband, he wasn't any different from a San Francisco kid in trouble.

Nate opened his briefcase under the boy's watchful eye. "Okay, Johnny. I'm here to help you. You got a last name?" Nate placed a yellow pad of paper on the tabletop.

Johnny didn't answer. He appeared to be deep in thought.

Damn. Maybe the kid had some sort of disability. If he did, this case would be over before it started. He scanned his notes. No mental eval had been done.

The boy eyed him suspiciously then his face lit up. He pointed his finger at Nate. "Did my grandpa send you?"

"Your grandpa?" *What the hell was he talking about?* "No, boy, the state sent me. I'm your lawyer."

Nate pushed back his gut reaction trying not to shout at the kid. "They said you couldn't afford counsel, so luck of the draw, you get me and I get you. I think you know what I look like by now. So how about you stop gawking and we get on with this."

"Know what you look like? I've looked at your face so many times, it's pathetic. I just didn't know you were real." Johnny put his hands over his eyes. "I think I get it. This whole thing's a nightmare."

"Real? What?" Nate asked. *Wow.* The boy must be delusional. "Johnny, you got some sort of *problem?*"

"*Problem?* Whatta you mean?"

"It's okay, son. You don't have to be embarrassed."

There was no doubt the boy comprehended that one. The words hit home. Anger flashed across Johnny's face. The fear that clouded his expression moments before was replaced with defiance. "There's nothing wrong with me, mister. I just got locked up by a bunch of dumb cops and I want to go home. If you're a real lawyer, then get me outta here."

"Slow down, kid." This was a little better. At least the boy was alive. "I'll ask you again. You got a last name?"

"I go by Lone Wolf," Johnny snapped.

"Lone Wolf, huh. Interesting name." Nate scanned the police report.

"That's what I want to be called." Johnny sized up Nate. His wrath had ebbed a little. He sat back, crossed his arms and relaxed his shoulders though some question still seemed to lurk in the shadows of his eyes.

Nate rubbed his chin and surveyed his new client. "How old are you Johnny. Excuse me, *Lone Wolf?*"

"Eighteen," the boy answered stonily.

Nate looked over the top of the police report and stared at the boy. "Shall I ask again?"

Johnny shifted in his seat and refused to meet Nate's gaze. "Okay. Fifteen."

Nate slapped the report down on the table. He leaned close and spoke in a stern voice. "Let's talk turkey here, Johnny. If there's anybody you better tell the truth to, it's me. I'm on *your* side. And I guarantee you, nobody else is. Get that straight now."

Johnny squirmed. "Sorry."

"Where you from, kid?"

"Chimayo."

"And where would Chimayo be?"

"You're not from around here, huh?" The boy rolled his eyes.

Nathan looked at him without responding to the question. Straight from nitwit to smart-ass, that was quite a transformation. The kid sure as hell didn't need this attitude to help him get into prison. His chances weren't great without it.

"North. Up two eighty-five toward Taos." The boy ran his hand across his face in a fatigued gesture.

"What were you doing in Santa Fe?"

"I came here yesterday with some friends. You know. We came to goof around in town."

"What do you mean goof around? What did you do?"

"Went to a movie, hung around the arcade, messed around down on the plaza for a while."

"Is the plaza where you were arrested?"

"Yeah. That's where them dumb cops stopped us and started shoving' me around."

Nate placed his elbows on the table. "Son, do you really know what you're here for?"

Johnny's eyes went hard and steely. "A long, long time if you can't prove to them I didn't hurt that girl."

"Wrong, boy. It's *we*." Nate rose from his chair and leaned toward Johnny. "If *we* can't prove you didn't do it. If that girl dies, a real long time could be the rest of your life, *if you're lucky*."

"Whatta ya mean by lucky?"

"I mean if the girl dies, you're history. Lose the attitude. It's not going to get you anywhere."

Johnny swallowed hard, crossed his arms and stared at the table. Nate ran a hand through his hair.

"What about the girl, Johnny?"

"I don't know anything about it."

"You brought it up. You must know something."

"I know just what I told you. The cops think I tried to kill some girl. That's why I'm here."

"What else?"

"That's it. Somebody hurt this girl real bad and they arrested me."

"And you know nothing about it?"

"That's right, mister. I'm dumb as a rock."

"Only if you think that's all there is to it."

Johnny's eyes narrowed. "Trust me, I know what this is about. You don't have to treat me like a kid."

"You don't want to be treated like a kid, huh? Then, boy, you better grow up and stop acting like one. Do you know the girl?"

"I don't know."

"What do you mean you don't know?"

"I mean nobody told me who she is."

Odd. Nate scratched his chin. "They booked you without telling you the assaulted girl's name?"

Johnny nodded. "They didn't tell me nothin'."

Nate thumbed through the police report and made a note. "Stella Sanchez."

Johnny gave him a blank look as if he didn't hear.

"Stella Sanchez. That was her name. You know her?"

Johnny's face went pale. He swallowed hard and nodded.

"Then you do know her?"

"Yeah, I know her." Johnny's voice was low and shaky. He frowned. "It's not Stella. It's Stellar. You know, like the stars."

Nate went back to his notes. "Hmm. Must be a typo here."

Johnny scratched his forehead and stared at the wall for a moment in silent contemplation. His breathing seemed shallow. "Is she going to be okay?"

"I don't know. She's in bad shape."

Johnny's brow furrowed. "But she—"

"She's what?"

"Nothin'. She's hurt real bad, huh?"

Nate bit the inside of his cheek. What did this reaction mean? What was the boy really feeling? Surprise or remorse for his actions? Was he totally ignorant of the crime? Or had he randomly chosen a victim without knowing it was his friend? Question after question poured through Nate as he tried to decipher the boy's actions and reactions.

"You said you were with your friends. Where were you between one and two o'clock yesterday afternoon?"

"I took a walk."

"Alone?"

"Yeah. What of it?" Johnny rubbed his eyes. "I'm allowed. I'm a big guy."

Nate frowned. "No, kid, you're a little guy, a real little guy. A grease spot when the DA gets through with you, if you don't wise up."

"Oh God, the DA." Johnny slumped in the chair.

"Yeah, bud, the prosecution. You get it?"

Johnny didn't respond.

"You got an alibi for where you were yesterday afternoon?"

"Alibi?"

"Yeah. Were you with somebody between one and two?"

"I just told you I was alone."

Nate leaned into Johnny's face. "Look, tomorrow morning at ten o'clock, you're going to go before the judge. And I'm the one who's going to stand up there with you and tell the world you're innocent."

"Yeah." Johnny pulled back as far as he could but Nate followed, keeping himself inches from the boy's face.

"You damn sure better be telling me the truth, Johnny. Don't you make an ass out of me, boy."

"I told you everything I know. Honest." His lower lip quivered, his dark eyes shot to Nate's and held them for a moment. "You gotta help me, mister."

Something in his look was pitiful and childlike. All evidence of the attitude he'd flaunted earlier evaporated.

A flash of sympathy ran across Nate's chest. *Dammit.* Under that snot-nosed attitude was just a kid. Only was he an innocent kid or a guilty one? That question had Nate's gut in a knot.

"Your folks know where you are?"

Johnny's eyes and his demeanor softened. "I don't think so. Can you tell my sister?"

"Your sister? What about your mom and dad?"

He shook his head. "Ain't got either. Just Mary and Grandpa."

"Where is your sister?"

"Chimayo. She's probably real worried by now."

"Didn't you or the police call her?"

"Mister, after what my sister's been through, I couldn't tell her something like this on the phone. And I never told the police how to find her. I didn't tell 'em anything. Not even my real name."

Nate shot him a piercing look. "What is your real name, kid?"

"Begay. Johnny Begay." Obviously, that tough exterior had a soft underbelly after all.

"Okay, Johnny. I'll go tell your sis and your grandpa."

"Oh no, sir, please don't tell my grandpa." The look of fear returned to his face.

"Why not? From what you said earlier, I thought you wanted him to know?"

"*No, sir.*" A sad, solemn look shrouded the boy's face. "Me being in jail, shames my grandfather, and his people. I'd rather go to prison than face that." If nothing else he'd said was truth, Nate had no doubt about this.

Nate paused. The boy was up to his neck in trouble and his biggest worry was his image before his grandfather's people. There must be something more to this boy than met the eye, even if what he'd seen so far hadn't impressed him.

"Tell my sister, but promise me you won't tell my grandpa."

"Okay kid." Nate shook his head and handed Johnny a piece of paper. "Write down your sister's name and address for me. I'll go tell her myself."

"Thanks, mister."

Johnny scrawled an address on the paper and passed it back. Nate folded it and tucked it into his pocket.

"I have to go." Nate looked down at his hands folded on the tabletop. "You know tomorrow is just the beginning."

"I didn't hurt *anybody*, Mr. Nakai."

"You know some people say they saw you?"

His face wrinkled into a disbelieving frown and his eyes became instantly cold and steely. "Then they're liars." His eyes met Nate's. "Do you believe me?"

Nate paused, the words hanging in his throat. "I don't know. I'll tell your sis and we'll talk more later."

"I have to stay here?"

"For now. There's not much I can do about that at the moment."

The boy nodded.

Nate closed his briefcase and gave Johnny a half smile. "Try to get some rest." Nate turned toward the door and knocked for the deputy.

"Mr. Nakai." The boy's voice was sharp.

"Yes, boy."

"Don't worry. Spirit is strong in my people."

"I'm not worried, Johnny." Nate squinted at the young man as the deputy opened the door and let him out into the outer hall. Johnny's smile was confident. Nate's gut wasn't so self-assured.

—◄——

"Nakai." A voice bellowed down the hall as Nate reached for the door to his office. A man in a brown-tailored suit made his way toward Nate, a slight limp hindering his approach. The gray-haired man squared his shoulders and reared back his head, reminding Nate of a rooster, standing guard over his territory.

"Jim Smith, Santa Fe District Attorney." He extended his hand.

"Nathan Nakai." Nate accepted the clammy handshake, sensing something in Smith's demeanor that made him ill at ease.

"I know who you are." Smith paused and cleared his throat. "Heard you got your first case."

Nate surveyed Smith through suspicious eyes. "Yeah. Guess that's what I'm here for. Have to earn my keep somehow." Nate smiled at Smith's furrowed brow. Smith showed no sign of sharing in his amusement.

"My office is going for murder one," Smith said, sternly.

"Unless you know something I don't, the girl's still alive." Nate rubbed the back of his neck and loosened his tie.

Smith's eyes narrowed. "I'm prepared for the worst. I suggest you do the same."

Nate gritted his teeth. "I'm still reviewing the case, Mr. Smith. I'd prefer to hold my comments until I'm finished." If this guy was trying to piss him off it was working.

"Three eye witnesses on this one," Smith said gruffly. "It's a sure conviction."

Nate set his jaw. "Last I heard the law still read innocent until *proven* guilty."

"Arraignment's at ten tomorrow morning." Smith gave a nod but the piercing look in his eye nailed Nate to the wall.

"I'll be there." Uncomfortably, Nate turned back toward his office door.

"Nakai." Smith's tone sounded more like an army drill sergeant. Nate rotated to meet Smith's gaze. "My office has a perfect record for convictions in murder cases. What kind do you have?"

Nate rubbed his chin and squinted as he held Smith's steely eyes. "A perfect record for finding out the truth. Whatever it is."

Smith's scowl would have melted the fainthearted.

Nate didn't flinch. "Excuse me. I have business to attend to. I'm sure our paths will cross again."

"You can count on it," Smith grunted as Nate closed the door.

What the hell's up with this DA? Nate placed his briefcase on the desk, popped it open and thumbed through the case file, pondering Smith's words. So far he had a mouthy kid with no alibi, three eyewitnesses, and a DA with blood in his eye. The stage was set, and the game just got more interesting.

A wave washed over him, an overwhelming feeling that there was something here he was missing, something between the lines he couldn't read. His gut tightened. What he couldn't see would ultimately mean life or death to Johnny Begay.

With a heavy sigh, Nate sat down in the chair behind the desk. He sat there for a few minutes contemplating his morning and his next move. Glancing at his briefcase, he saw the letter from his grandfather and remembered the package now tucked away in his desk drawer. He unfolded the handwritten note and read quickly through it a second time as the strangeness of it claimed him once again. The old man's repeated reference to his discomfort with forwarding on the family heirlooms, nearly alluded to a warning, though he swore he was not superstitious. Nate smiled. It seemed there was a lot of long-held superstition when it came to his great uncle.

In the midst of his move, Nate had tucked the package away. Maybe it was time he looked inside. Tearing away the packing tape, and layers of bubble wrap, he saw a lavishly decorated wooden statue of some sort. His first look into the face of the figure sent an eerie feeling through him followed by a bone-deep chill when he put his hands around it and removed it from the box.

He examined it, admiring the craftsmanship of carefully carved feathers comprising its costume that included a mask carved with a bird-like intention, complete with a beak protruding below strange lifelike eyes. It was a unique family heirloom, indeed.

A note was tucked beneath the arm of the carving. Nate opened it and began to read.

Nathan,

I regret I never met you, but I know that our spirits have been connected through this life. I have felt the special power of your soul. Your ways of thinking do not lend to the details that have brought this gift to you. That information has been handed to your brothers and will come to you in time.

You have long lived on the surface of this lost and misguided world and participated fully in its inequities. The changes about to take place in your life will show you a deeper and more meaningful side of your existence and lead you to your destiny.

The Eagle is symbolic in many Native cultures as a messenger of the gods. This Hopi kachina is a symbol of the spirits who watch us from beyond the clouds, awaiting their return. In the days to come you will begin a journey of spirit and this kachina will play a vital role in the answers you seek.

In this package is a small box, meant especially for you. Do not open it until you are ready to embark on the next phase of your life's journey. You and only you will know when that time has come and its meaning will then be clear. Go forward with courage.

Your great uncle,
Hosiah Nakai

Nate rubbed his chin, attempting to decipher the meaning of the odd message. Was the old fellow some sort of preacher? The oddity of what this uncle had apparently known about Nate's life, struck too close to home. He started to replace the kachina in the box then changed his mind. Placing it on the corner of his desk, he said aloud. "Well, one thing's for sure, you should feel right at home here."

He shrugged and disposed of the wrappings, tucking the smaller box and the letters away in his desk for deeper consideration at another time. This talk of his family's past and his destiny were all well and good but they seemed like a lot of idyllic words. For now, he had more pressing matters that needed his attention.

CHAPTER THREE

Nate drove toward Chimayo as the sun hung above the mountains to the west. The New Mexico landscape was barren here by his standards. The trees were sparse and small, native grasses and sage seemed to cry out for moisture in the harsh dry climate. Yet, something about it was mystical, enchanting. As if Mother Nature had somehow compensated for the lack of water by adding nourishment for the spirit.

He couldn't put his finger on it, couldn't explain what touched him in such a mysterious way. There was a blending of cultures, a mingling of ancient ways and modern times, a simplification of life and an opportunity for the spirit to take time to understand. Something he'd never had the chance or the time to do.

The deep red earth itself spoke of the heritage here of the area's native people. From the deep blue skies, to the mesas and unique rock formations, it all seemed to have come together as an offering to both heaven and earth. A light-blue pickup truck sped past, raising a dirt cloud that whirled into a dust devil and danced off into the distance, coming to life from nothingness much as the landscape itself appeared to have done.

Since he'd first set foot in Santa Fe, he'd experienced a strange kinship with the place, an almost haunting sense of connection to the land. Something stirred deep inside him when he looked out across the vast openness skirted by stately mountain peaks in the distance. A remote corner of his memory said he'd seen it before, walked these sands at some time, but that was ludicrous. Yet he couldn't shake the feeling. Here alone on the quiet highway it rambled through the alcoves of his mind.

In some ways, he regretted the new burden he'd taken on. It weighted his soul and his mind. Periodically, he glanced down at the notes from the police report that lay on the seat beside him. Tugging at him, it drew him back from the mysterious place that repeatedly tried to claim his mind.

A fifteen-year-old girl, Stella—Stellar Sanchez—had been attacked in an alley near the plaza. An attempted strangulation. *Stellar.* Johnny's words and his reaction troubled Nate's thoughts. Interesting. Three eyewitnesses claimed to have seen Johnny at the crime scene. The police arrested him an hour later walking with his friends on the south side of the plaza.

The police report was sketchy, but specific in its details about the positive identification of the assailant, Johnny Begay. Johnny may have been operating under the illusion that the police didn't contact his sister because he didn't tell them who he was, but the report was to the contrary. There was a discomfort in Nate's mind around the reasons why no one had called Johnny's family, but that was a question he'd pursue later. For now he had a mission of his own to complete.

The highway ran through the middle of the tiny town of Chimayo, nestled in the foothills of the Sangre de Cristo Mountains. To Nate's surprise, the landscape here was much different from some of the open sweeping countryside he'd seen south of Santa Fe. This area had many more trees and farmlands.

The town was quaint and charming with a distinct New Mexican flair. Adobe buildings dotted both the main street and the road into town, many bearing gallery signs and traditional bundles of dried chilies hung from shop doorways along the roadside. Nate shrugged. Not the kind of place you'd expect a murderer to grow up in, but fairy tales aside, no place was exempt from such things.

Nate pulled onto a narrow well-marked street lined with an assortment of small houses. Some of these were adobe others built of wood or brick. The road wound through a tree-lined lane, bordered by small farms and cornfields, and went on for a mile or so before he saw the house number on a mailbox.

A small tan adobe house sat in the middle of what appeared to be a fairly large piece of land. Behind the house sprawled an open meadow dotted with beige and black sheep grazing in the distance. A maroon Pathfinder was parked next to the house. Nate pulled into the driveway and walked to the door. Several Spanish-style pots filled with flowers and plants lined the path between the house and patch of scraggly grass that served as a lawn.

Summoning his courage for the bad news he was about to lay on this family, he rapped on the screen door. As he waited, a large yellow and white cat accosted his feet, rubbing and purring loudly. A black and gray Australian Shepherd dog sat at the corner of the house, ears cocked, eyeing him suspiciously. The door opened a crack and a young girl peered out.

"Hi. Are you Mary?"

She giggled. "No. Mary is inside." The girl spoke with a strong Spanish accent.

"I need to speak with her." He pulled a business card from his wallet. The girl opened the door wider and reached for the screen, then stopped in her tracks. Her eyes widened and she gave him a startled look. Johnny's first reaction to him ran through his mind, but he opted to ignore the girl's response. He had no clue what it was about his appearance that startled these people, but he didn't have time to analyze it. He parked the question in the back of his mind for consideration at a later date.

"Would you please tell Mary I'm here?" He pushed the card at her. She batted her lashes and swallowed hard, then reluctantly reached for the card. A troubled look haunted her round eyes as she composed herself. She read the card and rolled her lips together. "I'll—I'll be right back," she whispered.

The girl disappeared for a moment then returned and opened the door, avoiding his gaze, but keeping a wary eye on him. "She says to come in. She's working, but she will speak to you."

Nate shrugged and opened the screen door. He walked into the living room of the house, feeling like he'd just stepped through the looking glass into another time. A small sofa was covered in sheepskin. Various sized rugs, woven in Native American designs, adorned the floor and walls. An Indian drum and baskets woven in intricate patterns were placed around the room.

The wide-eyed girl peeked around the corner and motioned to him. "Come this way. Mary is back here." Nate followed her to a room at the back of the house. The room was small, but well lit and in the center a large loom had been constructed. A black-haired woman sat with her back to him, kneeling at the loom, her fingers busily moving strands of wool.

"Mary," the girl said. "This is the man who wishes to see you."

As the woman turned toward him, her dark eyes met his. Her stern expression melted. "Oh my." Her hand flew to her mouth, her eyes widened, and her jaw fell slack.

Nate's face warmed and a tingle shot through his chest. She was one of the most beautiful women he'd ever seen. Her flawless bronze skin and high cheekbones accented large dark eyes and full lips. Hair the color of a raven flowed down her back, all the way to her waist. Hers was not the beauty of fashion models, but a natural beauty that left him standing there with his mouth dry as cotton.

Words evaded him, but there was no self-consciousness in his hesitation as his eyes took her in from head to toe. Her reaction to him made him wonder as well as she stared silently back at him.

"I don't believe it," she whispered. She stepped toward him and reached two fingers toward his cheek, then pulled back. "You are here—in the flesh."

"What?" Nate stammered. *Was there some other way to be here?* He moistened his lips as reality took charge. "Excuse my manners, ma'am. I'm Nathan, Nathan Nakai."

Blushing, he extended a hand to shake hers. She accepted it, still looking oddly at him and saying nothing. The touch of her soft hand in his brought a surge of warmth. He pulled away, uncomfortable with the feeling that rushed through his body. Heat burned at the back of his neck beneath the collar of his shirt and tie, his face flushed. He was suddenly conscious of his own silence. "You're Mary Begay?"

She nodded, her long black hair moved softly. Looking up at him through large brown eyes, she batted her long lashes as if trying to force herself to focus. "I'm Mary. Begay was my maiden name."

Maiden name. Nate's heart sank. Hell, she was married. His head spun. Swiftly, he recalculated his priorities, getting a grip on his composure. He had to deal with the boy. "I came to talk to you about Johnny."

"You know where he is? I've been trying to find him."

"Yes, ma'am."

"I searched all morning in Santa Fe. I've been frantic with worry. He didn't come home last night."

"Johnny's gotten himself into some . . . trouble."

She shook her head, her face stern. "Not Johnny. He's a good boy. What's he done? Some mischievous prank?"

"Well—not exactly." Nate wished he could soften the blow. "Johnny's in jail."

Her eyebrows rose. "Jail?"

"Yes. He's accused of attacking a girl in Santa Fe."

Her eyes flew open and went dark. She wavered for a moment. Nate reached for her, thinking she might faint.

"Oh God—not again." She covered her face with her hands. "Not Johnny. He's just a child, a gentle child."

Again? Nathan's ears perked and his heart skipped a beat.

She turned away from him and stared at the floor, shaking her head and waving her hands animatedly, as if trying to comprehend what he'd told her. She whirled back to face him. "What you're telling me is a lie. He went into Santa Fe with his friends to see a movie. What you say can't be true."

"I said he was *accused* of attacking the girl. I didn't say he's guilty. It's my job to prove he isn't."

Her eyes flashed and darkened with something Nate couldn't interpret. She looked down at the card in her hand as if comprehending it for the first time. "You're *his lawyer?*"

"The court appointed me. Johnny told the police he couldn't afford his own legal counsel."

"The police. Another public defender." She closed her eyes and let out a heavy sigh, swaying slightly as if she were still unsteady on her feet.

Another public defender? Nate's eyes narrowed. The words stayed in the air.

She pursed her lips and her breathing quickened. An icy gaze coupled with a voice that sounded tight and restricted, as though she were swallowing the fury choking at her throat. Then, as if it all suddenly became too much to comprehend, her brows arched and her face clouded over with confusion and pain. "It's always about money, isn't it? Between Grandfather's illness and the gallery." She abruptly stopped the flow of words pouring from her. She swallowed hard.

"Forget about the money. That's taken care of."

She squared her shoulders and raised her chin. "Taken care of? My family, we take care of ourselves." Regaining composure, the look of shock left her face and in its place hard determination and anger formed in a set jaw. She turned away from him again, folded her arms and looked toward the loom.

Nate wondered what storm brewed beneath the surface of such a beautiful face. Somewhere beyond the shock he'd half-expected seemed to be an underlying volcano of mysterious pain and anger. An odd feeling hung over him as if in a few moments time he'd run the full gamut of her emotions. He'd gone from wondering if he'd just met the woman of his dreams to being her greatest revulsion in a matter of minutes. His radar screen was still jammed with blips from the barrage of curious comments she'd assaulted him with. Now wasn't the time to question her, but she was definitely at nosebleed level on his priority list.

Slowly, she turned to face him. She seemed to have calmed herself, but her face was hard, her look cold. "I'll get my things and go see my brother. I'm all the family he has. Our parents died years ago and I've taken care of Johnny ever since. Me and Grandpa."

"I forgot to mention the boy's adamant about not telling his grandfather."

Her dark eyes blackened as she lashed out with her words. "You needn't worry. I'll take care of Grandpa. And I'll take care of Johnny. Do not doubt this, Mr. Nakai."

The fire burning behind those fiery eyes left little doubt she spoke the truth. But her reaction and her words only deepened Nate's questions about the reasons that lay behind them.

While Mary gathered her purse and sweater, Nate headed for the front door. As he entered the living room, the girl huddled in a corner, looking at him with huge round eyes. He wanted to ignore her, but exasperation won out. "What's the matter?" he asked. "I'm not going to hurt you."

She frowned and cautiously stepped closer. Reaching a small brown hand into the pocket of her sundress, she pulled out a pale mauve business card and pressed it into his palm. "Go here. You'll understand." She turned and skittered away.

Nate glanced down at the card. "Summernight Gallery." He watched the girl slip into the kitchen. Then he let out a heavy sigh and tucked the card into his jacket pocket. Later, he'd check it out.

These people were sure a strange group. Maybe a mind reader would have been a more suitable choice than an attorney for this case.

Mary shifted in her chair as she sat in front of the glass. The room was a dreary gray, matching her mood. What was taking them so long to bring Johnny? She shot a glance at the broad-shouldered attorney who sat next to her scanning a police report. She had to avert her gaze from him. The initial heat of his presence was lost in this cold depressing place.

She wished she could go back to that first moment she'd seen him and stop the clock. The pleasant feeling that rushed through her when she saw him had evaporated within minutes. If only for a fleeting moment, she'd believed miracles really could happen. The picture from her mind had walked straight through her front door. But this form he'd come to her in put her heart in such a quandary. At first, she'd wondered if she'd seen an apparition, until he'd introduced himself. Then the truth reared its ugly head.

Why would the gods play such a dirty trick? Why would they send her the personification of her own perfect vision in this form—the form of another sleazy attorney? It was a cruel slap in the face that came along with the news Johnny was in jail.

Maybe these thoughts were a diversion she'd created to shield herself from the truth. She wasn't sure she could go through this again.

Part of her wanted nothing to do with Mr. Nathan Nakai, but she couldn't send him away—yet. Not as long as the possibility existed he could get Johnny out of this mess—the slightest chance history wasn't repeating itself and she wasn't really reliving a nightmare. The only thing she feared more was making a wrong decision for Johnny. Bombarded by a barrage of horrific memories, she had to remain reasonable and clearheaded. She had to be strong.

Those were the thoughts that pounded through her mind all the way from Chimayo. The legal system had screwed her family. There was no dainty way to put it. But one thing was certain. Hell would freeze over before she would let it happen again.

She wanted to see Johnny, to know he was all right. Something was wrong. *Very wrong.* Her brother wasn't capable of such a thing. She'd stake her life on it.

"Here's a list of the charges against your brother." Nate leaned closer.

She glanced at the list. The first item cut her heart in two. *Attempted murder.* Shoving aside the legal pad, she snarled in his ear, "Your words mean nothing to me, Mr. Nakai. My brother didn't do any of these things."

Nate shot her a steely look that softened when his eyes met hers. "I didn't create them. I'm just the messenger. Perhaps we should discuss this later. After you've seen Johnny."

The broken pieces of her heart fell to the pit of her stomach as the metal door on the other side of the glass creaked, then opened wide. Johnny handcuffed and bearing the look of a whipped animal, glanced at his sister and stepped through the doorway an armed deputy at his heels.

"Sit down, boy," the deputy barked and Johnny did as he was told. His eyes were cast to the floor, shame written on his youthful face as he sat on the other side of the pane of glass from Mary.

This wasn't the Johnny she knew. He came from a family that held their heads high and proud, not hung in shame. "Johnny," she said, biting her lip. "Are you okay?"

He nodded, his eyes at last meeting hers. A silent message passed between them, as he seemed to draw strength from her presence. He squared his shoulders and raised his chin. His jaw rippled with tension.

Her instincts kicked in. He was frightened. She could feel it. "What happened?"

Johnny looked at the floor then gave Nate a distrustful look under a furrowed brow. Mary knew he'd be guarded about what he said with Nate at her elbow.

"My brother and I need a moment alone." Mary gave Nate a sideways glance.

"Certainly," he said, rising to his feet, all six-foot-plus of him. "I'll step outside, but the three of us need to talk. And we need to do it today."

Mary's lips tightened and she held her tongue. Her brother wasn't going to be sucked in by some crooked lawyer. Nate left through the door behind them. Except for the guard posted at the desk, they were alone. Mary leaned close to the speaker in the window.

Johnny's face relaxed. "They think I did something terrible."

"I know. What happened?"

"I don't know. I don't know anything." His cuffed hands went to his face.

"Don't worry. I'll do everything I can. You know that."

"Mary, I'm scared." His hard dark eyes were childlike. A tear glistened in his eyelashes.

"I know that, too." Her words seemed empty, echoing the helplessness searing her heart. She put her palm to the glass and he leaned the top of his head against it.

"It'll be all right."

"But Angelo—"

She slapped her hand firmly to the glass and he stopped. "History will not repeat itself. Not in this family. I won't allow it to happen."

"What about the lawyer? He was here earlier."

"I don't know yet," she snapped. A response followed by a stab of remorse. "Say nothing more until I can be sure."

He was silent for a moment. "I want to go home."

She nodded. "I'll see what I can do, but—." She knew she didn't have that kind of money.

"I know, I remember Angelo."

Mary shook her head. "Hush. Put it from your mind. It *will not* happen this time."

The boy's eyes were large and sad. "Don't worry. I'll be strong."

She smiled. Her arms ached to hold him, her heart seared with his pain. "The lawyer wants to talk to us. I'll call him back in."

Johnny nodded, pulling himself upright in the chair. His eyes met Mary's and she silently prayed for his strength and his safety. She brushed away her own tears, rose and opened the door. Nate was on his feet immediately, collecting a handful of papers and bringing them with him.

"Five more minutes," the guard at the desk said.

"You okay?" Nate's gaze locked on Mary's.

"I'm fine," she replied coldly.

"Good. We're in for the long haul here." His gaze pierced through the wall she'd thrown up and he ignored her curt response.

He stepped near the glass, followed closely by Mary. "The arraignment's at ten tomorrow morning." He looked from Mary to Johnny.

Johnny's dark eyes stared up at him then went to Mary.

"They're charging you with attempted murder. Anything to say?"

"I didn't do it." Johnny's look was intent and his jaw set.

"Three eyewitnesses identified you and you still swear you weren't in that alley?" Nate glanced at Mary.

Johnny's eyes narrowed. "Yes, sir."

"Well, that's enough to get us through tomorrow. We'll put in a not guilty plea." Nate sighed, turned away from Johnny and faced Mary. "The rest we'll take one day at a time." His brow clouded with an expression that made Mary's heart sink to her feet. Nate wasn't pulling any punches. His body language told it all. Things didn't look good for Johnny.

CHAPTER FOUR

Nate arrived at his office at 6:00 a.m. and at the courthouse when they unlocked the doors. Mary's comments haunted him all night. What had her odd references meant? Why had she said *again*? Johnny had no prior record—that was easy enough to check. Damn, he should have pinned her down then, but he hadn't the heart when he'd seen the distress and sadness in the depths of her brown eyes.

What a sap. He could have saved himself a night's sleep, and by God when he saw her, he was going to demand an answer.

At ten o'clock sharp, Nate sat next to Johnny at a polished wooden table, facing the judge's bench. He glanced over his left shoulder, wondering to what he could attribute the honor of the presence of the DA himself. Jim Smith sat in the front row behind the prosecution. Something smelled fishy with this whole deal, but Nate wasn't sure he was getting the whole aroma.

Smith's smirk and Mary's comments, both stuck in his head and his craw. Considering the boy's record was cleaner than the DA's starched white shirt, two plus two kept equaling twelve. What he wanted were some answers and he planned on getting them today.

Mary had tossed and turned all night, unable to sleep, but refusing to let out her tears. Sometimes she wondered if she simply had no more left to cry in this lifetime. But there wasn't time for crying. It certainly wouldn't help Johnny. Johnny still had a chance. It was too late for Angelo. This brought it all back, brought the painful memories rushing to the forefront. She'd buried them two years ago, along with her husband. She twisted the Kleenex she held in her hand and waited.

The sound of the judge's gavel on the bench echoed through the courtroom, like the snap of a steel trap around Mary's heart. Johnny would be held over for trial, charged with attempted murder—provided the girl lived. The judge reiterated that the charge would be upgraded to first-degree murder if she died.

A minute later, she couldn't remember the exact words. They seemed slurred and unreal through the haze of anger and confusion raging in her mind. It was like the replay of a bad movie, only last time it was Angelo and they were talking robbery. This time it was Johnny and they were talking murder. *Murder.* Mary shuddered. *Sweet Jesus.* Could this be happening again? Would the repeating horrors in her life ever end?

Mary buried her face in her hands and summoned her strength before she rose to her feet. Johnny was being led away by two deputies. She wanted to touch him, hold him, and tell him it would be okay. Instead she caught Nate's eye on her, a discerning and suspicious look. She moved away quickly only to meet the smug and contempt-filled gaze of Jim Smith. Her insides lurched. There was no way she could tolerate him today. Her steps quickened as she walked down the aisle and out of the courtroom. Dear God, what was she going to do?

Nate waited outside the courthouse. Questions raced in his mind like minnows darting through a brook. He needed some answers from Mary and now was as good a time as any.

As Mary emerged through the tall doors, Nate caught sight of Jim Smith walking a few steps behind her, scanning the crowd. His eyes flashed when he saw Mary. Smith rushed forward and grabbed her arm. She tried to pull away. Nate bristled, but he couldn't get through the stream of people. Half of Santa Fe must have shown up for the preliminary hearing. The media reports had hit the airwaves and the papers immediately. It was likely to be a high profile case.

Smith pulled Mary close and whispered something in her ear. By the time Nate reached her, Smith had stepped back inside.

"What the hell was that about?" Nate demanded.

Mary gave him a stony look. "It's no concern of yours." Her face was flushed, her jaw set.

Nate took her by the elbow, directing her down the stairs and up the street toward the plaza. "I need to have a word with you."

Nate threw a glance over his shoulder at Smith who now stood at the top of the stairway watching them leave. Smith's puckered mouth and creased brow only added to Nate's questions.

Mary pulled away. "What's there to talk about? My brother's going to trial."

"Oh, I think we have a *lot* to discuss, unless you want your brother to finish growing up behind bars."

Mary looked straight ahead and said nothing. She kept walking. "Then maybe your time would be better spent finding the real criminal."

"My search starts here. I have some questions that need answers now."

Air escaped between Mary's teeth, an obvious sign of her annoyance. Nate could care less if he was inconveniencing her. He was going to get to the bottom of this attitude before he went any further. Grabbing her upper arm, ignoring the gush of warmth it sent through his body, he guided her into a white wrought iron chair at the table of a sidewalk café.

"I think we need a cup of coffee after that ordeal, don't you?"

Mary rolled her eyes at his sarcastic effort to normalize their conversation. She sat stiffly in the chair, clutching a woven wool Navajo handbag to her turquoise peasant blouse. She reached inside the purse, pulled out a pair of dark glasses and placed them on her face. Nate's gut tightened. Her actions reeked of someone with a million secrets. Did she think she could hide those expressive eyes that easily?

Nate rubbed his chin and tried to cool his temper as a waitress in a short green apron approached.

"Now what can I get for the two of you?" she asked cheerfully.

Mary peered over her sunglasses at Nate. "Ice water."

Nate raised an eyebrow and met Mary's defiant look. "Espresso, double shot."

The waitress looked from one to the other and shrugged, then went on about her business.

Nate folded his hands and leaned his forearms on the tabletop. "Ms. Begay—Mary. This got off to a bad start. Look, can we sit here and talk without the animosity, or would you like to tell me what that's all about?"

"What are you talking about?"

"This attitude, this anger you've got toward me. I don't get it. It isn't my fault your kid brother's in trouble."

Mary clenched her jaw. "I didn't say it was your fault."

"No, but you've acted like you're totally pissed off since you first laid eyes on me." He winced. "Pardon the language, but it's true."

Mary seemed to choose her words carefully. "Perhaps what you perceive as anger, Mr. Nakai, is merely distrust."

"Distrust? Have I done something to make you believe you can't trust me?"

Mary pursed her lips and paused as the waitress placed the drinks on the table. "You shouldn't take it so personally. My feelings are associated more with your profession than with you."

"Oh, I see." Nate nodded and forced back a grin. "You just hate lawyers."

Mary gave a sideways nod.

"Even if they happen to be trying to save your little brother's ass?"

A cloud of emotion shadowed Mary's face. Some of the coldness melted. For a few moments she sat quietly attempting to compose herself. Nate's eye took in the curve of her high cheekbones, the fullness of her lips as she moistened them with her tongue. The woman's hard as nails facade fell away for a fleeting moment.

She laid her sunglasses on the table. "This has been a very rough day for me, Mr. Nakai. Some hard things happened in the past—." She stopped, sizing him up before she went on. "I can only say you'll have to win my trust before I'll give it to you. In the meantime, forgive my coldness, but I can't feel any other way right now."

"If what's happened in the past is important to Johnny, we need to get it out in the open. Or," he paused.

"Or what?"

"Or maybe another attorney could better serve your needs."

"No." Her eyes flashed at him then looked away. "I mean I'll let you know if I find that to be true. Just give me time for all this to sink in."

"Okay. I'll give you space, but for Johnny's sake and the best interest of this case, I need answers."

"All right. Perhaps tomorrow."

"Tomorrow?" He rolled his eyes.

"Yes." She set her jaw. "I need to get to the gallery. We'll have to meet another time." She was almost flippant and seemed hell bent on setting the rules.

He let out an annoyed sigh. "Then tomorrow for sure. I don't have time to waste."

"Nor do I, Mr. Nakai." She placed her hand on the table.

"There's only one more thing, Mary."

"What's that?"

"Can you stop calling me Mr. Nakai? Nate would be my preference."

She shook her head, and dark suspicion shot into her eyes. "I'd prefer Mr. Nakai."

Nate sat there stunned by her coldness and distance as she rose from the chair and disappeared into a crowd moving in the direction of the plaza.

Nate put his head in his hands. What was this woman about? She bore such striking beauty, such depth of soul. Womanhood emanated from her and hovered in mysterious places in her eyes, yet it was wrapped in a cloak of secretive sadness. He was dumbfounded by her beauty, mystified by her attitude—and nervous as hell about what she might be hiding from him.

She had to get to the gallery, huh? *No time to waste on something as insignificant as the rest of her brother's life.* He snorted.

Gallery. Nate flipped open the brown leather portfolio he'd laid on the table when they sat down for coffee. From the tiny pocket in the front cover, he pulled the business card the girl had given him the day before. *Summernight Gallery.*

He threw a five-dollar bill on the table and headed down the street. He caught a glimpse of the turquoise blouse up ahead of him. He'd check out where she was going and see if it was the same gallery. Could lead him somewhere or just create another mystery. It was damn hard to tell with this woman.

Nate stayed close enough to keep her in sight as Mary wove her way down the narrow crowded sidewalks, dodging tourists. The adobe storefronts of the restored original buildings that were unique and charming seemed endless now and at each corner they crossed another cobblestone street. The music of a Spanish mariachi band came from an alleyway and intriguing smells wafted through the doorways of eateries as they passed.

Finally five blocks down, Mary disappeared into an entryway below a sign that read, "Summernight Gallery." *Bingo.* Now he was getting somewhere.

Nate stepped through the ornate doorway, out of the hot July sun and into the cool air-conditioned gallery. Several people milled around, nibbling on cheese and crackers and sipping wine from plastic cups. As he squinted and glanced around the room, a well-dressed woman pushed a tray of hors d'oeuvres into his path.

"Good morning and welcome," she said, flashing him a lipstick-covered smile.

"Morning," he muttered, glancing around the room and pushing the tray aside.

"Is there something I can help you find? We're honoring some of our local artists today. All of their works—"

"I'm just looking for . . . a painting," he stammered, distractedly mouthing a feeble excuse for his presence.

"Oh, I'm sure I can help you find something."

"No, no. I don't mean I'm looking for a painting. I mean I want to look at the paintings."

The woman raised her eyebrows and gave him an odd look. "Well," she said, quickly, "you've come to the right place." She half-smiled, threw him a look as if he had an extra head, and moved on to the next customer.

"Way to go, Nakai," he muttered. "Show 'em your cultured side." He rolled his eyes and resumed his quest. He wanted to see if Mary was here and what she was up to. But he was also curious what the heck was here the girl wanted him to see.

He scanned the walls while subtly searching to see if Mary was among the group milling about. Making his way across the larger main room if the gallery, he stepped through one of the many doorways that led into a small rooms in the back of the gallery.

He scanned the walls then stopped dead in his tracks. His mouth went dry. On the wall before him hung the portrait of an Indian warrior. The lifelike form seemed to spring from the canvas and meet Nate's amazement dead on. The painted brown eyes staring back at him were an exact mirror image. The cheekbones, the nose, every finely brushed detail of the mouth—all the way down to the small scar on his upper lip—were undeniably his exact likeness. My God, was this the reason for the girl's odd behavior?

At last he moved his spellbound gaze from the eyes and took in the careful details the artist had rendered on canvas. Dark wispy hair appeared to flow on an imaginary breeze. His eyes scanned the war-painted face above the broad chest and followed it to muscular arms spread to the edges of the canvas. Upon the hands, faintly brushed shadows of feathers appeared. Between the arms and body the pale image of wings disappeared into the background as if the warrior were in transition between man and bird.

"Beautiful work, isn't it?" A woman's voice near his ear jolted him back to reality.

"Absolutely awesome," he said, having difficulty finding his voice.

"Why, doesn't he look a lot like you?" the woman who had accosted him earlier asked in an annoyingly high-pitched voice. She pushed against him in the doorway trying to get a better look at Nate's face.

"No. Of course not." Nate turned quickly away from her and pretended to become involved in a painting on the adjacent wall. Much to his relief, the woman let out a disgusted little sigh and walked away.

Turning back to the painting, an odd feeling swept over him. The warrior's eyes—his eyes—were hypnotic and wild. They drew him in.

The white painted lines of the warrior's face looked so real. Nate's face felt oddly parched and his hand shot there for an instant, feeling the sensation of tight dryness on his own cheeks for a fraction of a second.

A low pulsing rhythm grew out of his heartbeat, then pounded softly in his ears, like the sound of drums. He turned his head and listened. Wow, he must be going nuts.

What a freaky coincidence. His face flushed at the near nakedness of the warrior and the bulging breach cloth. It was such a close likeness, it was like an invasion of privacy.

Squaring his shoulders, he loosened his tie and leaned forward, squinting to read the signature on the painting. "Summernight," read the graceful brush stroke. When time allowed, he must find this artist.

An uncomfortable feeling crawled up the back of his neck. Whirling around, he saw Mary standing behind a glass enclosed display case at the rear of the gallery. She stared at him for a moment, her eyes wide. She spun and darted into a doorway marked "Office" and closed the door behind her. Now what was he to make of that behavior?

Shaking his head, he walked back toward the front entrance. He'd had enough for one morning. It was time to move on. There was work to do and the sooner he shook off the strangeness of this whole event, the better.

Johnny needed his full attention. He'd have to table this bizarre encounter until later. As for Mary, he couldn't afford the distraction of her mysterious issues either. Business was still business and he had to keep it that way.

The man in the painting walked through his mind all afternoon. In between were pictures of Mary's face and her wide-eyed look. Why was she skulking around watching him, and why did she make a beeline into the office when he saw her? Okay, maybe skulking was too strong a term, but she definitely had been staring at him with that strange look in her eyes. Almost horrified, definitely not comfortable with seeing him there.

Maybe this had nothing to do with the case at all. But damn if there wasn't enough mystery about her already, now there was one more thing to add to the list. Why wouldn't she make time to talk to him? What did Smith say to her when she came out of the courthouse?

He glanced at the clock on his desk. It was almost two in the afternoon. A decent night's sleep sure wouldn't have hurt anything. Placing his elbow on the desk, he rested his chin in his palm. His eyelids grew heavy.

A young girl's face flashed in his mind. Her eyes were closed, a rope tight around her throat. She screamed. Nate jolted awake.

The picture came straight from his vision on the pier a week earlier. What a strange coincidence a strangling would have gone through his mind that night and now he had a similar case in his hands. But a coincidence was all it was. This entire journey up to this point had been filled with bizarre twists. From the moment he'd opened that package from his grandfather. *Nah.* All he needed was a good night's sleep to change his perspective. He closed his eyes.

"You Nakai?" A deep voice brought Nate from his fog. Standing in his office doorway was a broad-shouldered man with long black hair trailing out from under a black western hat.

"I am," Nate straightened in his chair.

The man stepped forward and extended his hand. "Pete Gorman. My office is down the hall. I'm the investigator assigned to the Begay case."

Nate accepted the firm handshake. "Good. Sit down and bring me up to speed."

Pete slid into the dark blue chair on the opposite side of the desk. "I tried to call you this morning. They said you were in court. I went out to the scene yesterday afternoon, not long after the call came in about Johnny."

"You seem familiar with the case already."

"I read the police report." Pete shrugged.

"And?"

"Not much to say. I wrote some notes. I'll get it printed and over to you by the end of the day."

"How about the alley? Find anything?"

"Picked clean." The man's eyebrow rose as he spoke.

"What do you mean *picked clean*?" Nate sensed the change in the tone of his own voice.

"I mean nothing was there. Not a footprint, not a hair, not even a scuff-mark in the dirt."

"You're sure?" A cloud gathered in Nate's brow.

"Dead sure."

"You said picked clean. You think somebody tidied it up before you got there?"

"Either that or a street sweeper came through and politely put the crime scene tape back when he was done."

"Might be some questions to be answered about that one down at police headquarters...or by our friends in the DA's office."

"So you've met our DA have you?" A smirk crossed Pete's face. He shifted back in the chair and stretched his legs in front of him.

"I have indeed had the pleasure." Nate grunted.

"Hmm. Some interesting history there." Pete ran his thumb and forefinger down his cheeks as if thinking out loud.

"Why do you say that?"

"I grew up in Chimayo. Went to high school with Johnny's sister. Her and the Smith family, well, they go way back."

Nate raised an eyebrow. "How so?"

Pete shook his head. "It's a long story. One I'd rather not go into at this point."

"I've got nothing but time if it sheds light on this case."

"Unless I'm sure it does, I'd rather leave the past where it belongs—dead and buried."

Great. Another closed-lipped character on the scene. Nate gave Pete a stony look. "If it pertains to the case, you need to spill it."

Pete met Nate's gaze with steely eyes and crossed his arms over his chest. "And if it doesn't, it isn't your concern. Spilling it, as you say, doesn't seem like a fair or honorable thing to do at the moment. Guess you'll have to trust me. Unless it bothers you to trust an Indian."

Nate frowned. "What brought that on? Buddy, I don't care if you're red, yellow, blue or green. Do your job and shoot straight with me."

Pete grinned and squared himself in the chair. "Just testing the water. Not everyone in this town feels that way."

"That's their problem, not mine. Don't bring it up again."

"Done. Let's get on with business. My main objective is to get Johnny a fair trial."

"At least we have a common goal. Some reason why you think he won't?"

Pete shrugged. "I guess we have to assume that's what will happen. Unless something proves otherwise."

"You got some qualms?"

"You bet I do. About the crime scene, the evidence and the kid's chances. Did you get the copy on record from the line up they did the night Johnny was arrested?"

"Line up? It's not in my reports." Nate shuffled through the papers in the folder on his desk. "I should have been told about it."

"There wasn't a copy in the file. But I know it happened. Three people made a positive ID on Johnny. They all claim to be eye witnesses."

"Saw that part. Didn't know they picked him out of a line up."

Pete winced. "Not good. I want to talk to all three."

"I want to be involved in that. Just tell me when."

"As soon as I can. I've got some other nosing around to do along with it."

"I want to interview the kids he was with earlier that day." Nate picked up a pen and underlined the item on his notes.

"Got them on my list, too."

"Let me know when you get all that arranged, Pete."

"Will do." Pete rose from the chair and stood in front of Nate's desk. "My friends call me Coyote. Reckon that could apply to you, too."

"Coyote, huh. Where'd you get that name?"

"Spent some time sniffin' around the rez."

"The rez?"

"The reservation. Did some time there as an undercover narc. It sucked. I didn't last long."

"Did some time? Interesting way to put it."

"It fits."

"Lousy job, huh?" Nate tapped his pen on the desk.

"It was, until I realized what the kids needed was help, not prosecution. Then I got the hell out."

Nate nodded. "Looks like you're still sniffin' around. I take it this is a better place to be?"

Coyote shrugged. "Sometimes I get a chance to help out an innocent kid. Kids are kind of my specialty. I spend my free time working to keep them off drugs and out of gangs. Makes me feel like I'm giving something back."

"Yeah. Or paying restitution for a guilty conscience."

Coyote looked Nate in the eye, then a grin spread across his face. "Wondered what a fancy San Francisco lawyer was doing here. Sounds like we might speak the same language."

"Or we're at least doing the same gig." Nate liked him. And he had good intuition.

Coyote moved toward the door. "Well, I've got work to do. I'll keep in close touch."

"One more thing," Nate couldn't hold his question any longer. "You said you know Mary, the boy's sister."

"Yeah. For a long time." Coyote shifted in his stance and his eyes narrowed.

"She seems a little tight-lipped. Didn't want to talk to me this morning after the arraignment."

Coyote crossed his arms as he contemplated his response. His eyes darkened. "Mary's been through a lot. I wouldn't read too much into it."

Nate took in Coyote's suddenly protective demeanor. "A lot? A lot of what?"

Coyote's brow furrowed and he waited for a long moment. "Mary lost her husband less than two years ago. All that's happened to Johnny in the last few days probably dredged up some bad memories."

"So Mary's a widow?" Nate rubbed his chin ashamed of the rush that raced through him. He paused, gathering his thoughts for the rest of his question. "I guess I'm missing something. What bad memories?"

Coyote rubbed his lips together and looked at the floor, obviously considering his answer carefully. "I need to get going," he said suddenly and moved toward the door.

"Wait." Nate was on his feet, still trying to come up with a connection.

"I'll check in with you tomorrow." Coyote was out the door before Nate could utter another word.

The questions in Nate's head went into overdrive. What history did Mary have with the DA? What bad memories had Johnny's arrest brought back for her? He'd bet his life they were the same "hard things that happened in the past" she'd referred to earlier. Another mystery was evolving in an already clouded picture.

He shook his head. *All this and three eyewitnesses. And not a scrap of evidence so far.* How the hell would he convince a jury the kid was innocent when he couldn't even convince himself?

He sat down roughly in his chair and let out a huff in frustration. It damn sure didn't help that it was so hard to get a straight answer out of anybody in this godforsaken place.

CHAPTER FIVE

The flame of the candle flickered as Mary sat silently in the dark living room. Not wanting to wake Grandpa, she'd shuffled softly down the hallway. For a second night, sleep evaded her.

It was impossible to turn off her mind as she milled over Johnny's plight and dredged up the old horrors and the old hatreds of the past. Chapters of her life she thought were closed forever haunted her every waking hour once more. She bowed her head. Would it ever end? Would the raw emotions ever heal? Would the ghosts of the past ever allow her and her family peace?

What was happening to Johnny wasn't related in any way to what happened to Angelo. She'd kept telling herself that over and over as she'd driven to Santa Fe and seen Johnny in jail. Even as she'd tossed, turned and walked the floor the previous night, she kept telling herself this was different. Johnny had been in the wrong place at the wrong time. This was a terrible mistake and the truth would come to light.

But as she'd left the courthouse, the glimmer of hope she held in her heart dimmed. Jim Smith was out for blood *again.* His hissing words were stuck in her head. "I didn't think we'd have the pleasure so soon." Her family's misfortune had played into his hands once more. Fate had given him yet another opportunity to seek his continuing revenge—to keep his vendetta alive.

What were the odds that so many horrific events could cross the path of one family? She'd played it through her mind a thousand times during Angelo's trial. Was it just her family's ill fate or did Smith somehow have his hand in both occurrences? But how? If he did, she had to somehow find the truth. She had to prove Johnny innocent and still keep her secrets from a devastatingly handsome legal apparition named Nathan Nakai. Speaking of odds and cruel jokes—.

Laying her head on the back of the sofa, she rubbed her temples and placed a cool cloth across her tired, burning eyes. Maybe she should never have come back to Chimayo. She'd made a clean break once. Hard work had earned her a college degree, a major in business and a minor in the arts. Along the way, she'd learned to express herself on canvas and at the loom. She loved working with oils and her weaving was an inherent art from her mother and grandmother. She'd recently taken it to the next level—owning her own gallery—and she was proud of the work she did. God had blessed her with a passion that made her a living, at least here in Santa Fe, one of the art capitals of the world.

When her father's failing health had brought her home, little did she know that her mother was ill, as well. In the end, Johnny was alone and Grandpa was too old to care for a nine-year-old boy. Now she couldn't escape the fact that her place was here with her family.

Even after everything that happened, this was still the place where her heart belonged. She'd finally found a way to walk the streets of Santa Fe with her head held high, to turn away from the few who still remembered and snickered behind her back. It didn't matter anyway. They didn't know the truth and they never would. The truth would go with her to her grave.

If she'd never come back, things probably would be different. Blaming herself wouldn't help Johnny, but she would always carry the guilt in her heart for the choices she'd made—and the pain for those made for her.

Not a single doubt existed in her mind about Johnny's innocence. He was not capable of hurting anyone and the how and why of all these false accusations had her dumbfounded. But she would find the evidence and clear Johnny or she'd die trying. Stellar of all people, Johnny had known her for years. It was ludicrous anyone would think he would want to hurt her. Dear God, what had really happened in that alley?

Nate walked gingerly past the dog on the porch and knocked on the door. The Australian Shepherd made little growling noises deep in his throat and watched Nate with a wary eye. No one answered. He knocked a second time.

This woman was about to drive him crazy. He could get no answer on the telephone and she hadn't contacted him about meeting today. As the hours ticked by into early afternoon, he was rapidly getting to the end of his patience with her. She appeared to be flat out avoiding him and he was damn tired of it. He pounded the door a third time, more from annoyance than from expectation of an answer.

An uncomfortable feeling ran through him. Whirling, he was confronted by a short stocky old man who hit Nate about mid-chest.

"I've been waiting for you," the man said abruptly.

"Pardon me?" Nate stepped back, trying to hide his surprise and reclaim his personal space. As the words sunk in, Nate rubbed his jaw. "Waiting for me?"

The elderly man nodded. "I knew you'd be back."

"How could you possibly know that?" Nate surveyed him.

The old fellow's white hair hung to his shoulders and was encircled by a folded green bandana. He wore a pair of blue jeans, a brown vest and a beige shirt pulled together at his throat with a bolo tie. He responded only with a crooked smile. His gaze made Nate feel like a windowpane.

"Actually, I was looking for Mary." Nate stepped off the porch, trying to avoid the piercing eyes.

The old man followed him. Ignoring the inquiry, he proceeded to circle him, looking him up and down as if he were a prize sheep he was considering purchasing.

"Is Mary here?" Nate asked, louder this time. Maybe the old gentleman was hard of hearing.

The man continued with his inspection and didn't respond.

Okay then, let's try again. "I'm Nathan Nakai." Nate extended his hand. "Pardon my manners, sir. You must be Mary's grandfather."

The old man grunted and ignored the gesture as he looked up from his ritual. "I know who you are."

Did he really know? Nate recalled Johnny's request not to tell his grandfather and hoped Mary had honored it. Nate looked back toward the house.

"If Mary was here, she'd answer the door." Grandpa stopped in front of Nate and put his hands in his pockets.

Nate nodded, tilting his head to one side. "Do you know when she'll be back?"

"When she's ready to come home, she will."

"But, Mr. Begay—sir—"

He smirked. "Grandpa will suffice, city boy. Save your misters for the court room."

Nate managed a respectful nod and an even tone in spite of his growing annoyance. "Look, Grandpa, I came all the way from Santa Fe to talk to her. Can you tell me when you expect her?"

"Wise men expect nothing except from themselves."

Great. Just what he needed, a philosopher. "This is getting us nowhere." Nate put his hands on his hips.

"Nowhere is a remarkable place to be from, but a poor place to be headed." The old man's face was somber, but his eyes twinkled with wisdom and amusement.

"Can you just tell me where to find her?" Nate looked at his watch. He really didn't have time for this.

"Nice watch," Grandpa said. "You in a hurry?"

"I have a very tight schedule most of the time. And the sooner I find Mary, the sooner I can get back to it."

Grandpa put his hand on his chin and nodded. "You sure are in a hurry for somebody headed nowhere. But you won't need your fancy watch where you're going."

"Grandpa, what are you talking about?" Nate's frustration meter had pegged out. "You know what, never mind. Forget it. I'll find Mary myself." Nate threw up his hands and turned to walk back to his car.

"Anger does not become you. Mary is at the Sanctuario." Grandpa turned in Nate's direction, arms folded across his chest.

Nate spun around. "The Sanctuario?"

"The old Spanish mission in town."

Nate rolled his eyes. "I'll look for her there. Thanks." He dared not ask for directions. He'd be here another twenty minutes.

As Nate turned away, Grandpa's words followed him. "If you wanted to know where to find her, you should have simply asked."

Nate stopped in his tracks. He was too tired and too exasperated to get into it again. "Okay, Grandpa. It's nice to meet you. I'm sure I'll see you around." Best to humor the old guy.

"You'll see much more of me in the days to come than you will care to." The old man's tone hit Nate with a strangeness that sent goose flesh down his arms.

Never mind, Nate, just walk away. Glancing over his shoulder, Nate moved toward the car. Grandpa watched. The hint of a smirk on his wrinkled face left Nate curious.

Nate stopped and looked back at the old Navajo man before he climbed behind the wheel. His gut gnawed as his mind flashed on the image of the warrior in the painting. The feelings dredged up by seeing his own likeness in the form of the warrior sprung back to haunt him. Something in him had shifted when that happened. Somewhere deep within, in his inner most being, he'd tried to connect with that half-naked, free spirit on canvas. For a fleeting second, something in his soul had remembered a piece of the far distant past.

Now that's silly. Why would this rambling old man make it run through him again? Unexplainably compelled to take one last look in the rear view mirror, Nate hit the brakes. The picture in the mirror was the ethereal image of an ancient buckskin-clad Indian man. Where Grandpa stood was the ghostly image of an old one with an age-wizened face and the wind in his white hair. Nate spun to look over his shoulder. Nothing was there. Where Grandpa had been and the image had appeared there was nothing. *Cripes sake.* Now he was seeing things. Nate shook his head. If he hung around this place very long, he'd soon be as strange as the rest of these people.

Gathering his scattered psyche and adjusting his seat belt, he forced himself to regroup. He had business to attend to. That was where his mind needed to be. Nate punched the accelerator as the strangeness threatened to creep back upon him. He had to find Mary and get on with building Johnny's case.

Several minutes later, Nate sat in the parking lot of the old Spanish mission, the Sanctuario de Chimayo, waiting for the afternoon service to end. He checked the time. He wasn't leaving without talking to her. And he'd be damned if he'd let her avoid him again.

From what he'd seen so far, he had qualms about Johnny's plea. Maybe they should be negotiating for a lighter sentence instead. If the kid hadn't convinced his own attorney he wasn't guilty, how would they be able to convince a jury? That said, maybe he shouldn't have taken the case. The thought had crossed his mind, but then there was Mary—

The narrow double doors of the old mission opened and people began to straggle out into the gravel parking lot. An old woman draped in black from head to foot held onto the arm of a younger woman. A small child walked behind them kicking at stones and scuffing his tiny feet in the dirt. Soon others filed out. A middle-aged couple, a young family, an elderly man and woman moved through the doors and out into the parking lot, but no sign of Mary.

He waited. Several minutes passed. A few more people came through the doors. He glanced at the clock on the dash of the car. He was due back in Santa Fe in an hour. The parking lot was nearly empty. Where was she?

He climbed from the car and approached the ancient wooden doors of the mission. Gravel crunched under his feet as he passed through the courtyard. The door squeaked as he pulled it open, breaking the complete silence inside the church.

The passageway at the entrance was narrow and dimly lit. Stepping into the musty smelling entryway, he took only a few steps before a tidal wave hit his mid-section and clasped a vice grip on his heart. Totally unexpected emotion flooded over him and washed from his throat into his chest—emotion that defied description.

White adobe walls below small stained glass windows displayed brightly colored Spanish crosses and crutches. There were crutches of all sizes ranging from very old crude handmade ones to modern metal ones that could be found at the local pharmacy. Intermingled with the crutches were orthopedic braces. Most were well worn from years of use on the limbs of their former owners.

Brightly colored Spanish and Mexican religious pieces and metal crucifixes were placed any where there was available space. After an unavoidable pause to take in the display, Nate cleared his throat and took a few more steps.

Just beyond the wall a small light shone above an opening in the floor where a hole had been dug in the earth about three feet in circumference. An elderly woman knelt by the hole and filled a tiny plastic bag with reddish brown earth. Clutched in her hand was a rosary. Caught off guard by his emotion-charged reaction, his previous sense of urgency was momentarily forgotten. He stopped at a plaque positioned on the wall next to the hole and read the brief message written there.

In 1810, a gleaming crucifix had been found here. Though stolen by thieves three times, all three times it had miraculously returned to the hole where it was found. Soon the soil from that hole was found to have healing powers. And so the mission was built around it.

Nate glanced at the crutches. Interesting. The brief history went on to explain that people made pilgrimages to the mission every year to collect soil from the hole and take it to the sick. Its miraculous powers could not be scientifically explained.

Nate rubbed his chin. Some things defied scientific explanation, as did the unlocked mysteries of the human mind. One thing was certain. This place touched his soul. And along with it, a distinct feeling gripped him that his presence here wasn't coincidental. He drew his hand across his face trying

to erase his emotions from it and glanced into the
church behind him. The pews were empty.

Ahead of him was an open doorway and a
churchyard beyond. A little fresh air sure couldn't
hurt. The weight in his heart distracted him as he
pushed ahead and out into daylight. Stepping into the
sun, the relief he was seeking did not come.

The courtyard had several large trees and an array
of hand-hewn wooden benches. People dotted the area,
some alone, some clinging to family members, most
openly weeping. It hit him that the service must have
been a funeral. Then his eyes took in the rest of the
story.

Around the perimeter was a wire fence covered with
heavy green mesh. The wire, the mesh and the
surrounding trees were plastered with tiny crosses and
photographs. Literally hundreds of photos were tacked
up, some with poems and short written messages,
some faded over time, others looking very recent. Old
people, young people, small children; their pictures
were everywhere. And he knew instantly they all had
one thing in common. They were all dead.

A whole new tightness accosted his throat. He
pulled a pair of dark glasses from his shirt pocket and
pushed them onto his face. It was impossible to be here
and not be moved by the emotion and faith
surrounding him, even a jaded, hard-ass attorney.

Across the churchyard beneath a large tree, he
spotted Mary. She knelt next to the fence. Nate
stopped, too moved to approach her and not wanting to
interrupt the moment of privacy she'd obviously come
here to find. He stepped behind a nearby tree,
watching Mary, but not wanting to be seen.

On the fence in front of her, hung four crosses. Two
were positioned side by side. A photo hung beneath
them. Another cross was hung a few inches away with
a photo beneath it as well. The fourth cross did not
have a photo. He couldn't make out any of the pictures

from this distance. He watched as she gently ran her finger down the lone crucifix with no picture and bowed her head. After a few minutes, she rose to her feet and walked back toward the church.

Crap. His own emotional response was unexpected and the timing was lousy. What now? Through the half-open door of the church he saw Mary stop to speak to the old woman who was still lingering by the healing hole with her bag of dirt. Unable to help his curiosity, Nate approached the fence where Mary had been.

He examined the photo under the two crosses. It was a picture of a middle-aged couple. He didn't know for sure, but he suspected they were the dead parents.

The photo beneath the other single cross was of a young Hispanic man. *Nice looking guy.* Was he Mary's husband? Coyote said she was a widow. A pang of jealousy ran through him along with a shot of pain. She must have loved him very much to construct this little temple in his honor. He wondered what the story was behind his untimely demise.

Who was the fourth cross? There was no picture to identify it. The tenderness that showed when she ran her finger across it indicated it was someone very special to her. Hmm. Maybe one day he'd ask. Today wasn't the day.

Hurrying back across the churchyard, he saw Mary walk on through the church. He tried to purge himself of the feelings that ran through him. He was very good at it. Years of training to put his emotions in a box had paid off in that regard. He'd become an expert at stonewalling his heart. It made him a damn good attorney.

Out in the parking lot, Nate took long strides appreciating the unavoidable view of Mary's hips rippling beneath her long skirt. *Something else that belonged behind that stone wall.* She pulled the keys from her purse and unlocked her car door.

"Hold on a minute," Nate called as he approached.

She turned in his direction. Her eyes flashed both with surprise and something he couldn't quite identify, an interesting mix of joy and second-thought loathing. She looked down at her feet and reached for the car door as if she were debating fleeing.

"You're a hard woman to find." Nate placed his hand on the side of the burgundy Pathfinder. "I'm starting to think it's intentional."

"Intentional? Why would you think that?" She refused to meet his gaze.

"I've been trying to get in touch with you all day. You promised we'd meet today. Remember? You have a brother in jail. Remember him?" He couldn't pretend any more. It was time to put it to her straight.

"You needn't be sarcastic, Mr. Nakai. I'm very aware where my brother is."

"Then why are you avoiding me like the plague? I'm the one whose job it is to get him out of this mess. And a little help from you sure as hell wouldn't hurt."

"I'm not avoiding you." Anger flashed in her eyes. "If it's your job to clear my brother, your time would be better spent doing exactly that instead of wasted tracking me down. How did you find me anyway? Did you follow me again?"

"Clear your brother? How about a reality check here? Your kid brother will be lucky if he gets out of this with less than thirty years." Nate shifted on his feet. They'd talk about him following her later.

Mary put her hand to her head and whispered under her breath. "Thirty years—"

"I said *lucky*. What do you think will happen if that girl dies, Mary?" He wasn't pulling any punches with her.

"Stop this. I don't want to hear any more."

"Whether you want to hear it or not, you can't hide from the truth."

"I've no intentions of hiding from the truth. Truth has been a faithful and cruel companion in my life. How dare you make accusations."

"I didn't come all the way out here to argue with you. We can't put off meeting any longer." Nate glanced down at his watch. "Dammit. I've got less than twenty minutes to get back to Santa Fe. I'm interviewing the witnesses in your brother's case. You meet me in Santa Fe tonight at the Coyote Café, seven o'clock sharp."

"So we've gone from requests to orders. Whom did you say was working for whom?"

"Just be there. I work for the state and if you don't show up tonight, they can find another idiot to keep your kid brother's ass out of the slammer." Nate whirled and stormed to his car. Slamming the door, he drove away leaving Mary standing there looking after him.

Her body language screamed of outrage. What had he ever done to her? He'd reached a point where he was just plain pissed off at her attitude. There was a good chance Johnny was guilty. Nothing Nate had seen or read thus far pointed any other way. And Mary hated his guts. Why the hell was he still on this case? Why couldn't he scrape together that stonewall in his heart when he really needed it?

———

"Did you check on the girl this morning?" Smith nailed the police officer to the wall with his gaze.

"Yeah. No change in her condition." Officer Gonzales avoided Smith's eyes as he took a seat on the other side of Smith's polished mahogany desk.

"Humph. Keep checking. Let me know if anything happens with her." He slid into his chair and leaned back. His exhausted body wracked with tension. Turning his chair, Smith noted the stress lines in

Gonzales' face, deepened by the shadow of reflected sunlight from the window. He was looking old these days.

"I'll keep you in the loop." Gonzales jotted a note in a small wire bound notepad.

"You'll do more than that. I want a report every day until she's better or she's—" Smith ran his hand down his face. "She's what? Dead? That's what you were going to say isn't it?" Gonzales frowned in disgust.

"What if it was? It could very well happen and you know it."

Gonzales rubbed the back of his neck. "Sure it could."

"Then what's your issue?"

"It's your tone of voice, Jim. You say it like you hope it'll happen."

"I never insinuated any such thing. It's a cold hard fact." Smith shifted in his chair. Was Gonzales trying to come across as some goody two shoes?

"It is a fact. But this whole case is cut and dry. Johnny Begay is going to prison. I don't see it any other way."

Smith's eyes narrowed. "That's the way it will happen."

Gonzales shook his head. "It's a shame. He's just a kid."

"A kid capable of murder."

"You can't let it go, can you? She's not dead yet."

"That was a slip of the tongue."

"I don't think so. Putting the Begay kid behind bars isn't enough for you, is it?"

"We have a legitimate homici—" Smith cleared his throat. "I mean, assault here. The kid is a danger to society and nothing will get in my way of getting a conviction."

"Christ sakes, Smith. You're like a dog with a bone."

"What are you getting at?"

"Come on. We both know what this is really about."

"If you think this has anything to do with what happened with Mary Begay a few years ago, you're wrong."

"Yeah, right."

Smith rolled his eyes. "Being a dog after a bone is what's made me the best damn DA this county ever had."

Gonzales avoided his eyes and looked down at the floor. "You've been the DA for four terms, and in this business for twenty-nine years. Maybe it's time to hang it up."

"Twenty nine years is something I'm proud of. I'm not ready for a rocking chair, yet."

"It's not all something to be proud of." Gonzales rolled his eyes and mumbled under his breath.

Smith rose from the chair as his face reddened. "I could hang your ass from the nearest flagpole if you give me reason. You know that. How dare you challenge my integrity."

"It's tough to challenge something that doesn't exist."

Smith clenched his teeth. "Guess that makes us peas in a pod. We both have things in our past best left under wraps. At least everything I've done has been for the greater good. I can't say the same for you and your kickbacks."

Gonzales's jaw rippled and he squirmed in his seat. "Leave it be, Smith. I know you have me by the balls."

"Good. Now that we've gotten everything back in perspective, I have one more thing I want you to take care of."

"What's that?"

"His name's Nakai. Public Defender's office."

Gonzales' frown deepened. "He has no case. What difference does he make?"

"I don't like him. I want him off the defense."

"Easier said than done." Gonzales rolled his eyes.

Smith ignored the gesture. "That's where you come in. You just volunteered your services in seeing he's gone."

"Smith." Gonzales grasped the arm of his chair and leaned forward.

"Sure would be a shame if I had to clean out my old records and came across some incriminating evidence about a crooked cop."

"Jesus. I'll see what I can come up with." A cloud crossed Gonzales' face as he eased back.

"Thought you might see it my way."

Gonzales' look threw daggers at Smith as he stormed from the office.

"And don't bungle it. I don't want anything popping up that isn't iron clad." Smith yelled behind him.

Jim Smith sat roughly back into the chair behind his desk and loosened his tie. It was a hot day, but the beads of sweat rolling down his neck weren't all from the heat outside. A part of him was almost giddy, while another part felt like he needed a bath. It was a feeling that would pass. It had before.

After all, the kid was a punk, another potential drunk the world was better off without. And once again, Smith had a golden opportunity to get to Mary Begay, the murderess gone unpunished. Nothing that had happened to her, yet, could equal his pain. She couldn't possibly hurt the way he had.

Ethan was his own flesh and blood, his dream, and his hope for the future, his only son. Ethan was all he had left in the world, the piece of him that was supposed to go on when he couldn't. Now it was gone forever. Gone in a split second of drunken Indian stupidity. His fists knotted in anger.

He'd made Mary pay once for her involvement. Made her pay where the system had failed him, but his heart had yet to find peace. He knew where the dirty feeling came from. But this too would pass. After all, none of this was his doing. The situation with Johnny Begay was a stroke of luck in his favor. A gift from a vengeful God that would once again see justice served against Mary Begay.

There was only one fly in the ointment. He closed his eyes, trying to calm the throbbing in his chest. Anxiety pounded through his body. What was it about Nakai that had him so cverwrought?

From the moment he'd seen the man for the first time, a band of iron had clasped around his heart. There was a familiarity there, yet he couldn't quite remember where it came from. He had this feeling they'd met before . . . and it wasn't good. A feeling of dread had shot through to his very soul, and hung there still.

He'd tried to analyze it. He had no real reason to believe Nakai was going to keep Johnny Begay out of jail. He rubbed his taught jaw. Maybe it was the instinct he'd so finely honed through the years. Or maybe there was something deeper. A chill ran through him and he shook it off. Either way, Nakai was trouble, a cancer that had to be stopped before it spread.

Smith loosened his tie and laid his head back on his chair. He simply had to learn to relax. Within a few moments he was fast asleep.

Crow Feather was up early. Crawling from the kiva to greet the first light of Father Sun, he'd chanted at the morning ceremony and blessed the day for his people. But his thoughts were on Lone Eagle. He wished to see the pain in his son's eyes by the light of day. It was worth the loss of an hour of sleep.

Of all his sons, Lone Eagle was the least like him. That was one of many reasons that last night had brought him such pleasure. Lone Eagle was right. Black Hawk was the one most like his father.

For a moment, across the village, he thought he saw Lone Eagle gathering his morning's nourishment from the cooking pots. He had to look twice, but to his disappointment it was Black Hawk. He'd confused the two many times.

Though the brothers were almost identical in appearance, Black Hawk had his father's eyes. Lone Eagle's were more like his mother's, but thankfully for all of them, he'd been spared the telling blue eyes of the ancient lineage from which he descended. The blue eyes would have meant certain death for all of them.

Two Birds, the youngest of his sons, ran between the cooking pots. He was still a few summers away from manhood. He had the look of his uncle, and at times Crow Feather wondered if Two Birds' mother had secretly mated with Raven—something he dared not ask his brother. Still, Two Birds showed promise. He, too, could possess the soul of his father.

The old man nodded with pleasure and continued to search the group gathered for the morning meal. Lone Eagle was not among them. This troubled Crow Feather. Where was his son this morning when he should be preparing for the hunt?

Smith jerked awake. He rubbed his eyes. What a strange dream. But these were strange times in his life. The dream had left him with an oddly satisfying feeling, though. He shrugged and shook it off. He had bigger things to worry about.

CHAPTER SIX

"What do you mean it was cancelled?" The heat rose beneath Nate's collar.

"The lady says she got a call from someone this morning saying the meeting had been postponed." Coyote stood in Nate's office, hands on his hips in exasperation. "I figured you made the call."

"It sure as hell wasn't me. I busted my butt getting back here." Nate shook his head. He'd left things hanging with Mary in order to meet with this eyewitness. How many obstacles could occur in less than a week?

Coyote shifted his stance and said nothing.

"Do you think the old lady was lying? Maybe she doesn't want to talk to us. What's your gut feeling?" Nate tried to calm his anger.

"I think someone called her. I think she's telling the truth about that."

Nate rubbed his jaw. "If it wasn't you and it wasn't me, then who?"

Coyote raised an eyebrow. "Maybe it was a mistake."

"Yeah. Maybe."

"You don't sound convinced."

"That's not all I'm not convinced about in this case. I'll get over it."

"Or not." Coyote laid the black portfolio he was holding on Nate's desk. "I've got a copy of her statement to the police. We can at least review it since we won't be going out to her house today."

"Nice of our friends at Santa Fe PD to finally shake loose of the reports." Nate snorted.

"I can't figure out why they weren't part of the original package. Maybe they screwed up."

"Screwed seems a fitting word for the situation."

Coyote's eyes met Nate's and his jaw rippled. He pulled several more pages from the pocket in the front of the notebook.

Nate took it from Coyote's hand and sat in the chair behind the desk. Coyote seated himself across from Nate and the room fell silent for several minutes as Nate read and reread the report. He laid it on the desk and leaned back in his chair.

"How many kids in black T-shirts and blue jeans do you suppose walk the streets of Santa Fe on any given Tuesday afternoon in July?"

"Indian boys with shoulder length black hair? Chances of there being more than one are definitely not that far fetched in this town."

Nate looked back at the report. "She picked him out of a line up. That's here, too."

"All three of them did. That's what's gonna kill us."

"Yeah. Hopefully it doesn't kill the girl." Nate ran his hand down his chin.

Coyote winced. "Bad choice of words."

Nate nodded. "The line up is the kicker. We have to interview these people one on one. We've got to find some holes in their stories."

"A reasonable doubt. That's what we really need."

Nate looked at the report and tossed it across the desk. "Not much to build a defense around."

"It's all we've got so far."

Nate brought his fist down hard on the desk. "Dammit. This thing's going nowhere fast."

"Easy man. It's still early in the game."

"Some games are over before they start." Nate regretted what he'd said before the words finished rolling off his tongue.

"What's that supposed to mean?"

"Nothing. Just having a bad day, I guess."

The skeptical look and the crease in Coyote's forehead didn't need words for clarification. "If you don't believe the kid, you aren't doing him any favors by staying on the case."

Nate ground his teeth. "What I believe isn't ultimately going to be the problem. It's what a judge and jury believe that decides Johnny fate."

Coyote leaned back in his chair, his lips taut and his brow creased. "And if you don't believe him, how the hell are you going to convince them?"

"I never said I didn't believe him. Don't think that. From the time I first looked into the eyes of that terrified kid, something inside kept saying he isn't capable of doing something like this."

"So what happened? When did you change your mind?"

"I haven't. But when I look through these reports I can't see how we're going to prove these witnesses wrong."

"You know that's why he needs you. You've been a lawyer long enough to know it's your job to find the one thing that doesn't fit."

"You're absolutely right. I'm letting the frustration get to me. Did you reschedule with Mrs. Savage?"

"Yeah. For tomorrow."

"Tomorrow." Nate blew air between his lips. "We can't afford to lose another day. You know as well as I do, the more days that pass the colder the trail gets and the dimmer the truth becomes in people's minds."

"Indeed I do. But there's nothing we can do about it today."

Nate stood and turned toward the window. "I'm going to go out to where it happened. Maybe there's something you missed."

Coyote shook his head. "There's nothin' there, but help yourself. You go on. I've got some phone calls to make to the other two witnesses. I'm gonna be sure they don't have any schedule changes unless they hear directly from me."

"I've got a meeting with Mary tonight at seven o'clock. Maybe I can still stir something up before this day is over."

Coyote's demeanor took an obvious change at the mention of Mary's name. "Mary." He shook his head. "She ought to give us plenty of reason to find some evidence."

Nate gave Coyote a questioning look. The same thought had been on his mind, but hopefully they were on different wavelengths. For now he'd assume Coyote's reaction was based on his long-standing friendship with Mary. His own was more about his failure to keep his primal urges in check. Mary stirred something in him he hadn't felt in a long time, at least not earnestly.

It was approaching five-thirty when Nate parked on the street around the corner from the alley where Stellar Sanchez had been attacked. Three days had passed and there was no longer any police tape around the area.

Coyote was right. There was nothing in the alley or the surrounding area that offered any sign of what happened a few days earlier. But it wasn't just clean, it was squeaky clean. Freshly swept was a very accurate observation. Not a grain of sand, not a wayward bit of trash, a tumbleweed or even a thread could be seen anywhere.

"Unnaturally clean" were the best words Nate could find to describe it. He jotted the note in a small notebook he carried in his back pocket. If there wasn't any evidence, perhaps that in itself would be evidence of some sort. The thought played in his mind as he carefully examined every crack and corner hoping to find something that had been left behind or perhaps more accurately, missed.

He scoured the approximately fifty-foot dead end alleyway between two one-story adobe buildings. A few small piles of bird excrement were on a short retaining wall at the opening into the alley and that was it. Nothing to base a case on. Last time he'd checked birds were allowed to poop anywhere they pleased. Of course, in Santa Fe, the DA might have something to say about that, too.

The comment Coyote had made about Smith and Mary's history and his own encounters with both of them weighed on his mind. Was there a connection between them?

A chattering screech interrupted his thoughts. Turning in the direction of the sound, he noticed a large black and white magpie standing atop a retaining wall. The bird conjured images in his mind.

The vision from the pier washed through him like the first wave of a Tsunami, unexpected and devastating in its force. The rope tightened around his throat—around her throat. The stifling suffocation brought the shadows of blackness that threatened to steal the sunlight. Fear ached in the pit of his stomach. The images of the girl raced through his mind like a movie. His body responded to those pictures, totally beyond his control.

His hands grabbed at his throat, trying to pull at the cord searing his neck. He fell to his knees on the rough cobblestones, the feel of their roughness all too familiar. Then the blackness poured over him, the release of the pain, the floating sensation.

Holy shit. What the hell happened? Nate opened his eyes. He lay sprawled on the ground. He sat up hoping no one had seen him. Brushing off his slacks, he rose to his feet and loosened his shirt collar. His throat was taut and parched. His knees were shaky. He wasn't a drinking man, but he could sure use one right now.

He walked to the short wall and leaned on it to steady himself. The bird still sat on its perch. Turning its head, its sharp black eyes looked into his. It chattered almost laughingly at him. An unexplained icy finger ran the length of his spine. Nate blinked his eyes as the bird flew away.

Nate mopped his brow with the back of his hand trying to make sense of what had happened to him. Then the full realization began to seep in. The vision he'd had in San Francisco could have actually happened, here on this spot.

No, it couldn't be. It wasn't possible. But the feel of the cobblestones beneath his body, the searing rope at his throat. It was a crazy idea, an insane prospect. His mouth went dry as cotton. It wasn't logical. There was only one way to put his mind at rest. He looked at his watch. He had to meet Mary in a few minutes, but he knew where he had to go first thing tomorrow.

He glanced around as his mind raced with possibilities. Only one thing he was sure of. He didn't want to be on this spot where evil stood three days earlier. Its presence was strong and undeniable, as if the vision had opened a hole in his psyche. He wasn't going to hang around and see if it had anything else in store for him.

"Are you okay?" Mary asked. "You look a little pale."

"Probably the light in here." Nate responded curtly.

She didn't believe him. He looked white as a ghost and seemed ill at ease. Nor had his arrogant attitude shown up. She wondered why and glanced at him occasionally from the corner of her eye, searching for clues to what was on his mind. Maybe she was being overly suspicious.

Obviously, he read her actions. "I'm a little tired. It's been a long day."

"Perhaps I should apologize for making you come all the way out to Chimayo today." Her mouth made apologies, but her heart lacked sincerity.

He shrugged and studied the menu silently.

Grateful to hide behind her own leather fortress, she pretended to be intent upon the selections. She had to get her thoughts together on how to prove Johnny innocent. *If this public defender could help her.* Well, that was why she'd come, the only reason why she'd come.

She tried to focus on her mission, but thoughts she'd prefer to suppress kept crowding her mind. Heat crept into her cheeks. Being near him made her uncomfortable. Nate's face had haunted her since the first minute she'd laid eyes on him.

Every detail, every line in his face and even the scar on his upper lip was an exact likeness to the painting. The dream warrior, whose very image on canvas made her blood boil, sat across from her in a dimly lit corner booth in the Coyote Café. Things like this just didn't happen.

Now that he'd seen the painting, what was he thinking?

"You spend a lot of time at that mission?" Nate interrupted her thoughts but never looked at her as he talked into the menu. Perhaps he also wanted to hide what lay behind his eyes tonight.

"I go there from time to time. When I need a place to be alone and think."

"All those crosses," Nate said softly. The words hung in the air.

"Remembrances of the dead. Tributes to loved ones. It's part of the energy and peace of the place."

Nate nodded. After a short pause he asked. "Ever wonder where that kind of energy comes from?"

Mary shrugged. "I don't know."

"Does it come from inside of us or out?"

"I guess I never thought about it."

His eyes narrowed. "Ever wonder if one soul can talk to another?"

A shiver ran through Mary. "That's an odd question." He'd stepped beyond her comfort zone. "I know you didn't want to meet to talk about the mission or its energy. What's your point, Mr. Nakai?"

"Sorry. My mind's wandering in some strange directions tonight."

Nate shot her a quick glance then fell silent. It was obvious he was deep in thought about something. There was a tug at her heartstrings. It was the first sign she'd seen so far that there was a human being inside of that all-business attorney with the high and mighty attitude. She wondered exactly what was running through his mind.

She was feeling unsettled, too. The trip to the churchyard hadn't helped to ground her. It always had before. It brought clarity and made life seem worth living, if not for herself at least for those entrusted in her care. Johnny and Grandpa.

But Johnny's fate hung in the balance and she had to do something about it. She knew in her heart he was innocent, but she didn't know how to prove it. That's why she needed this attorney—this apparition—this man who'd walked into her life two days ago and turned her world upside down.

She couldn't afford the distraction. It was time to put her questions, emotions and this damnable urge to run away, aside. Half of her despised Nathan Nakai and what he stood for and the other half was clawing at her insides like a tiger in heat.

Mary took a deep breath. She was in control. She was always in control of her emotions. She would sit here and have dinner with the man, who not only had lived in her imagination for years, but who possibly held her brother's life in his hands.

She lowered the menu. The long silence was becoming uncomfortable. "The enchiladas are very good."

Nate nodded absentmindedly. He was way too quiet. Where was the bulldog after a bone that had been pursuing her the last few days with his prying questions?

Nate finished his first glass of wine and poured a second from the carafe, pouring one for Mary before she could decline. It was the first wine she'd had in almost three years. She'd never had a problem with liquor, but she'd spent a lot of years blaming it for its repercussions on her life.

But the past was dead and it was time to bury it. It was time to bury it all.

When the second wine glass was empty, Nate poured a third and seemed to be relaxing. "Sorry, I haven't been very good company so far. I've got some issues on my mind."

"Involving Johnny?" Mary's heart stopped.

Nate paused. "Some of them. Don't panic. We've got a long way to go."

Mary let out a partial sigh of relief. "I don't think I can handle any more bad news."

"I wish I had some good news to tell you, but I haven't been able to come up with anything in the last two days. I'm hoping you can shed some light on what's bothering me."

Mary looked down at the table. "We'll see." She was aware the stoic tone returned to her voice. Her deflector shields were back in place.

Nate raised his eyebrows and squared his shoulders as the waiter approached the table. After placing their orders, he turned back toward Mary.

"Has Johnny been in trouble with the law before?"

"No, of course not. What would make you think that?"

"You alluded to it the first time we met." Nate pinned her down with his eyes.

Mary frowned. "No, I didn't."

"I believe you said something like, 'oh no, not again'."

His mimicking tone annoyed her. "I wasn't referring to Johnny when I made that comment. It meant nothing." God, she hated lawyers.

"It made me curious enough to check it out." His pale thoughtful look twisted into a smirk.

"If you've already checked it out, why are you asking me?"

"It's my job to ask questions—and get answers."

Mary nodded and rolled her eyes, but chose not to respond.

"What were you referring to?" Nate prodded further.

Mary pursed her lips. "That's of no concern to you."

"Is it of any concern to Johnny?"

Mary paused. "Not that I'm aware of, Mr. Nakai."

"No need to get testy. What about your comment about public defenders?"

"That wasn't about Johnny, either."

"Based on your answers you seem to have a lot of experience somewhere along the line you'd rather not talk about."

"That's the first *true* insight you've had, yet."

"Look, if there's anything here that relates to Johnny's case, I hope you care enough about your brother to lay it on the table."

"You can rest assured I'll share anything I believe will help Johnny. Everything else is my personal business and not something I intend to share with a complete stranger."

Nate's voice softened as he looked at his glass of wine and took another sip. "Then maybe the key is not to be strangers." A glint sparked in his eyes for a fleeting second as they met hers.

Mary's heart stopped and a warm rush threatened her deflector shields. Then anger flared and put them back in place. She closed her eyes and swallowed the retort that wanted to jump from her lips. *Damn*. This man couldn't seem to avoid her hot buttons. Composing herself, she made a careful reply. "The Navajo are a private people. We hold our cards close to our chests. It's part of my upbringing."

A threatening smirk told her he was avoiding the comment perched on his tongue. She'd left herself wide open with that remark. She was grateful he'd sidestepped it.

"Mary, I have a difficult job here. To be perfectly frank I haven't found one scrap of evidence that tells me your brother didn't try to kill that girl. Noble as your loyalty to him is, and the pride your people take in being secretive, your belief that he's innocent isn't worth a tinker's damn in court. That's about as delicately as I can put the truth."

Mary's face flushed. For two cents she'd tell him what he could do with his arrogance. If Johnny's life didn't hang in the balance, she'd damn sure give him a piece of her mind. Instead, she swallowed it along with a gulp of wine. But the vile stuff didn't make her feel any better. No matter how hard she tried, she blamed it for too much heartache.

Nate's face steeled. "What did Smith say to you outside the court house yesterday?"

"He merely said hello." Why was he asking about Smith? What assurance did she have Smith and Nakai weren't in cahoots?

"I don't believe that for a minute. I doubt he'd waste time exchanging niceties when he's out to send your kid brother to prison."

Mary flinched. He had her on that one. "He made some snide remark. I don't remember. I ignored it."

"Not very professional for someone in his position." Nate rubbed his chin. "Smith paid me a visit after I saw Johnny the first time. He came across like a stuffed shirt. A man with blood in his eye when it comes to getting the maximum sentence for your brother."

Mary snorted. She couldn't hold back. "Jim Smith's had blood in his eye when it comes to my family for years. He's not a stuffed shirt. He's a pompous ass."

The corner of Nate's mouth turned up in a half grin. His eyes snapped. Obviously, he knew he'd struck a nerve. "I heard you and your family have some history with the DA. Care to elaborate?"

"I do not. He's a prejudice, underhanded man. And he has been for the fifteen years I've known him. I have no use for him. It infuriates me that he has so much influence in the justice system in Santa Fe." She stopped, panting slightly from her angry outburst. "That's all I have to say on the subject. I have work to do at my gallery tonight. I need to be going." She picked up her purse and scooted out of the booth.

"Wait a minute. I'm not finished."

"Well I am." Mary whirled, nearly crashing into the waiter carrying their dinner plates.

"Dammit, woman." She heard Nate's comment as she sped between the tables, out the front door and into the dark street. To hell with this attorney and his prying questions. There would be no more meetings for the two of them. Clearing Johnny was up to her and her alone from here on. She wasn't exhuming any more of the ghosts from her past for Nathan Nakai or anyone else.

<hr />

Cripes sake. Either she had some serious hatred for Smith or this woman couldn't keep her temper in check if her life depended on it. What could be so damn important or so deep-seated she couldn't put aside her secrets and come clean even to help her kid brother? He just didn't get it.

Nate downed the remainder of the wine in his glass. This had been one hell of a day and he'd secretly hoped for a nice quiet dinner with an attractive lady. Well, that didn't happen.

He was actually getting used to Mary's cold shoulder. Expecting anything else was fruitless. Maybe she thought he was prying when he brought up the mission. Or maybe she had issues. Big ones.

The rumble in his stomach and the smell of the enchiladas reminded him he'd skipped lunch. *No reason to let it go to waste.* He picked up his fork and shoveled in the warm food. Mary was right. It was excellent.

"Aren't you Nate Nakai?"

Nate swallowed and looked up, wiping his mouth with his napkin. A tall Hispanic man stood next to the table dressed in a white shirt and gray slacks. "Yes, I am," Nate said after a quick drink of water.

"Nice to meet you, sir. I'm Detective Gonzales. I'm assigned to the Begay case." Gonzales extended a hand.

Nate's intuition meter instantly went on alert. The man's hand was clammy and cool. His eyes darted nervously.

"I just got off duty and stopped for a bite to eat." Gonzales seemed to feel the need to explain his presence.

Nate smiled and nodded.

"Mind if I sit down?" Gonzales slid into the booth before Nate could respond.

"Go ahead. But I'm almost finished."

"Yeah. Always got a case to investigate. Seems crime never slows down."

"Keeps us both employed."

"Yeah. Too bad about the Begay kid. Cut and dried case that one." Gonzales shook his head and made a clicking noise in his cheek.

"It's a little early to be so sure." Nate's insides twisted. Even if he had doubts, he resented getting this kind of commentary from the police investigator.

"I've seen these cases too often. Kind of surprised an attorney of your stature would get their name involved in a case like this one. Gang members and all. The media's going to have a hey day in the papers."

Nate looked across the table at Gonzales. "First I've heard of gang involvement."

"Oh hell. That's a lead pipe cinch. No doubt about it. Gangs are a huge problem here. This one's no different. That's what most of the problems relating to minors in Santa Fe are about."

Nate nibbled the inside of his cheek. This time he wasn't going to say anything.

"Three eye witnesses. Positive ID. Kid with no alibi. I guess this one's gang buddies aren't willing to lie for him. Sure wouldn't want to have my good name and career tied up with a low life like that."

"You seem to have an awful lot to say about this case." And it was way too much for Nate's taste.

"Oh, I didn't mean to run on. You'll get my reports in a few days. Just wanted to warn you, being new to town, this one could be a real bad thing for you. You know, while you still have time to get out of it without any questions being asked. Before the newspapers get hold of you. You ought to hand this one over to some rookie who doesn't know any better." Gonzales winked and bobbed his head in Nate's direction.

"Real thoughtful of you." Heat rose under Nate's shirt collar.

"No problem, man. Wanted to give you the inside scoop. You know, before it's too late. Us good guys have to stick together." Gonzales winked.

"Speaking of late, I need to be going." Nate had his fill of both the enchiladas and Gonzales' line of bull.

"Yeah, I gotta be going too." Gonzales got up nervously and left as abruptly as he'd appeared.

Wasn't that interesting? Thought he came in to get something to eat. Apparently not. It seemed his real mission was to deliver a snow job. Nate's curiosity peaked about who sent the message. He had a suspicion, a stinking suspicion at that.

It had without a doubt been one hell of a day.

CHAPTER SEVEN

The stark contrast of the white hospital sheets next to her bronze face made the girl look small and frail. Monitors surrounded her and their intermittent beeps were all that broke the silence. Digital numbers and green wavy lines ran across their screens. Tubes ran from bags of fluid to destinations under the covers tucked neatly beneath her chin.

Nate's blood ran cool for more than one reason as he stood at the foot of the bed. Her eyes were closed, her breathing steady and even. The comatose sleep that claimed her was blessedly peaceful. Except for the red marks around her neck, no other outward signs alluded to the violent horror that had besieged her a few days earlier.

Hands tucked deep in his pant's pockets, Nate asked himself why he had really come here. Seeing the young victim in person tore at his heartstrings and heightened his commitment to find the truth. Silently, he prayed for the girl and that he wasn't defending the person who'd put her here. Coming here was against his better judgment. It wasn't in his or Johnny's best interest for him to feel what he was feeling.

He wasn't sure what drove him. A burning curiosity and something deep in his gut drew him to her bedside. And worse yet, no one else was here. No one sat with her, as he would have expected. Perhaps they'd just stepped out. The absence of flowers, or any personal effects in the room made that theory seem shallow at best. In every sense of the word, the girl was still a child, fragile and alone.

The knot in his belly formed because it was his job to defend the boy accused of putting her here. But ironically, he sensed an unexplainable connection to her, a possibility that had haunted him all night. And yet a faint feeling of guilt hung over his heart for coming at all.

He wasn't sure how long he stood there studying the minuscule details of her face and her black hair splayed across the white pillow. There was a similarity to his vision, and yet, how could he be absolutely certain she was the girl who'd walked through his mind and being? The one who'd devastated him for a fleeting moment in time as he'd seen a horrendous crime through her eyes, the eyes of the victim.

Maybe the impact of the vision was the reason for the connection he felt. Perhaps there was nothing more to it. The thoughts that danced in his mind defied logic. He should be more concerned with what was going on with the DA and an overly friendly investigator named Gonzales, more grounded in the details of the case.

Silently, he watched her breathing softly, in and out, in and out. Her chest rose gently up and down. The hospital was surprisingly quiet. There was an occasional squish of shoes on tile floors as nurses moved through the corridor and the steady blip of the monitors.

He tried to remember the face from his vision and distance the debilitating emotion threatening to claim him. It was like walking a tightrope.

"Are you family?" A soft female voice spoke next to his ear.

A small blonde nurse in a colorful pink smock entered the room without his notice.

"Yes—err no. I'm actually assigned to the case." Nate stumbled over his words pulling himself back to the moment.

"Such an awful shame, isn't it?" The nurse removed a clipboard from the foot of the bed and checked the girl's vital signs.

"Yes, it is." He didn't welcome the interruption or feel like making polite conversation.

"At least she's stabilized."

"What about the coma? Any sign she might come out of it?"

"Not yet. The longer she's in this state, the smaller the chance she'll come out of it. But it's still early. There's time."

"I'm curious. Does she have family?"

"Her mother was here for a while. Seemed more concerned about who was going to pay the hospital bill than with her daughter's condition. I haven't seen her since the day Stellar was brought in."

"Too bad." Nate bit his lip.

Tuning in on the emotion Nate was trying to keep at bay, the nurse gave him a thoughtful look. "You said you were working on the case?"

"Yes."

"Well, this has been on my mind. I don't know if it means anything or not." The nurse opened the top drawer of a small bedside table and removed something in a paper towel.

Nate stepped closer as she carefully unwrapped the contents.

"This was in her hand when they brought her in. Not sure if it has any significance or if it was something she was carrying. ER labeled it as personal belongings and it ended up here." Opening the towel, a large black and white feather lay in the folds of white paper.

Nate staggered as intense white light flashed through him and an image jumped into his mind, the blurred picture of a boy in a black hat.

"Are you okay?" the nurse asked.

"I'm fine," Nate struggled to clear his head, and quickly regained his composure.

"Do you recognize it?"

"No—not really." He wasn't prepared to explain his experience.

Taking the feather in his hands, he examined it closely and glanced over at the tiny form buried in the pillows next to him. For a fleeting moment, the girl opened her eyes and looked at him. His gut wrenched and his heart jumped to his throat. The color drained from his face along with any doubt from his mind. *Good God, it's her.*

"Did you see that?" Nate managed to squeak out the words, realizing the girl's action was important.

"See what?" The nurse was immediately alert.

"She opened her eyes."

"Really. I didn't see it. I was watching her, too. I guess I could have missed it, but I don't think so."

"Well, she did. I'm certain she looked at me."

"If she did, it's a positive sign. But she's a very sick girl."

"What's the prognosis?"

"Not good."

A heavy sigh escaped from Nate without warning.

"I'll leave you alone," she said. "I hope you find whoever put her here. Whoever it was is an animal and needs to be behind bars."

As quickly and quietly as she had appeared, the nurse left, like an angel disappearing into the night. Nate looked at the feather in his hand. She was right. He needed time alone to sort this out. The revelations of this morning went far beyond the realm of the legal aspects he was up against. His heart and soul vibrated at a rate he'd never known before.

The smells of the hospital suddenly hit him and he
had to get away before he was physically ill. He
hurried from the room, trying to keep from running,
desperately in need of fresh air.

———

Mary looked pleadingly into the eyes of the boy as
they stood on the wooden porch of the mobile home.
"Luis, I know you're upset about this, too. But if
there's anything, anything at all you can remember
that might help Johnny, he really needs you."

"I wish I could help him. But like I said, and like I
told the police the other day, Johnny left by himself
while we were at the arcade. I honestly don't know
where he went. He joined back up with us just before
the cops came and hauled us all away." The boy's
shoulders slumped beneath his white T-shirt and the
morning sun highlighted the slight growth of dark hair
on the Hispanic boy's jaw line.

Mary sighed. Luis and Johnny were both boys
showing the first signs of their journey into manhood.
"You're Johnny's best friend. I know you'd do anything
for him. I was hoping you'd remember something."

The boy batted long black lashes as red circles crept
around his eyes. "I can't believe any of this. Stellar
was with us for a while and she left to go home. Said
her mom was gonna be real mad if she didn't get home
and do her chores. God, I hope she's going to be all
right."

"That was the last time you saw her?"

"Yeah." The boy's large eyes mirrored his shocked
disbelief.

"And Johnny?"

"He left a few minutes after she did, when we
decided to go goof around at the arcade for a while.
Said he didn't feel like hanging out there."

"Really." Mary's stomach turned and her mouth was dry as desert dust. She had no doubt about Johnny's innocence, but she also knew how this must sound to the police. She'd been caught in this trap of false assumptions before.

"They're not going to send him to jail are they?" Luis' voice raised several octaves. "Mary, I know he didn't do it."

Mary tried to still her trembling hand as she placed it on his arm. "I know it, too. But what we both know in our hearts, won't stand up in a courtroom."

"It's not fair. None of it's fair." Luis ran his hand down his face avoiding Mary's eyes. She knew he was trying to be strong and hide his tears. No matter how hard he tried, the pain he was feeling for both of his friends oozed from his body language.

"It's going to be okay," Mary said in a more comforting tone. "We need to find some substantial evidence."

"The police questioned us all on Tuesday afternoon. None of us could tell them anything." Luis shook his head. "I can ask the guys again. We were all scared to death that day. You know none of us have ever had any run-ins with the law. And poor Stellar—"

"I know. This is some horrible mistake. It has to be. I'm going to get to the bottom of it. Don't worry. Okay?"

The boy nodded and forced a half smile, but the depths of his eyes were dark and sad. Mary couldn't stand it any longer. She gave Luis a long hug, and walked back to her Pathfinder. So where was she to turn next?

"Man, you don't look so good." Coyote came up the stairs as Nate opened the door to his office. "You tie one on last night?"

"Of course not," Nate replied coarsely. "I'm not a drinking man." He flinched remembering the way he'd polished off the carafe of wine last night. At least he wasn't unless he had a damn good reason. Either way, he knew his current appearance had little or nothing to do with that.

Coyote shrugged. "Just wondered. You look like warmed over death. Or maybe you ran into a ghost in the lobby."

Nate shook his head and blew out a sigh of disgust. The ghosts he'd encountered in the last two days lived in his head, not in his office building.

"You find out something new on the case?" Coyote prodded.

Nate hesitated. "Not really, but come on in. I've got a couple things I want you to check out."

Plopping his briefcase roughly on the desk, Nate slid into his chair. "I want you to scour the police report and see if you can find anything about a hat."

"A hat?" Coyote positioned himself in the chair across from him and leaned forward with his elbows resting on his thighs.

"Yeah. A black one."

"Don't recall seeing anything about it."

"I don't want recollection. I want you to be absolutely iron-clad sure. I want to know if any of the eye witness reports mention one and if the boy had one in his possession when he was arrested."

"Okay, man. No need to get uptight. You find some new evidence?"

Nate avoided Coyote's eyes. He didn't want them prying into the place this was coming from. "Maybe, maybe not. It's your job to find out if there's anything to it."

"All righty. I take it from your mood your dinner last night didn't go too well."

"That's another subject entirely. That woman wears me out. She and the visitor I had for dessert were pretty much a night full of nonstop entertainment."

Coyote raised an eyebrow. "That good, huh?"

"Mary Begay is the most secretive, high and mighty woman I've ever met. She's come up with every avoidance in the book to keep from coming clean with me. Even using her damn heritage as an excuse for clamming up. I've got enough of a challenge just to find *any* evidence in this fricking case without her being tight-lipped as a damn mummy."

"Hey, bro, back up a few expletives. And easy on the heritage bit. Navajo's mine, too."

Nate rubbed his eyes. "Sorry. I didn't mean to unload on you."

"Maybe if you throw out a few more details in between the frustration here, I could help you sort through this. Unless of course, you're not in the mood. Or maybe there's something too personal going on under this thing with Mary."

"Personal? I could only wish." Nate regretted that remark before it ever saw the light of day. His entire emotional state was an open book after this morning. He ran his hand up his forehead, into his hair and leaned into his palm. He felt his hair roots stifle a scream as he pulled hard on them and swallowed his heart along with his raw feelings.

"You sure you're all right?" Coyote leaned closer.

"Yeah. It's just been a real rough morning."

"All right. I think you need to spill some things here. Especially, if it effects my job. Calling Mary secretive is like sunshine calling the canary yellow."

Nate managed a smile as he looked at Coyote around his hand. "Sunshine and canaries? How fricking corny is that?"

"Corny, but original." Coyote removed his hat and sat it on the chair beside him. "Okay, spill what's on your mind. I got all day if we need it."

Nate looked down at his desk then leaned back in his chair. Running his finger under his shirt collar and taking a deep breath, he tried to relax. Maybe Coyote could clear up a few questions, if he was willing to talk. But only those grounded in reality and that pertained to the case.

"The meeting with Mary was a disaster. I tried to ask her some questions and she ended up getting mad and storming out without having dinner. I wish I knew what she was so touchy about all the time."

"What did you ask her?"

"She keeps making references that lead me to believe Johnny might have been in trouble before, but she denies he ever has. I checked it out and I can't find a thing."

"Johnny? No way. He's always been a real quiet kid. Goes to school. Gets good grades. Definitely has no record." Coyote pulled a toothpick from the pocket of his denim shirt and popped it into the corner of his mouth. Rolling it in his fingers, he looked as if he were thinking hard about something. He shook his head, but his demeanor had taken a serious turn. "Can't figure that one out. What was it she said?"

"The day I went to tell her about Johnny she said something about it was happening again and when I introduced myself she said, 'not another Public Defender'."

Coyote's face went solemn and his jaw tightened on the toothpick. A frown crossed his brow. He considered his answer carefully before he spoke. "I'm afraid I'd have to agree with Mary. Some things are best left buried. If it doesn't pertain to the case, then Mary owes you no explanations."

Their eyes met. "It doesn't involve Johnny?"

"It has nothing to do with him." Coyote looked sincere, but uncomfortable. He chose his next words carefully. "Nate, sometimes people have painful chapters in their lives they never want to reopen. That should be Mary's choice. Please let it be."

Nate nibbled the inside of his cheek. He took a deep breath. "All right. I have no idea what all the secrets are among you people, but I'll take you on your word and let that sleeping dog continue his nap."

Coyote nodded a silent thank you.

"What do you know about her and Smith?" Nate rose from his chair and walked to the window. "He said something to her when she came out of the courthouse the other day, but she refused to tell me what it was. She freaked on me when I pushed her about it."

"She's under a lot of emotional strain. I wouldn't read too much into it." Coyote leaned back in his chair and raised his right foot to his opposite knee, exposing a black cowboy boot. His answer seemed defensive in contrast to his laid back demeanor.

Nate turned and looked out the window. "You seem very protective of her. Something going on there I should know about?"

"No, sir. Like I told you, I've known her a long time and I don't want to see her hurting any more than she has to. Simple as that."

"After she left, I was paid a visit by a man named Gonzales. Odd sort of conversation. You recognize the name?"

"It's pretty common here. I can't say it means anything to me."

"This Gonzales works for the Santa Fe PD. Told me he's the investigator on this case." Nate turned to meet Coyote's eyes. "You ever work with him?"

"No. I do remember seeing the name Gonzalez on some of the police reports. Didn't register at first. Definitely didn't stand out for any reason."

"Well, he had a lot to say last night. He was pushing real hard to convince me to quit Johnny's defense."

Coyote looked surprised. "Why? What did he say?"

"Tried to tell me I was making a big mistake getting my name mixed up with this one. Told me Johnny's sure to go to prison."

Coyote's jaw rippled. "Interesting comment from someone who's supposed to just be gathering facts."

"I thought so, too. Also said Johnny was a gang member. You know anything about that?"

"Gang member? Not Johnny. Santa Fe's had some problems with gangs in recent years, but so have lots of other places. I'd bet my new boots Johnny's not mixed up with any of them."

"I want you to check it out anyway. Dig around, question his friends and see if there's any validity to it. It could be something."

"I'll do it. Still don't believe it, but I'll check it out anyway."

Nate rubbed his chin. "Do a real thorough job of it, please." He paused. "I went to see the girl this morning."

Coyote couldn't hide his surprise. "I don't think that was a good idea, but I'm not the boss. That why you look like hell?"

"Part of it. I don't know if she's going to make it."

"Damn. This could end up being murder one after all."

"Yes, it could." Silence fell like the drawing of a curtain.

"Well, I'd best get after this." Coyote picked up his hat and positioned it on his head. "Let me know if you need anything else."

Nate only wished the something else they needed was within Coyote's grasp. It seemed the more Nate learned the worse things looked for Johnny. And the most incriminating evidence seemed to exist inside of Nate's own mind.

CHAPTER EIGHT

Nate shifted in his chair. He'd lost track of how long he'd sat there. Combing through the police reports, hoping to find some tiny detail he'd missed earlier, he'd searched for any clue that could disprove the connection between his vision and the accounts of the crime. His failure to find any discrepancies weighed heavy on him. There had to be some explanation. Exhausted and numb, he leaned his elbows on the desk and rubbed his temples.

The whole thing made his mind a maze of incomprehensible thought. In the last twenty-four hours he'd been confronted with the unbelievable possibility that he'd stood on a pier in San Francisco and psychically seen a crime committed in Santa Fe. It was more than he could comprehend.

He was a logical, educated man. Things like this didn't happen in his world. His was a world where black was black and white was white, and only solid evidence was acceptable—and permissible in court. His head throbbed.

The shadows on the carpet and outside the window grew long. Several hours must have passed. There were things in the reports he should follow up on. But he was caught between two worlds in this case, between the real one and another that existed only in his own soul. And he'd find it a lot less unsettling if the two didn't cross over.

He had to admit he was hiding here because he was too stunned to function. For the first time in his life, he had to admit he was too emotionally and mentally exhausted to be of any use.

As if stepping straight from this surreal world he was caught up in, the form of an old man with long white hair appeared in the doorway of his office. He entered the room quietly and seated himself in the chair across from Nate's desk.

"Grandpa?"

The old man nodded.

"What are you doing here?"

"All things happen in their own time. It's time for us to talk."

Nate put his hand to his face, closed his eyes and pushed against them. Was this yet another vision? He removed his hand and opened his eyes. No, the old man was still there. Pulling himself from the distant state he'd been in all afternoon, he rose from his chair and extended his hand.

"I'm sorry, sir. I didn't mean to be disrespectful. You caught me off guard."

The elderly gentleman stood and took his hand. He shook it firmly, placing his other hand on top in a more intimate gesture. "Sir is not necessary. Grandpa will do just fine. Please sit down. My old bones were enjoying the rest."

Nate smiled and returned to his seat. "What brings you here, especially so late in the day?" Frankly, the old fellow was a welcome distraction.

Grandpa squinted slightly, scrutinizing every detail of Nate's face before he spoke. "I'd say Navajo and some sort of Pueblo in your blood. Although you're on the tall side for either."

"Actually, that's pretty good. My brother, Alex, the archaeologist, tells me we're Navajo and Hopi." He shook his head as he remembered his childhood. "But we were never taught much about our heritage. Pretty Americanized bunch, me and my brothers."

"Aw, Hopi." Grandpa nodded. Then the kachina on the corner of Nate's desk caught his eye. Grandpa leaned closer and a crease crossed his brow. "May I?" He pointed to the kachina.

"By all means," Nate replied.

Grandpa took the kachina carefully in his hands and turned it over, examining it thoroughly. He placed it back on the desk and gave Nate a discerning look. "Now I see. Your friend tells me much."

"See what?" asked Nate.

"This was not what I expected though I knew when I first saw you there was something special about you."

Nate shrugged. "Special?"

"Too much time has passed for some. For others, events in history were too painful to be passed to a new generation. The lack of knowledge about your heritage is a shame, but of little concern now. I could feel your Native blood the first time I saw you."

"Really?"

Grandpa nodded and wrinkled his nose. "It's been tainted a bit, but in your soul there's a fire that remembers. We all struggle to go forward until we first acknowledge where we came from. For you it's far more than a connection to your past. It is about your inevitable destiny."

Nate was aware he was staring at the old man. Something in Grandpa's words rang of truth and stirred some odd sense of peace in him. "Destiny?" Nate smiled, "You know, Grandpa, that's about the furthest thing from my mind at the moment. Tomorrow is about all I can get my head around right now."

Grandpa's eyes twinkled with an odd light as he grinned at Nate. "Your answer doesn't surprise me. What haunts your mind seems irrelevant. But it has a far greater and farther-reaching meaning than you can possibly comprehend at this moment. I cannot explain, but in the days to come you'll understand. In the scheme of things, it's all connected." He patted the kachina on the head.

Nate looked at him dubiously. Was Grandpa reading his mind? "I seriously doubt what's in my mind has any relevance, Grandpa. I don't see how it could."

"Heritage and ancestry are funny things. Even if we're unaware, they affect us. We don't have to acknowledge them for them to creep into our lives. We all come into this world with a purpose to fulfill. For some it is pre-destined before we take our first breath."

Nate gave him a questioning look and approached the subject with caution. "Like what?"

The old man's eyes were sharp as his mind. His look and his words pierced straight through Nate's protective barrier. "Mysterious things that run through our minds, or pictures we see in our dreams can be voices we need to hear. They connect us to the past, or they can be inherent powers passed to us from long dead ancestry. They are more than meaningless functions of our minds. They are very real—even if you do not believe in the world and the power of the spirit."

Nate pulled back and righted himself in the chair, uncomfortable with the old man's apparent ability to reach inside his head. For once, Nate was at a loss for words.

Grandpa smiled, as if he knew his words had hit home. "You see, it's all part of the soul circle you are traveling in."

Nate raised his eyebrows. Grandpa's words were seeking out uncharted territory for him. Cautiously, he asked, "Soul circle? What's that supposed to mean? Is that some Navajo thing?"

Grandpa shook his head, a smile still on his lips. "It's far more a lesson from the journey of life than a Navajo *thing*. It's not my job to explain it to you. Your unanswered questions will in time resolve themselves."

"Grandpa, I don't have the faintest freaking idea what you're talking about."

"I know. But when you're ready, this conversation will come back to you and you will seek me out. I will be there when the time comes." Grandpa rose from the chair and walked back to the doorway. Turning back toward Nate, he winked. "It's time I go, but I want you to know I'm glad you're back among us."

Nate stared at the doorway contemplating Grandpa's words. "Back among us? What the hell?" he whispered, eyeing the kachina.

In a crazy sort of way it made sense, at least as much as anything else that had happened to him in the last two weeks. He sighed. Frankly, he didn't have the strength left to chase any more wild rabbits tonight. He gathered his briefcase, turned off the lights and locked the door on his way out. It was time for a hot meal and a good night's sleep. If only he could turn his mind off long enough to accomplish both.

"Give him some time. At least let him stew on it for a while." Gonzales leaned closer and spoke in a hushed voice. "I've been keeping the witnesses playing cat and mouse. That has to be frustrating the hell out of him. I still think he'll come around."

"It's been two days. Nothing's changed." Smith placed an arm on the round café table and played with his coffee stirrer.

"It hasn't been two days. I just talked to him yesterday." Gonzales rubbed his jaw.

"Time enough, in my opinion."

Gonzales shrugged. "He's from San Francisco. I heard he had a pretty lucrative practice there. Guess we can't assume he's a wuss."

"*I* never assumed that. I thought I was sending a man to do a man's job. Maybe I was wrong." Smith glowered at him. Sometimes he wished his pickings weren't quite so slim when it came to puppets. Smith rolled his eyes. Of course, his source wasn't exactly prime stock.

"Look. You don't like it, do it yourself. You left it up to me. Don't complain, unless you've got a better idea."

"I could come up with a better idea in my sleep." Smith snarled.

"Fine, then do it. But do it without me."

Smith looked over the reading glasses perched on his nose and stared at Gonzales. "You got a yellow streak up your spine?"

"No, but this isn't exactly in my comfort zone either."

"Being outside the law never bothered you before," Smith whispered, glancing over his shoulder and scanning the dimly lit corner of the coffee shop. "And maybe it's still preferable to the truth."

Gonzales crossed his arms and let out a disgusted sigh. "Maybe."

"I'm implementing Plan B. Let's tighten things up a little. You know, really get his attention this time." Leaning closer, Smith spoke in a hushed voice. "You did one thing right. You laid the groundwork. But the professional angle's not going to do it with him."

"Okay, then what now?"

"Now make it look like a gang is to blame for some sleazy escapades. Make him think a gang wants him out of town."

"I don't know about this. I don't see Nakai as a coward," Gonzales whispered.

"He had a cushy practice in California defending a bunch of rich spoiled brats. I've looked at his background. Turn up the heat and he'll go running back to his soft life in a heartbeat."

"And who's going to pull all this off?"

"I don't see that as a big problem. Surely you've got some friends in the right places. Ones that owe you a favor."

Gonzales scowled. "I swore I'd never contact them again. You know that."

"This is an exception to the rules. All bets are off."

"You got me where you want me and you keep digging the hole deeper, don't you? I'd have been better off taking the rap, than getting involved in this."

Smith shrugged. "I guess that's still an option if you want to take it. I don't see you're in a place to be choosey. I figure a couple of your old pals would no doubt be willing to rough him up a little."

Gonzales snorted. "For a price maybe."

"I never said money was an object."

"Shit, man, you're crazy. You're going to have both of us in prison before you're done."

"You've trusted me this far. Do what I say and you'll be around for your retirement party from the force. You willing to give that up along with everything else in your life?"

Gonzales hesitated. "You know I'm not or I wouldn't be here. I've got damn near twenty years of my life on the line."

"Good. We're on the same page. Tomorrow night I want something to come down." Smith rose from his chair. "Be in my office at seven a.m. day after tomorrow. I want a report."

Gonzales' grim look seemed embedded in the lines of his face and the depths of his dark eyes. He was a man out of choices and it was clear he'd do what he needed to do.

Smith threw two crisp one-dollar bills on the table and walked to the door, Gonzales followed a few steps behind.

Mary turned away from the window and laid the straw hat on the counter. Once Smith had passed, she watched him walk out into the darkness. He ambled along with his unmistakable limp. It was Smith all right. The voices had been so hushed she wanted to be absolutely certain.

With her hair up and tucked under of the loose-woven cowboy hat, he obviously hadn't noticed her sitting there. She'd thought of it more as a fashion statement this morning, but apparently, it had been a very effective disguise.

Too bad she couldn't hear everything he was saying. Only the beginning, before they started whispering. Then it was bits and pieces, but enough to hear the name Nakai. She distinctly heard his name. "Outside the law. Plan B. Tighten things up. Get his attention this time." Then they'd talked so low she couldn't make out their words. What the hell were the two of them up to?

The man with Smith certainly wasn't happy. She'd heard them discussing Nate's background before their voices became inaudible. She needed to do a bit more checking into the Public Defender's background herself.

With the shock of Johnny's arrest, she hadn't really thought about all there was to do. But thanks to this encounter, she was thinking now.

It was time to do a little homework of her own and maybe, just maybe, she'd show up for Smith's meeting the day after tomorrow. If he were up to something that related to Johnny's case, she'd damn well know about it before the day of the trial. This time she and her family weren't going down without a fight.

Nate stared at the ceiling of his dark bedroom. He squeezed his eyelids together trying to stop the storm in his head and force sleep to come. Images of Stellar ran through his mind. The small form was so young and vital, but now frail and vulnerable, as she lay there clinging to life. He was haunted by the startling moment when she'd opened her eyes and he knew she had walked through his mind.

Pieces of the vision were crystal clear, Stellar's face and the black hat. The rest of it was hazy. Dimmed, or obliterated by the intense pain and horror of what happened next.

He closed his eyes and struggled to remember, wanting to bring the face under the hat's brim into focus. There was no memory of the seconds that preceded the intense searing pain at his throat—at her throat—

He tossed in the bed. Things like this happened in the movies. They didn't happen to real people. Another nagging question hung in the back of his mind. If Stellar was the girl in his vision and he'd seen the attack in exacting detail, what about the case? His knowledge would cripple his ability to fairly defend Johnny.

If at some point he could recall the face of the attacker, was his vision credible evidence? But, if it were Johnny he'd seen, why wouldn't he have had a similar reaction when he'd met him the first time. Why would he remember Stellar and not Johnny?

If he divulged the information, he would sound like some self-proclaimed psychic. If he didn't, he would have to live with the consequences. If he could just see the face under the hat, he would know for sure. His mind would either be put at ease and he could get some rest—or he'd be in the midst of a hell that would keep him up for a month. God, he wished it had never happened. His job would have been a lot easier without it.

The feather that brought on his last insight lay on the nightstand beside his bed, the same feather that was found in Stellar's hand. He shook his head. Where had it come from?

Somewhere in the wee hours of the morning, exhaustion won out and he dozed.

Feathers blew around him like a storm of giant airy snowflakes. He turned in a circle as if caught in a whirlwind. Delicate soft fuzz and sharp quills peppered his bronze arms and bare chest, pain and pleasure.

He reached skyward toward an eagle soaring overhead. Just in front of the eagle was a black and white bird, screeching as if being pursued by the larger bird. The wind subsided and he fell gently toward earth.

Nate jerked awake. He rubbed the back of his neck. What a crazy dream. He thought of the warrior turning into an eagle in the painting and of the bird in the alley. The storm of feathers had been part of his vision. Somehow in his screwed up psyche, they must have all melded into a confusing dream.

The first light of day was breaking. He threw back the covers. He wasn't going to lay here long enough for his head to start stewing on his quandary. This whole thing had gone far enough. It was time to get back to work on tangible things and events. Visions and dreams had to go on the back burner—unless they proved themselves to be more substantial than they had so far.

CHAPTER NINE

"Mrs. Savage, are you absolutely certain the boy in this picture is the one you saw in the alley standing over the girl." Nate held the mug shot up for her to see.

"Yes, I am. I told you that three times. My friend Florence and I had come out of the bookstore and were walking back to our car. And there he was. Standing in the alley, hovering over that poor child laying there on the ground." Mrs. Savage clicked her tongue and shook her head. "Poor thing."

"And you got a clear look at the boy?" Nate placed his arms on the elderly lady's kitchen table and made eye contact with her.

"Mister, I'll never forget those evil eyes. They'll haunt me in my grave."

Damn. There wasn't a jury on the planet that wouldn't believe this sweet old lady. Even his insides were churning from her convincing honesty.

Nate looked at Coyote. Coyote's look was grim as he sat to Nate's left with arms folded. He'd watched the woman carefully throughout the questioning.

Coyote spoke for the first time in the interview. "Have you and Florence been talking a lot about what happened? I imagine this was a frightening experience for the two of you?"

"Why of course we have. Like to scared the liver out of the two of us. We both live alone and now we're terrified to look out the window at night."

"I can see that. You and your friend exchange details about what you saw?"

The older woman's brow creased. "Some."

"You both remember it exactly the same way, did you?"

"Exactly. At least I'm pretty sure we did."

"Florence gave the same account. Did you and she discuss anything about what you saw before you were called in for the line up?"

"Well sure. We rode down to the police station together. You see my friend Florence doesn't drive much so, I took her."

Coyote nodded. "And there was no doubt this boy is the one you saw in the alley?"

"I told you that before." The old lady was getting annoyed.

"I know you did, ma'am. But you have to understand in our business we need to be absolutely sure of what you saw." Coyote flashed her a suave handsome smile.

She smiled back. "You know, I might be old, but I'm not stupid. You're trying to make it sound like Florence and I talked about this until we got our stories confused." She leaned toward Coyote and set her jaw. "Well look here, sonny, I can't speak for Florence, but I can speak for me. My mind is clear as a summer desert sky and so is my vision. That evil boy in the picture was there in that alley with the girl and I'd bet my life on it. You got any more questions about the accuracy of my eye sight or my memory?"

"No ma'am. I do not."

"Well good, because I got things to do." She nervously brushed away some crumbs on the white tablecloth in front of her. "You people keep calling me and changing your mind until I don't know when to expect you and when not to. If you hadn't told me to ignore the phone calls, I'd have been off to the market this morning."

Nate looked at Coyote then chimed in. "Did someone call you again about our meeting today?"

"Damn straight, they did. And I didn't half know whether to believe them or not. Seems you folks think an old lady doesn't have a life or something. Your office must not do much talking to one another. Or you wouldn't have so much trouble getting your appointments straight."

"We're sorry about the confusion, ma'am. We're not sure who has been making those calls, but I assure you it was without our knowledge. We're grateful for your patience and for you being here this morning so we could talk."

The old lady was huffy. It was obvious the interview was over.

"I know we've worn out our welcome, but I do have one more question."

"All right. But just one more."

"Was the boy wearing a black hat?"

She scowled. "I don't recall one, but then the boy had such black hair and the black shirt and all. You know he might have."

"But you're not a hundred percent sure?"

"You know it all happened so fast." Mrs. Savage ran her hand across her mouth.

"I understand. You think about it and if you remember, please give me a call." Nate pulled a business card from his shirt pocket and laid it on the table in front of her. He closed his briefcase and rose to his feet. "Thank you for your time, Mrs. Savage. We'll be in touch if we need further information."

Mrs. Savage showed them to the door. Her hospitable attitude had cooled considerably.

As they descended the stairs from her front porch to the street, Coyote looked over at Nate. "Well, that went great," he said in a sarcastic tone.

Nate snorted. "Great isn't the word I was thinking of."

"Pretty convincing witness, huh?"

"That's an understatement. We'd be better off with the Pope."

Coyote shook his head. "I went after the only angle I could think of."

"You did fine. It just didn't pan out."

"Yeah. But I still think it might be viable."

"Could be all we have."

Coyote reached for the car door. "What about that black hat angle you're after. Where'd that come from?"

Nate frowned and opened his door. "Call it a hunch. You come up with any more on that?"

"Not yet, but I'm still looking into the stuff we talked about yesterday." Coyote pulled a toothpick from the pocket of his denim shirt and chewed on it as he stared straight ahead. "You still seem to have a lot on your mind. Let me know when you're ready to talk about it."

Nate started the car and put it in gear without responding. There wasn't anybody he dared share his thoughts with at the moment. He wished it wasn't coming through so strongly to Coyote.

The pictures in his head and the haunting vision had been at the forefront of his mind all morning, a completely unsubstantiated thing that was becoming about as believable as Johnny's innocence. But it was undeniably his job to prove it wrong—unless, of course, he opted to take Gonzales' advice.

He glanced over at Coyote. In that respect, they were both cut from the same cloth. They were both in it for the long haul. His personal challenge was going to be keeping his emotions and the vision from skewing his opinions until he could check out the facts. Getting involved on such a ground roots level wasn't in his or Johnny's best interest. It was time to tuck his heart and nagging mind in his shirt pocket and move on to the next witness.

Mary shut down the computer in her office at the gallery. She leaned back in the mauve desk chair. Nate was the most pressing thing in her thoughts at the moment. The San Francisco papers she'd pulled from the public library site had yielded a few items mentioning his name.

She'd scanned a few legal web sites to track some of his cases. They were long-winded and filled with legal jargon, but thanks to past experience, she was able to interpret some of it. The one thing most had in common was they involved young people, several in Johnny's age group. She didn't know if it was coincidental or not. Maybe it was his specialty or just his preference.

The trial and legal records were way out of proportion to the articles in the media, but scanning the papers in search of information did yield one interesting fact. Many of the names listed on the legal sites, the last names anyway, correlated with names mentioned in other articles in the San Francisco news.

When she'd noticed it, she'd combed the newspapers and purposely looked for matches to the names in the trials associated with Nate. Several were matches. They were apparently names associated with people of stature in the community, doctors, city officials and a few bigger name politicians.

She'd taken it a step further and searched arrest records. Several mentioned Nakai as the defense attorney. Her gut said maybe Nate's real expertise was sweeping teen problems under the carpet for people who didn't want the publicity. She had no real basis for the assumption, but her gut was seldom wrong.

Maybe her suspicions about Nate were unfounded. She'd been through so much in the past with people in the legal system of questionable honesty, maybe it was skewing her perception.

She had reason to believe he'd been in San Francisco as far back as ten years. Then she tracked him back to Los Angeles and UCLA. She discovered another man named Nakai who was a professor at that University, possibly a relative. An Angelina Nakai served on the city council there for a number of years.

And there was a divorce record for a Nathan Nakai, actually an annulment, in San Francisco about seven years ago.

So what had she learned? Maybe nothing pertinent, but it was enough to make her wonder how he would have gotten mixed up with Smith in Santa Fe. Nate had only been here a few weeks. Johnny was his first local case. A connection to Smith wasn't impossible, but it seemed unlikely to her.

Public defenders were definitely on her low life list. And why not, after the scumbag who'd defended Angelo. She knew he was in cahoots with Smith but she'd never been able to prove it. That was another gut feeling she couldn't substantiate with rock solid facts.

Rising from the desk, she walked out into the gallery and stood before the painting of the half-naked warrior. The eerie eyes haunted her. The uncanny likeness of the man on canvas to Nate ran goose flesh down her entire body.

She had to admit deep in her heart she wanted to prove Nate was who he appeared to be and that he really did have Johnny's best interests at heart. If she could come to grips with that question, what would she feel? If past experience was influencing her opinion of him, then what?

The heady rush when she'd seen him the first time was so strong. Different from anything she'd ever experienced. So much like she was seeing someone she'd known for a lifetime, after a long separation. It was frightening in its intensity.

God, she'd gotten so good at stuffing her emotions into her purse for the sake of survival that she didn't know how she would react if she actually gave herself over to her own feelings. But did he affect her this way because she'd seen him for so long in the painting? Was it because she'd secretly fantasized about that body next to her own—or because the thought of him as her dream warrior had gotten her through so many lonely nights?

Her suppressed emotions and hormones were pushing hard to override her logic and she knew it. She couldn't be too careful. She'd trusted in the past, loved and believed in people she shouldn't have. She'd placed her heart and her future in hands that crushed her hopes and dreams and she couldn't take that risk any more.

Still, there must be a way to find out more about this attorney Nakai. And then it occurred to her. She hadn't seen Coyote Gorman in several months, but she'd heard he'd recently taken a job at the Public Defender's office. She hated to call on him when she needed a favor, but maybe it was time to buy him lunch. She sure wasn't getting anywhere trying to clear Johnny on her own. He could have some ideas that might help her—and information about Nakai.

Coyote had been her trusted friend for years. She didn't know why she hadn't thought of it before. No doubt, there were too many things on her mind.

She gave a longing and wistful last look at the painting, sunk her teeth in her lower lip and turned away. There was a phone call she had to make and a lunch date to arrange. It wasn't much, but it gave her one thing. Hope.

Nate walked the pathway through the park. The path and its shadows were dark and eerie tonight. Large trees bearing an abundance of summer foliage blocked the surrounding streetlights. Unable to find any sanctuary in sleep, he'd decided to retrace the parts of the vision he could remember and try to encourage other parts to recollection.

He remembered the path through the park clearly. The shadows of the leaves on the bricks, and the sound of shoes against stone were alive in his memory. The absence of daylight and people, and the presence of the moon above the silent plaza square, created a different picture. That was okay. This way he could be sure his own sensory perceptions didn't influence the pictures in his mind.

Crossing at the corner, he proceeded down the side street. Dear God, the detail of the vision was almost more than his logical mind could absorb. He'd walked this street, this very route in his mind, or in someone else's mind, a week earlier. It was uncanny, unbelievable.

He was rapidly approaching the alley. Inside his head he heard a bird screech. He stopped and strained trying to clarify the images. They were foggy and distant. There was the black hat. He'd visualized it at least a thousand times since his visit to the girl a day earlier.

Reaching into his shirt pocket, he grasped the feather. It had been in Stellar's hand, touched her skin, perhaps it could help him connect to something his psyche. Who was the face beneath the brim of the ominous hat? The vision always stopped here. Stepping deeper into the alley, he beckoned the darkness to help restore the mental picture.

He pointed his face skyward and closed his eyes. This was where the vision had returned to him. He waited silently, half-expecting, half-hoping for a repeat of the previous experience.

A soft shuffle from the dark corner behind him caused him to open his eyes a split second before a blow to the back of his neck sent him reeling. He staggered backward into a solid form standing behind him. Before he could get his bearings, two massive arms encircled and clamped his elbows behind him. A dark figure jumped in front of him.

A blinding punch slammed his mid-section. His breath flew from him. The second blow brought an audible crack from his rib cage. Debilitating pain rushed through his torso. The arms released him. He staggered and fell to the ground. Doubled with pain and struggling to breathe, he rolled to one side.

A kick to his mid-back thrust his survival instinct into action. Defense mechanisms clicked on. Fighting off the pain, he got to his feet. Facing his attackers, he confronted two black ski masks.

"Begay was on our turf. Get off the case." The hoarse deep voice hissed from beneath the mask. "Or it's gonna be hazardous to your health."

The second dark figure, clad in a black T-shirt, rushed at Nate. Nate pulled back his arm and took a hard swing. His fist made solid contact with the face beneath the ski mask. A groan followed. "Shit," he groaned.

As the punch made contact, a body slam hit the middle of Nate's back. He fell, sliding across the alley on his left shoulder blade. His shirt and his flesh tore. Blood and searing pain ran down his back. A quick deep breath and Nate lunged to his feet. A blow to the back of his head sent him first to his hands and knees, then to his belly. Face down on the street, blackness threatened to pull him under. The sound of footsteps running away faded into oblivion. Time stopped.

What seemed like moments later, a cool soft hand reached from out of a dream world. As it soothed his forehead, he struggled to open his eyes. The blurred image of a woman's face seemed ethereal. Was she real, or part of yet another vision?

"Oh my God. Are you all right?" Mary knelt in the alley. Her heart pounded against the walls of her chest. "Oh sweet Jesus, it's you."

Nate's eyes opened momentarily then closed again.

"I'm going to call an ambulance," she said, starting to rise to her feet.

His hand grabbed hers as she moved it from his face. "No. I'm okay." His voice was strained and raspy.

"Are you sure? God, look. Your face is bleeding." She caught a trickle of blood with her fingers as it ran from his eyebrow toward his eye.

"I'll be all right. Give me a minute to get my bearings." Wincing, he rolled onto one shoulder, then put his hand on the street and slowly pushed himself up.

"What happened? Were you in an accident?"

"No. A couple of punks thrashed the crap out of me."

"Why on earth would they do that? We need to call the police."

Nate managed to sit up. He put his hand on hers. "Not yet."

"What? Someone attacked you."

"Look. Can you help me get some place where I can get cleaned up, then we'll think this through?"

Exasperated, Mary shrugged. "Sure. I'll take you to the gallery. It's down the street."

"That's great." Turning slowly, he gingerly got to his feet, grabbing his rib cage as he did and letting out a ragged breath.

His shirt was torn and spotted with blood. One sleeve hung open where the buttons had been ripped off. He couldn't seem to straighten up as he held one arm across his middle and wobbled slightly as he moved toward her.

"If you aren't a sight. Here, let me help you." She slipped in under his free arm and pulled it around her neck, allowing him to lean against her as she pointed him in the direction of the gallery. Her arm wrapped around him and she could feel the back of his shirt was torn open and damp with what she thought was blood.

"I think you need a doctor."

"Let's wait until we get into the light and I can sit down. Let's don't overreact."

"Overreact. Yeah, right." Her womanly instincts were doing back flips. What the hell was he thinking?

She helped him hobble down the sidewalk a block and a half to the gallery. Digging in her purse for the key, she opened the front door and helped him into a chair in her office.

"Sit here. We've got a first aid kit in the bathroom. I'll be right back."

He nodded, his eyes glassy. She knew he was unconscious when she found him. She wondered how long he'd been there. Even in this state, he was too damn stubborn to let her call for medical help. *Men.* They were all alike in that respect.

She hurried into the bathroom and grabbed the first aid kit from under the sink. Wetting several paper towels with warm water, she rummaged around until she found a bottle of rubbing alcohol. That was going to burn like crazy, but maybe it served him right. He'd scared the daylights out of her.

Back in her office, she set the first aid kit and the alcohol on the desk and went to work on his forehead. The cut didn't look so bad once the stream of blood was mopped up. "Why would someone do this to you?"

"I have a pretty good idea, but I'd rather not say anything."

"That was a nice noncommittal answer. But then you're a lawyer so I suppose you have a whole book full of them." She selected a small bandage from the kit to place on the wound.

He managed a half smile. "I have another book full I use in my personal life. You hadn't figured that out yet?"

"I thought as much. Guess it's just feminine intuition." She dipped a cotton ball in the alcohol. "This is going to sting a bit."

"No probl—yeoww!!! Holy shit, what are you putting on there?"

"Alcohol to clean it out," she said as she dabbed the cut.

"Damn, it feels like battery acid. Leave it alone, would you?"

"Stop being a cry baby. A big tough public defender like you, I thought you'd be hard as nails."

"That's got nothing to do with it." He shifted in his chair. "Go ahead and clean it some more if you need to."

She smiled and shook her head. "I'm all done with that one. Now let's take a look at your back."

"Now that one smarts a little." He stood and turned his back to her. The shirt hung in shreds between his shoulders. Blood soaked the material in a long v-shape that ran almost to his waistline.

Mary took a deep breath and swallowed. She hoped it was like the one on his head and looked worse than it really was. "Off with the shirt so I can see it."

"Huh?"

"Take off your shirt. I need to get to it to clean it."

"Oh, sure." He unbuttoned the shirt slowly and pulled it off his shoulders, revealing smooth rippling muscle across the broadness of his back. The room suddenly got warmer. He flinched as he pulled the shirt the rest of the way off favoring the left side of his mid-section.

"Ribs still hurt, huh?"

"Yeah, they're pretty sore."

None of this was new to her. She'd cleaned Angelo up several times after bar room brawls. She recognized the symptoms of bruised ribs. Hopefully, nothing was broken. She carefully cleaned the gash and abrasion on his back.

"Did you get a good look at the thugs who did this to you?"

"Not really. They were wearing ski masks."

"And their reason?"

"You already asked me that. I still have no comment." He winced as she touched his back with the damp paper towel that by now was getting cold.

"Sorry. I'm almost done. I don't think this gash needs stitches."

"That's good."

"There is one large cut, but it's mostly an abrasion. Looks like you skidded across the alley on your back."

"That, I remember clearly."

"I'll clean it with the alcohol. Ready."

"Yeah. Go ahead."

He moved slightly when she first started cleaning the wound, then he seemed to relax. As her fingers moved across the smooth muscle, working the cotton ball along the jagged scratch, she felt him lean into her. She moistened her lips. It really was warm tonight.

Finishing the task, she pulled a fresh towel from the center of the stack on the desk, wanting to complete the job without causing him discomfort. She moved the warm moist towel in a circular motion around the outlying area of the wound.

"That feels nice," he whispered.

She said nothing, savoring the opportunity to touch his beautiful male flesh, if even for a moment. She'd almost forgotten how pleasant it was to be so close.

He turned to face her and pulled her to him. "I wasn't quite finished," she said in a low voice.

"I know," he said softly, his lips inches from hers. "You're quite a nurse."

The heat of his bare chest, a heartbeat from hers caused her to flush. "Nursing isn't my thing."

"Could've fooled me." He wet his lips.

"I just wanted to help you." She moved her face closer to his, and lifted her chin as she met his deep brown eyes.

"I'm glad you were there."

"Me, too."

His lips were so close she could almost taste them. His breath was warm on her skin. He bit his lip and stepped away.

Letting out a ragged breath, she picked up his shirt from the desk and handed it to him. "Think you'd better put this back on."

He took it from her and gingerly pulled it on, his eyes intent upon her as he did.

"I'm still concerned about your ribs. You may need to have them looked at."

"I think they'll be all right. I just need some rest."

"Yeah. It's very late."

"What were you doing here this late at night?"

She hesitated. "Some research." She busied herself with putting the first aid kit back together. "What were you doing in an alley in the middle of the night?"

His jaw rippled and he straightened his collar. "Some research."

She nodded and closed the small white box with the red cross on the front.

"I'll walk you to your car."

"Thanks. I'd appreciate that."

The door lock clicked in place and their eyes met momentarily, then they silently turned toward the street. Neither spoke as they walked down the side street. It had been a strange night, filled with more than one unexpected event.

Mary watched Nate hobble to his car after he'd seen her to hers. Who was Nathan Nakai really? Why had he appeared in her life under such bizarre circumstances?

She shook her head. Johnny was her number one priority. He had to be. He should be all she was thinking about. But the flame smoldering in her heart tonight had admittedly been a welcome distraction, even if she could permit it to last only for a moment. Tomorrow reality would reign. And she had to decide where to go from here.

CHAPTER TEN

"It's done." Gonzales glanced over his shoulder then down the hall as Smith unlocked the door.

"Calm your nerves. No one else is in, yet." Smith opened the door and led the way through the reception area and into his office. Sitting his brief case on the mahogany desk, he observed Gonzales' nervous dance with amusement.

Gonzales closed the inner door, looking around outside as he did. He turned toward Smith and spoke quickly. "They took care of it. I talked to them late last night. Beat him up pretty good, I guess."

"Good. Then it went off as planned." Smith settled into his chair.

"But one thing bugs me. He didn't call in and report it. I checked the overnight police reports early this morning. There was nothing."

Smith scratched his chin considering what that might imply. "It could be a good sign. Seems he's pretty predictable."

"How so?"

"He's probably thinking about it. If he bought the gang angle hook, line, and sinker, maybe he's afraid they'll come after him again if he rats on them. That's what we want."

Gonzales twitched nervously. "It could also mean he suspects I had something to do with it."

"Cripes. Stop being so damn paranoid. You gave him no reason to suspect any such thing."

"I don't like it. That's all. The whole thing isn't right. Having some guy beat to a pulp isn't normally part of what I do."

Smith opened his top desk drawer, pulled out his pipe and stuffed it full of tobacco from a red and blue pouch. "I don't necessarily like it either, but it is our job to insure this punk Begay gets put away for good."

Gonzales slid into a side chair. "This feels like a funny way of accomplishing it."

Smith hadn't figured on the hand holding Gonzales required, but he was getting the job done. "You said it yourself. The man had a hell of a practice in San Francisco. He might get the kid off. That's why I want him out of the picture." Smith lit his pipe with a silver engraved lighter from the desktop and leaned back in his chair as the smoke drifted around his head.

Gonzales observed Smith. "In other words you'd prefer to pick the kid's lawyer."

"What the hell are you talking about? You know the law doesn't work that way." Smith rolled his chair into the desk and lowered his voice. "I have nothing to do with what goes on in the Public Defender's office. Everybody in this judicial district gets a fair unbiased trial."

Gonzales shifted in his chair. "Not exactly how I heard it. Or maybe your version of the law only applies to those named Begay—or Summernight."

Smith's eyes flew open and he glared at Gonzales. "I don't know who you've been talking to, but it will cease. You'd better have iron clad proof before you start throwing around insinuations."

"You mean you'd like it better if I didn't talk to anyone else you've got in your pocket."

"I mean, if you don't shut up, you'll be eating your next meal off a utility tray in the county jail. And I can make the same arrangement for the low life who put all this crap in your head."

"Look. I'm not the only one in this town who knows what happened. It isn't that no one's sympathetic to your cause—"

"Shut up. Shut up, now. This isn't about sympathy or anybody's cause. It's about the law and seeing justice served. Don't cross me on this or justice will be beating down your front door and taking you into custody before the sun sets. Mark my words. I mean business."

"Okay, okay. I shouldn't have brought it up. I just think it needs to end somewhere."

"There's nothing to end. Got it?" Smith slammed his fist on the desk. His face was hot. His pulse pounded in his temples. "We're doing what we're doing in the interest of upholding the law and seeing the guilty do not go unpunished. I've never done anything in this office that wasn't in the interest of achieving that end. Is it perfectly clear to you?"

Gonzales' face paled. He looked at Smith from under a wary brow. "Yeah. It's clear."

Smith tried to relax his shoulders as he loosened his tie. He laid the smoldering pipe in its holder on top of his desk. Removing his handkerchief from his shirt pocket, he wiped the beads of sweat from his brow.

Dammit. People didn't seem to see things his way. And he was tired of trying to convince them. He leaned back tentatively in his chair, prepared to verbally thrash Gonzales again if he needed it. The man was becoming a worry to him. Still breathing hard, he mopped his brow. It was time to change the subject. "What have you heard about the girl?"

"Still the same. No change."

Smith nodded. "How many days?"

"Five or six. I don't know."

"Keep me informed."

"Yeah." Gonzales pulled at his shirt collar. It was obvious the heat of the room and the conversation were affecting him, too. "So what's next?"

"We wait."

"How long are you going to give him?" Gonzales squirmed in his chair.

"Who?"

"Nakai. How long to change his mind?"

Smith propped his elbows on the chair arms and folded his hands. "I don't know. We'll see how it plays out."

"I've done all I can."

"We'll see about that, too. You'll hear from me when I need you again."

Gonzales' head bobbed. "Can I go? Today's my day off and I promised the grandkids I'd take 'em to the park."

"Yeah. We're done—for now."

Gonzales looked relieved, rose from the chair, and reached for the door handle.

"Gonzales."

"Yes, sir."

"Remember what I said about that friend of yours. You both have as much to lose as I do."

"Understood. Not likely I'll forget." With that, Gonzales hurried out.

Seconds later, Gonzales burst through the door. His eyes were wild and he spoke in a loud whisper. "Somebody was in the outer office. I heard a door close when I went out in the hall."

"What?" Smith got up from his chair and followed Gonzales out into the hall. "I don't see anybody."

"I swear. There was somebody listening. They ran when I came out."

Smith shook his head. "I think you're imagining things." The last thing he wanted was to let the paranoid son-of-a-bitch see he was concerned.

Smith proceeded down the short hallway. Carefully, he tried the doorknobs of each of the four offices on the right side of the hall. They were secure. Gonzales followed close, watching over his shoulder as he tried the doors. Gonzales had his hand stuck in his jacket pocket, something hard inside bumped against Smith's elbow.

Smith whirled. Grabbing Gonzales by the throat, he pinned him to the opposite wall. "If you've got a gun in that pocket, you better get your hand off of it. What are you going to do, shoot me or shoot yourself in the foot?"

"You know I carry it on the job and I know how to use it. If somebody's skulking around here, we might need it."

"Brilliant deduction Sherlock," Smith whispered. "If somebody is here, they probably work in this office. If you panic and shoot somebody, do you have any idea what will happen? Dammit, Gonzales. You're going to give me a fricking heart attack."

Gonzales pulled his hand from his pocket and Smith released him. Smith's head pounded. His pulse beat in his temple. Gonzales was about as trustworthy as a schizophrenic rattlesnake.

Smoothing his clothes and recovering his composure, Smith leaned toward Gonzales and spoke in a low voice. "We'll check the bathrooms and if anybody's there, I'll do the talking. You keep your mouth shut and your hand off the pistol. Got it?"

"Got it." Gonzales' voice was shaky.

"Good. Follow me." Smith stepped into the men's room and stood in front of the mirror. He motioned with his head for Gonzales to check the stalls. No one was there.

They stepped outside and down one door. "If anybody's in the ladies room, we're gonna have to handle it tactfully."

"Sure. You take the lead. I'll follow."

Smith opened the door a crack and peered in. There weren't any women on this floor except his secretary and he knew she wasn't in. They went a step further and listened. There was complete silence.

Stooping, his eye ran along the bottom of the stalls. *Nothing but toilet bowls and tile.* Gonzales watched him, then stepped around him. Throwing a quick look around the corner at the washbasins, he shook his head and let out a long sigh.

"There's nobody here. It's your mind playing tricks on you. You need to chill out," Smith said as they both walked back out into the hall.

Crouching with her feet on the toilet seat, Mary struggled to control her heavy breathing and her pounding heart. She was still as a statue, holding her breath until the voices were gone and the door closed. Mary had ducked into the ladies room trying to shut the door quietly. But the door had slipped and obviously made an audible sound.

She let out a shallow shaky breath and soundlessly stepped from her perch. She glanced at her watch. It was 7:15. She'd wait five or ten minutes and slip down the stairs at the opposite end of the hallway.

Stepping quietly out into the main bathroom, she looked at her reflection in the mirror. She adjusted the bandana holding her hair up and removed the large round dark glasses. Would the makeshift disguise and the blue shirt she'd taken from the janitor's closet at the gallery have been convincing if they'd found her? And what would Smith and the man he'd called Gonzales have done if they had?

She took a deep breath and blew it out, shaking her head at the funny looking woman in the mirror and the grim look on her face. How the hell had she ended up playing super sleuth?

Whatever force had driven her to come here against her better judgment, knew what it was doing. Now that the crisis had passed, she knew why she had to come.

It had been difficult to hear through the closed door. Again, she couldn't hear the whole conversation. The man Smith was meeting with was named Gonzales. It appeared Smith was bribing him. At least, that's what it looked like. But part of the conversation made her stomach sick. They'd had someone beaten last night. And she was willing to bet it was Nate. But why?

She'd also heard them make a reference to Begay and Summernight. Her greatest fear had been that Smith wasn't ready to let his revenge against her family die. The muffled names renewed her fear to a heightened state.

In her mind, her suspicions had been partially confirmed and two things were certain. Destiny had brought her here, and she had to talk to Nate. She took a deep breath and quietly opened the door. Maybe if she'd been less of a doormat last time and more aggressive about chasing her suspicions, she could have changed her destiny—and Angelo's.

Smith closed the door and let out a puff of air. A tiny noise had brought him back out to the hallway. But it was only a cleaning lady, headed down the back stairs. He'd caught a glimpse of the back of her shirt. Probably what Gonzales had heard earlier. If Gonzales kept it up, he'd have him paranoid, too.

He slipped back into the chair behind his desk thinking about the morning and their conversation. The sun hung above the horizon to the east. Its early morning rays peeked through the plantation blinds, casting long strips of shadow on the deep green carpet. Smith stared *at the patterns on the floor.*

Grandchildren, indeed. It was easy for Gonzales to pass judgment on Smith's actions when it wasn't his life that had been destroyed. This case and the

Summernight trial weren't the same. They were different as night and day.

Smith picked up the smoldering pipe and clenched it between his teeth. He'd been right in all he'd done. Where the law had failed, he'd helped it along. He'd helped to bring the guilty to justice and seen they paid for their horrible crime.

God wouldn't fault him for what he'd done, nor should anyone else. It was a special circumstance. A case where the victim deserved restitution, and needed to see payment made for the pain they'd lived through. It just so happened in this case, he was the victim.

———

Mary looked at her watch. She'd changed her clothes and went in search of Nate, but he wasn't in this morning. That had her concerned. It was now past eleven thirty. Across the plaza she recognized the familiar stride and the black cowboy hat. Coyote Gorman's look hadn't changed in fifteen years.

Even with what transpired this morning, she needed to follow through with this meeting. She smiled as he walked in her direction. In all the years she'd known him, he'd never once let her down. She hoped he could help her now.

"Mary. Everything okay with you and Grandpa?" Coyote's face was full of concern.

"Yes. We're doing okay."

"Good. You had me worried when you called." He gave her a hug and took a seat at the table of the outdoor café. "Tell me what you have on your mind, pretty lady."

"I'm sure you heard about Johnny."

Coyote's brow furrowed. "It's an awful thing."

She nodded. "It's been all over the papers."

He leaned closer. "Mary, I've been assigned to the case."

"Oh." She was genuinely surprised. "I'd heard you were working in the Public Defender's office, but I had no idea."

"I didn't think you knew. It's all right. I wish I could punctuate that for you with some words of encouragement. Unfortunately, I can't."

Mary ran her teeth across her lower lip. "I actually feel much better knowing."

"It's a tough deal. I'm not sure what to say."

"You've known Johnny a long time. You know he isn't capable of such a thing."

"What I know isn't what counts. Rest assured, I won't leave any stone unturned. It's all I can do, I only wish I could do more."

"Maybe you can be more help than you think."

"How so?"

It was time to blurt it out. "What do you know about the Public Defender?"

"Nakai?" Coyote raised his eyebrows. "Well...he seems like a good guy. I haven't known him very long."

"I tried to check him out on the Internet. Guess he came here from San Francisco?"

Coyote scratched his head. "That's what I've been told. Most of my dealings with him are business."

Mary pressed him harder. "You think he's trustworthy?"

Coyote shrugged. "Seems like a down to earth person. I know he's working hard on the case. Haven't you talked to him a couple times?"

"We've had some discussions." Not to mention there were also a few Band-Aids between them. "I wanted your opinion. I trust your judgment."

A smile turned the corners of his mouth. "I just have one question. You checking him out, or *checking him out*?"

Mary's mouth flew open. "Coyote. I'm talking business here." She folded her arms in exasperation.

"I was just asking. Don't get huffy."

"Stop teasing. It's not funny. I have a genuine reason to be concerned." She planted her arms on the table.

Coyote put up his hands. "Okay, I'll stop. Don't get your feathers ruffled."

"I want an honest answer. Is he on the up and up?"

"I guess I'm not sure exactly what you're getting at."

Mary was sober. The horseplay was over. "When Angelo went to trial, he and I went through hell with the Public Defender assigned to his case."

"I was still working out on the rez then. I didn't know about all that."

"It was awful, Coyote. He told us one thing and when we got to the trial, he did something totally different."

"In what way?"

"I could never prove it, but I think he threw the case."

"You're kidding?"

"We were working on an appeal when I got the call from the prison."

Coyote's jaw was rigid. "I had no idea. Why do you think he threw the trial?"

"It's all conjecture, Coyote. Isn't that the term the legal system uses when you can't prove something? If you can't prove you were framed then led down the primrose path by a crooked lawyer?"

"I don't understand why he would do something like that."

"That question has haunted me for over two years. I keep trying to talk myself out of the *who* I think is the primary suspect."

"I'm not following you."

"Coyote. Who in this town hated Angelo and me more than anyone else."

Coyote shook his head. "You don't think—he wouldn't have."

"I don't know. I could never prove it."

"Nobody knows better than I do about Smith and his prejudice. And I know everything that happened around you and Ethan in high school—and what happened after you came back. But I can't believe Smith would go that far."

"Maybe none of us know how far Smith would really go." Mary raised an eyebrow. Coyote didn't know the half of what had happened between her and Ethan Smith that senior year of high school. That was a secret no one could ever pry from her heart and soul.

Coyote pushed back his hat. "My dad was an investigator for the Santa Fe PD for years. He worked a lot of cases with Smith. He never once said anything like that about him."

"I know all about your dad. He testified at Angelo's trial."

"Sorry. I didn't mean to bring that up."

"It's all right, Coyote." She reached across the table and touched his arm. "I never blamed your dad. And I certainly never blamed you."

"I know that. I'm sorry for the way things worked out. It happened when I was on the res. Maybe I never knew the real truth."

"Sometimes, I wonder what's truth and what isn't. In fact, I'm not sure of anything anymore. I want the past dead and buried. I can't change it, so I have to let it go." Tears stung the backs her eyes.

Coyote shifted in his chair. "Okay. Let's be logical here. You're right. Now isn't the time for exhuming old ghosts. We've got to focus on Johnny." Coyote was steering her away from the issue, but shadows hung in the back of his brown eyes that told Mary he'd already heard more than he wanted to.

Mary cleared her throat. "Johnny is the most important thing. But I have to make sure what happened in the past doesn't repeat itself."

Coyote clasped his hands under his chin and made a tent of his fingers, pressing them against his lips. She knew the pose. He was either thinking very hard or trying to find a way to tell her something he'd rather not.

"Mary, I know what you've been through has been pretty awful, but I have to tell you this. I've been working on Johnny's case and it doesn't look good. We can't let the past interfere with what's happening now." His eyes locked on hers. "If we're going to get Johnny out of this, neither of us can afford a distraction."

"I guess that brings us back to my original point. You think Nakai is all right?"

"I can't give you a written guarantee, but if he's half the attorney I think he is, I honestly think he's the best chance Johnny's got. I don't think we have any other options. Not at the moment."

"Okay. I'll have to put my faith in your judgment. I don't know where else to turn."

"I can only promise you I'll keep an eye on him as much as I can. I'm in a place to do that for you."

"I can't ask for more." Mary mustered a smile.

Coyote looked at his watch. "Guess I'll have to take a rain check on the lunch."

"I'm sorry. I didn't mean to take up so much of your time."

Coyote shot her a wink. "It's all right. That's what old friends are for."

She nodded. "I'm sorry. I didn't ask about your dad's health. I heard he wasn't well."

Coyote shook his head. "He's not. We're taking it a day at a time."

"I'm sorry to hear that."

"I've got to get back to work. But there's one more thing I want you to do."

"Sure. Anything."

"If there's anything you can tell Nate that could help Johnny, tell him." Coyote was as stern as she'd ever seen him.

Mary raised an eyebrow. "Has he been talking about me?"

Coyote scratched behind his ear. "Seems he might have mentioned your name."

"Well, he needs to keep his opinions to himself." How dare Nate say anything about her behind her back, especially to Coyote. "This is a business relationship and he needs to treat it as such." The heat rose in her face as the words left her lips. Business had been the furthest thing from her mind last night.

Coyote grinned and rose from his chair. "That's my girl. Remember you're the boss and you'll be able to handle him just fine."

"Trust me. That's something I won't let him forget."

Coyote gave her a quick peck on the cheek. "See you later, sunshine. Don't let the past drive you crazy and hang in there. You aren't alone."

With that Coyote hopped the wrought iron railing enclosing the café tables and trotted back across the street. It wasn't much and the news wasn't good, but in a way he'd put her mind at ease.

He was right about one thing. She had to bury her fears. Johnny's best chance lay in her joining forces with Coyote and Nate. It was logical, it was sound thinking, and bottom line, she and Johnny didn't have any other viable options.

As for this morning's incident, she'd take it directly to Nate. Getting Coyote involved in what happened last night wasn't the answer, and it wasn't her place to tell him. The two of them were too close as friends and there were a few skeletons in their past she hadn't considered. In view of Coyote's circumstances and her own, this wasn't the optimum time to dig them up.

Sometimes it was best to let sleeping dogs lie. From what both Nate and Coyote had told her, she needed all of her strength focused here in the moment, and on getting Johnny out of this mess. *If that was possible.*

CHAPTER ELEVEN

"Man, you look like crap." Coyote whistled as he stepped into Nate's cffice and leaned forward to examine the bruise on the side of Nate's face. "What the hell happened to you? Step in front of a Mack truck?"

"A couple of members of Johnny Begay's allegedly nonexistent gang kicked my ass last night," Nate grumbled. He knew eventually someone in the office was going to see him and ask questions. And he wasn't in a particularly jovial mood this morning.

Coyote looked stunned. "What? No way."

Nate leaned back in his chair carefully. He winced as the pain grabbed his rib cage. "You heard me right. Last night I was checking out the alley where the girl was attacked and a couple of thugs jumped me."

"They did a number on you. What was that you said about gang members?" A look of disbelief was on Coyote's face. He reached behind him, pulled up Nate's side chair and sat down.

"Two punks in ski masks. One of them said something about Johnny and their turf. Sounded like gang lingo to me."

"So why did they come after you? Did they say?"

Nate gritted his teeth. "They want me off the case."

"Well, I'll be damned." Coyote folded his arms across his chest. His face was one giant question mark.

"No. *I've* apparently been damned. This ass hole said if I don't, I'd get more of this." Nate pointed to the bruise on his face located below the throbbing cut on his head. He was tired, in pain and exasperated.

Coyote was silent for a few moments. His face clouded with concern.

Nate attempted a half smile, and winced. "Don't act shocked. This stuff happens all the time in the big cities."

"The fact somebody beat the shit out of you isn't what's bothering me."

"Well, that was nicely put."

Coyote didn't acknowledge Nate's attempt at humor. "I came by this afternoon to tell you I checked out the gang connection." Coyote paused again.

"And?" Nate prodded.

"And I found nothing. Johnny's never had anything to do with any gangs." His expression hadn't changed. The shock seemed ingrained in his face.

"Then I'd say your sources are wrong. And I've got a whole lot of black and blue marks to prove it." Nate rubbed his arms. That seemed rather obvious.

Coyote shook his head. "But they're never wrong."

"*Never* seems a little meaningless in this instance."

"No, Nate. Like I told you, I work with these kids. I've got connections. I put the word out on the street. Johnny Begay's a squeaky clean kid, not a gang member." Coyote ran the fingers of one hand down his cheeks to his chin. "Ten minutes ago, I'd have staked my life on it."

"Well, let's don't stake my life on it. Okay?" Nate groaned softly, moving in the chair and trying to shift his weight to any place that didn't hurt.

"You're really in pain, aren't you?"

"Got a couple broken ribs. Nothing serious. They'll heal."

"Then what are you and your busted ribs doing here?"

"I saw a doctor this morning. He gave me some stuff. It'll kick in pretty soon."

Coyote shook his head slowly. He seemed to be talking more to himself than to Nate. "I'm still having a hard time believing this. My sources have never let me down." He shot Nate and exasperated look. "Damn, if they'd steered me right, maybe I could have prevented this."

"I doubt you could have stopped them. It just happened. We move on from here." They'd labored the topic enough. Nate was done.

Coyote looked at Nate with steely eyes. "Oh, don't worry, I'll get to the bottom of it."

Nate truly believed he would. And leaving it in his capable hands was one less thing Nate had to think about. "You do that. I'm going to knock off early and get some sleep. It was a long night."

"I can imagine." Coyote rose to his feet. "You said they told you to get off the case. You going to?"

Nate looked up at Coyote. "Hell no, I'm not."

Coyote smiled. "I figured as much." He started toward the door. "You call the police and report this?"

"Nope."

Coyote stopped and pushed back his hat. "Why not?"

"I'm thinking on it. Sometimes things fit together too perfectly. You know what I mean?"

"I do. I'll get back with you on what I hear from my snitches on the street."

Nate nodded as he watched Coyote leave. He hadn't come across one cut and dried thing since he'd set foot in Santa Fe. He wasn't fool enough to assume this situation was any different.

An hour later, Nate eased into bed. All he wanted was for the pain prescription to kick in and let him sleep. He glanced at the clock. It was a quarter before four in the afternoon. A nap would help. He didn't think he'd slept two hours out of the last day and a half.

There were a hundred things he should be thinking about, but not one of them was strong enough to override the pain in his ribs. A little sleep and he'd be able to deal with it. He closed his eyes.

Nate stood in the alley. There was a shuffling noise behind him. He whirled. Behind him stood a boy in a black hat, his back turned toward him. Nate realized he was carrying something in his hand. He glanced down at the black and white feather lying in his palm. He grabbed the boy's shoulder and spun him around. Looking up, his eyes met the boy's evil ones. The words rasped from his tight throat. "Johnny. It's you."

Nate sat straight up in bed. The searing pain in his side obliterated by the hammering of his heart. Dear God, he'd finally seen the face. *Holy shit. It was Johnny.*

He put his hand over his mouth and laid back. Struggling to regain his breath, his heart pounded like a drum against his chest wall. He closed his eyes again. All he could see were those evil eyes. Eyes like an animal—and Johnny's face, just as it had been in his vision. Carefully he rolled over, then sat on the side of the bed.

Dammit. What now? He pounded a palm against his forehead. He'd wanted to know the truth, but that was truly the last thing he'd wanted to see, the last thing he wanted to remember. He should have been prepared for the answer, but he wasn't. *Especially not after last night, and selfish as it seemed, Mary.*

He'd tried to recreate the picture in his mind for days. Maybe he'd tried too hard. He picked up the pill bottle from the nightstand and slammed it back down. Nothing like a bottle of prescription assistance to finally bring it all back. Rising from the bed, he pulled on his slacks and went to the kitchen for a glass of water.

Mary reluctantly rang the doorbell. This was going to be awkward, but she had to come. The receptionist told her Nate had been in the office for a while this afternoon. She'd missed him. What she had to talk to him about couldn't wait.

She listened intently for sounds from inside. Again, she rang the bell. This time the lock clicked and the door opened a crack.

"Mary?"

"Hi. Sorry to bother you, but I have to talk to you."

Nate's look was a mixture of surprise and hesitation. After a second, he opened the door and motioned for her to come in.

Mary stepped inside. Nate moved gingerly as he closed the door.

"You don't look so good. How are you feeling?"

"Like ten pounds of crap in a five-pound sack." He attempted a smile, but refused to meet her eyes. "But thanks for asking."

Mary lifted the paper bag in her hand. "I brought you some dinner. Thought you might need some nourishment."

"That was thoughtful of you."

Mary was uncomfortable. Nate was distant. Maybe she shouldn't have dropped in on him, but what she had on her mind couldn't wait.

Nate put his hands in his pant's pockets. His shirt was untucked and his hair rumpled. He looked down at his bare feet. "Sorry, I wasn't expecting company."

Mary shook her head. "I'm sorry to pop in on you. I have an important reason for being here. Otherwise, I wouldn't."

"No, no. It's all right." He seemed sincere, but she sensed something was bothering him. "I was just going to get a glass of water. Do you want something?"

"Water would be fine, thank you."

"Please have a seat, while I get you some."

Mary turned toward the living area and set the paper bag on the coffee table. Then noticing the expensive finish, she moved it to the floor. She took a seat on the black Italian leather sofa and glanced around at the rest of the masculine upscale furnishings and simple modern design of the room.

She cleared her throat. The contrast between their lifestyles was a glaring chasm. She wasn't sure what she'd expected. The apartment was in a nice area. She raised her eyebrows and her gut tightened. Being an attorney must be a lucrative business.

"How did you find me?" Nate called from the kitchen, above the clank of ice cubes against glass.

"I have my ways. It pays to know the right people."

Nate came into the room carrying two tall glasses of ice water. "For some reason, that doesn't surprise me."

She took a glass from him and placed it on a black stone coaster on the table in front of her. "I didn't mean to intrude. I know you were probably trying to rest."

He ran his hands through his hair. "What would make you think that?"

They both laughed. It was a relief to Mary that he wasn't upset with her for seeking him out. But he wouldn't look in her eyes. She felt awkward. "You have a very nice place."

"Thanks. But I have a feeling you didn't drop in to see it and bring me food." He eased into the black leather recliner across from her. "What's on your mind?"

"I have some information I don't think can wait until you're feeling better."

Nate raised his eyebrows and looked at her expectantly. "And that would be?"

"I have reason to believe what happened to you last night might have been arranged."

Nate turned the cold glass in his hands. "Arranged? I'm not sure I'm following you."

"I overheard a meeting between Jim Smith and another man at a coffee shop the night before last. I couldn't be sure what they were talking about then."

Nate ran his forefinger across his chin. "And now?"

"I heard them arrange to meet again this morning, so I dropped by to satisfy my curiosity."

"Really?" Nate's eyes narrowed and his expression was sober as he listened intently.

"I'm positive they were talking about what happened to you. They said someone had been 'beat to a pulp'."

"Well, the description fits."

"Nate, I heard them mention your name both times they met. I couldn't hear every word, but I feel certain enough." She stopped as their eyes met for the first time since she'd come through the door. "That's the reason I had to find you."

Nate's eyes darkened and a cloud seemed to cross his face. "Interesting."

She nodded. "You didn't change your mind and call the police did you?"

"No. Nobody knows about this except you and me."

Her mouth twisted. "Then, if they didn't have something to do with it, how would they have known? And all the more interesting, one of them was a police officer."

Nate shook his head. "I don't know. I'm not sure it proves they knew about it. Especially, since you couldn't hear the whole conversation. What if they were talking abut someone else?"

"I can understand why you're skeptical but I want you to be careful." She glanced at him, then down at her hands folded in her lap. All afternoon she'd considered the possibility he wouldn't take her seriously.

Nate shook his head. He obviously was milling the information around in his mind. "The only other person who knows about this is Pete Gorman, but that wasn't until this afternoon."

"Pete?" Mary put her hand over her mouth to suppress a snicker. "Nobody calls him Pete."

"Okay. Okay. Coyote. It just didn't sound professional."

Mary was silent for a moment as she ran her finger around the rim of her glass. "I'd hoped we'd gotten beyond professional after last night."

Nate glanced at her, then looked at the floor. A trace of a smile crossed his face, but the troubled look in his eyes was more vivid than ever.

"Is something else bothering you?" Maybe it wasn't appropriate to ask, but after this morning she was past that stage of her life. She was getting nowhere hiding under a rock.

"No. But what is Smith's motive?"

Mary nibbled the inside of her cheek. There was a lot she had to say about Smith, but maybe this wasn't the time. If she gave Nate only the facts, and let him put the pieces together for himself, no one could say she or the past had played a role. It was probably best to let this incident stand on its own and hope Smith would go down for the scumbag he was.

She wasn't ready to bare her soul to Nate or anyone else. If Nate was all he was cracked up to be, let him prove it. Let him track down the truth. *Bandages, near kisses, and untamed hormones aside, the rest of the story wasn't any of his business.*

"You're awfully quiet. Nothing more to say?" Nate pried her from her thoughts.

"I think I've said enough." She reached down and picked up the bag by her feet. "You ought to eat this, while it's still warm."

Nate looked at her across the room. He bit his lower lip and hesitated. "Only if you'll stay and have some with me."

Secretly, she'd hoped he would ask that very question, and the reason why she'd come prepared with plenty of food. But she was bothered by his hesitation and would rather he'd have shared what was on his mind than his meal. Reluctantly, she nodded in his direction. "I'll take it to the kitchen and put it on some plates if you'd like."

He rose stiffly from the recliner and took the bag from her hand. "No need. I'll take care of that."

She held onto the bag as he pulled at it and met his eyes. "You don't let anyone take care of you, do you?"

"Only when I can't reach the bleeding to stop it myself." He smiled smugly and tugged at the bag.

She tightened her grip. "Sometimes it's okay to let someone close enough to help you."

"Funny. A few days ago, I thought the same thing about you."

She raised her eyebrows and released the bag. "Touché, Mr. Nakai."

Nate returned in a few minutes with chicken breasts, rice and vegetables divided on two square black plates. He placed them on the coffee table and turned on a floor lamp by the sofa. "Guess we can eat right here if you don't mind sitting on the floor."

"That's probably going to be easier for me than you tonight." She slid from the sofa and sat cross-legged at the low table.

He nodded, easing himself down slowly next to her. Picking up his fork, he didn't look up. "So you never answered my question."

"What question?"

"Why do you think Smith would do something like this?"

Mary busied herself with her food. "I don't know that I can answer. That's why I didn't."

Nate appeared to be considering her response. "You said you showed up for his meeting this morning. You must have had some reason."

She avoided his eyes. "I was curious, that's all."

Nate nodded. "How did you pull that off anyway?"

"Well, I didn't actually attend. I kind of eavesdropped."

"Eavesdropped? Another coffee shop get together?"

She thought for a moment. "No. Smith's office."

"That's a risky place for a public figure to have a meeting like you're talking about."

"Not at seven o'clock in the morning."

"But you got in and listened. Through the door, I'd assume?"

She stuffed a piece of chicken in her mouth and nodded. "Um hmm."

"That makes me even more curious."

"Curious about what?"

"Why you'd take a chance like that?"

Suddenly, she wasn't feeling hungry. The smoldering ember from last night had lit an urge in her to be close to Nate. Now she feared it had driven her to make a bad choice.

Nate wiped his mouth with a napkin and laid it on the table. "The conversation seems to always stop at the same place."

She met his eyes. "Do you always have to be a lawyer?"

He looked down at the table.

"It's getting late and you need to rest. It's time for me to go."

He touched her arm. "Mary, I—"

The warmth of his touch tempted her, but she listened to her head instead of her heart. She pulled herself back onto the sofa. He followed, wincing and putting his hand on his ribs.

She got to her feet and he stood in front of her, looking into her eyes.

"You don't have to leave." His lips were very close.

"I need to check on Grandpa." She turned her head away flushing at his closeness, and knowing she should keep her distance. Hungering for one more moment near him, she whispered. "I've made a decision."

He moistened his lips and put his hands on her arms, pulling her to him. "Mary."

She put her index finger to his lips. The heat between them was intense as his body touched hers. "I want to help with Johnny's case in any way I can. I'm sorry I've been distant, but I want to help you find the real assailant."

His eyes flashed. As if she'd flipped a switch, his grip on her arms relaxed. Leaning away from her, his jaw rippled and the softness in his eyes was replaced with a troubled look. He took a step backward and swallowed hard as he ran his hand through his rumpled hair. His voice was hoarse when he spoke. "We can talk about that tomorrow."

She was both relieved and disappointed. Much as she wanted to taste his kiss, she wasn't sure it was the right thing. His reaction confused her, but she really did need to leave. "Tomorrow sounds good." She reached for the doorknob.

"One more question." Nate's hand was on his temple. "I forgot to ask if you knew the man Smith was meeting with."

"I've never seen him before. But I heard Smith call him Gonzales."

Nate looked as if he'd had the second slap in the face of the night. "I should have known."

Mary observed him curiously. "You look exhausted. Get some sleep." She turned the door handle, then closed it quietly behind her. She should never have come. This building desire made them both uncomfortable.

Mary shook her head as she walked across the parking lot. There were too many issues from the past living in her soul. Too many unresolved things, she hadn't left behind.

She wasn't ready to make her life an open book, or face its ghosts. Doing so would destroy any hopes of a future with someone like Nate. She had to get a solid grip on reality. He wasn't her dream warrior. He was another attorney on a mission.

CHAPTER TWELVE

Nate stood staring out his office window, one hand in the pocket of his trousers, the other around a cup of strong black coffee. He took a sip of the hot bitter brew trying to clear the cobwebs and the narcotic fur from his brain. The prescription pills had stopped the pain and forced him to sleep, but with the new day came the dawn of a whole new set of complications.

Now the vision had come to full clarity. He'd walked in his mind through the brutal crime Johnny Begay had committed. How could he with a good conscience stay on this case? And how the hell was he going to tell Mary he had to walk away?

Was he insane to believe he'd had a full blown and credible psychic experience? It truthfully wasn't something he'd ever believed in, yet, how else could it be explained? He knew in his heart it was too much to be a coincidence, and too intense not to be connected to reality. Still, the attorney in him couldn't come to grips with it as solid evidence.

He removed his hand from his pocket and massaged his temples. Even if he were just fricking nuts, he'd never be able to stand in front of a jury and defend Johnny after he'd seen him commit the crime in his vision. Be it psychic vision or be it lunacy, a fair trial and a viable defense had both evaporated into a mystical vapor.

His throat grew tight and raspy. The emotion was too strong, too embedded in his soul. There was no way he could defend Johnny. He took another drink of coffee.

"Good morning." A soft gentle voice spoke from behind him.

He immediately recognized it. He cringed and his stomach knotted. He didn't have the courage to turn to face her. "What are you doing here so early?"

"We're short-staffed today at the gallery. I was on my way there and thought I should stop in while I had the chance."

He was silent. Still looking out the window, he said nothing.

"You said we would talk today...about Johnny."

Her words caused physical pain to his ribs as tension shot through his body. "So I did." He could avoid her no longer. He turned to face her. Words stuck in his throat. He stood there silently taking her in from head to foot.

Her long black hair hung loose, framing her face. A sheer white blouse over a form-fitting white tank brought his lower regions inconveniently to attention. Now was not the time for this.

She looked away and color rose to her cheeks. She seemed uncomfortable with his quiet stare and frankly, so was he. "Are you feeling better?" she asked. "You still look a little under the weather."

"I'm doing much better today. Thanks." He was lying through his teeth. He'd have volunteered for another beating in exchange for the conversation they were about to have.

"Like I tried to tell you last night, I feel as if I behaved badly when you asked me to help you with Johnny's case. I guess I let it get to me."

Nate wet his lips. He'd often had to choose the right words to say to a jury. God, if he could only find the right ones now.

She shot him a wary glance. He knew she was wondering why he didn't respond.

"Anyway, I've come to my senses. I want to do whatever I can to help." She gave him another quick look, folded her hands behind her and paced back and forth in the area in front of his desk. "I've been out to talk to Johnny's best friend."

"Mary," Nate interrupted her.

She didn't look at him or pause. She just kept talking. "They were together that day, but he doesn't know where Johnny was when it happened. I think the next thing I should do—"

"Is find another attorney for your brother." He finished the sentence for her, and waited for her to react.

She stopped in her tracks. Her eyes flashed as she turned to face him. "What?" she stammered, a stunned expression on her face. "Why?"

"I'm not the best choice for this case. I can't—"

"Is this because of what's happened between you and me? Nate, I didn't let you kiss me—"

"Kiss you? That's ridiculous."

"You're telling me."

"You don't honestly think I'd walk away over that do you?"

"I don't know. I don't know how to read any of this. One minute you're following me around and accusing me of trying to hide something that could help Johnny. The next you try to get close. Then you decide to desert Johnny when you're the only hope he has." She threw up her hands. "No, Nate. I don't understand."

"Don't lay any guilt trips on me. I'm not deserting anybody. Dammit, Mary. I can't defend Johnny because I believe he's guilty. It's not fair to him. And after what I've been feeling for you, it isn't fair to you either."

If he'd slapped her across the face, her look would have been no different. It appeared she only heard one sentence he said.

"My brother is *not* guilty, Mr. Nakai. You know nothing about Johnny. And you don't need to resign from this case. I'll have you removed before another day passes." With anger seething from her gestures, she squared her shoulders, spun on one foot and stomped out of the room.

My, that went well. But it was pretty much what he expected. The sexiest, most beautiful woman he'd ever known had just walked out of his life. His first case in Santa Fe was out the window. And it wasn't nine o'clock in the morning yet. It was shaping up to be one hell of a day.

Mary stormed down the street. Tears stung her eyes, but she refused to let them fall. Her heart pounded and her ears burned. Anger surged through her entire body.

She'd been right all along. Nathan Nakai was bad news. Letting down her guard, permitting him to touch her heart had been her second mistake. Allowing another public defender to represent a member of her family had been her first.

She was short on cash, but she'd find a way. Her money was invested in the gallery and in Grandpa's hospital bills from his bout with pneumonia last winter. The one thing she had that could provide the funds she needed for a retainer to hire a new attorney was something she'd told herself she'd never part with. But as of fifteen minutes ago, it meant nothing.

Unlocking the glass door to the gallery, she marched inside. She turned on the computer and quickly printed a note card that read, "Eagle Dancer, $7,250." Purposefully walking to the back room, and avoiding the dark painted eyes that always beckoned to her, she slipped the new card over the top of the one that read, 'Not For Sale.'

She went back into her office, trying to keep from thinking about what she'd done, and locked out the feeling she'd cut off a body part. Grabbing the phone book from her desk, she opened the Yellow Pages to 'Attorneys.' It was time for practicality—time to let go of the fantasy—and time to realize dream warriors simply didn't exist.

Coyote strolled into Nate's office, parked himself in the side chair and propped his cowboy boots on the corner of the desk.

Nate looked at him without raising his head from the file spread in front of him. "Make yourself at home. Don't let me get in your way."

His sarcastic tone brought a smirk from Coyote. "You get up on the wrong side of the desk this morning?"

"Maybe. Or maybe you could at least say good morning before you plant your dirty shit kickers in my work space."

"You know you wouldn't be so cranky in the morning if you had a good woman in your life." Coyote adjusted his hat. He had a knack for knowing which nerve was raw.

"I seem to have a finely tuned skill at avoiding that very thing," Nate grumbled and flipped a page in the file folder, pretending to concentrate on what it said. Truth was, he'd had it in front of him for almost an hour and hadn't read a word.

Coyote raised his eyebrows. "Sounds like a sore subject."

"Leave it be. Okay?"

"Sure. Stopped in strictly on business, anyway." Coyote grinned. "Thought you might want to know. I got the low down on the gang you were socializing with the other night."

Nate looked up.

"There's definitely no gang involvement when it comes to Johnny Begay. Word from the street sounds suspicious. Those two guys got a payoff from somebody. They've apparently been going around town flashing some extra cash since yesterday. The whole deal smells bad to me."

"You know who they are?"

"No. But I know someone who does. He wouldn't rat them out, but he told me enough."

"What reason would someone have to want the crap kicked out of me?"

"I don't know, man. Maybe it's the wild party life you keep after hours."

Nate rolled his eyes. "Could you be serious for five minutes?"

"Maybe ten on a good day." Coyote pushed back his hat. "You're either in a really bad mood or you got something heavy on your head. I've never seen you like this. You all right?"

Nate rubbed his chin. "How much do you know about Smith and the investigator from the PD? Gonzales is his name."

"Smith's been here for years. Long as I can remember. My dad worked with him when he was an investigator for the police force." Coyote shrugged. "Gonzales, not so much. Found out he worked the beat for a while, but I don't know anything else about him. Come to think of it, my old man mentioned his name a couple times, but that's about it. Why are you asking?"

"Some inside information. It seems the two of them were overheard talking about me, and somebody being 'beat to a pulp.' I believe those were the exact words they used."

"Hmm. Interesting, but not necessarily anything fishy."

"No. Except nobody else knew about it. What reason would Smith have to be after me? The whole thing makes no sense."

Coyote frowned. "All those two gangsters wanted was to get you off the Begay case, huh?"

"That's what they said." Nate rose from the chair and walked to the window. "The first time we met you said a couple of things that started eating at me last night. I think maybe it's time for some clarification."

"What was that?"

"You said Mary Begay and the DA went way back. You've sidestepped my questions. Maybe it's time you told me what you meant."

"I didn't figure it was anybody's business, but Mary's. Still don't."

"Well, if somebody beat the shit out of me over it, that might make it my business. Don't you think?"

Coyote nodded and looked uncomfortable. He removed his feet from the desk and situated himself in the chair. "When I made the comment, I was thinking a long way back. Smith's son Ethan was in the same class as Mary and I. Smart-ass. High school jock. You know the type. His old man was a prominent citizen and he thought he was God's gift to Santa Fe." Coyote snorted. "At least to the women of Santa Fe."

Nate moved away from the window and sat on the corner of the desk with his arms folded as he listened.

Coyote went on. "Ethan always had eyes for Mary. And why not, she was the prettiest girl in school. Anyway, Mary and him became an item for a time. I actually thought Ethan might straighten up his act, but it didn't happen. The biggest problem was Ethan's dad."

"Smith didn't like Mary?"

"Smith didn't like anybody who was Indian. My old man worked with Smith almost every day. He came home angry a lot of times over things Smith said. Racial slurs and the like."

"Your dad was Indian. I can see why that wouldn't sit well."

"It didn't. But my dad had a good job and he didn't want to jeopardize it, so he took it. But it made him hopping mad."

"So what happened with Ethan and Mary?"

"They broke up. It was the best thing for Mary. But Ethan still hung around her. I knew the reason for it. Smith had a fit over his precious son dating an Indian girl. Carried on about how a squaw wasn't fit for his superior son. Said so much it got back to Mary." Coyote paused and tipped his hat back on his head. "Mary's a proud woman. And she was proud back then, too. It tore her up pretty bad, and Smith's big mouth had the whole town talking."

"Sounds like small town gossip. The whole thing happened so long ago, why would either one of them care anymore?"

"It never went away. And it got a whole lot worse."

"A high school romance doesn't seem like grounds for a fifteen-year grudge. I don't get it."

Coyote shook his head and got to his feet. "Then you need to ask Mary. It isn't my place to tell you any more." He walked toward the door.

"Then I may never know the rest of the story. I doubt if I'll be seeing Mary Begay. She was pretty angry when she left earlier."

Coyote turned back toward Nate. "Man, you keep calling her Mary Begay. That's her maiden name. She goes by Mary Summernight now. I've got to go. I've said too much already. And Mary's got enough headaches without dredging up the past."

Nate stood there with his mouth hanging open as Coyote's words sunk in. *Mary Summernight. Summernight Gallery. Holy shit.* It was Mary's signature on the painting. What an idiot he'd been not to connect the dots.

—◀—

Mary walked up to the door of the law offices. She glanced at her watch. She was fifteen minutes early. The sooner the better. This issue needed to be resolved as quickly as possible. She reached for the door handle. An arm wrapped around her and a hand covered hers. She stopped in her tracks and whirled around.

"Grandpa. What are you doing here?"

"Keeping you from making a mistake." Grandpa stepped back and adjusted his bolo tie.

"A mistake? But you don't know what's happened."

"I know you're here to replace Nakai as Johnny's lawyer."

"Grandpa. I promised Johnny I wouldn't tell you about any of this." Mary's heart sank as she moved away from the door.

"And you didn't. That doesn't mean I don't know." Grandpa's face was stern and she could tell he was upset with her for trying to hide Johnny's plight. "I'm an old man, but I'm not oblivious to what's happening around me. You didn't think you could keep this a secret did you?"

Mary winced. The fine line she'd been walking between Grandpa, Johnny and Nate was wearing on her. "I've never been able to hide anything from you. You've always known about things before they happened." She crossed her arms. "I was a fool to think I could keep you from finding out."

"You're no fool. But it would be a foolish mistake to replace Nakai."

"You don't understand. He thinks Johnny's guilty. He's another public defender Smith has in his back pocket."

Grandpa shook his head. "I think you know better."

She wished Grandpa would let her handle this. "But he's too unpredictable and he believes Johnny hurt Stellar."

"You need to give him some time. There are things you don't understand and things he doesn't understand. Not yet, anyway."

Time. Mary sighed. She was tired of playing games of cat and mouse. But when she looked Grandpa in the eye, her heart melted. "Then what do you propose I do?"

"Wait to take action. In time, he will find his way."

"This has gone on long enough. I can't work with him. And you tell me not to let him go. Being around him is very uncomfortable."

There was a twinkle in Grandpa's eye. "Things closest to us are the most uncomfortable."

"I meant, because he thinks Johnny did this awful thing." Mary put her hand on the side of her face. "I guess, I'm guilty, too. Guilty of letting the past dictate how I feel about what's happening."

Grandpa looked to his right as if he were seeing something beyond the tangible. "There is far more to the past than either you or Nakai realize. Until you fully experience and understand its impact on your lives, you will not be able to resolve the problems of the present."

"That makes no sense." She looked at the business card in her hand. "I know you mean well, and I know you'll end up being right. But I don't get it."

"And you won't until you understand all that is playing a part in the direction of your life. I will say no more now. I only ask you not to make this decision, today."

Mary nodded reluctantly and slowly turned away from the door. Maybe she was jumping the gun. She didn't have the retainer yet. Taking Grandpa's hand, she pulled out her cell phone and dialed the attorney to cancel the appointment. She'd have to honor the old man's wishes and tolerate Nakai one more day.

She let out an exhausted sigh. Why had she let Grandpa talk her out of it? She wasn't sure. Aside from the nagging fact that she couldn't remember a time when Grandpa's words didn't ring true, she was at a place where she had to put her trust in someone. There was no choice in the matter.

CHAPTER THIRTEEN

Nate rubbed the stubble on his chin. His five o'clock shadow was rapidly approaching the midnight hour, but that was the least of his worries. Coyote's words echoed in his mind. The impact of them had settled upon him.

The puzzle had finally come together. Johnny's comments and actions when they first met now made perfect sense. The boy must have thought Nate was an apparition. The uncanny coincidence of the painting hammered inside his head. The phenomenal scenario seemed impossible, but then so was seeing Stellar and Johnny in his vision.

His concept of the world as a logical, concrete place was teetering on the brink of collapse. Some force beyond his own understanding was walking through his life, pulling him toward the unknown, unexplored regions of his soul.

Mary's grandfather had sat in his office days earlier and talked to him about the native blood that flowed in his veins. It was something he'd taken for granted in his thirty-six years of living. But he was rapidly realizing it had a major role in this bizarre mystery that was playing out. Now, in this time and this place, it was undeniable, and looking back at him from a face painted on canvas.

He placed his hand on the kachina on his desk and turned it to face him. "What the hell is this all about? Somehow I think you know."

Grandpa's words tumbled through his mind. Talk about inherent special powers, connections to the past and destiny that had seemed like superstitious mumbo jumbo at the time. Grandpa knew something when he saw the kachina. This was no dime store trinket. The Eagle Dancer Kachina was a symbol of something more. And it was far more than a coincidence that the painting bore the same name.

He'd dreamed a few nights ago of being caught up in a whirlwind of eagle feathers. In it, his own physique was Indian bronze, not just his California suntan, but alive with the color of his heritage. His hair had been its natural color, jet-black. Not lightened to diminish the hints of gray at his temples. Tell tale signs of both the high stress life he was trying to leave behind and his effort to be someone he wasn't.

With elbows on his desk, he ran his hands across his temples and down the back of his head. Maybe he was going off the deep end. Part of his job was sniffing out the facts. He needed to slow down and consider all the possibilities. He'd immediately assumed Mary was the artist of the painting. He turned his chair toward his computer. Mary was a widow. What if her husband painted the warrior?

A few mouse clicks and he was searching the Santa Fe newspapers for anything with the name Summernight. There it was, two years ago, an obituary for Angelo Summernight. Sure enough, the same picture was on the fence in the churchyard. He read on. "Died two days ago in the New Mexico State prison." Nate's brow creased as he read the rest. "Details surrounding his death were not available."

Nate searched for more information. The next item was six months prior. He scanned the article searching for more. "Angelo Summernight, husband of Navajo artist, Mary Summernight, was convicted today in the armed robbery of a liquor store in Santa Fe. No comment was available from the office of the Public Defender."

A couple of huge pieces of Mary's puzzle slid into place. Nate leaned back in his chair. *Again. Another Public Defender.* Mary's words echoed through his head. She hadn't been through this before with Johnny. She'd been through it with her late husband.

Mary. The stubborn, hardheaded, fiery woman had earned every right to be that way. She was the widow of a convicted felon. Her parents had died and left her to care for a little brother and an elderly grandfather. He shook his head and wondered at the question in his mind. Who took care of Mary?

His heart felt a pang of remorse. He'd been hard on her, prying into her world. No wonder she'd been hesitant to tell him. Yeah, it was his job. Or it had been. Now he was deserting her, too. Leaving her to fight the world—and Jim Smith—on her own. Coyote's story about that didn't compute, but it was too much on his mind tonight.

Nonetheless, it came down to the inevitable—and the painting of a half-naked warrior hanging on a gallery wall. Somehow it had to be connected to the how and why of something bigger and deeper, something tainted with shadows of the past and covered in the fingerprints of the hands of fate.

Nate thought of Mary standing in his office early that morning. Her long black hair flowing down her back, the white tank top hugging her breasts. The tightness he'd felt below his belt earlier, returned. How could she have painted his exact likeness, the mirror image of a total stranger? How could it have been inside her head, and flowed from her fingertips with such accuracy?

Heat boiled inside him. A deep down fire surged. He'd suppressed it longer than he cared to remember. Raw primal thoughts of Mary washed over him, along with the image of her painting the details of her warrior—the details of his body—burned in his mind. The memory of her gentle hands caring for his wounds engulfed him, of bare flesh against bare flesh, of his flesh against Mary's. The intensity brought beads of sweat to his brow. He wiped them away with his fingertips.

Mary wanted nothing to do with him, but there was one thing he could do. He wasn't sure how it would be received or where it would lead, but there was only one way to find out. He glanced at his watch. It was almost 6:30 p.m. He had very little time to get it done.

When Mary arrived at the gallery, it was 7:30, half an hour before closing time. She'd been out more than in most of the day. Bev, her assistant manager, was busy cleaning the glass jewelry case. Mary laid her purse on the counter and walked around to the register. "Sorry to be gone so much. I came in to close so you could go home."

"No problem. I knew you had things to take care of." Bev turned toward her with a smug grin on her face and a twinkle in her eye. "I'm glad you came back though. I have some great news."

Mary eyed her suspiciously. "Oh God. You're not getting married and quitting your job are you?"

Bev wrinkled her nose. "Oh please. I've done that marriage thing enough times to learn my lesson. Trust me, the third times not the charm, or the fourth, or the fifth—"

"Okay, okay. That was a lousy thing to guess. So what's the big news?"

Bev's eyes grew large and the words fairly burst from her perfectly painted red lips. "I sold one of your paintings."

"Which one?" Mary asked.

"*The* painting."

Mary's heart skipped a beat. "The Eagle Dancer?" She asked cautiously, secretly fearing to hear the answer.

"Yes. And you would never have believed the guy who bought it. He was the one who was in here the other day."

"There have been dozens of people through here the last few days." Mary was only half-listening. She pretended to straighten the money in the cash register.

"Anyway, the guy came in here less than an hour ago, and hardly looked at it. Told me to wrap it up, he'd take it with him tonight. And guess what else?"

"I've no idea." Mary tried to listen, but her thoughts were whirling as the realization set in that she would miss seeing the painting of her dream warrior.

"He insisted on paying *more* than the price you had on it."

"More? Nobody does that."

"Look, there in the register. His check is under the drawer. Look how much it's for. And he wouldn't have it any other way."

With trembling fingers, Mary pulled out the black metal tray and sorted through a few checks and large bills. The one she was seeking stood out among the rest. At first, all she could see was *$10,000. Oh my, God.* Then she saw the name across the top. *Nathan Nakai.*

Mary's blood pressure pounded its way to the top of her head. Her face flushed. "Damn that man," she whispered under her breath.

"Isn't that wild?" Bev picked up her bottle of glass cleaner and went back to work on the other side of the counter. "I knew you'd just be beside yourself."

Beside herself indeed. How dare he do such a thing. Mary turned abruptly. "You can go now. I'll see you in the morning." She struggled to keep the emotion out of her voice. Her cheeks burned like two hot coals as she tried to contain the anger surging through her. Her breath came in short puffs. She had to be alone.

"Well, if you're sure, I'll take off." Bev tucked her cleaning supplies away and grabbed her handbag from under the counter. "You okay? You look flushed?"

"I'm fine. Now, go." Mary feigned a half smile and motioned toward the door.

As Bev walked out, Mary looked down at her shaking hands. How could he? The fact he'd purchased the painting was hard enough for her to deal with. But how dare he pay more than the asking price. It was a blatant insult.

He knew she was out to find Johnny a new lawyer. Buying the painting to help her raise the cash was totally unnecessary and absurd. She didn't want or need his help. That was for damn sure.

She picked up the check and put it in her purse. Pushing the register drawer closed, she knew she'd have to come back later. But she didn't care. At the moment, she had something more important to attend to, namely, some things to get straight with one Mr. Nathan Nakai.

No matter what she'd promised Grandpa, no one was going to treat her like a charity case. She stormed out of the gallery, dimming the lights and locking the door behind her.

Nate sat on the foot of the bed. He'd lost track of how long he'd been there, staring into the painting propped against the adjacent wall. Both the hot July night, and a strange need to feel kinship with his near-naked counterpart on canvas, had compelled him to remove his shirt.

He was mesmerized by the artist's skill and the realism of the painting, but even more so by its exacting duplication of every one of his features. It was

like looking at his   reflection, a mirror image in a
brook, or in a window looking into a different world.
Goose flesh ran the length of his arms.

Where had the imagery come from? What had been
the source of the picture in Mary's mind? It was a
question he wanted Mary to answer. Something about
it was hauntingly familiar, and the more he gazed into
the painting, the more odd pictures and images played
through his mind.

A loud knock on the front door startled Nate and
jarred him from his trance. He chose to ignore it the
first time, but the second knock had greater urgency.
He slipped on his shirt. Who could it be at this time of
night? At the front door, he looked through the
peephole.

Mary stood on the other side. Tightness washed
through his upper body. He'd half-hoped she'd seek
him out, but really believed she'd take the money and
run. He certainly didn't expect her to come here
tonight.

Mary raised her hand to rap on the door as he
opened it. Her barrage of angry words hit him before
he could say hello. "What on earth do you think you're
doing? Who in the hell do you think you are?"

"Come inside, Mary. Please."

"Why would I want to come in after what you've
done?"

Nate scratched behind his ear. "Well, maybe so you
won't disturb the neighbors."

Mary glanced over her shoulder and marched
through the open doorway. "Very well. I'm inside, but
it doesn't change what I have to say or why I've come
here." She reached into her purse and pulled out the
check he'd written earlier. "What is the meaning of
this?"

"Calm down. Is that what you're riled up about? It's
a check, in exchange for the painting."

"I know very well what it is. What I want to know is what gives you the right to walk into my gallery and act as if I'm some pauper who needs your contributions."

"I didn't mean it that way. Don't take it like that." Nate stood with arms crossed as Mary paced in front of him, shaking the check in his face.

"What other way would I take it? You knew I left this morning to go find your replacement. How dare you act as if I didn't have the money to do it without your help. How dare you patronize me with your donations. I'm not a nonprofit organization or your favorite charity. I'm a businesswoman and a damn good one. I don't operate off of yours or anyone else's handouts."

"Are you done?"

"I'm done all right. Done with people who think they're better than I am because they have more money. Through with living my life being treated like I'm somehow a lesser being because I'm a woman or because I'm Navajo. You're damned right I'm done." She whirled and headed toward the door.

Nate caught her by the arm and pulled her toward him. "Hold on one minute. Wanna back up that truck you just ran over me with?"

Her eyes were full of fire and her nostrils flared. Squaring her shoulders, she placed her hand over his and firmly removed it from her arm. With her hands on her hips, she looked in his face with jaw set and lips tight. Her look was expectant. Obviously, she was giving him permission to speak his piece.

"Could you settle down so we can talk about this like two civilized adults? I have some good reasons for what I did. None of them have a damn thing to do with your being Navajo, or with me treating you like a charity. They have more to do with you being a magnificently gifted artist, and a giving and loving person who could use a break for a change." He looked deep in her eyes. "And it has *everything* to do with you being a woman. One of the most beautiful women I've ever known."

She looked away. He could see her swallow hard as her eyes flashed around the room. She blinked. His words had hit home.

She wet her lips. "You shouldn't say these things. You don't know who I really am. You don't understand where I've been."

Nate spoke softly, wanting to touch her, but he dared not. "I may understand more than you think. Things aren't always what they appear to be on the surface and neither are people." He moved closer. "But I never knew until this morning that you painted the warrior. I had no idea it was your work."

"I guess, I thought you knew all along. You came into the gallery—"

"But I didn't make the connection. It never registered. I didn't know your last name was Summernight until today. Maybe I'm dense."

"Or preoccupied? Or too busy chasing things that either didn't concern you or didn't exist." Mary sighed.

"You haven't exactly been above suspicion, you know, but I think I understand some of it."

"Understand? How could you understand?"

"I know about Angelo. When I finally connected the name, I did some research and found out what happened. I'm sorry for what you've been through."

Mary searched his face. "I don't want your pity any more than I want your money. The past is dead. I want to forget and move on."

"Johnny's situation makes that hard too, doesn't it?" He reached out and gently touched his fingertips to her forearm, stroking it gently.

At first she flinched, then relaxed, looking at his fingers on her skin. She spoke in a low tone. "It's like reliving a nightmare. How could it not be on my mind?"

"I don't know the whole story, but the last thing I want is to make this worse for you." He sunk his teeth in his lip. "I had a hell of a time telling you this morning."

"I was angry at your words and I still am. It isn't true you know—what you said about Johnny."

He couldn't look her in the eye. He wouldn't spoil this moment. She'd let him in, let him touch her and they were finally communicating. "I've got some issues of my own to work through. But I've had some time to think."

She shook her head. "I'm not sure I want your help now, even if you've changed your mind."

His words caught in his throat. How could he possibly explain his reasons to her? "Mary, like I said, things aren't always what they seem."

"No, they aren't. Funny, I heard those exact words earlier from Grandpa."

"Grandpa sounds like a wise man."

"We'll see. He's the only reason I didn't replace you today."

Nate laughed softly. "Well, then maybe he's also the reason why you're here. I'll have to thank him."

She shook her head again and at last stepped away from his touch. "Not really. I'm here because you make me furious."

"It truly wasn't my intention. Let's don't go there. Not tonight."

She folded her arms and looked around the living room. "Where is he?"

"He?"

She smiled. "The warrior."

"In the bedroom. I've been in there for an hour staring at the painting. It's amazing." Nate shuffled his feet and buttoned the bottom buttons of his shirt. "Sorry, I've been relaxing."

Mary looked at the check she still held in her hand. "I think you should take this back."

"I don't want it."

She opened his hand and stuffed it into his palm. "I think for now it would be best."

"And you want the painting?"

"I haven't decided. You keep it for tonight. And keep the check until we can come up with a more equitable arrangement."

He nodded, walked over to a table in the entryway, and placed the check on it. Turning back toward Mary, he asked. "Where did it come from Mary?"

"What do you mean?"

"The painting—the warrior? I mean the inspiration for it. It's the weirdest thing that's ever happened to me—close, anyway."

"It came from some place deep inside me. Most artwork is that way. I can't say I know its origin."

"It just came to you one day? Even the face?"

An odd expression washed across her face and she spoke softly. "Hmm. I can only say, his face has lived in my memory all my life."

Nate raised an eyebrow and tried to keep the strangeness of how her comment hit him from showing. Yet, he couldn't stop honesty from escaping his own lips. "I felt the same way when I saw you the first time."

She gave him a questioning look. Their eyes met. It was so very strange.

"It seems we have some things to talk about." Her own words surprised her. It showed in her expression. Quickly, she corrected herself. "About Johnny and such. I have to finish closing the gallery. It's late." With a slight reluctance in her movements, she walked toward the door. She turned toward him, deep in thought and avoiding his eyes. "Perhaps another time?"

"Perhaps." Nate nodded.

Mary left quietly.

Obviously, the conversation and their feelings had both gone way beyond their comfort zones. It was time to call it a day. But the unanswered questions hanging in the air and swimming in Nate's mind were not the kind that could slip silently away into the night.

An hour or so passed. Haunted by everything that had happened since he'd come to Santa Fe, Nate couldn't shake his thoughts of Mary, the painting, and the mystery of how it came to be. He drank a cup of coffee, thankful to be alone.

He had some major decisions to make around Johnny's case. He hadn't come to peace with it. Had he been too hasty? Basing everything on his vision, something that truthfully wasn't concrete, bothered the part of him that was a hard-nosed attorney.

His world revolved around solid evidence and, frankly, he'd have had a heyday with the thought of such a thing a few weeks ago. He'd put it aside until tomorrow. All things looked different in the light of day.

Walking back into the bedroom, he stripped down to his shorts. He needed to get some sleep for a change. Not wanting to allow the eyes to capture him again, he tried to avoid the painting. Turning toward the bathroom, his own image appeared in the mirror on the door. In the reflection, the painting sat ominously behind him.

A movement caught his eye and he spun around. Startled, his heart pounded. Something in the painting had moved. That was ludicrous. The eyes of the warrior met his. He looked away then back to the mirror.

The mirror was clouded with mist, like a heavy San Francisco fog. But the fog was behind him, too. It seemed to rise from out of the mirror and the painting to engulf him in its white wispy tendrils. Pictures raced through his mind so quickly he staggered backward.

Enveloped by the hazy mist and lightheaded, he wobbled and fell to his knees. A wave of dizziness washed through him as his own consciousness seemed to drift away into the distance.

He had the sensation he was pushing through the fog. Making his way through the clouds of mist, it began to dissipate. Feeling water droplets on his skin, he looked down at his bronzed nakedness. Only a breach cloth covered his lower region.

The war cry tore from his throat and pierced the silence. Heat rushed through his shoulder as he threw the spear he held with all his might, a shocking contrast to the cold desolation that closed around his heart.

"He will not have you, even if I have to kill him." The words poured from his mouth. His body shook with rage. Clenching his fists, he fell to his knees in the dirt, prostrate with anger and helplessness.

"Eagle," Mourning Dove stroked his hair as she knelt beside him. "You can't do that." Her red-rimmed eyes told of the pain in her heart and her sweet young face had taken on the look of an older woman. "Crow Feather would only find you and kill you, too. If Raven's people didn't find you first."

"Why would my father do such a thing? A spear through my belly would have been kinder than this."

"Kindness does not live in your father's heart. The only thing that brings him joy is another's pain. And yours seems to delight him most."

Eagle moved into a sitting position and sat cross-legged looking into Mourning Dove's face. "Since my mother's death he is much worse. He seems to think of nothing else."

"Your mother is no longer here to protect you, to take his wrath and devious acts upon herself."

"He is the reason she took her own life. She couldn't take it any more." Lone Eagle brushed a stray tear

from the bridge of his nose. The ache in his heart was nearly unbearable.

"She loved you, Eagle. Never doubt that." Mourning Dove grasped his upper arms in her hands.

"I know that she did, but sometimes I think I, too, would be better off dead."

She placed her fingers over his lips. "Please don't say such things. I could not go on without you."

"I'd rather be dead than watch Black Hawk with you, Mourning Dove. Than know he'd made love to you, and watch you bear his children. There are things a man cannot do, and I cannot watch that happen."

Mourning Dove's eyes filled with tears. "I feel the same way about your brother. I cannot bear the thought of him touching me. What can we do?"

Grasping her hand, he kissed her fingertips. "But what are our lives to be like? Crow Feather has at last found the one thing that has the power to destroy me. Life without you."

Mourning Dove leaned into him. He pulled her to him and kissed her feverishly. Tasting the sweet nectar of her lips, he kissed her over and over. He whispered, "I could never love another as I love you." Suddenly, he pushed her away. *"I'd rather take my chances against Raven's band than stay here."*

"But, Eagle, I could never bear to leave you," she whispered.

"We must leave here together. It's the only way."

"But what about Raven? We'll be killed."

"If we leave under cover of night, I believe we can work our way South until we escape from Raven."

"But where will we hide? There are so few remaining villages. No one on the mesa will help us. They know you as Crow Feather's son—and know of your kinship to Raven. We've been told stories of those who will hunt us down and destroy us if we leave."

"And I believe much of it is only that. Stories told to us so that we can be controlled. My mother told me once

that her brother's mate, the Princess Snowcloud, made a journey somewhere far to the South and returned after many days. She spoke of other clans who lived there. I believe we can find safety among them. It's a chance we must take or live forever in the hell Crow Feather and Raven have created for us."

Mourning Dove shook her head. "I don't know. I'm frightened." She bit her lip and hesitated. "But I'm more frightened of the life your father is creating for us here than I am of dying. You're right. We have no other choice."

A sound in the bushes caused Eagle to start. A boyish figure darted toward them from the junipers and deer brush.

"Two Birds," Eagle said, a dour look crossing his face.

The boy's eyes glowed with the same wicked light as Raven's. "Father sent me. He wants me to go with you to hunt for the bear." Two Birds' lips curled in an evil grin.

Mourning Dove winced and glanced at Eagle. He read her thoughts. Had Two Birds heard their plans?

Eagle didn't know the answer, but it was a chance they'd have to take. Their eyes met and his silent message passed to her.

I could never love another as I love you—a chance they'd have to take—

The words faded away into the distance as his mind raced back through the mist.

Nate opened his eyes slowly and looked at the ceiling. He was lying on his back in the middle of the floor. Directly in front of him stood the ominous mirror.

He rose up on his elbows, and tenuously looked at his reflection. He looked normal—at least for a guy lying on the floor in his under shorts. He rose to his feet, noticing as the light caught the water droplets clinging to his body.

"What the—" He ran his hand down his thigh and looked at the moisture on his palm.

What the hell happened? A feeling of desperation clung to him. He felt hung over, but he knew he hadn't had a drink. Half stumbling across the floor to the bed, he ran his hands down his chest. His mouth was dry as cotton.

Sprawling across the bed, he stared at the ceiling fan. His mind and his world whirled faster than the fan's blades. Undoubtedly, he'd had another vision, but where had he been and who were the man and woman? What were they talking about? He raised his head, looking into the eyes of the warrior.

"It was you, wasn't it?" he whispered. "Where the hell did you take me?"

CHAPTER FOURTEEN

Mary stared out the window at the small herd of sheep grazing in the field behind the house. Peacefully, they moved around the meadow. From the taller grasses already beginning to yellow from the summer heat, to the short grubbed green carpet near the small creek that crossed the lower corner of the property, they dined on a smorgasbord of wild grasses and weeds.

Their wooly coats were growing out and it wouldn't be long before she could shear them for more wool for her rugs. Few people still kept sheep or spun and dyed their own wool. For her it was a labor of love, something that tied her soul to the past. She glanced down at the steaming cup of coffee on the kitchen counter. Life would have been a lot easier if she'd been a sheep.

Outside the back door, a gray wisp swirled up through the smoke hole of Grandpa's hogan. The small six-sided adobe building, rounded on top, had sat on the family's land for as long as Mary could remember. When she was a child, her grandparents lived in the structure. But after the death of her grandmother, and several years later, her parents, she'd convinced Grandpa to move into the house.

Ever since, Grandpa had risen before dawn and gone out to the hogan. He built his fire, drank his morning coffee and watched the sun rise through the doorway facing east. It was his ritual to greet Father

Sun every morning. The hogan was his sanctuary. The place he went to be alone and where he performed his ceremonies. It was his tie to the old ways, just as the sheep and weaving kept her heritage alive in her own heart.

It was a simple life. At least it should have been. Her childhood memories were happy and sweet. But things had changed drastically from her seventeenth year on, sometimes it seemed like another lifetime.

Seventeen. It was an age of innocence and a time when she should have been focusing on getting an education. But the education she received from her love affair with Ethan Smith haunted her to this day.

Why was that on her mind today? Maybe the stroll down memory lane was a distraction. Perhaps her thoughts were helping her with the avoidance game, avoiding the present issues. Creating a diversion from the decisions she had to make and the face that floated through her head all night. *Nathan. Nathan Nakai.* No matter how hard she tried, no matter how he angered her, he was stealing her heart. Was she ready for that? And, worse yet, was she putting him in danger?

"A penny for your thoughts." Grandpa's voice came from behind her.

Mary hadn't heard him come in. She glanced over her shoulder and smiled. "It would take a pocket full of pennies to cover my thoughts this morning. I'm trying to sort through them all. And wishing Johnny was back home with us."

"He will be soon. But your sorting would be easier if you would sleep. I heard you up again last night. You need some rest." He patted her shoulder.

"I will in time, Grandpa. I can't seem to turn off my mind. How do you keep so calm? You must have a secret."

"The secret is to trust. And to know nothing happens without a reason." Grandpa poured coffee into a large stoneware cup. "Everything in life is a lesson. Something we need to learn. What causes us worry is trying to intervene in other's lessons."

"That sounds good, but you know I have to help Johnny. We're all he has."

"Johnny does need our help. It's our responsibility to do what we can. But he isn't the one I was referring to. I think the attorney keeps you awake as much as Johnny."

She cast him a sideways glance. "Yes, he does. I have to decide what I'm doing about him."

Grandpa gave her a crooked smile. "In more ways than one?"

Mary tried to ignore the remark. "I know you don't want me to get another lawyer. But I'm not sure that's for the best."

"Things are best left as they are. Johnny needs him and so do you." Grandpa took a seat at the kitchen table.

Mary frowned. "I can find someone else capable of defending Johnny. One who doesn't cause me so much grief."

"What pains you doesn't have anything to do with Johnny. What Nate stirs in you is what you fear."

Grandpa's words squeezed at her heart. Hiding anything from him was impossible, he knew her too well. "What I feel has no resemblance to fear. Sometimes, I think I hate him."

"You may not recognize it, but fear is what it is. You built a wall around your heart a long time ago to lock out the hurt. Maybe it's time to let yourself feel." Grandpa took a sip of coffee. "He bought the painting, didn't he?"

Mary was silent. Tears threatened and her throat tightened. She stared out the window. "I don't know how you know these things, but, yes, he bought the painting. So what now?"

"Wait. He will come to you."

"You mean leave him on the case?"

"Even though you don't like what he says, you need to leave things as they are."

"And Johnny?" Mary turned to look at him.

"I know you are struggling, but our lives at this moment are in the hands of the masters—those who walk through our souls in the middle of the night and touch us with ancient memories we can't quite grasp." Grandpa's eyes twinkled with an odd light. "I knew it the minute I saw the kachina. Clarity will come to you in the next few days and so will Nathan Nakai."

She shot him a questioning look. "Kachinas? Masters?"

"The masters from the spirit world, my dear. It simply means it's time to open your heart and listen with your soul."

Mary rubbed her temples. "I'm not sure what you're saying, Grandpa, but I've learned one thing for certain in this lifetime. When you speak, I listen. I'll wait."

"And trust." He nodded and took another sip of coffee.

Mary stood in front of the window, noticing how the house fell eerily silent, as if awaiting the coming of Grandpa's masters, Nathan Nakai and some monumental event.

Nate rolled over and pulled the bedspread around him. He was still laying crossways on the bed. The air conditioning was still blasting, the ceiling fan was still spinning and he was still stripped down to his shorts. It felt like July all right—in the Arctic Circle. It had been a night he wouldn't soon forget.

The morning sun peeked through the white plantation blinds on the bedroom windows. Nate squeezed his eyes shut, trying harder to avoid his oil-painted counterpart than the sunlight. His neck was sore and his eyes gritty from lack of sleep. And the last thing he wanted to see was the face on the wall. His face—by some bizarre coincidence.

When exhaustion had finally claimed him and sleep had won over, he'd thrown the spear and cried out at least a hundred times over in his dreams. Phrases from his glimpse into that other world repeated over and over in his mind all night like a bad CD stuck in the CD player. He'd experienced the pain as deeply as if it were his own—and the desperation.

He'd been there. He'd stood on a mountainside and screamed out his lungs and the agony in his heart. Where? When? Why did it seem so real? What did it mean? The vision about Johnny and Stellar had been like that, so vivid—and so true. Nate stopped himself. He couldn't go there. If it wasn't foretelling the future, could it be revealing the past?

Struggling, he tried to remember the woman's face. It was cloudy, blurred and distant. She was crying. He remembered both her tears and her kiss, vividly, and the feel of her lips on his and the warmth of her body pushing against his.

He squeezed his eyes tight together. Maybe if he focused, he could see her face. Her skin was soft and bronze. She was dark and beautiful. She was Indian.

"Indian, just like me," he whispered.

Grandpa's words echoed in his memory. "I could feel your Native blood the first time I saw you." Was this somehow connected? Connected to his ancestry and the heritage he knew so little about?

He shook off the thoughts and tried to recreate the woman. Trying to force the picture into his mind, a face began to take shape. It was bronze. The hair was long and blowing softly back. She turned to face him. The image crystallized. It wasn't her. It was the old Indian man he'd seen in the rear view mirror at Grandpa's house.

"In your soul there's a fire that remembers." The words pounded in his head. "Soul circles." He pressed his hands against his closed eyes. The voices continued to echo in his mind.

Nate opened his eyes and sat upright on the bed. "When you're ready, this conversation will come back to you and you will seek me out." The words of the mysterious old man faded into the distance. Nate scratched his head. There was one thing, if anyone could explain the craziness going on in his head, it might be Grandpa.

Nate got up quickly, refusing to look behind him and in the direction of the haunting eyes. Taking a hot shower to warm his chilled body, he dressed and shaved.

Heading to the kitchen for a hot cup of coffee, there was only one other thing on his agenda this Saturday morning. Finding answers was his specialty. It was about damned time he went looking for some of his own. And since his mission for the day involved unanswered questions, he and Mary had some things to discuss. He smiled. The warrior was going to take a ride out to the ranch.

"I didn't expect you so soon," Mary said as she opened the front door.

Nate gave her a sly smile. "I didn't know you were expecting me at all."

"And you brought a friend." Mary quipped as Nate carried the painting into the living room.

"Yeah, my twin brother seems to be keeping me up at night. Thought maybe he should hang out here for a while." Nate turned toward her and his eyes took her in from head to toe.

Warmth rushed to her cheeks and she pushed her hair behind one ear. Glancing down at the white blouse and turquoise broomstick skirt, she felt self-conscious. "I was just getting ready for work."

"Sorry to pop in on you, but I need some answers." His brow creased and he looked as if he really hadn't slept. His comment may have been more than a joke. "In fact, I may lose it if I don't get to the bottom of some things." Propping the painting against the couch, he stepped back and looked at it with a discerning eye.

Mary tried to stop the shadow of a frown she knew crossed her face. "Did something happen? Is Johnny okay?"

"Johnny's fine. It's me, that's not all right." Nate stopped and ran his hand through his hair. He let out an exhausted sigh. "Any way you can take some time off today so we can talk?"

Mary relaxed and shrugged. "If it's important."

He turned back toward the painting. "I'll be honest. I've got some strange questions to ask you, and I think they're very important. To me—and to us." His eyes turned toward her, piercing her with their intensity. "I'm sorry, if this is bad timing."

Mary's chest tightened at the look in his eyes. Her heart sped up and the strangest words came from her mouth. "Let me make a phone call. Don't worry about your timing. Grandpa told me to expect you."

Nate raised an eyebrow and watched her as she dialed the gallery. He was silent, his arms crossed over his chest. The morning sunlight was behind him as it filtered through the living room window. It framed his tall stature and broad shoulders in yellow light and dimmed the details of his modern clothing.

As she talked on the phone, her mind marveled at his likeness to the picture in her mind, the inspiration of her painting. It was unbelievable, yet, here he stood in her living room.

With the call made and all else forgotten, she moved near him. She stepped close and looked into his dark brown eyes. "What's on your mind," she said softly.

She tingled from his closeness. A tight knot formed at the base of her throat.

"You," he said, leaning closer and hovering over her mouth.

"That's why you came?" she whispered breathlessly.

"No," he said, running his gaze across her hair and touching it lightly with his hand. He swallowed audibly. "You and that damned painting are turning me into a crazy man."

She wet her lips. "I don't understand it, either. It's almost too much to be a coincidence."

"I don't believe in coincidences. And after last night I'm not sure I know what's real and what isn't any more."

"What happened? I can see it in your eyes. Something's there that wasn't before."

"I had some crazy dream, I guess. God, Mary, it was so real, and it came out of that painting." He pointed at the warrior and his eyes darkened. "It was more than a dream. It was like a window into his world. Only, I was there. I was him." He took a step back.

Mary stared at Nate. He was different than she'd ever seen him. He was shaken and vulnerable. And he'd come to her. The hard-nosed lawyer with his straight talk and difficult questions was like a disoriented little boy.

"I'm sorry, you must think I've lost it." He straightened his shirt and tried to compose himself. She could almost feel the draft as he closed the door on his emotional openness.

Mary's arms ached to pull him back and hold him to her breasts. Her mouth wanted for the taste of the kiss that had almost been. She regrouped, too. For those few minutes he'd been her warrior, close, virile and completely irresistible. And she'd been there, internally panting for his touch.

She stopped and retraced her own thoughts. The painting was affecting them both. She stared at the artwork. For Nate, it had come to life in a dream last night. For her, it had happened when she put the warrior on canvas. He'd been a hauntingly real figure who'd walked through her mind and brought her ailing womanhood back to life. Who was he? And how could he have such power over them?

She looked at Nate. Except for the transition from ancient times to present, she'd have sworn the warrior stood here in her living room. She could feel the warrior's affect on them both.

Now that was crazy. Maybe they were both nuts. Nate gave her a bewildered look as if he were reading her thoughts. They stood silently looking at the man in transition to bird, and his eyes gleamed with a beckoning light that continually drew them in.

———

"The time has come." Grandpa's voice came from behind them.

Nate nodded. "I'm here. I can't say that I know why."

"You don't have to know the why. The why will come soon enough." Grandpa walked around him and looked at the painting. "It seems your friend brought you here."

"Or *drove* me here seems more appropriate."

A shadow of a smile crossed Grandpa's face. "You look exhausted. You've come in search of answers."

"I'd sure like to find someone who has some." Nate rubbed his eyes.

"I only know of one place to look for that." Grandpa motioned toward the painted warrior. "Bring him along. He seems to have a starring role in all this."

"Where are you taking him, Grandpa?" Mary asked.

"To the hogan. And you're coming, too. It's about time we went in search of an explanation for what's been keeping you both awake at night." Grandpa headed for the back door.

Nate glanced at Mary, and Mary nodded. Nate picked up the painting and followed Grandpa and Mary out into the yard. The large brown and black Australian shepherd joined the parade, following close at Nate's heels. Grandpa ducked as he pulled back the Navajo rug covering the low doorway leading into a small dome-shaped building. Mary followed with Nate and the dog bringing up the rear.

Once inside, Nate looked around the room. On one side was a cot, neatly made and covered with a brightly colored Pendleton blanket with a Navajo symbol at its center. To the left of it a small white refrigerator hummed away next to a wooden table and two chairs. Behind him a television sat on a square cart.

On the wall next to the television was a shelf. The shelf was lined with an assortment of pottery in various shapes and sizes. Some had lids and others were open. Below the shelf, hung an assortment of brightly decorated ceremonial pipes.

At the center of the room, several large rocks formed a circle and inside it were ashes and some charred pieces of wood. Directly above it was a hole in the roof that revealed a piece of blue-sky overhead. Beneath their feet was a cushion of warm Navajo wool rugs much like the one that Mary had been weaving the first time Nate saw her.

Grandpa waited quietly as Nate took in the interior of the hogan. He finally spoke. "Never seen one before, I'm sure."

Nate shook his head and smiled politely. "It's nice."

"It's tradition," Grandpa said and bowed slightly, motioning for Nate and Mary to sit. Mary moved to her left and sat down facing the fire pit. Nate started in her direction, but Grandpa put a hand on his arm. "Women to the south. Men to the north."

Nate gave him a puzzled look.

"I will face the east and Father Sun."

Nate nodded. "And where would you like him?" he asked and lifted the painting.

"Lean your troublesome friend against the east wall, facing me."

Nate pulled up a small stool and propped the warrior against it. He felt as if he'd stepped through the doorway and into another time. For certain, he'd stepped into a new culture. But the place had a good feel, warm and welcoming. Perhaps, it welcomed him because it was his culture, too, one he'd never had the privilege of getting to know.

"A man of your years should know something of his past." Grandpa said as he situated himself cross-legged on the floor and motioned for Nate to do the same. The dog lay down next to Grandpa's left knee, paws pointed forward and ears alert.

"I'm at a disadvantage here. I was never exposed to anything like this growing up."

"It matters more what is in your heart than in your memory. Today an open mind will be essential."

"An open mind was never my problem. I grew up in LA. My parents and grandparents didn't talk much about where we came from. I guess, I was always more interested in where I was going than where I'd been."

"Sometimes, we reach a point in our lives where we can go no further without looking back." Grandpa took some pieces of kindling from a small pile of wood beside him and laid it in the fire pit. "Do you know the real reasons for the silence around your heritage?"

"I know pieces of it. I remember a few things my own grandfather told me when I was small. Truthfully, I was always more interested in playing ball than listening to his stories. Sometimes, I regret I didn't listen closer."

Grandpa nodded. He lit the kindling and placed a small log on it. Flames licked at the log and colors of orange and blue slowly wrapped around it. "I'm going to tell you some things you may or may not know, things you should know because they are a part of who you are. Something that comes with the blood flowing in your veins."

Nate watched the fire, thinking it was a rather warm summer morning to be sitting by the fire, but the coolness of the earthen room made it enjoyable. Staring into the fire, perhaps his eyes played tricks on him, but he could have sworn he saw faces in the flames.

Grandpa began to speak as he looked into the fire pit. "Your great-great grandmother was the daughter of a Navajo chief, your great-great grandfather the son of a Hopi holy man. The times they lived through were a horror for the Native tribes. It was a time of upheaval when The People were gathered and moved across the country like herds of cattle and put on reservations. Many died and those that didn't, lived through hell."

"I've read about that."

Grandpa nodded toward him. "Our trail of tears. The peoples of all tribes were given designated pieces of land to live on. Reservations. A *gift* from the government. That same government formed schools to educate the children of the savages they'd rounded up. But the people had no choice about sending their children to the schools, either they willingly gave them up or they were taken by force. Not a pretty part of our history, either the white man or the Indian."

"Your ancestry fell victim to that horrible cleansing of the Native Spirit. To complicate matters further, the Navajo and the Hopi were not friendly with one another. The Navajo believed the Hopi had befriended the white eyes that had ultimately stolen their land. Stripped of all the symbols of their culture, shamed by the whites for who they truly were, they were part of a generation caught between a white world where they didn't belong and an Indian world they couldn't return to. Small wonder, they found their only peace in one another."

Nate was silent and thoughtful. Grandpa's words stirred his soul. At last he spoke, aware of the emotion in his voice. "I never heard the story told that way before. How do you—"

"How I know doesn't matter. What is important is now you know it. Remember the message, to go forward from here, we must begin by looking back. Billie," he said to the dog, "bring me my pipe."

The dog rose to his feet and walked to the wall where the pipes hung. Taking the one hanging in the center with his teeth, he pulled it from its place on the wall and brought it to Grandpa, placing it gently in his lap.

"Good dog," Grandpa praised him. "Now bring me my tobacco." Billie walked over to the shelf and rising onto his back legs, he pulled down a small white cotton bag with a drawstring and carried it to Grandpa in his teeth. "Thank you." Grandpa patted the dog on the head and he lay back down in his spot next to Grandpa's knee.

Grandpa proceeded to fill the pipe with a mixture from the bag. The pipe was about a foot and a half long. It was carved out of wood and had several feathers hanging from it.

"Grandpa," Mary said in a half-scolding tone. She raised her eyebrow as if she knew what was coming and wasn't particularly pleased.

"Sometimes the spirits need a little assistance," Grandpa said matter-of-factly as he continued to tamp the mixture into the bowl of the pipe. Picking up a small stick from the wood piled next to him, he lit it in the fire and transferred the flame to the pipe.

Tiny plumes of smoke rose from the pipe as Grandpa inhaled and drew the flame into the tobacco.

Taking several hearty puffs, Grandpa offered the pipe to Nate.

Nate shrugged. "I don't smoke."

"You do today," Grandpa said.

Nate took the pipe and inhaled for the first time since he'd tried his father's pipe under the back porch as a kid. The smoke filled his lungs and he coughed. Its taste was odd on his tongue. He couldn't find a word to describe the flavor. Woodsy? Or weedy? "That's different," he sputtered. "What kind of tobacco is that?"

"Oh, it's not tobacco. It's peyote," Grandpa said as he took another puff. "It will help you on your journey back in time."

Mary sat on the other side of the fire and gave Grandpa a look of disapproval. "Nate, you don't have to do this—"

"So," Grandpa interrupted, pointing to the painting across the fire. "Tell me, what's been happening between you and your friend."

Nate took a deep breath and another drag from the pipe. He glanced over at Mary. If he told the truth he risked alienating her. If he kept this thing inside, he risked losing himself. All eyes were on him, Mary's, Grandpa's and his own, staring out of the painting from somewhere in the past.

CHAPTER FIFTEEN

Grandpa bit his lip and waited. Nate shifted around. There was no getting comfortable for this one.

"You said, you had a dream about the painting," Mary coaxed. "But it sounded like more than a dream."

Nate looked into her warm dark eyes across the fire. "I came here because I have to know where *he* came from." He glanced at the painted warrior, then at Grandpa who was quietly listening. "What was it that brought that picture into your mind?"

"Like I told you last night, it was like he was somewhere in my memory. I'd seen his face over and over and at last I painted it." Mary glanced at the warrior, a soft gleam in her eye.

Was it pride in her work or was it something else? "Whatever this memory was, it must have been pleasant," Nate said. "You're smiling."

Mary shook her head. "The odd thing is I can't say that I know. I mean, I remember and yet, I don't. That sounds silly but I can't explain it any other way."

Their eyes met. The question and its curious answer hung between them. Simultaneously, they both turned toward Grandpa who was puffing on his pipe and staring into the fire. His eyes were hazy as he passed the pipe back to Nate.

Nate shot a questioning glance at Mary and asked in a low voice. "Is he stoned?"

"No," she whispered. "He's seeing things in the flames."

Grandpa reached into the cotton bag filled with peyote and pulled out a small handful. He threw it into the fire. Smoke plumed up and floated around them. Three more times he threw the leaves into the fire. Through the haze hanging in the room, Grandpa began to speak.

"I want you both to close your eyes and free your minds of all thoughts of the present day." His voice was smooth as he chanted the words. "Relax and clear away everything. Let it go."

Nate followed Grandpa's instructions releasing his tension and relaxing his thoughts.

Grandpa went on. "Your mind is a clear blue sky. Picture it. Breathe deeply. You are light as a feather. Your movements are effortless. Do you feel it?"

Nate nodded in an almost subconscious gesture as he imagined himself floating. He inhaled the strange aroma of the peyote.

"Now visualize yourself climbing a staircase that leads you deeper and deeper into Father Sky. With each step you leave this world further behind. Climb. Climb. You're floating up the stairs. Keep climbing. Climb until you reach the top step. At the top of the stairs is a door in the sky. Reach out and open the door. Look inside. Tell me what you see."

Nate was the first to speak. "I think it's a village. I see stone buildings with rows of square rooms. There are openings like windows, but no windows. The whole village is built inside an alcove in a cliff. Actually, I think it sits in a canyon wall, surrounded by trees, mostly evergreens. It's very old."

"How old?"

"I'd say ancient. But it isn't crumbled. It isn't a ruin."

"What else do you see? Move closer."

"There are people moving around in the village."

"Tell me about them."

"I see a naked child playing with a stick. And several women gathered in a circle. They seem to be working, but I'm not sure what they're doing."

"What was the first thing that came to your mind?"

"This was my home." Nate spoke the words without hesitation and without comprehending them fully.

"And mine." Mary's voice came from across the fire.

"Good." Grandpa said. "Now I want you both to concentrate and try to see yourselves in the picture. Tell me what you are doing."

"I'm wrapping some things in an animal hide," Mary said. "I think I'm preparing to leave."

Nate strained to see himself in the picture. He focused on the image he'd seen last night of himself in a loincloth.

"And you?" Grandpa asked. "What do you see, Nate?"

"Nothing. I don't see myself."

"Maybe you're trying too hard. I'm going to stop talking and let you concentrate."

Nate relaxed and took a cleansing breath. He could see the village. The picture began to spin, and he felt light headed. He had the sensation he was falling. Very slowly—falling. Suddenly, everything plunged into blackness.

He huddled on the cold stone floor, his legs tucked close to his body and encircled by his arms. Five feet into the mouth of the cave, he sat tense and motionless, listening for the sound of footsteps. It was a cool moonless night and the world outside was as black as the one within the cavern.

A twig snapped somewhere out in the darkness. He held his breath and listened until his lungs burned. Was it a wild animal prowling the forest floor? Or was it her? His worst fear crept up his spine in the form of a chill. Or was it a two-legged predator coming in search of them both?

He could hear nothing. Letting out his breath as quietly as he could, he shifted as bits of rock cut into bare flesh. Silently, he prayed to the gods of the night to bring the woman he loved safely to him.

A scuffle somewhere outside made him listen once more. "Mourning Dove, is it you?" he whispered. No answer came.

He settled back. The mournful howl of a coyote far in the distance broke the silence. The four-leggeds of the night would soon be out. Darkness had not been upon them long.

She would be here soon.

To pass the time, he closed his eyes and pictured her. Her long raven hair flowing down her back as she moved soundlessly through the forest on her way to meet him. Her breasts moving beneath the rawhide dress as she stepped softly, watching for night creatures and stones on the path. Sure feet and strong beautiful legs would serve her well as she made her way through the cloak of night, her only thought to be with him.

He envisioned her running to him, kissing him feverishly and holding him as she would for the rest of their lives. She was giving up everything to be with him. They were both risking it all to be together. And it was the right thing to do, the only thing they could do.

A sound came from behind him. He jumped. A forceful blow struck his throat. His head jerked back, knocking him off balance. A second later, he fell against a hard, warm, human body. A sweaty forearm tight around his neck entrapped his throat. The cold stone blade of a skinning knife pressed into the side of his head.

"You are a fool, Lone Eagle." A voice hissed into his ear. A voice much like his own, one he knew all too well.

"Black Hawk. What brings you here? Combing the forest floor for worms with the other snakes?" He

choked out the words in spite of the pressure on his throat.

Black Hawk tightened his hold. "I was looking for worms. And it seems I've found one."

Lone Eagle struggled for breath beneath the pressure. "Let go." A raspy half-human sound came from his mouth.

Black Hawk snickered and tightened his grip. Patches of stars flashed before Lone Eagle's eyes and his knees buckled. Black Hawk released him. Lone Eagle fell onto the rocky floor of the cavern. Stone scraped his knees as he tumbled. He gasped in a breath of air and lay motionless in the darkness.

Black Hawk's foot hit his rib cage. The bare foot, wrapped in a yucca sandal, served more to anger him than hurt him. Flipping onto his back, he grabbed in the darkness, catching his brother's foot behind the heel and pummeling him down on top of him.

"Rattlesnake," Black Hawk spat. The skinning knife was against Lone Eagle's throat. "I could kill you." He pressed the knife tighter. "But I'd prefer to torture you first," he hissed.

"I thought you'd be back at the village preparing for your wedding." Lone Eagle pushed hard against him.

Black Hawk moved the knife closer. The sharp blade grazed the tender flesh of Lone Eagle's neck. The shallow cut burned. Lone Eagle pulled back as much as he could, flattening himself against the stone. Black Hawk laughed softly. "Did I hurt you, little brother?"

"Hurting me is all you've ever done for as long as I can remember." But no physical pain he'd ever endured hurt as much as the painful thought of Mourning Dove being Black Hawk's wife. He'd rather Black Hawk slit his throat than live to see that happen.

He lay breathlessly, the knife touching his throat, and wondered where she was. She was coming. Coming to meet him. She must be near. He listened for her footfalls.

*"Cutting your throat would be too easy. Too kind."
Black Hawk pulled back and Lone Eagle pressed
against the weight of his brother. Black Hawk was his
height and their bodies equally matched in size and
form. But Black Hawk had always been the stronger of
the two. His strength and the weight of his body seemed
massive at this moment. As Eagle raised his head, a
fist came from out of the darkness and struck him
square on the chin.*

*For a few moments he lost consciousness and the
strength to fight back. His head whirled and he
struggled to keep his eyes open, fearing what would
happen if he let the sleep take him. But somewhere in
the darkness it stole him away.*

*As his head cleared, he found himself lying on his
belly. His hands were pulled behind him and bound
with strips of rawhide to his feet. His legs were bent
and drawn up almost to his backside. An agonizingly
tight strap lashed his wrists to his ankles. A wide strip
of gamey tasting rawhide was crammed into his
mouth. Another strip was tied tightly around his head.
The strip was long and it too was anchored to the strips
around his hands and feet pulling his head backward
as far as it would go.*

*There wasn't a muscle he could move nor could he
make so much as a sound. He lay on the cold musty
smelling floor struggling against the bindings. The
tough rawhide cords were tied so tight they cut
painfully into his flesh. He listened. He wasn't sure
where Black Hawk had gone.*

*"Eagle, are you there?" a whisper came from the cave
opening. Lone Eagle's heart leapt to his throat.
Mourning Dove. His gut knotted. He tried to move, but
it was useless. The position of his throat and the vile
mouthful of rawhide prevented him from uttering a
sound. How could he make her hear him?*

*So this was Black Hawk's plan. Mourning Dove
would think Eagle hadn't come. The cave was so dark*

Eagle couldn't see her. She would never find him. He struggled again, trying to at least make a noise to get her attention.

"Here." A whispered voice answered further back in the pitch-blackness of the cave.

Black Hawk. Lone Eagle's heart sank. He hadn't left after all.

"I knew you would come," she said in a low, relief-filled tone. "The night is so dark. It took a long time to find my way."

Eagle heard her steps as she moved deeper into the cave.

"Come to me," Black Hawk whispered.

Lone Eagle held his breath, listening.

"I'm trying. I can't see a thing in here."

"All the better to hide us." Black Hawk's whispers continued.

Don't go to him, Mourning Dove. Don't go. The voice inside of Lone Eagle's head was screaming, but not a sound could come from his mouth.

"Where are you, Eagle? Talk to me. I'm frightened."

"Come slowly toward my voice." Black Hawk spoke above a whisper now, but low and hoarse.

Lone Eagle's gut knotted as he lay helplessly listening to Mourning Dove's deerskin moccasins scooting across the cave floor. A rock rolled as she struck it with her foot. Please stop, Mourning Dove. Don't go any closer.

"Can't we light a torch?" Mourning Dove asked.

"No," came Black Hawk's quick retort. "Someone might see it."

She might see you, you weasel. Every muscle in Lone Eagle's body burned from the force he exerted against his bindings. They didn't give.

"Oh. There you are." Mourning Dove's voice was filled with relief.

"I've waited for your kiss." Black Hawk's whispers were louder. No doubt, they were intentional torture meant for the ears of his captive brother.

Pain shot through Lone Eagle's heart. His stomach lurched. How dare Black Hawk steal her kiss under these pretenses. The moment of silence that followed seemed an eternity as the heat of anger burned a hole in Lone Eagle's soul.

"Are you all right?" Mourning Dove asked.

"Yes. Why do you ask?"

"You seem strange. Your body is so hard and tense."

She's touching him. Damn you, Black Hawk.

"I was worried about you. That's all."

"You're too sweet," she laughed softly.

Why hasn't she discovered it's Black Hawk? Lone Eagle's anger continued to build. He tried to force a sound from his throat but only a small raspy snort escaped.

"Did you hear something?" Mourning Dove asked.

"A four-legged out in the night."

There was another long silence, punctuated by breathing sounds from their direction.

Lone Eagle's heart was beating faster. It hammered in his ears blocking out the sounds he strained to hear. What are they doing? Why are they so quiet?

"Your kiss is sweet as nectar."

Her kiss. A scream tried to escape from Lone Eagle's throat, but was strangled back by the massive wad of rawhide stuffed half way down his throat.

"Shouldn't we be going while the night covers us?"

"We'll wait here awhile. Sit. I brought a buffalo robe to keep you from the cold floor."

"Buffalo. It feels nice."

"You feel nice."

"Eagle. What are you doing?"

"Sharing your warmth."

If I live to the end of this night, I will kill you Black Hawk. I vow, I will kill you. Lone Eagle could not bear to think what Black Hawk was doing. The pictures in his mind were too painful to allow in. *Why, oh why, doesn't Mourning Dove know? That pained him more than anything else.*

Soft sounds came from Black Hawk and Mourning Dove as the drums of war beat within Lone Eagle's ears. Hammering throbbed at his temples, his head pulsed as if it would explode. He tried again to scream, this time making a slightly louder sound. But it went unnoticed. *I hate you Black Hawk. Stop this.*

"Eagle, be careful. You're hurting me." Mourning Dove's whisper was loud enough to echo in the chamber.

I would never hurt you. Don't you know it isn't me? It isn't me—

His throat burned and a tear made its way down his nose. This helpless agony was more than he could endure.

The noises and breathless whispers continued. Lone Eagle's gut contracted. His gag reflex was blocked by the mass in his mouth. He pulled against the rawhide strips until blood trickled down his wrists. His scalded heart thrummed in his chest.

There was only one thing that could hurt Eagle worse than knowing Black Hawk would make love to his woman, and that was to be there when it happened. *Black Hawk, you are pure evil. I will never call you my brother again.*

If he had to listen to Black Hawk's grunting any longer, unable to stop what he knew in his heart was happening, he might go insane. One final attempt to scream yielded a noise like a muted buffalo's bawl.

"What was that?" Mourning Dove said. "I know I heard something."

"It was your lover." Black Hawk spoke aloud for the first time.

"My what?" Mourning Dove stammered.

"Your lover. My brother. You remember him. Although after me, he won't be hard to forget." Black Hawk's evil laugh echoed through the cavern.

There was the sound of scuffling in the darkness. *"Black Hawk. No. No."* Mourning Dove screamed. *"You horrible man. What have you done to me? What have you done?"*

"I tricked you. You little witch." Black Hawk's laughter roared through the chamber and out into the night.

"You bastard," she screamed. *"How could you? Why would you do such a thing?"*

"You'd have been mine anyway, and you know it. But at least this one time I had you the way he has you. I know what it would be like if you loved me as you love him. That is why I did it."

"What have you done to him?" she screamed. *"Where is Eagle?"*

"Tied up in the dark, listening to me take you, unaware."

"You horrible, vicious thing. You aren't human. You are lower than a snake." Mourning Dove screamed. *"I hate you, Black Hawk."*

At that moment Lone Eagle realized only hers equaled the pain in his heart. What a cruel, evil joke. His brother was pure evil.

"Eagle, where are you?" Her voice pierced the darkness.

Eagle made the bellowing sound.

"I hear you. Don't stop. I'll find you."

Black Hawk roared with hideous laughter. *"I'll leave you to find your big brave warrior. I've had what I came for,"* he taunted her. *"I'll be outside waiting. When the two of you are ready to go back to the village, I'll be sure you get there. Unless you'd prefer a spear in your back."* His scuffling steps faded away.

"Eagle. Eagle. I have to find you." Sobs choked her desperate voice.

He grunted as loud as he could. She stopped and listened, then a few short steps came in his direction. Each shuffle grew closer. The sliding sounds and scattering small rocks were interrupted by soft sobs and an occasional sniffle. She would be here in a moment and when she freed him, he would kill the deceitful man who did this to her.

He continued to make the noises. Now that she knew he was here, they were audible enough for her to hear. Swish. Swish. Her moccasins shuffled as she carefully groped her way across the stone-riddled floor.

At last, her bare leg brushed his shoulder. Her hands fumbled in the darkness and tugged at the bindings. "Oh, Eagle, what has he done to you?" Her voice was low and shaky. "What has he done to us?"

He wanted to hold her and comfort her. Only he wasn't sure he could ever soothe this pain. And the armed menace was waiting outside to take them back so he could hurt them even more. Over and over and over—their father wouldn't have it any other way.

CHAPTER SIXTEEN

"Nate. Nate. Are you all right?" Mary tried to shake his six-foot plus frame without much success. "Grandpa, what have you done to him?"

"I have done nothing. It is the spirits who have done this." Grandpa sat by the fire, stroking the dog's head and appearing quite unconcerned.

"And I suppose the spirits are to blame for the peyote too?" Mary put her hand on her hip and gave Grandpa a perturbed look.

Nate still didn't move. A series of strange noises had come from his throat, but his breathing was normal. She couldn't tell if he was trying to speak.

When she'd opened her eyes after Grandpa had stopped talking, Nate was lying on his back. Grandpa said he'd toppled over and started making peculiar sounds.

"Put some water on his face. It will bring him back from wherever he's gone."

"Grandpa he hasn't gone anywhere. He's right here."

"His body is here, but his spirit has gone on quite a journey."

"How would you know that?" Mary rose to her feet and went to the small sink in the corner. She picked a towel from the counter and wet it with cool water and went back to Nate. Kneeling beside him, she patted his face with the moist cloth. He tried to open his eyes.

"Not too quickly," Grandpa said. "Bring him out of it slowly."

"You've seen this happen before, haven't you?" she scolded. "And you did it to him anyway."

Grandpa nodded, then shrugged. "It doesn't happen often. Don't be angry with me. I do what the ancients tell me. They are the ones who wanted Nate."

"I think he's waking up."

Nate opened his eyes and looked at Mary. He grabbed her hard and started to pull her toward him. "Mourning Dove," he said, his eyes wide. "I'll kill him for what he did to you."

Mary pulled away and patted his cheek. "Nate, it's me, Mary. Wake up. Are you okay?"

Nate let go of her and rubbed his eyes. He blinked several times as if trying to get his bearings. "I'm sorry," he said. "I don't know what happened. I must have fallen asleep or something."

"Or OD'd on Grandpa's happy smoke," Mary puckered her mouth and rolled her eyes in Grandpa's direction.

"It was enough to relax him. No harm done." Grandpa patted the dog again.

"I sure had one crazy dream." Nate said as he sat up and looked over at Grandpa with a questioning look in his eyes.

"Oh, you weren't dreaming," Grandpa said in a matter of fact tone.

"Let him get his head back on straight before you lay anything else on him." Mary shot Grandpa a disapproving look and turned toward Nate. "I'll get you something cold to drink. Is there anything in the fridge, Grandpa?"

"Some beer." A mischievous grin tugged at the corners of the old man's mouth.

"I think not," Mary retorted.

Nate put his hand on Mary's arm. "It wasn't a dream, was it?"

"I don't know," she said looking him in the eye, but saying no more. She stood and went back to the kitchen and pulled a cold can of lemon-lime soda from the refrigerator. "Actually, you may need something stronger if you hang around Grandpa any longer."

After giving Nate the beverage, she went back to her seat on the other side of the rapidly dwindling fire. She was glad.

The normally cool earthen house was beginning to get very warm.

Nate took a long drink. "What did *you* see?" he asked Mary. His expression and his eyes were deadly serious.

"I saw the ancient village same as you." She rubbed her forehead, recalling the realistic details she'd seen in her mind. "Then it was dark. Nighttime. I was running through a forest. I don't know where I was going, but I came to a cave and went inside."

Nate's eyes darkened. "And then?"

"Someone was in the cave. Then it was gone." She turned her face away. She'd seen the face of someone she'd recognized, but she certainly wasn't going to mention it to Nate. Nor could she bring herself to tell him what had happened to her in the cave. Not here, and not now. "And you?" She wanted to change the subject.

Nate shook his head. He was silent and thoughtful. His questioning eyes went to Grandpa.

Grandpa met his gaze. "You are the best person to interpret your visions. The messages in them are meant for you, alone."

"Then why do I feel like you know exactly what I saw?"

Grandpa shrugged. "If I did, it wouldn't mean the same to me. I don't walk your path. You do."

Mary raised her eyebrow at Grandpa. Did the old man know what had gone on in Nate's mind? Worse yet, did he know what had passed through hers? Grandpa looked at her and smiled.

Nate got up. "I think you're right about one thing. I need to digest this experience before I go any further. I need some time alone."

As he turned away from her, Mary spoke. "When you woke up you were talking. You called me Mourning Dove. Why?"

Nate turned back toward her. "Because I thought you were her." He paused, studying her for a moment, then moistened his lips and said in a low voice, *"You were her."*

Mary shot Grandpa a look she knew was filled with confusion. The old man only grinned. She watched as Nate ducked under the short doorway and walked out into the sunlight.

What was going on in Nate's head was as much a mystery to her as what he'd seen as he sat at Grandpa's fire. Though nothing had materially changed in the past few days, there was definitely something in Nate's demeanor, and in his eyes, that was different. She didn't know where it was leading, but she knew without a doubt she'd be going along on the ride.

She looked over at the painting, propped against the chair to her right. If she didn't know better, she'd swear the warrior was smiling at Grandpa. But after what she'd experienced, even that wouldn't surprise her.

—◆—

Nate drove away from Chimayo. Coming to the fork in the highway, he stopped. He rubbed the back of his neck, then his chest. What was happening to him? Images still walked through his head. Nameless faces and shadows danced in the firelight cast on stone walls that seemed to exist only inside his mind.

Drumbeats hammered with each beat of his heart and each throb of the pulse in his ears. Beneath the rhythm, a distant voice whispered his name. An undeniable impulse struck him. Instead of going left toward Santa Fe, he turned right and headed toward Taos. At Taos the fuel light flashed on and he hurriedly filled the car with gas and kept driving north.

He couldn't say he knew where he was headed. Following some burning in his soul, he kept driving. Tiny towns rolled by, strange places with strange names, meaningless blurs as they whizzed past. Still headed due north, he came to the Colorado State Line, then Highway 160, pausing only for a moment before turning left.

As he headed west he began to notice some of his surroundings as they began to change from distant flat topped mesas, squatty round cedars, and buckhorn cactus to snow capped mountains, pines and aspen trees. Occasional lavender-tinged meadows and farms dotted the roadside landscape; a dappled horse, a windmill with an arrow pointing west, rusted train tracks bridging a gulch. It all rolled by. He was cognizant of what he saw, but it wasn't what he was searching for.

He drove on like a man on a mission, but sensed only his spirit knew the reason and destination. A strange need drove him on, pushing him toward some unknown interlude with destiny. The voices still whispered to his soul. He stopped next to a sign that read Wolf Creek Pass. Laying his head on the steering wheel, he asked himself why he was doing this, and where he was going. But no answer came. An insatiable desire to keep driving consumed him—and he drove on.

At the summit of the pass, something wild and needy stirred deep in his being. Pulling out into a turnout, he turned off the engine and listened. He was totally alone. Climbing from the car, he walked a short distance and inhaled the intoxicating aroma of cold, pure mountain air. He stepped over the guardrail and walked a short distance, taking in the lofty pine trees clinging to the mountainside like a baby to its mother's breast, drawing nourishment from the source that gave them life.

Kneeling, he drew his hand gently through the soil, letting it pass between his fingers. It was rich and brown, moist and cool to his touch. He let it sift through his fingers. Grabbing a handful of fresh pine needles, he crushed them to his palm, inhaling their intoxicating pungency.

Earth, at its purest. Life as it was intended to be in origination, the ultimate gift to man from his Creator. The air was crisp and fresh, not tainted with car exhaust and factory smells. Touching the face of God could not be much sweeter or pure. He picked a wild flower and inhaled its sweet scent and stroking its delicate petals. No doubt, it was the Creator's model for the delicate and beautiful flesh of a woman.

He closed his eyes. To run here, wild and free, unencumbered by the inconvenience of clothing and society's sense of propriety, to be just who he was as a man. Civilization was wonderful but it too had come at a cost to the freedom of the soul.

Realization seeped into his being as he sensed the pull of the virgin earth around him, beautiful and untouched, but wanting—aching to share her spirit with his. And he was reciprocating by communing with this wild heart of what was once an untamed land.

Though he knew others had come this way, he sensed the undisturbed wildness of the mountains and forest as it must have been experienced by the first to walk her soil and taste of her sweet pure waters. He was living that journey in his mind's eye, as if through some ancient memory, distant but filled with a distinct oneness of man and his land, of man and the unknown.

He righted himself and listened to the wind whispering in the treetops. There was no doubt something called his name. Something told him to keep going. He ambled over the guardrail and slid back behind the wheel. He glanced at where he'd stood. What an odd transition his soul was experiencing. No doubt, he was getting closer to what called him, but it wasn't here. It was somewhere ahead.

On the other side of the pass, he stopped at a small store in the town of Pagosa Springs. He sipped an icy cola as he paid the clerk. A rack of brochures caught his attention. One in particular seemed to jump out at him. Among many far more colorful ones, one alone pulled him in. The words written across a tan and brown background read 'Mesa Verde National Park.' Suddenly, he knew where he was being led.

Grabbing it from the display, he waved it at the store clerk behind the cash register. "How far?" Nate asked.

"A little over a hundred miles. Just stay on 160. You can't miss it."

"Thanks," Nate called over his shoulder and headed back to the car.

Nearly two hours later, Nate handed the ranger at the park entrance a twenty-dollar bill. "How late is the park open?" he asked.

"Closes at seven," the man answered, as he made change. "You've still got a couple of hours, but the park pass is good for seven days." He handed Nate his change, a handful of brochures and a green cash register tape.

"Thanks. A couple of hours is all I have."

"Ever been here before?" the ranger asked.

"Not in this lifetime," Nate replied, surveying the scrub oak by the roadside. The words hung strangely in the air. The euphemism he'd used many times now sounded odd.

The ranger shrugged. "Enjoy the park."

Nate drove along the winding road looking from one side to the other. He passed trees and bushes, yuccas and signposts; searching, but not knowing what he sought. Hell, he didn't even know for sure why he was here. Something had brought him to this place, and whatever it wanted to show him, his challenge must be to find it.

A strange new side of him had surfaced now that he was willing to let go and take the risk. It was a different world, one he'd never allowed to have a voice.

Stopping at an overlook, he got out of the car. At the rocky ledge he looked down into the canyon. Tucked in a weathered sandstone alcove below the opposite rim were the remnants of an ancient village. Stones the tan color of the canyon, hewn by ancient tools into square rooms and circular chambers, long since crumbled to rubble, but still undeniable evidence of life that once existed and thrived on this mesa.

A strange feeling came over him. Pictures flashed through his mind, pictures of the village he'd seen that morning inside his own head. His was a village alive with activity, a place much like this had been nearly a thousand years earlier.

Nate closed his eyes and visualized the plaza full of children playing and women cooking over open fires. The old ones looked on with wrinkled faces and wizened eyes. He inhaled deeply, the odors of smoke and roasting wild game playing in his mind as if he remembered it all distinctly.

This wasn't the exact spot. He looked down the canyon as far as he could see. The place he'd seen was out there somewhere among the cliffs and rocky terrain. Cedars, scrub oak and earth no doubt buried it now. The hands of time would have gently covered it over. And in his heart dwelled this amazing feeling. Once he had called this place home—

He got back in the car, feeling the need to move on, still seeking something he couldn't describe and wouldn't attempt to explain. Rolling down the car window, he let the breeze blow through his hair. If he closed his eyes and listened to the sounds of the land, he could feel its familiarity in his soul. The drums started again in his head.

High on the mesa top, he pulled over and stopped. All the drama back in Santa Fe seemed part of another world. San Francisco was a distant memory. A superficial and insignificant existence compared to something bigger he was on a quest to find. He did not understand what had shifted in his soul, at almost the exact time when he'd received the kachina and the letter from his grandfather—

For the first time in his life, he felt truly grounded, strangely in touch with who he was and where he'd come from. Excitement gnawed in his gut as if he were about to touch the face of his creator.

As if he'd transcended time and merged with the spirit of the man in the painting, nearly naked and bronzed by the sun. A man like him, only primitive and struggling, trying desperately to hold on to and protect the only things of true importance, the thread of life and the woman he loved.

The primal need of a man for a woman was something that hadn't changed since the beginning of time. His own manhood stirred. A hand tightened around his heart at the thought of how he'd neglected those deep down desires. Regret nagged at him. Mary awakened that need in him and brought it to the forefront of his life, where it belonged. He'd trained himself well to push it aside, to always be in control of his whole world. That part of him needed to change, too.

He unbuttoned his shirt and pulled it off, throwing it through the open car window. He stood in the quiet of the late afternoon hours, listening to the birds chatter in the trees and feeling the sun on his back. The world here was so basic, so real, so unencumbered by the modern complications of life. Perhaps that was why he'd been brought here. He needed to remember what was truly important.

He walked several yards down a gravel pathway cut through small trees mingled with deer brush and wild currant bushes. Kicking at the earth and inhaling the smell of cedar, he reached the end of the path. There stood a partially crumbled structure, the remains of a small ancient dwelling surrounded by a protective stonewall.

Studying the partial reconstruction in the enclosure, he was struck by its simplistic nature. *Shelter.* It was all that was required. Now this was the only evidence remaining of an ancient people and a way of life, a people whose lives must have been unbearably hard.

He thought of the past few days, of the faces and the emotions that had passed through his mind and his heart. He'd long surpassed the need to question their origin. It was blatantly apparent. He was seeing the past. The warrior was key to that connection. What he'd seen this morning, he'd lived through. He'd lived through it with Mary.

Mary and the Indian woman were vivid in his mind. Lying helpless in a cold damp cave, his heart had yearned for Mourning Dove. The thought made Nate's heart yearn for Mary. *Two lovers. Two lifetimes. One love?* Was such a thing possible?

Flashes of memories, pieces of the past, and a soul connection to Mary. Fragments. It was like dumping a jigsaw puzzle out of the box and starting the slow process of constructing a picture.

Over the past weeks he'd wondered numerous times if he was losing his grip. Today, he didn't think so. Today he was a vessel. A vessel being filled with information in preparation for something, but that something eluded him.

He sat down on the stone wall. Picking up a pebble, he tossed it into the deer brush. That's all he was. A pebble. *A pebble among millions of other pebbles.* So why would the universe single him out for this special ability to see things from another realm—or visions from this one?

What was the reason he'd been pushed to make a six-hour drive? What was here that he was supposed to see? *Show me. Please, just show me.* Nate glanced at his watch. Maybe he should move on, his time was growing short. Rising from the wall, he started back down the path toward the car.

Something rustled in the brush and Nate stopped and listened. He heard it, again. From out of the thick scrub oak and small trees, a few yards up the path, an animal emerged. A brown and gray Australian shepherd bounded onto the path and stopped. Was it the dog that belonged to Grandpa? If not, it was identical.

Nate's mind whirled for a moment. The dog couldn't be here. It couldn't have followed him this far. That was impossible. But it was possible that Grandpa or Mary had followed him.

The dog stood in the pathway ahead of him and raised its ears. Damn, if it didn't act like it recognized him. Nate scratched his head. "Here, boy," he called softly. "Here, Billie."

The dog started toward him, wagging its stub of a tail. Somewhere in the distance a woman's voice echoed through the forest. "Billie. Come Billie." The dog turned in the direction of the voice and bounded away.

Following his gut reaction, Nate went after him. If that were Mary's voice, the dog would lead him to her. Through thick bushes, past wiry cedar and small pines, Nate ran, barely keeping the dog in sight. Glimpses of gray and tan flashed ahead of him as Nate navigated over rocks and fallen logs. He strained to hear the voice, but the crunch of tree needles and twigs in the gravelly soil, along with his own heavy breathing, drowned it out.

Follow the dog. Don't let him get away. Those were Nate's only thoughts as the dog led him further and further from the path and deeper into the wooded area. He ran some distance before he lost sight of the animal. He stopped. "Billie," he called. "Here, boy."

He listened. There was no sound. "Billie," he yelled. "Billie." A dog's bark echoed somewhere in the distance, to Nate's left. He turned and ran in the direction of the noise. Emerging from the dense trees and brush, he stepped into a clearing. He stopped in his tracks. There before him stood a mass of red stone. A strange sensation swept through him.

A chill ran down his spine that went soul deep. His mind whirled, and sped back in time. He remembered—then it slammed him into a brick wall. The force of it was so intense it left him reeling. Breathless and stunned, he doubled over, dizzied by what had happened. He caught his breath, but his brain wouldn't stop.

His mind had flashed on something from the distant past, but refused to let him see what it was. Pulling himself upright he walked slowly to the stone. His logical mind tried to overcome his feeling. It was just a rock. What was the big deal?

The stone was the intense color of fresh rust forming on a nail, looking out of place among the surrounding terrain. It stood about ten feet tall, was a yard wide and a foot thick. There was no denying its effect on him.

Surveying it cautiously, he laid a shaky hand upon it. Intense emotion flooded him. *Sorrow. Dread. Fear.* The emotions vibrating through him were deep and powerful. His body trembled and his soul surged.

Was it giving him energy or drawing energy from him? His hands were warm, hotter than the sun-baked stone itself. The stone's rough texture begged his hands to run across it. He closed his eyes and a picture formed. *An ancient warrior clinging to the stone in the dark of night.* The picture was vivid. There was pain in the young man's heart. The heaviness transcended to his own.

Following his first impulse, he pressed his cheek to the rock. Allowing the pictures in his head to claim him, an unexplained force flooded through him. He saw himself as the warrior. His bare chest melded with the stone. He wanted to feel what was in the warrior's heart. Nate pressed closer, releasing his own will.

"At last you have come home." The thought jetted through his mind. Was the thought his or the warrior's—or did it come from the stone?

"Tell me why you've brought me here," he whispered.

The air was eerily silent.

Nate pulled away and glanced around. Had a voice spoken the words or did they happen in his head?

"Grandpa? Mary? Are you here?" he called, not sure if he wanted a physical being to answer him or not. Had someone spoken?

Not understanding what was driving him, he wrapped his arms around the stone. "Speak again," he said loudly. He pushed harder against the rock but nothing came to him.

"Dammit. I've come all this way," he said. He dropped to his knees and studied the designs embedded in the rock. Deep red lines ran across it like veins in a gigantic appendage. They looked like tiny red rivers drawn on a map, blood red and spread across the entire face of the monolith.

Pressing his hands hard to it, moisture formed on his palms. Did the stone bleed, or did it cry? Sadness and anxiousness washed through him. Was the stone trying to tell him something? *Danger.* The word flashed through his mind.

"Caw. Caw." The sound above him caused him to glance up. A large black bird perched on the rock scrutinized him through dark, beady eyes. The bird turned his head to one side then to the other, examining Nate with a curious eye. It spread its wings and took flight. As it gracefully lifted into the sky, a large black wing feather floated down and landed next to Nate. He reached down, picked it up and held it to his palm.

"Crow feather," he whispered. "Crow Feather." The words rolled from his tongue lingering strangely in his heart, a shadowy feeling of sadness and anger.

Shaking his head, he grasped the feather. Examining it, he thought of the feather the nurse had given him. As he rose to his feet, a fierce wind suddenly caught him and nearly overpowered him. He clung to the stone to keep from losing his balance. From a clear blue sky overhead, a bolt of lightning reached down. An electrical jolt ran through his arms and into his body, knocking him to the ground.

A string of words echoed through his mind. *The power of the ancients is yours. Follow the signs.* The deafening roar of thunder followed and vibrated so fiercely his entire body rattled. From out of nothing, large white flakes fell around him. Confused and stunned, he held out his hand. Was it snowing? The realization quickly came that the blizzard was made up of feathers. "What the hell?" he asked in amazement. Within seconds, the storm stopped.

For several minutes he stood grasping the stone. Struggling to regain his wits and compose himself from the shock, he stepped back. Realizing in the confusion, he'd dropped the black feather, he looked down at the ground. Right in front of his feet, near the base of the rock, was a smoldering square of earth. Inside the square, five feathers lay crossed at the quill and spread out in the shape of a star. The crow feather from his hand had fallen and landed perfectly among them.

Follow the signs. The words reverberated through his psyche. Stunned and confused, he knelt and studied the burned earth and the perfect arrangement of the feathers. Acting on instinct, he carefully picked them up, one by one.

Shakily, he glanced at his watch, realizing it was after six thirty. He needed to find his way back to the car. His body trembled and exhaustion weighed heavy on him. The stone and the lightning had drained him. Instinct told him he'd found what he'd been led here to see. Perhaps, in time it would make sense. He looked at the stone mass he still knelt before.

A hand grasped his shoulder and he started. A voice came from behind him. "What are you doing way out here?"

Turning quickly, Nate saw a tall man in a brown uniform hovering above him. "I guess I got off the path." He let out a sigh of relief and rose to look the park ranger in the face.

"You all right?" The ranger eyed him rather suspiciously.

"I'm okay. Just got a little turned around."

"You're in a restricted area. But you're a long way from the trail. It took me twenty minutes to find you."

"Sorry about that." Nate sensed the ranger was irritated and could feel a lecture coming.

"Dangerous business wandering around out here. There's a reason we don't allow people to roam off the trails like this. A man last week broke his leg when he fell into a buried kiva."

Kiva. The word brought on a strange feeling. Stone walls and flickering firelight flashed through his mind's eye for a split second, then was gone. Nate forced a smile and shrugged. "I'm sorry. I guess I didn't realize I'd gotten so far off course."

"I could give you a stiff fine, but I don't think you did it on purpose. I thought I saw something running through the brush earlier. When I came back to check it out, I saw your car."

"Didn't mean to cause you any grief, sir. It was a mistake."

"If you ever come here again, you need to understand there are lots of ruins that have been uncovered by recent fires in the park. Some of those old ceremonial chambers are big and covered over with dirt so you can't see them. Dangerous things to fall into. You were lucky. Better stick to the trails."

Nate followed the ranger back through the heavy brush and trees. He pulled his shirt from the front seat of the car and put it back on. Remembering the feathers clenched in his fist, he turned away from the ranger and slipped them into his pocket. The ranger was already ticked off enough without him seeing Nate taking anything from park property.

"You need to head for the main entrance. The park closes in ten minutes." The ranger's arms were folded and his voice was stern.

"Yes, sir. Thanks for helping me out." Nate shook his head. He sounded like a schoolboy in trouble with the principal, but it was no time to burn any bridges. In his heart he knew he'd journey back here. The exploration of his soul was far from over. In fact it was just beginning.

As he drove back down the winding road, myriad images flashed through his mind, a black and white bird and the face of a boy in a black hat. They'd both been in his original vision. The feather the nurse had found in Stellar's hand was black and white. Now here, first the crow feather, then when he'd asked for answers, a bolt of lightning had delivered a handful of feathers in the shape of a star. *Birds. Feathers.*

It all seemed convoluted and crazy, but there was some mysterious connection to it all. There was far more here than bizarre coincidences. He just couldn't get his head around what he felt in his soul. But he just might know an old man who could help him make things clearer.

Nate pulled onto the highway wondering if he had the fortitude for the six-hour drive home. Out of the blue, an uncomfortable sensation washed through his heart, a feeling of foreboding.

A picture of Stellar lying in the hospital bed flashed through his mind. Stellar was the only one who knew the real truth about Johnny—the only one who knew the truth about his vision. A shadow loomed over her. His heart jumped into his throat. *Danger.* The words riveted in his mind.

He jammed on the gas. His detour was over. He needed to get back to Santa Fe as quick as he could.

CHAPTER SEVENTEEN

Jim Smith sauntered into the kitchen in his robe and slippers with the Sunday paper tucked under one arm. He tossed the newspaper onto the kitchen table and poured himself a cup of strong black coffee. He took a sip and shuddered. It was lousy. He never could make a cup of coffee as good as his ex-wife. Maybe he should have kept her around for that.

Fifteen years later and he was still trying to convince himself he'd had a choice about her leaving. She was stupid to go. It was her loss. He'd made a good life for her. The wife of a prominent well-to-do man in the community, she'd had everything.

But she'd harped at him all the time, telling him he was prejudice and manipulative. Then she'd accused him of controlling her and Ethan's lives. The last time he'd seen her was at Ethan's funeral. After that, she'd moved away.

He remembered how good she looked in that black dress, even then, racked with grief at the loss of her only son—their only son. She was a beautiful woman. He'd likely never see her again. Maybe he should have tried harder, tried to change—but then she was wrong about him.

He wasn't guilty of any of the things she accused him of. All he wanted was the best for her and Ethan. A Navajo girl wasn't good enough for his boy. He was right about that, no matter what anybody said.

Staring into the cup of steaming coffee, he took another sip. *Bitter.* Just like him. Maybe a little sugar would take the edge off. A hot cup of crappy coffee in the morning was almost as hard to handle as a cold empty bed at night. Dipping a spoon into the sugar bowl, he sprinkled some into his cup and turned back toward the table. The coffee he could make tolerable. The rest of his life wasn't so easily remedied.

He sat in a chair and picked up the newspaper, scanning the headlines about the latest happenings in Washington, D.C. and more gloom and doom about the economy. There was nothing new under the sun or in the paper these days.

Flipping it over, a headline caught his eye. "Boy sought in murder of Los Alamos girl." *Damned kids. Couldn't they stay off the streets and out of the gangs?* In his day, no parent would have tolerated it.

He started to read the article. The phone rang, startling him and interrupting his thoughts. "Who the hell—" he muttered. Rising from the chair, he grabbed the phone from the kitchen counter.

"Hello."

"Smith. It's Gonzales."

"Why are you calling me on a Sunday?"

"Just got off my shift. Something interesting happened last night."

"It better be damn interesting."

"There's an APB out on a kid who murdered a girl in Los Alamos."

"I saw it in the paper. So?"

"An Indian boy, mid-teens, dressed in black from head to foot."

An uncomfortable feeling ran through Smith. "Like I said. So?"

"He pulled the girl into an alley and strangled her with a cord. It hit me, it was almost verbatim the call that came in on Johnny Begay."

"Bull shit. The last thing I need is for you to start fabricating a bunch of crap. We live in New Mexico. There are thousands of Indian kids that fit the description on any given day."

"Strangling girls in alleys with cords? Whatever. Thought it might be worth checking out."

"The only thing worth checking out is what that stupid public defender is up to. It seems there's a lot of unfinished business you should be taking care of instead of turning over rocks looking for a worm."

Gonzales cleared his throat. "I haven't seen him in days. Don't know what he's been up to."

"Well, he hasn't resigned from the case. I can guarantee you that. If he had, I'd have heard by now."

"Maybe he left town and didn't tell anybody."

"Right. You and I aren't either one that lucky. Find out what he's been doing. We'll meet for coffee tonight. I want a report."

"All right."

"And what about the girl?"

"Barely hanging on. Doctors don't give her much hope of waking up."

"Hmmph. Damn shame."

"That it is. I'll see you, tonight."

Smith set the phone back in its cradle and turned toward the paper on the table. There were tons of kids fitting that description in New Mexico. *Strangling teenage girls.* Gonzales' words rang in his ears. It was a coincidence. He had the lousy scumbag in jail who'd attacked the girl here in Santa Fe.

He picked up the paper from the table and scanned the article. "The boy was described as Native American, possibly Navajo, in his early to mid-teens, about five foot six and of lanky build, last seen wearing a black T-shirt and black jeans." *Could be any one of a hundred kids.* They all looked the same to him.

He pulled the page from the paper and angrily tore it to shreds and crammed it into the bottom of the kitchen trashcan. What if Nakai were to get hold of that information? Regardless of its relevance, it was enough to put a question in the minds of a jury. He hoped Nakai was out of town.

Smith chewed at the inside of his cheek. What Nakai needed was another push toward the exit door. This time, one he couldn't ignore.

Beads of perspiration formed on his upper lip. Nothing was going to keep him from putting Johnny Begay behind bars and putting another nail through Mary Begay's heart in the process. The damn shame was something or someone couldn't hasten the process. He scratched his chin, uncomfortable with the thought running through his mind.

———

Mary rubbed her eyes and tried to get the Sunday morning cobwebs out of her head. As she left the mission parking lot after the Sunday services and drove toward Santa Fe to open the gallery, she realized she'd been in a strange hazy world for the past few days. A lost world somewhere between imagination and blatant reality had sucked her in— and apparently devoured Nate.

The truth of the matter, Johnny was still in jail and his lawyer was nowhere to be found. She'd gone to Santa Fe in search of Nate yesterday afternoon, to see if he was okay. But he wasn't home and he wasn't at his office.

Wandering through the shops in the plaza, the park, and the scene of the crime, she'd finally given up, at a loss of where else to look. She'd tried to call him, well into the night, but there was no answer. Concerned for his well being after yesterday morning, quite truthfully, she was beginning to worry.

If what he'd experienced in the hogan had been anything like what she'd seen, she had good reason. It haunted her. She had to admit that. But she was far too embarrassed to tell anyone about what had gone on in her mind.

In the pitch-blackness of a cave somewhere a long time ago, a heinous trick had been played. It affected her so personally, so distinctly, that it was like a distant memory of something that actually happened to her. But it wasn't possible. Every detail was real. She shuddered.

It seemed long ago, in an ancient world. And yet, the face that flashed in her mind at the end certainly didn't belong to the ancients, but very much in her own, not so distant past. *Ethan Smith was definitely part of this lifetime.* The thought hit her strangely. She shook her head. She didn't want to think about it. It was ludicrous.

She didn't know what those feelings and pictures meant, any more than she knew what to do about Nate. She couldn't stop thinking about him. No matter how much the situation with Johnny and her own suspicions pushed them apart, there was a force and a feeling in her heart that kept drawing her to him. He'd even proclaimed Johnny guilty, and she was still here, still trying to find Nate, still trying to help him, and still not willing to walk away.

It was crazy. The whole thing was insane. From the mysterious insights and visions Grandpa had conjured at the fire, to the fact that a man from a painting was handling Johnny's defense. It was enough to drive her nuts. There was one phenomenal coincidence after another. But were they coincidences? Or simply things meant to be—

She drove on. Glancing at the clock, she wondered where Nate was now. Had he come home last night and where had he gone?

Nate opened his eyes and ran his hand across the stubble on his chin. He stared at the textured ceiling above his bed, trying to clear the sleep from his brain.

In the wee hours of the morning, he'd gone to the hospital to find Stellar's condition hadn't changed. Everything appeared to be okay there. He couldn't explain his earlier concerns. He'd come home and collapsed from exhaustion. Everything that happened yesterday combined with the long drive had taken its toll.

Dreams of screeching birds, swirling feathers and phantom shadows in the darkness of a cavern, haunted his sleep. He clung to the red stone and whispered words echoed indiscernible messages.

Nate thought of the lightning strike and the feather storm. The four feathers that came out of his bizarre experience were in the car. No doubt, the unexplainable events of the last two days had brought on the devastating dreams. His jaw tightened. He couldn't allow them to have the same effect on his world. Enough was enough.

He ran a hand through his hair. He had to pull himself away from whatever had a hold on him. Friday, Saturday—and today was Sunday; two crazy days had past. He wasn't going for three.

He snorted. The feeling about Stellar hadn't played out. Lightning seldom came from a clear blue sky—but stone didn't weep or bleed either. Nonetheless, when he could he must return to the mesa. Next time he'd find Alex. Alex had experienced a strange transformation there as well. But Alex had said in his letter he was on his way to a new site. Some remote place called The Canyon of the Dead.

Had the messages been from a world beyond? If what Grandpa said was true, and the spirit world had something to say to him, it needed to get on with it. Either way, he had no choice, but to get back to his life.

Rolling from the bed, he climbed into a hot shower. The water spilled over his body, revitalizing him and bringing back more normal thoughts. He couldn't get Mary out of his head. His nakedness brought a rush of thoughts and longing. How long had it been since he'd been with a woman?

His mind flashed to the darkened cavern in the vision he'd experienced yesterday. He thought of the woman, the Indian maiden, who had been totally fooled into making love to the evil brother of her lover. It couldn't be. It couldn't happen.

No woman could be so taken in, so fooled into such a thing. Surely she'd intimately know her lover's touch, his kiss, she'd know how he held her, and the way he made love to her. Could two brothers be so much alike physically to trick a woman in that way?

This was nuts. It was just another dream, another vision. But it sure as hell seemed real. He grasped his throat, thinking of the rope from his vision and the marks on Stellar's neck. He looked down at his wrists where he'd known the same kind of burn from the rawhide bindings. What kind of crazy worlds had he tapped into, worlds where he felt things as if they were happening to him? A place where he experienced others pain as if it were his own.

A burning sensation caused him to look down. His feet were sore. Red streaks ran up his lower legs. They must have come from the lightning strike. The thoughts played in his mind as the water rained down on his body until the shower ran cold.

Twenty minutes later, Nate leaned into the car and retrieved the feathers from the seat. He looked at them in the sunlight. Besides the black crow feather, there was a large, brown and white one and a smaller, more delicate gray. The third was also black, not as large as the first, but with a slight brownish tint.

Each had a distinct shape, size and texture. What did they mean? Why feathers? They must have some significance to have come to him in such a bizarre way.

Grandpa's words were in his head, something he'd said about things coming to him in their own time. The old man was quite a philosopher, if only he wasn't always so full of riddles.

Nate picked up the newspaper and walked back into the house holding the feathers in one hand and the paper in the other. In the kitchen, he made himself a cup of espresso before retiring to a more comfortable chair in the living room.

He rubbed his eyes. Maybe, he'd hang out and relax for the rest of the day. He wanted to clear his head. Being emotionally caught up in this case wasn't necessarily a good thing for his career. The old Nate wouldn't have allowed this to happen. Tomorrow, he had to force himself back into reality. He had to make a final decision on what he was going to do about Johnny.

He unrolled the paper and glanced over the front page. Preoccupied with everything that had been going on in his strange world of late, he hadn't checked out what was happening on the rest of the planet. A headline caught his eye. A girl had been murdered in Los Alamos. He read the first few words of the article when the doorbell rang.

Laying the paper aside, he opened the door. On the front step stood Mary.

"You're finally home," she said in a relieved tone.

He smiled. "You were looking for me?"

She rolled her eyes and smirked. "Let's say I was concerned about you." She brushed against him as she stepped through the doorway. "I'm glad you're all right."

The scent of her perfume sent a warm rush through him. "Everything okay?" he asked as he took her in from head to foot. She was dressed in a white summer dress that hugged her bosoms. Her long black hair was tied at the back of her neck with a turquoise scarf then draped over her right shoulder. A turquoise necklace sat in the 'V' at the base of her throat.

She must wear this stuff to tantalize me. Damn, it was hard to keep his mind on the conversation when she looked and smelled so good.

"Everything's fine. I was worried when you left yesterday. You seemed to be kind of preoccupied. Kind of out of it, if you don't mind me being honest." She perched on the arm of the sofa. "I came looking for you and tried to call you half the night, but I couldn't reach you."

"Sorry. I didn't mean to worry you. I needed some time alone. Time to sort things out."

She smiled and looked at him with bewitching eyes. "And did you?"

"Still sorting, I'm afraid." He had an impulse to scoop her up from the couch arm and kiss her, but when he locked into her gaze, she looked away. Even though she'd started to loosen up around him, there seemed to still be something mysterious hiding behind her eyes.

She sensed what he was feeling. He was sure of it, but every time they were alone, she retreated into her shell. Like a turtle, popping out its head, then pulling it back just as quickly.

"I was on my way to work and I was wondering if you were home. Now that I've seen you're okay, I better be going."

Nate moved a step closer, not wanting her to leave so soon. "You have time for a cup of coffee?"

She glanced at her watch and shrugged. "Maybe a quick one."

Nate went to the kitchen and prepared a small pot in the drip coffee maker. "It'll only take a few minutes to make some."

"Okay," she said, sounding a little distracted.

Nate finished making the coffee and pulled out two cups from the cupboard. He walked back into the living room to find Mary reading the newspaper. As he came into the room, her eyes shot to him and she pushed the paper toward him.

"Did you read this?" she demanded.

"What?"

"The article on the front page. The one about the girl in Los Alamos."

"I started to, but I didn't get a chance to finish it."

"Well, you *need* to finish it."

"Why?"

"Read it. You'll see."

Nate took the paper from her and scanned the article. Looking up when he'd finished, he asked, "And?"

"Doesn't it sound familiar to you? Maybe *too* familiar?"

He gave her a half nod. "Possibly."

"Possibly? It sounds like what happened to Stellar. And the boy sounds *very* similar to Johnny."

"Mary, you know Johnny's in jail—"

"I don't mean that. I mean there could be a lot of people in the world who could fit his description."

"It's probably just a coincidence."

"Well, I don't believe in coincidences. And when something jumps in my face, I think maybe there's a reason why."

Nate shrugged. His own thoughts on coincidence were congruent with that. He rubbed his upper lip below his nose. "Okay. I'll look into it further in the morning."

"What's wrong with now?"

He looked into her eyes. They were fiery with excitement, or anger. He wasn't sure which one. He looked back at the article and reread the description. It did sound like Johnny. It wasn't impossible for descriptions to be generic enough to fit a lot of people, but the glaring truth was they had three positive IDs from eyewitnesses. It was a coincidence. There was that word, again.

"You didn't answer me. What's wrong with now?"

"I'm not sure any of the agencies I need to contact would be open on a Sunday." He fumbled for an official sounding excuse to put her off.

"And what are your other options?"

"Mary. I promise to look into it. I'm not going to blow you off."

Her eyes flashed. "Damn straight you're not." She glanced at her watch. "I'll give you until tomorrow to see what you can find out. I'm going to the gallery now, and I'll use tomorrow to get things squared away. If you don't come up with an answer by tomorrow night, I'll go to Los Alamos on Tuesday and chase it down myself."

"Mary. I don't know if this warrants—"

Nate's mouth watered and he bit his lip. A thought tugged at the back of his mind. There was a chance to be alone with Mary for a few hours, away from everything. His pulse quickened and a surge of warmth ran through him. "I'll see what I can find out," he said, avoiding her eyes. "But a trip there isn't a bad idea. If you decide to go on Tuesday, I think I should go along. You may need my help."

She looked at him suspiciously. "I'm going with or without you, but there's only one way I'll allow you to come."

He looked at her under a furrowed brow.

"You have to be in earnest about sticking it out with Johnny. No matter what we find. And your heart better damn well be in it, or I'll have no choice. We'll have to go our separate ways."

"Is that an ultimatum?"

"Sounds like one, doesn't it?" She set her jaw and met his gaze.

He sidestepped the question. "I'll call you tomorrow and let you know what I find out."

"And what you've decided?"

Nate gave her a nod. His heart was in a quandary, but he couldn't tell her.

For a moment, her face reflected what was in his heart. Turning quickly, she was half way to the door, when she answered. "I'll talk to you tomorrow then?"

He followed and watched her walk away. The white skirt rippled as her hips swayed beneath it. His chest tightened and his hormones responded in kind. He had to make a decision, but if he could be alone with her, away from Santa Fe and Johnny's pull on her heartstrings, maybe they would be able to sort out their feelings for one another. She'd put him between a rock and a hard spot. If he dropped Johnny's case, he'd probably never see Mary again.

The trip on Tuesday might well be a challenge, being so close to her. But, frankly, it was all he'd be able to think about whether he went with her or stayed behind.

He glanced at the paper in his hand. A strange sensation came over him. The face from his vision flashed through his mind. Maybe, the story was worth checking out. It was a long shot, proving to a jury a description could fit a lot of boys. Especially, with three witnesses looking him in the face and testifying to the contrary. On the other hand, the way things were shaping up, there wasn't anything left to lose, for himself or for Johnny. He'd follow through with his promise to Mary and check it out.

Smith glared at Gonzales. "He's back. I knew it."

Gonzales shrugged. "Don't know where he's been."

"Doesn't matter. He's still a thorn in our side." Smith chewed on his coffee stirrer.

Gonzales glowered at him. "A thorn in your side maybe. Not mine."

Smith raised his eyebrows. "And I would be the pain in your ass that makes him your problem, too."

"I can't deny that."

Smith's lips curled. "I'm through playing games with you and with him. Things just got serious."

Gonzales rolled his eyes. "More serious than those two thugs? They damn near put him in the hospital."

"Apparently, it wasn't enough to convince him. He's still around. Should've sent a real man to set up the job."

"Oh, you got another idiot lined up to do this shit? I should be so lucky." Gonzales snorted. "Did you ever stop and think that it might make him dig in his heels? I've seen guys like Nakai before."

Smith gritted his teeth. He'd seen Nakai before, too. But damn if he could remember where or when. Especially, with what had come up in Los Alamos over the weekend, he had to get Nakai out of the picture. Permanently. And do it before Nakai could find a loophole and blow the whole case out of the water. Even Gonzales had picked up on the similarities between the two cases. And he was about as bright as a burned out light bulb.

Nakai could take those parallels and craft a defense out of them. He damn sure didn't have one now. Smith had been in this business long enough to know what a keen-eyed defense attorney would look for and that incident was prime for the picking. It was risky business, letting Nakai hang around.

Nakai had gone somewhere. Chances were he hadn't seen the paper. But Smith couldn't take a chance. He had his hands around Mary Begay's throat once more and nothing was going to stop him from hurting her—from making her pay and pay and pay—

Gonzales broke the silence. "You're awfully quiet. What's on your mind?"

"What was that guy's name at the garage? The one you caught switching out bad parts on people's cars to drum up business."

Gonzales squirmed. "I don't know what you're talking about."

"Yeah, right. Don't play stupid. I know he was paying you to look the other way."

"That's here say. You can't prove it."

"Stop doing the dance. I'm not trying to nail your ass for it. Not right now, anyway."

Gonzales stared at his hands. "Ernie. Ernie Gomez."

"Ernie, huh? Well, it seems to me Ernie owes you a favor."

Gonzales shrugged. "Maybe."

"At least one, huh?" Smith smiled. "I want you to pay him a visit. Come up with something he can do to Nakai's vehicle. Something with the potential to end this once and for all."

Gonzales's eyes shot to Smith. "You're out of your fricking mind."

Smith squirmed in his chair.

Gonzales went on. "I don't want any part of this anymore. You're losing it, man."

"Losing it? Maybe. But not quite as much as you and Ernie have to lose." Smith swished the coffee in his cup and set it on the café table.

"Go to hell. I want nothing to do with this. Messing around with his car is dangerous business. What if he gets killed or kills some innocent person?" Gonzales crossed his arms and huffed.

Smith rubbed his chin. "Nakai's condo is in a pretty quiet area, and a little way out of town. What time does he leave for work?"

Gonzales looked at him through leery eyes. "He's an early bird. Gets up with the chickens. Leaves for the gym about five in the morning."

"Well, there you go. Not many out and about that time of the day. So Ernie does the deed in the dead of night and it's all over before the sun comes up. It'll work out okay for everyone." Smith sneered. "Well, maybe everybody, but Nakai."

"You use the term *dead*, pretty loosely don't you?" Gonzales shook his head. "You never answered my question. What if you kill the son of a bitch?"

Smith glanced around nervously. "I can't control the outcome. We set the stage and let providence take it from there. But it's gotta look like a mechanical failure. An unfortunate mishap." Smith rubbed the stubble on his chin. "At the very least, I want him out of commission long enough to get Begay's case reassigned."

"So say he does run into a tree or something, and he comes out without a scratch? It could happen. Then what about me and Ernie—and you for Christ's sake?"

"To me, it's worth the risk." Smith shrugged. "I'm sure your friend Ernie won't flinch. Did he kill anybody with his part-switching scheme? Did he ever get caught?"

"Of course he never killed anybody. And I caught him."

"Well, then I'm convinced he could make it look like a freak accident. Something that happened naturally. You know—natural, like wear and tear."

"I don't know. What makes you think he'll even do it?"

"I'll sweeten the pot for both of you. Keep both of your butts out of the legal system once and for all and throw in some cash. I know Gomez has a whole passel of kids to feed. That's what got him into this to begin with."

Gonzales's eyes narrowed. "How sweet are we talking?"

"Enough to feed his kids for a year. All in cash. No questions asked. And no worries that anyone will ever find out about his underhanded dealings. Or yours— I'm off his back and yours *forever*."

"You mean that?"

Smith nodded. "It's the last thing I'll ever ask you to do."

Gonzales let out a sigh and rubbed his chin. "You promise?"

"I'm a man of my word. I'm out of your life."

"What about those files you keep threatening me with?"

"I'll turn everything over to you. You can burn them, shred them, I don't care. Either way, they no longer exist as far as I'm concerned."

Gonzales's jaw rippled. Smith had him thinking. "This one last thing and it's over?"

Smith nodded. "I'll give you until tomorrow to think about it."

Gonzales rolled his eyes. "Yeah, like you've got some other jackass lined up to do this if I don't."

Smith gritted his teeth. "Tomorrow."

"And if I say, no?"

Smith chuckled. "You and Ernie get to be roomies at the state pen?"

"And if I say, yes?" Gonzales growled.

"You and Ernie can cross me off your list—and spend the rest of your natural days playing with your kids and grandkids."

"There's only one thing you could offer me that would make me go this far and you know it."

"Yes, sir. And I've laid it on the table." Smith wasn't sure how it had gotten this far, but he couldn't let anything stop him. He wiped his sweaty palms on his trousers.

Gonzales nodded as he rose from his chair. "You'll hear from me."

Smith opened his wallet and threw a five-dollar bill on the coffee shop table. He smiled. He had a real good feeling about this deal. If he got rid of Nakai, he'd have no use for Gonzales. Gonzales would do anything to be

free of his past—and Smith. It was like taking candy
from a baby.

.

CHAPTER EIGHTEEN

Mary rolled over in bed for what seemed like the thousandth time. She pounded the pillow with her fist. She couldn't get Johnny off her mind. Faces ran through her head. *Johnny. Nate. Jim Smith—and those ever present suspicions.*

She'd tried her best to forgive him. Smith had lost his son. Her heart went out to him. But no matter how she tried, she couldn't forgive his evil obsession to avenge his son's death, a son he'd turned into a saint in his own mind. If only he knew the real truth about his idolized offspring.

She remembered the vision from the encounter by the fire. Ethan was much like the evil brother who'd betrayed the woman in the cave. *Betrayal.* It had been Ethan's specialty, too. They were so much alike it was uncanny. Perhaps, somehow in the eerie world of the vision, her mind had twisted that evil into Ethan. She didn't want to remember the vision or the wickedness Ethan and his father had brought into her life. Wanting to forget it, she squeezed her eyes closed. Somewhere in the darkness, sleep eventually claimed her.

She was floating, seeing what was around her, but not totally comprehending where she was or what was happening. She tried to move her hand, but it was as if it belonged to someone else. While her other hand twitched and shook as if it had a mind of its own. How strange. How very, very strange. But she was floating and oddly, she didn't care.

Ethan and a boy she didn't know stood across the room. The boy sneered and spoke in a hushed voice. "What are you so serious about? You know you had to do it. Your old man would kill you if he ever found out. He told you to stay away from her."

Ethan threw him a distraught look. "Yeah. I know. There isn't any other way."

Unable to speak or control her motor skills, Mary lay on a hard table covered with a sheet. It wasn't comfortable, but she couldn't seem to clear the fog from her mind enough to move to a different position. Two silver stirrups loomed ominously at her feet. Her mind was functioning to a degree, enough to recognize what they were, but she had no idea where she was or why she was here. Nor did it concern her. The world was in a fog, but she could hear them talking about someone. Her dashingly handsome Ethan. Why was he standing so far away and who were they talking about?

"She ain't good enough for you, anyway. She's a dumb Injun girl."

"You sound like my old man." Ethan glanced her way and ducked his head.

"Well, he's right you know. They ain't like us."

"What if she tells?"

"She ain't gonna tell. More than likely she won't know what hit her. Even if she did, nobody would believe her. The son of the DA wouldn't have nothin' to do with some squaw."

Ethan was silent as he looked at her. "Yeah. I guess no one would believe her." Ethan folded his arms and drummed his fingers. "I hope this lady hurries up. What if the stuff wears off before we get her back to Santa Fe?"

"We gave her a lot. She should be out of it for a good long while."

"Hope you know what you're doing," Ethan muttered.

"Trust me." The boy flashed him a smile.

There was the sound of a door opening and closing as someone entered the room.

"So this is your sister?" A woman's voice came from somewhere near her feet.

"Yes, ma'am."

"So why did you bring her here?"

"We don't have anyone else, ma'am. Our folks are dead." Ethan cast a nervous glance in her direction. "My sister isn't right in the head. I mean she's badly retarded."

Who was he talking about? She didn't know Ethan had a sister. His suave actions and his sad sincere demeanor made her feel sad for this sister she'd never met. Poor thing. Why hadn't he told her? She wanted to ask, but she had no voice when she opened her mouth. She had the strange sensation she was hovering above her own body lying there on the sterile white table.

"She's been like this since she was born?"

"Yes, ma'am."

"Too, bad. What a pity. I can see why you don't think she's capable of caring for a child, and the baby could be—like her."

Ethan glanced at the boy, his nervous expression fading and a self-assured look taking its place. His suave voice carried through the room. "Why, I don't know what I'd do. I could never take care of them both."

"Well, don't worry. I'll take care of it for you. I'm surprised you couldn't have this done through the proper channels—considering the circumstances." A woman with short brown hair wearing a white smock stepped into Mary's view.

Who's she? What were they talking about? Couldn't they be quiet and let her drift in this euphoric state?

Ethan looked at the woman with pleading eyes. "Ma'am, I tried everything. No doctor would touch her. That's why I'm so grateful we found you."

The woman shrugged. "I'm not surprised. No parents and her only being seventeen."

"Yes, ma'am. It's a real hard situation. I don't know where else to turn."

"You know what happens here today is outside the realm of normal medical practice. You must never tell anyone about it—either of you."

"Oh, yes, ma'am. I'll take this secret to my grave." Ethan's eyes and demeanor were genuine.

"Me, too, ma'am. I swear, I'll never tell a soul." Ethan's friend spoke up for the first time since the woman had come into the room.

"And there's the matter of the fee."

"I have it." Ethan reached inside his leather jacket and pulled out a white envelope.

The woman took it from him and opened it enough to examine the contents. "You boys wait outside. This shouldn't take long."

A strange sensation boiled up through the fog in Mary's head, a feeling that she needed to get up and run away. Unexplainable fear grasped at her throat. Her arms and legs responded like those of a rag doll.

She tried to speak, to cry out, but it seemed her mouth and brain couldn't connect. The sound coming from her was an animal-like groan. She could feel drool running down her chin. What was wrong with her? It was the fog, if she could only get out of the fog.

The woman came over and laid a hand on her arm. She was fuzzy, distant looking. Her voice echoed in an odd manner. "She seems to be getting overwrought. I'm going to give her a local and a strong sedative. It will be safer."

"Ma'am," Ethan was out of sight, but his voice came from somewhere in the room. "Could you give her

enough of that so she'll stay under until we get her home?"

The boy chimed in. "Yeah, it's a long way and I reckon she'd be real hard to control if she got out of hand."

"Don't worry. I'll give her enough to keep her sleeping for several hours. That will help you get her safely home."

"Oh, thank you, ma'am. We really appreciate all of your help."

The door closed. Mary struggled against the instinctive fear in her gut. She faded in and out of reality. Another moan came from deep in her throat, but she was unable to form it into words.

"Now, now. I'll give you a shot and it will be over soon." *Those were the last words Mary could remember. There was a prick in her arm. Seconds later the fog intensified and everything disappeared.*

Mary jerked awake. Beads of perspiration poured down her face. Disoriented, she felt around in the darkness. Relief flooded her when she found herself warm and safe in her soft bed, not awakening on the hard, cold park bench drenched in chilling rain as she had on that night fifteen years earlier.

That cursed nightmare. The nightmare she'd lived through and miraculously survived. Her unborn child hadn't been as lucky. And all these years later, her heart still ached for what had been stolen from her.

She hadn't had the dream in several years. She'd hoped it was gone forever. No doubt, Ethan's memory had been stirred by everything that had happened in the last few weeks. His wretched deed had scarred her life. She could never forget. No matter how she tried to put it behind her, it would forever be part of her past, a secret passage in her life history.

She pulled herself into a sitting position, her heart hammering in her chest. She let out a sigh. Even though she hadn't had the nightmare in a while, it was as vivid as the day she had lived it. Every detail. *The voices, the exact words, and the horrific feeling of returning to reality.* The emptiness and devastation that engulfed her later.

Whatever Ethan and his friend had given her that day, she had perfect memory of what was said in that room, every word. She was unclear then of what was happening, but it didn't matter. The drugs had rendered her helpless to do anything about it.

She'd done some research in her college years and figured out how they'd devised their plan. She'd narrowed it down to one prime suspect. Rhypenol, better known as the date rape drug. Slipped into her soft drink with a little alcohol, it had become a devious tool to help Ethan do what he did best—avoid his father's wrath. Both the plan and the drug had rendered her helpless in more than one way. A Navajo girl, especially a seventeen-year-old, couldn't take on Santa Fe's well-respected DA and his golden child— not unless she was crazy.

She'd done the right thing by not telling anyone. Her mother would never have understood, nor would her mom have had the courage to stand against Smith. It was for the best she never knew.

Mary's mind flooded with sweet memories of her mother and her childhood. It was a simple world, so different from what had followed. A deep need came over her as she remembered the days of her youth. A need grew inside to feel the happiness and safety that existed before everything had changed—drastically.

Throwing back the covers, she climbed from the comfort of the bed, her feet sliding silently across the hard wood floor. Intermittent creaks came from the floorboards as she stepped from them onto the woolen Navajo rugs scattered in the hallway.

Silently, she opened the door and slipped into the room she rarely visited these days. It was filled with too many memories. Memories of her father and mother and of a life and place she could never return to.

The moonlight illuminated the room through the window next to the bed. She stepped to the bedside, stroked the woolen coverlet and clicked on the sturdy wood lamp on the night table.

Turning, she opened the closet door, pulled a box from the closet shelf, and set it on the bed. Adjusting her silk pajamas, she situated herself, cross-legged, and dove into the box of memories.

Inside the box, the family photos were arranged in neat stacks. Her mother had always intended to put them in albums, but fate had other plans. Instead, they were placed in tidy piles. She flipped through a stack of pictures of her, reminiscing about happier times when there were no cares and no problems. When the biggest worry on her mind was what to wear to school the next day.

Picking up another, she found Johnny's baby pictures. A warm glow flushed through her as she remembered his first year. It was that joy, along with her artwork, that helped her recover from her own trauma and move on with her life. She'd regretted being away at college during those days, but it had been the pictures and the letters about Johnny that kept her connected to home and to the joy once residing in this simple house.

Sweet Johnny. The child who had been both a healing force and a reminder of what Ethan had stolen from her. It was her duty to take care of him—even now. And he needed her more than ever.

Mary thumbed through the pictures. *Three months. Six months.* Her mother had photos all the way through his elementary school years. He was a nice looking boy. And he was a good boy. He always had been.

Mary reached back in the box. A large yellow-brown envelope was tucked in the bottom. Pulling it out, she opened the clasp and the contents spilled onto the bed. Her parent's marriage license and their birth certificates were among the papers. Mary sighed and tucked them back into the envelope. Those were of no use to anyone, but she'd keep them forever, just the same.

A carefully folded sheet of white paper remained on the bed along with an envelope. She unfolded the paper and spread it on the blanket. It was Johnny's birth certificate. A crease formed in her brow as she scanned it. It was odd. Some of the information had been covered with white out and typed over. In fact, the whole document was covered with white splotches.

Her eyes stopped at the county. San Juan, not Santa Fe? That had to be a mistake. She shook her head. It was definitely Johnny's birth certificate, but how weird to see a legal document so sloppily prepared and the wrong county listed.

She shrugged it off. Laying it aside, she chose the white envelope and turned it over. Scrawled on the front of it was a note in her mother's handwriting. "For Mary *only*. To be opened *only* in the event of my death." She bit her lip. She hadn't realized this was among her mother's things.

Carefully, she ran her nail across the top and opened the sealed envelope. She removed two folded sheets of paper. The top sheet was a short letter from her mother.

Dearest Mary - If you have opened this envelope, the worst has happened. I've taken this secret to my grave for a reason. I must protect Johnny, and you must do the same. I must entrust this secret to you, for there is only one other living soul who knows. One day the truth may have to come to light, and one day it may be safe to let it be known. Until then, please honor my final wish. Know that I love you and I regret placing this on your shoulders. Mother.

Mary's hand trembled as she pulled aside the piece of paper. Shock washed over her as she read the words at the top of the next page. *Certificate of Legal Adoption.* Her parent's names jumped off the page, and Johnny's, too. She read the dates. They had adopted Johnny when he was six months old.

Emotion clenched at her throat and her eyes burned. Her mind swam as she tried to get her head around what she was reading. Why would her mother do such a thing? Why would they lie to everyone, especially her? And what was the meaning of the note? None of this made sense.

Johnny was adopted? Had she been so preoccupied with her own issues back then she'd not figured this out? She thought back to the days when it happened. Johnny was born several months after Mary left for college. She'd gotten the news, quite suddenly and quite unexpectedly. She hadn't known her mother was pregnant.

She'd been aghast at first, but the explanations all seemed logical. Her mother had told her that she didn't know herself until late in the pregnancy. Being a large woman, the doctor's had believed she was going through menopause. When the pregnancy was confirmed, she chose not to tell anyone, because it was a risky pregnancy. Her mother was in her forties and her health issues made for a bleak prognosis for the child.

But Johnny was healthy and happy—and she never asked again. She never questioned the story. Why would she? Mary had no reason to doubt her mother's word. Something was wrong, very wrong. This couldn't be true.

She reread her mother's letter and swallowed hard. But how could she deny her mother's message from beyond the grave? It had to be fact.

She looked back at the birth certificate, then to the adoption papers. She didn't know what to make of it.

Noticing a small piece of pink paper lying on the bed, she picked it up. It must have fallen from the envelope, but she wasn't certain. It was a telephone message. Her eyes ran across it. It was dated a few days after Johnny was born. "Louise—Call Irene Choya in Shiprock. *Immediately.* She says it's an emergency." Then it listed a phone number.

Shiprock? Mary's mother was born in Shiprock. Mary pulled out her mother's birth certificate and read the county. She was stunned when she saw San Juan County there, too. How odd. Her mother had lived there when she was a girl, but to Mary's knowledge had only visited a couple of times since.

Her mind tried to make sense of what she was seeing. Was Johnny adopted? Was he born in Shiprock? She started to scratch at the white out on the birth certificate, but she stopped. Whatever her mother's reason for asking for secrecy, it must be something important. She couldn't violate her mother's wishes. It was the one thing she would never do.

She secured the rest of the papers carefully back in the box with the photos. The birth certificate, the note, and the adoption papers, she folded and tucked back into the large envelope they'd come from. Securing the box closed, she put it back on the shelf and left the room with the new mystery clutched in her hand. None of it made sense.

Glancing down at the papers, she wondered what she should do. What was the reason for the deep secrecy and the serious tone of her mother's letter? Had she touched up the birth certificate to keep Johnny from finding out? It was crazy.

If she could, she would sleep on this one. She rationalized. None of this would help Johnny. And he had enough problems without bringing the skeletons out of his closet. If she hurt this way, how would he feel if he knew? At a loss, she sighed. Until she could get her head and her heart around this, she couldn't pursue it. She would honor her mother's request, but she wished she'd have explained the reasons behind it. Even so, it wasn't the most important thing going on at the moment.

Tomorrow, she had important decisions to make. She had to get the gallery ready so she could go to Los Alamos on Tuesday. It was a trip she had to make. What if there was something there? It might dictate the rest of Johnny's life. She couldn't lose sight of the importance of the trip no matter what else had happened. Nate was probably right. The description in the paper could fit a hundred kids, but she wasn't ready to give up.

The papers in her hand didn't change anything. It certainly didn't change the love in her heart for her little brother. And damn it all, she was going to move mountains if necessary to keep him from going to prison.

She ran her fingertips down her eyelids. Falling asleep had been difficult before, but it was totally out of the question tonight. If she stayed up, Grandpa would ask too many questions in the morning. Questions she had to table, for the moment. Best to get back in bed and pretend she could turn off her mind and get some rest. *Yeah, right.*

Nate adjusted the blinds above his desk, directing the morning sunlight out of his eyes and onto the desktop. He took a sip of coffee trying to medicate the emotional hangover he had from the weekend. His head was filled with confusion and his heart pulled him to places he'd never been.

He rubbed the sleep from his eyes, pushed the button on the CPU, and waited for the computer screen to come to life. Too bad he didn't have an on and off switch. That would make this a lot easier.

He watched the screen dance through its programs. This was a long shot. It was ridiculous. Was he following up on the article to satisfy his own curiosity or simply to please Mary? And to keep from closing what seemed to be the inevitable door between them.

He was still hoping to pull a rabbit out of the hat. Johnny's guilt was clear as the New Mexico morning sky and the longer he tried to avoid what was destined to come, the harder it became.

The weekend's surreal fallout clung to him like a sweater two sizes too small. He didn't have the luxury of staying in that realm. The rest of his life needed his attention. He'd feel better about what had happened the past few days if he could explain it, or make some connection. The sheer heart wrenching impact told him this must have some major significance. Otherwise, why? Why this and why now? *It's too much to be coincidence.* There it was, again.

The computer screen flashed asking for his login. Within seconds he was scrolling through the online version of the Los Alamos newspaper in search of further details. The Sunday news said the crime happened on Saturday night. The Monday paper had no new details, but referred to page four. One mouse click and the blood stopped in his veins.

His heartbeat quickened. He blinked his eyes in disbelief. In the middle of the article was a composite drawing. A drawing that bore a freakish resemblance to Johnny Begay. Then a more bizarre thing struck him. The boy's head was covered to above the eyebrows by a hat, darkened in the pencil sketch to almost black. A strange feeling came over him. A face flashed through his memory, but not with complete clarity. He rubbed his eyes and looked again.

"Holy crap." A voice came from over his shoulder. "What's Johnny's picture doing in the Los Alamos paper?" Coyote had come in unnoticed and stood behind Nate, observing the website from over his shoulder.

If not so stunned, the voice would have startled him. Nate turned away from the screen. "How long have you been standing there? No wonder they call you Coyote. You're stealthy as one."

"Sorry. Didn't mean to sneak up on you. What do you make of that?" He gestured toward the screen.

"I don't know, but I aim to find out." Nate glanced back toward the monitor trying to comprehend what it meant. The jaw line was the same. The nose was almost exact. A whirlwind of thoughts raced in his mind.

Mary's words echoed in his head. "When something jumps in my face, I think there's a reason why." Did Johnny have a double? Was it strong enough evidence to convince a jury? If he did use it to build a case, and he was wrong, could he live with himself if he set a potential cold-blooded killer loose on the streets?

"I saw Johnny this morning. He's having a hard time being in jail." Coyote tilted his head to one side and looked at the computer screen. "Do you think those witnesses could be wrong?"

Their eyes met. Nate chewed at his lip. "Not likely, but stranger things have happened." Glancing back, the hauntingly evil eyes of the drawing hit him like a bolt from the blue. Mrs. Savage had said she would never forget the eyes. Even in the pencil sketch, the look sent a chill down Nate's spine. And still, he wondered—

Coyote scratched the back of his head. "And there's your black hat. What do you make of it?"

"I guess I'm more curious about who the hell's wearing it." He had to leave it at that. The hat's origin wasn't a topic open for discussion.

Nate glanced at his watch. It was after ten. He hated to wait until morning to head to Los Alamos, but there was a mountain of paperwork on his desk he had to get through. Then there was Mary.

His insides twitched. The drawing bore more than enough resemblance to merit an investigation on the premise of mistaken identity. The rest of the similarities between the two cases were freakish. He could certainly justify checking it out. He shook his head. *Great.* His legal ego had just granted his hormones official permission for a road trip with Mary. He forced himself from the haze to listen to Coyote.

"I'd go up there for you, but I came by to tell you I'll be in and out this week. My dad's in bad shape—and I gotta be there."

Coyote's words pierced Nate's concentration. Embarrassed by his lack of presence in the moment, Nate looked in Coyote's direction as his words sunk in. "Sorry to hear that. Take care of what you need to. I'll handle things here." A pang of remorse ran through him as he considered his motives and lack of attention.

Coyote nodded and walked toward the door. Nate turned toward the telephone. He'd gladly handle it...and Mary. He clenched his teeth. Those damnable traitorous hormones refused to leave him alone.

———

"Mary?" Nate's voice came from the gallery phone like a welcome song to Mary's ears.

"Yes." Her breath caught in her throat.

"I'm heading for Los Alamos tomorrow morning at seven."

Her heartbeat quickened. "So you've found something?"

He hesitated. "Not necessarily. "I don't want to leave any stone unturned."

"I like your answer." She cleared her throat. "I'm going with you. You know that."

"I like your answer." His words hung in the air. After a moment he broke the silence. "I can pick you up in Chimayo."

"No. I'll come to you. I'm not going to tell Grandpa. I don't want to get his hopes up. I want him to think this is another buying trip for the gallery."

"Okay. However you want to handle it. But I think you're pretty good if you can pull the wool over Grandpa's eyes." He chuckled.

"The trick is to say nothing. The more you talk to him the more he can read your thoughts. I'll prepare as I always do for one of my trips and kiss him goodbye. That way I'm not lying to him and he's not trying to get inside my head. Trust me, I've had to learn how to keep a secret before—" The words tumbled off her tongue, but left an odd taste in her mouth.

Nate paused. "It seems to be a finely honed skill you've acquired."

"I'll be there at seven," she said, cutting the conversation short.

"By the way, bring along a picture of Johnny." Nate added.

"I can do that. I'll see you then."

She put down the phone. Her knees wobbled, but she blamed it more on fatigue than the sound of Nate's voice, even if the timing was more than coincidental.

The prospect of being alone with him made her insides knot up and sent a warm gush through her. As long as he was working on Johnny's behalf, she could relax for one more day.

But she'd have to watch herself. Emotions between them were strong—and dangerous.

Jim Smith flipped open the cell phone and put it to his ear. "Hello."

"Ernie's in. We'll take care of it, tonight." The words from the whispered voice at the other end curled Smith's lips into a twisted smile.

Smith spoke in a low voice. "Thought you'd see it my way."

"We'll come through on our end. You just come through on yours."

"You've got my word on it."

"Yeah. Your word. As long as it doesn't come with a knife in my back."

"You know better."

There was a click on the other end and 'call ended' flashed across the tiny screen on the phone.

"Oh well." Smith smiled broadly. God must be helping him out. *Helping me all the way to hell.* The thought raced through his mind.

Leaning back in the chair, he glanced at his watch. Four o'clock. He'd make arrangements to get the cash in the morning—when the job was done. He had faith in his own creativity to pull it off without a hitch, too. He wasn't a bad man. He wasn't evil. The world owed him this after what it had taken from him. After what he'd lost, he had one more chance to get even coming to him.

Gonzales and Ernie Gomez would get their money. When the deed was done. When Nakai was out of the way for good. Nakai and his haughty attitude and that hauntingly familiar face. Where had he known him before?

Smith let out a deep breath and tried to roll the tension from his shoulders. What did it matter? After tomorrow Nakai's brief history in Santa Fe would be done. There was a lot at stake, if things didn't go according to plan.

His head throbbed. His blood pressure must be through the roof. It would be over soon, but not soon enough. Damn, Nakai, anyway. He laid his head on the back of his chair and closed his eyes. Forcing himself to calm down, exhaustion claimed him, and he dozed.

Crow Feather surveyed his sons across the fire. There was a look of satisfaction in Black Hawk's eyes tonight. He had grown into a fine young warrior. One day, he would follow in the footsteps of his father. Soon Crow Feather would name him Hunting Chief. It would train him well to lead the tribe one day.

"Tomorrow Mourning Dove will become your mate. There will be ceremonies and feasting. I had planned a special gift for the occasion, but the plan has changed. And Lone Eagle has failed me, we must go on without it."

Black Hawk's lips curled in an evil grin. "I've already had my gift, Father. One I will long remember."

Crow Feather nodded. Whatever this gift, no doubt it pleased Black Hawk greatly. The evil gleam in his son's eye told him he must have taken a great trophy.

His eyes turned to his younger son, Two Birds. A dark shadow fell across his heart. There was something sinister about the child. The similarity of Two Birds to Raven angered him. But his deceitful brother was capable of anything. Mating with one of his brother's women was nothing compared to the hundreds of murderous acts he'd committed. There was nothing to do but keep silent and raise the boy as his own. Still, he would always wonder.

The boy's dark eyes flashed with impatience. "Why have you brought me here, Father?"

"To praise you for helping Black Hawk to find Lone Eagle and Mourning Dove. You have done well."

The boy beamed with pleasure. "I only regret he was not man enough to bring you back the bear."

"That is of no concern any longer. I brought you here for another purpose."

Two Birds leaned forward, listening intently. It was obvious the boy enjoyed the devious missions his father

*sent him on. Crow Feather smiled. At least, the boy was
useful to him.*

*"Raven came to me this morning. A small clan
moved into the valley. Strangers from the south. A pale
strange people who come in the name of peace." He
snorted. "Raven believes they have come in search of
others hiding here on the mesa. He believes their intent
was to seek him out and destroy him."*

"And my uncle has allowed this?"

*"Certainly not. He has killed them. But a child
escaped. He believes the child may lead him to the
others or they may try to help the girl. He wants you to
find the child and follow her."*

*Two Birds face lit with delight. "Will he kill them
when we find them?"*

*Crow Feather nodded. Uneasiness ran through his
heart at the boy's sadistic joy. There was little doubt he
was Raven's spawn.*

*Two Birds rose and turned back toward his father.
"What is to happen to Lone Eagle? Will you punish
him?"*

*Crow Feather raised his eyebrows. "I will see Lone
Eagle gets what he deserves. He will not deceive me
again." His laughter echoed through the stone
chamber.*

Smith opened his eyes. A sense of deep satisfaction
settled in his heart. Nakai would get his.

Wha—what? He must still be dreaming. The sound
of laughter reverberated in his ears. His heartbeat
quickened. He shook his head trying to pull himself
together and clear the fog from his brain. Was he still
asleep?

Realizing the sounds came from the outer office he
let out a sigh. Maybe he needed to lighten up on those
sleeping pills the doctor had prescribed. They were
causing him to doze off during the day—and they sure
made for some crazy dreams.

CHAPTER NINETEEN

Nate slid into the driver's seat as Mary fastened her seat belt. She was quiet and preoccupied.

"Why did you change your mind?" she asked softly. "Did you find something you haven't shared?"

Nate glanced over at the beguiling eyes looking in his direction and pretended to adjust the mirror. He shrugged. "We'll see." *Damn.* He was in trouble already.

But there was no point in raising her hopes or making any commitments. After all, it was just a drawing. The chance someone looked that much like Johnny was pretty far fetched.

Still, he couldn't get those eyes—or that hat—out of his mind. Frankly, he wasn't sure what he was looking for. Or how he would explain it, if he found it.

He glanced at Mary. She was nestled in the passenger seat in a white tank top and a pair of snug fitting jeans. Her raven hair was loose and pulled over one shoulder. A pair of dark glasses hid the mystery behind her eyes. Was it hot in here or was it him? He rolled the window down half way.

"I brought the picture of Johnny like you asked." Mary said as she tucked a large envelope next to her purse.

"Good." If they'd done a composite drawing, there was a witness out there somewhere. He wasn't going to mention the drawing, not yet, anyway.

Nate glanced at the clock on the dash. It was just after seven o'clock. He stretched a kink from his neck. He'd had too many other things on his mind this morning to go to the gym. Exercise was his way of relieving stress. It was rare he missed a workout, but today he'd made an exception.

He turned the key in the ignition and the engine purred. A smile spread across his face. He liked the feel of Mary beside him. The scent of her soft perfume tantalized his nose.

The car eased out of the parking lot and onto the street. The area was quiet as they passed through the twenty-five mile per hour speed zone. A man in sweat pants and a T-shirt crossed his lawn and picked up the morning paper glancing up as they passed. A young woman in spandex shorts walked a small black dog down the quiet street in the near-new neighborhood of stucco homes with classic flat Spanish-style roofs.

For the first time in his life, Nate realized he wouldn't mind settling down in a neighborhood like this. He was thirty-six years old. He'd sown his share of wild oats and had his share of wild, stuck-on-themselves women. Mary's exact opposite.

Mary had a simple and unpretentious beauty that drove him crazy. The woven handbag she carried he was certain she'd made herself. It had the slight scent of wool, typical of Navajo weaving. A scent he'd noticed the first time he'd seen her in her studio working at the loom. The smell of natural fiber mingled with oil paint. The aroma vivid in his memory, as was the picture of that first time he'd seen her. Strikingly beautiful, natural and somehow—so familiar.

Her eyes shone with a mystery and magic. She looked at life simply and gleaned her joy from the products of the earth and the work of her own hands. It was something he found unique to the hustle and bustle of the big cities he'd lived in all his life. Perhaps that was what drove him to help her and to want so badly to take the weight of Johnny's plight off her shoulders.

Even then, somewhere deep behind those eyes always lay a sadness and a sense of suspicion he couldn't seem to conquer. Perhaps the sadness was for the husband she'd lost. Nate wondered if Angelo still haunted her heart. A living competitor for her affection would have been easier for him to deal with. Taking on a memory was dicey business at the very least, even the memory of a man who had died in prison. What dreams that would never be and what unsatisfied emotions lived in her heart?

Taking a swig of coffee from his travel mug, he forced back the inner heat threatening his composure. He pushed the button to close the window and turned the air conditioner to high.

"Let me know if you get too cool," he said.

She shot him a half-smile and nodded, gazing out the window distractedly.

"Everything okay? What's on your mind this morning?" he asked, finally growing uncomfortable with the long silence.

"Johnny," she replied and said nothing more.

What could he say to make her feel better? "I wish I could guarantee he'll be all right. Or at least reassure you, but I can't. Not now."

She nodded, a sullen expression washing over her face.

Nate pushed his thoughts aside. He didn't want the negative to cloud the day. If he could pull Mary from her shell today—maybe at least a small portion of it could be about them—after they'd gone to Los Alamos.

They left the residential neighborhood and moved into the open country. The city lay just a couple of miles away, down the road that led through a small canyon. Nate concentrated on the road lined with small pine and cedar trees. Yes, this place was beginning to grow on him. Dry climate and all, it had a charm of its own. For the first time in his life, he'd actually had time to explore the inside of his own head—and heart.

Nate touched the accelerator and the car sped up along the straight stretch of highway. Sixty, then sixty-five. Approaching the curves up ahead, he let off the gas. The car didn't respond. He took his foot off the accelerator pedal and went for the brake. Pulling hard on the steering wheel, the tires squealed as he navigated the forty-five mile per hour curve at sixty-five.

He was aware Mary shot him a concerned look under a creased brow. On the other side of the curve lay an incline. Shifting in his seat, he hit the brake and the car slowed, but they were still going way too fast.

Nate's mind raced. Something was wrong. Why wasn't the brake working? No, the accelerator wasn't responding. He tapped the pedal and the car lurched forward. *Seventy. Eighty. Holy_shit.* They were flying down the hill. He focused his mind on the next sharp curve. Taking the outside lane, they swerved around it at breakneck speed. The tires screaming as he forced them to turn. The brake pedal was on the floor, but with no effect.

His mind flashed on the next incline ahead and the curves at the bottom. His sweaty palms froze to the wheel. Adrenaline raced through his body. All his mental faculties focused on keeping the car on the road.

The car screamed over the top of the next hill.

"Nathan—" Mary grabbed the handhold on the car door.

"Something's wrong. Hang on." His heart hammered in his chest. Beads of perspiration trickled down his forehead. Moving his right foot to the brake, he tried to get his left under the accelerator pedal. They were gaining speed on the hill.

"Dammit," he cried out over the scream of tires. *God, don't let anyone be coming.* Every muscle in his upper body tightened. He pulled the wheel with all his strength. The car barely made the curve. As he rounded it on the other side, a car flashed by going the other way. A few seconds earlier and—

"Dear Jesus," he whispered. *What the hell do I do?*

The hills were behind them. The car roared into a short straight stretch that lay between them and the horror in the back on Nate's mind. *A hairpin turn.* Nate pumped the brakes. The car slowed slightly. *Eighty-five. No freaking way we'll make it.*

The turn was coming up fast. He tried again to get under the accelerator pedal, but the toe of his boot was too thick. It wouldn't go under. If he took the turn too wide, he risked hitting the soft shoulder. Rolling the car would be eminent.

From the corner of his eye, he saw Mary's hand reach for the emergency brake. It would never be enough.

No more time to think. They were on the curve. It was worth a try. "Now," he screamed. She pulled the brake. The car skidded sideways. The tires screamed. They were dangerously close to the shoulder. He prayed the trees lining the roadside would keep them from flipping. But the impact alone would probably kill them. He braced for the crash.

In an eye blink, Mary's hand went from the brake to the ignition key. The engine stopped. The brake engaged. The car lurched to the left. Nate pulled to the right.

The sheer momentum forced them onto the soft shoulder and into the tree-lined curve. A tree limb smashed through the window on his side of the car. They skirted the side of the road, scraping the forest edge as they did. The car slowed and finally came to a stop partially off the roadway.

His first thought was of Mary. "You all right?" he blurted.

She let out a long shaky breath and nodded. "What on earth happened?" she asked, looking at him aghast.

He shrugged, making an animated gesture with his hands. "I don't know. The accelerator. Something broke, I guess."

"We could've been—"

He cut her off. "Don't say it. I know."

"Your head's bleeding." Mary reached and touched his temple.

Nate put his hand on his forehead and wiped at a scratch from the limb that came through the window. "It's nothing. I'm fine," he reassured her.

Mary put her trembling hand on the door handle and Nate climbed over the console. Moments later, on wobbly knees, they both stood next to the car and surveyed the damage.

"That was terrifying," Mary whispered.

"To say the least."

"What do we do now?"

"Call a tow truck." Nate pulled his cell phone from the back pocket of his jeans. Overcome by emotion, he pulled her to him and held her close for a moment. Kissing her on the forehead, he whispered. "Thank God, you weren't hurt."

He was surprised when she stepped into his arms. Clinging to him, her body trembled. She seemed small and vulnerable in his arms, though he knew better. It was the first time he'd ever seen her let her guard fall away. Only the second time he'd ever seen the stoic facade give way to female emotion. They stood there for a moment and she stepped away.

"You better make the call."

By eight forty-five they were standing in the lobby of Santa Fe Automotive. Nate was at the counter filling out some paperwork. A man in a pair of greasy blue coveralls had the hood of Nate's car up and was looking at the engine.

"I don't know what happened," Nate was saying to the man behind the counter. "It kept speeding up. I couldn't get it to stop."

Mary stood at the window watching for the taxi they'd called to take them back to Nate's condo. *Wow.* It had been a morning.

The man in the coveralls closed the hood and walked back into the shop. He wiped the grease from his hands with a red rag then rubbed his chin thoughtfully.

"Well?" Nate asked.

"Oh, it's repairable. It won't be cheap, but I'll write up an estimate for your insurance company. Probably be out of commission for at least a week though."

"Okay. I'll call my agent and get things rolling." Nate flipped open his cell and laid it on the counter. He pulled out his wallet and thumbed through it in search of his insurance information.

The burly bearded man observed him for a few seconds. "That'll fix the body, but it won't get you on the road. You got another problem there."

Nate nodded as he looked at a business card and began dialing numbers on his phone. "I know something went wrong mechanically. I'll have to get that fixed."

Mary observed the man in the coveralls. He seemed to be contemplating something. He rubbed his beard and looked back out the window at the car. He turned toward Nate again, this time with a frown on his face. "I can tell you what's wrong with it. It doesn't take a master mechanic to see the problem."

Nate looked up from what he was doing. "What happened?"

"You need a new throttle spring. That's why you couldn't stop."

"Really? I wonder what made that go bad."

The man raised one eyebrow. "Mister, I've been working on cars all my life. The spring in that car didn't go bad. It was cut in the middle slicker than a whistle."

Nate stopped and closed his phone. A concerned expression enveloped his face. "You're sure?"

The man scratched under his ear. "Sure as I'm standin' here in a pair of greasy coveralls. I'd bet my reputation on it."

Nate looked at Mary. She stood there stunned. *Cut?* The word hung in the air. How could such a thing happen? A knot formed in her stomach and fell to her feet. Her eyes met Nate's.

Nate stepped next to the man and spoke to him in a low voice. "I work for the Public Defender's office. I'd appreciate it if you kept what you told me under wraps for the moment."

The man shrugged. "Sure."

"Park it in one of your garage bays and I'll have someone come out and take prints as soon as possible. Proceed with ordering what you need for the bodywork. I'll get in touch with my insurance company and we'll take it from there."

"Yes, sir. We'll do just that."

"Thanks," Nate said as a white and black taxi pulled up by the door. He nodded to Mary, retrieved his briefcase from the floor next to the counter and the two walked purposefully to the cab.

Nate rattled off the address to the cabby and slammed the door. He was silent and thoughtful.

Mary couldn't stand it any longer. "And what do *you* make of what he told you?"

Nate nibbled the inside of his cheek. "I think somebody is damn determined to get me out of the picture." He paused. "Or—"

"Or what?"

"Or to keep me from going to Los Alamos. What do you think?"

"I think you're right, but I don't believe it matters which 'or' you choose. Either was done to accomplish the same end. So what do we do now?"

Nate's jaw rippled. "We go ahead with the day's plan. Only now you're in charge of transportation."

Mary nodded. "I agree." Her mind was doing back flips. If her chief suspect was capable of something like this, what else had he been capable of in the past? She'd always suspected Smith was manipulating her life. Now, it seemed she'd finally found someone who wasn't going to let him get away with it any longer. And they might have solid proof since it was affecting someone other than herself. He'd gone too far this time.

Half an hour later they were back on the road and on their way to Los Alamos. Nate had done a quick once over on her Pathfinder to be sure there were no signs of tampering.

He was quiet and thoughtful. They were both shaken from the accident and apprehensive until they got past the last of the curves coming down the road from Nate's place. Once they hit the highway and headed north, the tension seemed to ease.

"You know, Mary, I'm going to be honest with you. I had hoped this day would give us a chance to get to know one another better." He spoke as he looked out the passenger window. His elbow rested on the door and his hand cupped his chin.

Mary ran her teeth across her bottom lip. "If I told you the thought hadn't crossed my mind, I'd be lying." Her insides still vibrated from fright, but she'd composed herself. The realization both their lives could have ended that morning was fresh in her mind.

"I never dreamed it would start off the way it did. I'm sorry, if I put you in danger." Nate shook his head.

"Quite the contrary. I think it's me who has put you in harms way."

He turned toward her. "I'm sorry, I didn't take you seriously earlier. I'm not a hundred percent sure who or what we're up against here, but I want you to know I'm in it with you. As of this morning, it became my problem, too." He slid his hand across the seat. Grasping her right hand, as it rested on her knee, he gave it a squeeze.

A flood of warmth and a rush of emotion shot through her. She didn't know if she was ready for the feelings that wanted to bubble up inside her. After the beating and tampering with his car, she knew he wasn't working for Smith. That was no longer a wedge between them. But there was a hesitation in her heart.

"Are you saying you'll stay with Johnny and finish the case?"

"It appears to me somebody is trying to make damn sure he's convicted. So much so, they'll do anything to buy insurance to make it happen."

"And you? You didn't answer my question."

"Me? I'm determined to find anything I can that will get Johnny acquitted. And—" He shot her a suspicious look.

"Yes?"

"Then I'm going to find out what else is going on here."

Mary shifted in her seat, uncomfortable with the intense way he was looking at her. His eyes seemed to pierce right through her. "First things first," she said. "Let's see what we can find in Los Alamos. We'll be there in ten minutes."

Nate nodded and looked out the windshield. His jaw was set and she knew he was thinking hard about something. For now, she'd like to keep them both focused on Johnny. She was glad he wanted to know more about Smith, but she wasn't sure how he'd react when he knew the whole truth. More important, she wasn't sure how he'd feel about her if all the skeletons came out of the closet.

Maybe, she liked things better the way they were. Mystery was sometimes much more romantic and charming than the cold ugly truth. She pretended to be intent upon the road. An unsettled feeling pushed its way from her heart into her stomach. She didn't know Nate well enough to predict how he'd react to her past.

—————

The girl had been walking alone on a side street in downtown Los Alamos. She was pulled into an alley and strangled. Witnesses saw a boy run from the scene. Star Romero was the girl's name. The scenario was the same, only she hadn't been as lucky as Stellar. If you could call the state Stellar was in luck.

Nate sat in the passenger seat of Mary's Pathfinder and compared the police report from Santa Fe to the one written days before in Los Alamos. The police chief had been cooperative and Nate was grateful. He'd provided Nate with a copy of the report without the slightest hesitation.

Nate scanned the details. The suspect had long black hair—just above the shoulder—and was described as being of Native American decent. Too generic, Nate thought. *Way too many holes to build a defense around.* A black T-shirt and black jeans—both were as common as brown eyes. A million kids dressed like that.

He ran his finger further down the report. "Witnesses described the boy's eyes as strange and wild looking." Nate recalled the old woman's comments about Johnny's eyes. She said she would never forget them. But then came the million-dollar question. Were the eyes she'd described Johnny's?

Mary sat behind the steering wheel, leaning over the console and trying to read bits and pieces of the report. He knew he wasn't being accommodating, but he preferred to select the information he passed to her. If she read the report herself, she would make way too much of the similarities...and make judgments based on what she was hoping to find here. He was protecting her in his way, hoping to cushion the fall of disappointment if this turned into a wild goose chase.

She pressed closer. Not quite touching, he could feel the warmth of her body close to his—or else he wanted to so badly he imagined he did. Her breast brushed lightly against his arm. He glanced over at her. He was sure it was her breast. Nate pulled at the collar of his shirt. It sure was one hell of a hot day, and it was getting hotter by the minute.

He tried to focus on the report as he ran his forefinger across the words. There it was, the witnesses' description. "The boy wore a black hat— pulled low over strange looking eyes." It was in the drawing. He knew it had to be somewhere in the pages. His heart jumped to his throat as he read the words that followed. "Something was hanging from the brim. I believe it was a feather. Yes. A black and white feather."

Nate's mind flashed. A picture blazed in his memory. The detail he'd been unable to pull from the vision embedded in his psyche. That image of the hat had been there—the feather hanging from its brim was the missing piece.

Nate put his hand over his eyes and rested his head back on the headrest. Emotion tightened his throat as the realization swept over him. Why hadn't he been able to pull that detail from his own mind? He swallowed hard.

Mary leaned closer. "What is it?"

Nate shook his head. "Later," he said through constricted vocal cords.

At that moment, a policeman clad in a dark blue uniform approached Nate's side of the car. "Mr. Nakai?"

Nate nodded his response.

"The chief asked me to bring you this. He thought it might be helpful."

Nate reached out the window as the officer handed him a copy of the composite drawing.

Mary gasped as it passed into Nate's hands. "Oh, my God," she whispered breathlessly. She glanced at Nate in complete amazement. Her index finger pushed against the indentation of her upper lip as she stared at the picture in stunned silence.

Nate's reaction surprised himself. The uncanny likeness of the boy in the sketch to Johnny was more prominent with the drawing in his hands than it had been viewing it on the Internet.

"How can it be?" Mary asked. "Johnny was in jail in Santa Fe on Saturday night. He was nowhere near here."

"I don't know," Nate replied. "The resemblance is amazing."

Mary turned her head to one side. "He's Johnny, but his eyes aren't Johnny's." She shivered. "The eyes are like a wild animal."

Nate nodded.

She nudged him. "You haven't said much. What are you thinking?"

Nate considered what was on his mind. Maybe it was time to share what troubled his soul. He reached around the seat and pulled his jacket from behind him. From the pocket he pulled a small plastic bag. Nestled in the protective covering were the five feathers, the four he'd brought from Mesa Verde and the one the nurse said was found in Stellar's hand.

He reached into the bag and pulled out the black and white one.

"What's that?" Mary asked.

"Stellar had it in her hand when she arrived at the hospital."

Mary took it from him and examined it. "I'd say it came from a magpie. A lot of them hang around the lean-to where the sheep shelter. I see feathers like these all the time."

A picture flashed through Nate's mind of the magpie he'd seen in the alley where Stellar was attacked. It was possible Stellar had picked it up off the ground before she was assaulted. It would be a bizarre coincidence if the feather on the boy's hat was a magpie feather. Nate rubbed his chin.

"Why do you think it's important?" Mary asked.

"The boy who killed the girl here had a feather hanging from the brim of his hat."

Mary looked back at the drawing. "There isn't one in the picture."

"No. But there's one in the witnesses' statement in the police report."

"Where?"

Nate skimmed the paragraph he'd read and pointed to the section. Mary took it from him.

"A black and white feather." She laid the report in her lap. After a moment of contemplation she spoke softly. "Johnny owns a black hat."

Nate's gut tightened. "He does?"

"Yes. But it isn't round like this one." She pointed at the drawing. "Johnny's is a cowboy hat."

"Mary. You know I have to ask this." Nate looked out the passenger's window as the images from his vision chased through his head. "Was he wearing it when he went into Santa Fe with his friends?"

"No."

"You're positive."

"Absolutely. It's lying on his bed. I saw it the other day."

"Well, then," Nate sighed. "That would bring us back to the feather. And the drawing." Nate studied the picture in his hand.

He considered the drawing, the police report and the feather. It was entirely possible he had enough to build a case for Johnny. His heart suddenly felt a little lighter.

Mary ran a hand through her black hair and rested an elbow on the steering wheel. Nate could tell she was deep in thought about something. She reached down and picked up the envelope she'd brought with her and pulled out the photograph of Johnny. She held it next to the drawing.

With the exception of the eyes, it could be Johnny peering out from under the hat. Mary looked at the feather. "The hat bothers me. And the fact you asked me about Johnny's hat? I've read the police reports and the eyewitness statements. There wasn't anything about a hat in either of them."

"No, there wasn't," Nate replied. "But the boy who attacked Stellar was wearing one."

Mary gave him an odd look and shook her head. "Why do you say that?"

He ran his hand down his chin. "Mary—"

"Yes?" She leaned closer.

"I haven't told you everything about this case—" He moved nervously in his seat avoiding her eyes. How the hell could he tell her the truth? His view of the crime didn't exactly fall in the norm.

"What are you getting at? I have a right to know if you've uncovered some new evidence."

His gritted his teeth and his jaw rippled.

She seemed to sense he was contemplating telling her something important. Frustration made its way into her voice. "Look. I read the police report. There was no mention of a hat. This is the first I've heard of it. It makes me angry when you act as if what's going on here is none of my business."

Nate nodded and leaned toward her. Making her angry wasn't what he wanted, but he'd be taking a bigger risk if he told her how he knew. There had been enough barriers between them. He couldn't justify adding anymore. Not now. She was there with him, within the touch of his hand, alone with him for a few more hours, if he didn't blow it.

Nate looked into her brown eyes. Shades of green glinted in them as the sun beams danced through the windshield.

She met his gaze, an odd expression forming behind her eyes. Her face was so close. He couldn't help himself. He put his hand on her cheek and leaned closer.

Nate's cell phone jangled in his jacket pocket. *Lousy timing.* He answered when he saw it was Coyote calling.

"What's up, man?"

"Got your message about the accident. You two okay?"

"Luck was with us. Did you get down to the garage to fingerprint the car, yet."

"No, but I'll get on it. I actually called for another reason."

"You sound serious. What's going on?"

"DNA tests came back on the tissue samples from under Stellar's fingernails. It was a perfect match." Nate's mouth fell open. He dropped his hand to his lap with the cell phone in it. It was like a slap across the face.

"Hello. Hello." Coyote's voice came from the phone. Mary shot a concerned look at Nate. She must be reading the look he knew was on his face.

For her sake, he had to get it together. "Thanks for the info." His voice was shaky.

"Don't give up. You know it may not be admissible in court. I'll check out the car and get back to you."

"Thanks." Nate flipped the phone closed. Where did that leave him? At last he'd found a glimmer of hope and suddenly it was snatched away. In his mind, DNA evidence didn't lie. A person who looked like him was possible, someone with the same DNA, not a snowball's chance in hell.

"What's wrong?" Mary demanded. "Something's happened. I can see it in your face."

He needed time to think this through. How could he stop it from ruining this day? The only day he might ever have with her. He shook his head and reached for her hand.

She pulled away. Fire flashed in her eyes. "Why do you constantly avoid my questions?"

Nate opened his mouth and the words seemed to spew out without any restraint. "I want you to understand something, Mary. I know you love Johnny. But there are times when I think it's best not to share things with you." He forced his hand into hers. "Your love and devotion for him are the reasons I sometimes chose to keep my silence. On the other side of the coin, you know more about him than anyone else on earth, so I look to you for answers. It isn't my intention to make you angry or frustrated." He wasn't going to tell her about the DNA no matter how angry it made her. Not now. Not today.

She was stunned by his outburst. She pressed her lips tight together and rolled her eyes. "I heard Coyote say DNA. They did a DNA test and it came back positive, didn't it?"

Nate let out a sigh. Her intuition was too right on, for her own good. He nodded. "It hurts my theory. I can explain the fact this boy looks like him." He held up the drawing. "I sure as hell can't explain the DNA."

Her jaw rippled. She grew silent. Obviously, something was working in her mind. Sunlight glistened in a tear that trickled from the corner of her eye. "Well, you were dead on about one thing. I know

Johnny. Or at least I thought I knew all there was to know about him—" A cloud crossed her face and he detected a tremble in her chin.

"What are you talking about?"

"It probably isn't important," she said the words so quickly, he knew better. She stared out the driver's side window and chewed on her thumbnail.

He wondered what it was she wasn't saying. But when it came to being honest, he had no room to call her on the carpet. Guilt crept into his insides. With the DNA test results, he was feeling uncertain about his decision to steal time with Mary. This was a dead end case, and it looked bleaker all the time. He glanced at the picture in his hands. Even with the close resemblance, the DNA proof was bound to screw them in court.

The relationship he wanted with Mary violated his code of ethics as an attorney and put the case in jeopardy. Using this opportunity to steal time with her and maybe steal her heart, betrayed his personal code. Without something more to go on, he should pull the plug on it here. But one piece of evidence remained. Johnny was in jail on Saturday night. At the same time this boy killed his victim in Los Alamos.

This was something Nate had to chase down, but he had to do it alone. He couldn't risk involving Mary, or getting involved with her. It was time to end the adventure. And time to stop the charade and step away.

"I think it's time we head back to Santa Fe," he said. His heart jumped into his throat at the sound of his own words.

Mary turned the key in the ignition. "I'll take you back, then I have some business to attend to."

"Something for the gallery?" he asked, attempting to make small talk.

"No. Something personal—in Shiprock." She glanced at the envelope on the seat beside her and rubbed her lips together.

"Oh," he said. "How far away is that?"

"Four hours or so." It was obvious to him the conversation was forced. Something was heavy on her mind.

"Long drive by yourself." He hadn't meant to say it. He couldn't seem to get his mouth or his brain to cooperate.

She nodded, nervously tapping on the steering wheel as she got back on the highway and headed slowly back in the direction they'd come.

"I have important things to do today, too. Otherwise—"

"Otherwise, what, Nate?" she demanded.

"I'm not being honest with you," he replied. "Johnny's case doesn't have a snowball's chance in hell with those DNA results. I want to follow up on this drawing, but I don't know if it's enough alone to turn this case around." Emotion took over, and his logic and propriety stepped aside. "Dammit. I don't know why you're going to Shiprock, but I want to spend the day with you."

Quickly, Mary brushed moisture from her cheek and repositioned her sunglasses over her clouded eyes. She struggled with the words. "Something's been on my mind. And now with this drawing—" Reaching into the envelope that had held the photograph, she pulled out several sheets of paper. She looked at him sternly. "Sharing this with you isn't easy. And you have to promise me that you'll never tell another living soul— unless it will keep Johnny from going to prison."

Nate raised his hand symbolic of taking an oath.

She handed him the papers. "I found these when I was looking through my mother's pictures."

"What is it?" Nate asked.

"Johnny's adopted. And I never knew."

A thick silence hung in the air as Nate thumbed through the pages. He had to say it. "But he's your brother. How could you have not known?"

"That's a long story. The point is, I didn't."

"So what now?"

"It seems there are some things I don't know about him and I'm thinking, with this DNA stuff surfacing, it could be important to find out more about where Johnny came from."

Nate scratched his jaw. "I agree."

"Well, the papers say he was born in Shiprock. I'm going there. I can take you back to Santa Fe first, but I'm going today."

Nate shrugged. "You know. I've stuck with you and Johnny this long. I'm not bailing now." He could justify following through on this. Maybe he could get his ethical attorney to sit in the backseat for one day.

Mary shot him a half-smile. "Good. I could use your help."

She turned the car around in the street.

CHAPTER TWENTY

Ten miles outside of Los Alamos, Mary pulled off the road. The Pathfinder bumped across the pavement edge and through the rutted dirt at the side of the highway. A tumbleweed skittered across the asphalt followed by a small dust cloud, both carried by a hot breeze.

"Something wrong?" Nate asked.

"I need some air." Mary got out of the vehicle and stood by the roadside. Her head was beginning to pound and she was queasy. She stooped forward, resting her hands on her knees.

Nate followed. "You feeling okay?"

She nodded. This sick feeling had begun to build the moment they left Los Alamos and headed for Shiprock. A stone had settled in her stomach.

"Maybe you're having a delayed reaction from the accident. The day didn't get off to a good start. I guess a brush with death before breakfast could set the tone for the whole day."

"To say the least." Standing upright, she put her hand on her forehead. "I think my mind's on overload and it's trying to escape through my ears." She tried to smile and make light of the physical symptoms she knew were manifested by an emotional storm brewing in her heart.

"That can't be good." He grinned.

He was silent as he watched her stretch and take a few deep breaths.

"There is something bothering me. I can't do this."

Nate looked surprised. "What do you mean?"

"I can't go on to Shiprock. We have to turn around and go home."

Nate scratched his head. "What?"

She looked at him. She was making a fool of herself. Of course, they had to go. She fumbled for an excuse for her behavior. "I don't know what to make of that sketch and now I've got us flying off half-cocked to chase down this crazy lead. I'm not even sure what we're looking for."

"Sometimes leads take you to dead ends, but every lead is a possibility." Nate shrugged as he leaned against the vehicle with hands in his pants pockets. "I'd rather chase dead ends than miss the one thing that can turn a case around. Come on. I'll drive and you can formulate a plan for when we get there. Maybe, that will help you relax."

She nodded reluctantly. She would feel better if he were behind the wheel. Trying to shake off the tension and her misgivings, she got into the car.

Mary sank back in the seat, hoping to calm herself. Nate buckled the seatbelt and adjusted the mirrors. Glancing at him from the corner of her eye, she wondered if he would understand if she told him what was gnawing away at her insides. "I don't know if I'm doing the right thing," she said.

"Why would you say that?" he asked, his brow deepening. He was serious and her comment seemed to hit him wrong.

Mary looked in his intense eyes. She hesitated. Maybe this wasn't the time to share her innermost feelings with him. Nate appeared to be a man on a mission.

He reached for the envelope on the floor and put it in her lap. "See what information you can glean from the birth certificate that will help us when we get to Shiprock."

Mary reluctantly pulled out the document. She laid it in her lap and looked at it.

"Well?" he asked as he started the car.

"Well, what?"

He frowned. "There's obviously been a lot of white out slathered on there. What say you scratch some of it off and see what it's hiding."

Mary held it in her hand and turned it over. His flippant attitude grated on her. It wasn't his family's personal affairs about to be split open and dissected. "I'm not sure I can do that."

"What?" He turned toward her and looked perplexed.

"I'm sorry. I don't feel right about this."

"But you have to do it. That piece of paper is all we have to go on."

She nodded. "I know."

"Then what's the problem?" Annoyance crept into his voice.

"Look, Nate, I've got a knot in my stomach the size of Texas because I'm caught between two things very important to me. I'd do anything to help Johnny but I'm violating a sacred trust."

"Sacred trust? That sounds pretty dramatic."

"Don't criticize what you don't understand." Mary struggled to keep her tone calm. "My mother asked me on her death bed to take care of Johnny. And that's what I'm trying to do." She put her hands on her head. "But there was a note with the papers begging me to keep his secret safe. In my heart, I know there had to be a good reason. I have a bad feeling she wouldn't want me to do this."

Nate's face softened with understanding. "For what it's worth, I think she'd forgive you under these circumstances."

Mary fought the tightness in her throat. "My mother never lied to me. And until the night before last, I didn't think she'd ever kept a secret from me.

The magnitude of this is hard for me to fathom. I shouldn't have shared this with you, but I didn't know what else to do. How would you feel if you suddenly found out your brother wasn't your blood relative?"

Nate paused and looked her in the eye. "Does it change anything?"

She shook her head and looked down at the papers in her lap. "Of course not. He's my brother regardless of what it says on a piece of paper."

"Then nothing else matters. I'll lay it on the line. Johnny's case is a dead end road and we're fresh out of options." He took a deep breath and stared out the windshield. "It's your decision. Your mother isn't here to give you her blessing. Are we going to Shiprock or not?"

Mary bit her lower lip. Her heart was in her throat. "Of course, we are. I just pray to God this knot in my belly isn't an omen of what we're going to find."

Nate put the car in gear and pulled back onto the highway as a brown lizard scurried across the road.

"Did you see that?" Nate's effort to change the subject was obvious.

"Grandpa says if a lizard crosses in front of you it means there's a big rain coming." Mary took a deep breath. Truthfully, she was glad to think about something else.

Nate raised his eyebrows. "Grandpa, huh? Something he came up with while smoking his peyote?"

A soft laugh escaped her lips. "No. These things are part of his Navajo upbringing. He still practices the old ways of our people."

Nate was silent for a few moments. "Do you believe in omens?"

"Sometimes. You?"

"A month ago I'd have said no, but I've had reason to question their validity since."

"So what changed your mind?"

He pursed his lips. "A painting, your Grandpa—and a handful of feathers. That'll do for now."

Mary picked up the bag containing the feather he'd shown her earlier. Curiosity wouldn't allow her to keep silent as she examined the contents through the plastic. "There's more than one feather in here. Do the others have some significance, too?"

Nate shrugged. "I don't know—yet."

"I believe feathers always have significance. They usually carry a message. More so when you find them in numbers like this."

"Then you think these could mean something?" Nate appeared to be listening intently.

"A storm of feathers is said by the elders to mean the spirits of the dead are trying to communicate with you." An unexpected shiver ran through her. She rubbed the goose flesh on her arms and went on. "Usually, it's a relative or your ancestry offering guidance or delivering a message."

An odd expression crossed Nate's face and he turned pale. He didn't speak.

Mary went on. "Perhaps the feather from Stellar's hand came to lead you to the truth."

Nate ran his hand across his chin, a look of deep thoughtfulness on his face. "They all came to me in a strange way, but I haven't found their importance, yet."

"Feathers bring us answers. There's an old prayer of my people that says to keep the feather near you all day and the next day you will find what you seek. When your answers come, thank the feather and return it to the Earth Mother. Instead of throwing these in the backseat, maybe you should put them in your shirt, near your heart." She looked up from the bag and observed his attentive expression. "I may be wrong, but I think it's your heart that's searching for answers."

Nate glanced away from the road for a second and met her gaze as he took the bag from her. He tucked it between the buttons of his shirt. "Next to my heart," he said softly.

She wasn't sure what he was looking for, but her intuition said it was far more than he'd shared. Under his strong and proud facade, she sensed a newfound vulnerability had surfaced. In the short time she'd known him, she'd seen changes in his demeanor and a side of him that would be dangerously easy to love—if only her heart were free of the past.

Closing her eyes, she laid her head back on the headrest and pushed away the thoughts racing through her pounding head.

Goose bumps ran the length of Nate's spine when the towering stone mass came into view. He pulled to the side of the road and climbed from the car. Something stirred in his soul when he saw it, as if the earth moved beneath his feet. "*De ja vu*," he whispered. The words tumbled from his lips before they registered in his mind. He had seen this rock before. Its energy was familiar to him—too familiar to push aside as a passing thought.

"*Tse Bi dahi*," Mary said. "Rock with wings. That's the name my people gave it long ago. The name Shiprock came later."

"Then you've been here before?" he asked without taking his eyes from the rock.

"Once, when I was a small child." Mary stirred in her seat. "My mother actually grew up on the Shiprock reservation."

Nate forced his eyes from the magic of the pinnacle that jutted from the barren New Mexico desert. "Then, why does the possibility of Johnny being born here surprise you?"

"My mother hadn't been here since she brought us here...not that I know of. That would have been more than ten years before Johnny was born."

"Still, she must have known someone here."

Mary shook her head. "All her family had moved on. There was no one she kept in touch with. But then it seems there were things I didn't know about my mother." She gave him a half smile, but there was a sad look in her eyes.

"I didn't mean to wake you by stopping," Nate apologized. "It was the rock."

"It obviously affected you deeply or you wouldn't have reacted as you did."

"I have a strange feeling I've seen it before." He glanced over at her wondering how she would react. "But that's silly, I guess. I've never been here." Looking down, he scuffed his shoe in the sandy dirt by the roadside.

"I don't think it's silly. One never knows when the spirits will choose to speak. Or what they will choose to tell us."

The cold chill once again raced up his backbone. "You're starting to sound like Grandpa."

She smiled. "Sorry. Guess it runs in the family." She stretched and pulled her long black hair over one shoulder. "I didn't mean to sleep most of the way. I guess I was more exhausted than I realized."

Nate shot her a mischievous smile. "It's okay, you didn't snore—much."

He climbed back behind the wheel. "How much further do you think it is to Shiprock?"

"The map says ten miles."

"Good. We'll stop and ask some questions."

She glanced down at the papers in her lap. "I got some of the white out off, but it's awfully heavy and stuck tight in places. I'll keep working on it."

"Hard telling how long it's been there. It may be tedious to get it to come off without damaging the print underneath."

Fifteen minutes later they pulled into the town of Shiprock.

"Well, since my co-pilot's been slacking and we don't know where we're headed, I'd say a pit stop is in order." He glanced at his watch. "It's after two o'clock. How about we get a bite to eat while you decipher the evidence?" He pulled into a parking space in front of a sandwich shop sporting a sign sporting two giant green chilies that read, "Best Subs in New Mexico."

"You're on. I'm ravenous." The rest appeared to have done her some good. The stress lines in her face had relaxed and her eyes didn't look as tired. He shot her a wink.

She gave him a genuine smile for the first time all day. A rush of warmth shot through him. She was a beautiful woman. Despite her secrets and her hang-ups, she touched his heart in places that had been cold and dark for a long, long time. He hadn't told her, but he could have cared less if she slept all the way. Most important, she was with him. That alone made him feel good inside. It just seemed right.

Nate shook his head. Even if it was just for the day, he was content. He'd never allow himself to think someday he might break through the stone wall she kept around her, but that smile momentarily gave him hope.

Nate got out of the car and walked around to open her door. The glint in her eye told him she was both surprised and pleased by the simple action. His gut said not many men had treated Mary the way she deserved to be treated. As they walked into the restaurant, a question came into his mind. Her first priority was always caring for Grandpa and Johnny. He wondered who took care of Mary, or if anyone ever had.

Mary took a seat in a booth and spread the birth certificate on the table. "Order me something and I'll keep working on this goop."

Nate nodded, but kept his eyes on her as he stood at the counter and ordered Southwest chicken subs and lemonades. She pulled her long black hair behind one ear and scratched at the page in front of her. With her face close to the paper, she gently brushed away the chips of dried white out as she went. It was going to be time consuming, but today he was in no hurry. No hurry, whatsoever.

"I don't know," she said as he approached the table carrying the tray of food and drinks.

"Did you find anything?"

"I'm not having much luck with the parent's names. They're covered with so much of this stuff."

Nate scooted the certificate across the table and looked at it. "That kind of looks like a 'c' and an 'h' under the physicians name. What do you think?"

"C-H?" Mary reached into the envelope and pulled out a pink slip of paper. "I found a note with the name Irene Choula written on it. Do you suppose?"

A boy in a tan shirt shook his jet-black hair back from his face as he wiped down the booth across from them. He stopped for a second and looked in their direction.

"Irene Choula?"

Nate ran his nail across the words. "Could be. What does the note say?"

"Yeah. It was to my mother and basically says call Irene Choula in Shiprock. It was dated five days after Johnny was born. It said it was urgent."

"Any idea who she is?" Nate reached for the note.

Mary shook her head.

The boy looked over at them again, stopped what he was doing and approached their table. "Sorry to eavesdrop on your conversation. Do you know my Grandma Irene?"

Mary shot Nate a surprised glance. "Your grandmother?"

"Irene Choula. You know her?"

"No." Mary shook her head. "I found her name on this piece of paper."

The boy glanced at the birth certificate and smiled. "She's signed lots of birth certificates. Delivering babies is what she does."

"Really," Nate interjected. "Could you tell us where we can find her?"

The boy shrugged. "She lives next door to me. I get off in twenty minutes, if you want to follow me, I'll take you there."

"Well, if you think it's all right," Mary stammered and looked over at Nate. "I wouldn't want to show up at her house out of the blue."

Twisting the white towel he'd used to wipe the booths, he thought for a moment. "I can give her a call and tell her we're coming," he called over his shoulder as he turned toward the counter.

"Well, I'll be damned," Nate said. "I didn't think it would be that easy."

Mary raised her eyebrow. "Or else fate had a hand in it."

"We were obviously given a bit of luck from somewhere."

"If she's delivered all the babies he says she has, she may not remember." A crease furrowed Mary's brow.

"Well, one thing's for certain. If we don't talk to her, we'll never know. Maybe, what we have will help her memory."

Mary scratched more intently at the paper. "I'm afraid to press too hard for fear I'll make a hole in it."

Nate took a dime from his pocket and slid it across the table. "Here, see if this helps."

Mary took the coin and chipped gently at a white blob. In a few minutes she'd uncovered Irene Choula's name. As he ate, she continued to work on the other sections. "Lonewolf," she whispered after a few minutes.

"What?" Nate's attention peaked.

"The father's last name. It looks like Lonewolf?"

An uncomfortable feeling ran through Nate. He'd heard that name before, but he didn't want to say anything yet.

The boy walked out from behind the counter and Mary picked up her purse. "My grandmother says she'll talk to you if you want to come by. Follow me."

They walked outside and the boy climbed onto a black bicycle leaned against the side of the building. "It's a couple of miles outside of town." The boy called as he pedaled down the street and Nate and Mary got into the car. Nate kept the boy in sight as they maneuvered down the main street of the small town. In a few minutes, they were out in the country. They passed several signs that referred to the Shiprock Reservation.

Mary was silent.

"What are you thinking?" Nate asked.

"It's strange to be here. It's a place my mother kept distant from our family."

"I know this is bothering you. But we're doing what we have to do. We'll know later if it's right." He reached over and squeezed her hand. Her hand seemed small in his. She didn't return the gesture, but this time she didn't pull away. He was pleased with that simple milestone. If nothing else, he'd learned to appreciate baby steps when it came to Mary. There was no fast track to this woman's heart.

A short distance out of town, the boy turned onto a dirt road and headed west into the sun. Though Nate squinted to see ahead of him, the scrubby dried grasses and the dry arroyo that skirted the roadside sent their own message about the hard life of the Navajo who claimed this as their homeland. Two brown and white paint horses grubbed at the grass several yards away. Their ribs were startlingly visible through their taut hides.

"Kind of on the thin side, aren't they?" Nate observed.

"Animals here live off the land, like the people. It is the way of things."

"Oh," Nate said. Her matter-of-fact tone didn't leave much room for continuing conversation on the subject. He glanced over at her.

"It's not for those from the outside to judge the ways of the Diné. It's best not to question what you don't understand."

Nate nodded. The only word of Navajo he knew was Diné. *The people.* He thought of Alex's letter and Grandpa's visit. They both said Navajo blood flowed in his own veins. The kachina was Hopi—his other bloodline. Grandpa's words echoed in his ears, his destiny was tied to that connection. He'd grown up in a place and a culture a million ethnic miles away from the simplicity of this place, but somewhere in his heart beat the drums of a native people he was beginning to get to know—and to find his way back to. His throat tightened as the thoughts stirred his spirit.

The boy pulled up to a small modular home. A few yards away was a white trailer. He climbed from his bike and walked over to the Pathfinder. Pointing to the trailer, the boy said, "Grandma Irene lives over there. She knows you're coming."

"Thanks for your help." Nate acknowledged the boy, then took a deep breath and looked over at Mary.

"Well, here goes," she said.

Opening her door before he had a chance, she walked with determination around a shiny dark-blue pickup truck parked next to the front porch. Clutching the envelope and her purse to her chest, she navigated around a gangly, but friendly, brown dog and knocked gently on the front door.

A middle-aged woman with long black hair opened the door. "Yes?"

"Are you Irene Choula?" Mary took the lead as Nate sauntered up the wooden stairs to the trailer and the dog gave a low throaty growl, eyeing him suspiciously.

The woman offered her hand. "I'm Irene. My grandson said you wished to speak to me." Irene was slightly taller than Mary, about five-foot-six by Nate's estimate. She wore a denim shirt loosely over a white blouse and a teal broomstick skirt that hung to her ankles. She certainly didn't look old enough to be the boy's grandmother.

Mary graciously clasped the woman's hand. "Thank you for letting us come. My name is Mary and this is Nate. Nate Nakai." Mary nodded toward Nate and the woman acknowledged him as she listened. "We've come from Santa Fe in search of some information about my brother."

"I don't know that I can help you—"

Mary pulled out the birth certificate and held it out to Irene. Taking it in her hand, Irene took a pair of reading glasses that hung from a gold chain around her neck and perched them on her nose. She squinted and examined the paper closely then looked at Mary with a question in her eyes. "This boy is your brother?"

"Yes. I've recently learned that my parents adopted him. I know nothing about where he came from. If there's anything you remember about him, it might help."

A crease formed in Irene's brow as she looked at the certificate then back to Mary. Nate could tell by the cloud on her face and the ripple of her jaw that something was working behind her dark eyes. She rubbed her chin and studied the document in silence.

"My mother lived here on the Shiprock reservation when she was a child," Mary offered.

"What is your mother's name?" Irene asked.

"Louisa Begay. Louisa Joseph was her maiden name."

Irene looked back at the papers. A smile tugged at the corners of her mouth. "I remember Louisa. She was a good woman." A grim look quickly overtook the smile. "Lonewolf." Her eyes darkened. "Perhaps you should come in." Irene opened the door. As Mary stepped into the trailer, she cast a glance at Nate. "Him, too." Irene motioned toward him. "Come inside, out of the heat."

Nate followed her into the small home. The trailer was clean and cozy. Colorful Navajo rugs covered the floors and hand painted pottery adorned a simple wooden shelf in a corner of the dining room. A big screen television occupied one end of the living room where a red sofa and a large black leather recliner were arranged in front of the screen.

"Please sit." Irene motioned toward the chairs at the dining room table. Nate and Mary sat and Irene pulled up a chair directly across from them.

"Perhaps, I should first ask you what you want to know." Irene spoke carefully.

"If you knew my mother, you must know something about—the adoption," Mary formed the words carefully. Nate knew this was one of the most difficult things she'd ever had to do. Breaking her mother's trust wasn't something she'd done lightly.

Nate studied Irene as she rubbed her cheeks, curious what lay behind her reluctant gestures. Whatever was on her mind wasn't pleasant. She shot him a concerned look.

"I think we'd like to hear anything you can remember about the birth and the family," Nate prompted. "We're looking for the facts."

He didn't have a good feeling about Irene's body language, but for Johnny's sake he had to let the chips fall where they would. He glanced at Mary. Even, if it meant he had to pick Mary up afterward.

CHAPTER TWENTY-ONE

The air was filled with the familiar scent of pine incense and ethereal flute music floated softly from a CD player on the kitchen counter. The woman and her home were both open and friendly. But Mary's heart was beating faster than normal. She wanted answers yet, she was afraid to hear the truth. She hadn't accepted what she'd learned about her family in the last days. Truthfully, she wanted to turn back the clock and not know any of it.

Nate glanced at her. Did he have any idea how hard it was for her to be here, to ask these questions? She thought she detected a soft glint in his eye, hiding behind his hard as steel demeanor that typified his professional side. His questions were all business. Hers came from an aching heart.

"I don't know what I'm looking for. I want to know how Johnny came to be with my parents." Mary reached into the envelope and pulled out the slip of pink paper she'd found among her mother's pictures. "When we started this trip, I didn't know your signature was on the birth certificate. I only found that out this afternoon. I found this telephone message with my brother's adoption papers. It and the Shiprock place of birth brought me here."

Mary handed the note to Irene. She read the message. Her face changed as she scanned the words. It seemed a storm rose up from her soul and settled in her features.

"Oh my," she said, as she let out a long breath.

"Then, you remember this?" Mary's hopes rose, but her woman's intuition had picked up strange vibrations since they arrived.

"Not likely, I'll ever forget." Irene shook her head and handed the paper back to Mary.

Mary's eyes went to Nate's and a sinking feeling washed through her. The look on the woman's face said, whatever it was she would never forget still troubled her fifteen years later.

"Then, there are things you can tell me about my brother?"

Irene raised one eyebrow and spoke at last. "Your brother Johnny was born here on the reservation. I caught him in my own two hands when he was pushed from his mother's womb." She looked down at her hands as if envisioning the moment. "I'm a midwife by trade, but I knew your family long before."

"Then you know who his real mother is?"

She sized up Mary before she answered. "I *knew* her."

"Oh. She's—" Mary was aware a shadow crossed her face.

"Dead. Yes." She nodded.

Mary bit her lip. She had to go on. "That explains why you signed the birth certificate and why he needed a home. But how did he end up in Santa Fe with my mother and father?"

Irene appeared to choose her words carefully. She spoke slowly. "I knew Johnny's mother and I knew your mother, too. His mother also lived here on the rez when she was a child. I was thankful when your mother took Johnny. The poor thing. Who knows what might have happened to him if she hadn't."

Mary's heart wasn't satisfied. "That doesn't answer my question. Why my mother?"

"The circumstances around adoptions are kept confidential for a reason. I've probably already told you more than I should."

"I'm Johnny's legal guardian. Doesn't that give me a right to know?"

Piercing dark eyes stared back at her from beneath a clouded brow. It was obvious Mary's questions brought unpleasant memories to Irene's mind. She scooted forward in her chair, adjusting the long teal skirt as she did. Her pink tongue appeared briefly as she moistened her lips. "Tell me why you feel you have to know."

She couldn't control the emotions that boiled from her core. The words burst from her. "I've been kept in the dark for fifteen years. I want to know why."

Irene's teeth sunk into her lower lip as she considered Mary's outburst.

Mary took a deep breath and reclaimed her composure. "How my brother spends the rest of his life is in our hands." She indicated Nate with her eyes. "Until two days ago, I thought I knew everything there was to know about Johnny. Now I find something this important, I never knew. We came here searching for a needle in the proverbial haystack."

"For God's sake, and for Johnny's, if you loved him enough once to help him, please find it in your heart to help me learn the truth." Mary quickly brushed a tear from her nose and went on. "I have no idea if you know anything that will make a difference, but I'm all he has. I can't stop until I've explored every single possibility and know everything there is to know. If I don't follow through with that, I'll never forgive myself." Mary suddenly became aware that Nate's hand was on her arm.

The woman was obviously deeply moved. Her eyes glistened with tears. "Some questions are best left unanswered. Mysteries better left unsolved.

Sometimes opening an old wound to eliminate the scar tissue only creates an even uglier scar."

Mary didn't know how to answer. Irene's fears didn't change anything. Mary looked deep in the woman's eyes. "Both my parents are dead. So is Johnny's mother. Please find it in your heart to help the living—"

Irene bit the inside of her cheek and surveyed Mary. "Johnny's mother was your mother's sister."

"My aunt?" Mary looked perplexed. "I heard my mother speak of her, but I never knew her."

"Your aunt was nothing like your mother. I don't mean she was a bad person. She was just wild. A restless girl who ran away from home when she was quite young. Your family didn't know where she was until she surfaced one day back on the reservation, a short time before Johnny's birth."

"Did my mother know this before Johnny was born?"

"I called your mother in Santa Fe a few days after your aunt arrived here. It wasn't a good situation, but I thought your mother and your grandparents should know."

"Grandpa," Mary whispered. "He knew this, too."

Irene nodded. "I called her on a Sunday evening. That night Johnny was born. Your mother and grandparents were to come on the following weekend to see her. But by the time five days had passed, it was too late."

Mary was stunned. She listened, but she was having trouble comprehending. "I didn't even know until two days ago. All these years I believed he was my mother and father's child. I was away at college when he was born. Everyone knew, but me."

"Precious few knew the real truth." Irene paused and looked down at her hands folded on the table. "I shouldn't be surprised you were kept outside the secret. It was no reflection on you, rather protection for

Johnny. Don't blame yourself, and don't ever blame your mother."

"I can understand why she might not want Johnny to know. He was a baby, only a few days old, when she brought him to our home. But surely she realized one day he might find out the truth. Adoption isn't usually kept this secretive."

"You must believe what I tell you is truth. Your mother took this secret to her grave. Surely you, of all people, must know she had good reason."

Mary's head spun with each new revelation. The story grew more incredulous to her by the minute.

Nate cleared his throat and shifted in his chair. He held the telephone message in his hand. "According to this message, you called Mary's mother when Johnny was five days old. I'd assume his mother's death was the family emergency you called about."

Irene nodded, sadness in her eyes.

Nate scratched the side of his head. "I'm curious. She obviously didn't die during childbirth. Did she die from an infection or something?"

"Indeed. It was an *infection* that killed her." Her lips were taught and her eyes flashed with hatred. "A disease. A scourge and a poison upon the face of God's earth."

Nate glanced at Mary and she met his eyes. Both had the same look of concern on their face.

"You needn't look so shocked. I've lived in the city just like you. Hideous things happen. The rez and the tiny town of Shiprock aren't exempt from the devil's work either."

"Then Johnny's mother was murdered?" Nate's words hung in the air and Mary had the sensation she was watching a movie. It seemed surreal and distant.

Irene smoothed her dark hair. "Johnny's mother came home with a man she met who knows where." She threw her arm up in a shrugging gesture. "A drifter, but worse. Far worse. She said he was

Johnny's father. Of course, he wasn't decent enough to make her his wife." She turned toward Nate. "And that man's very look oozed wickedness. It was his eyes." She shivered. "I knew in my soul, the first second he set foot on the rez, he was bad news. No. Not bad news. *Pure evil.* There is no other way to describe him." Her eyes turned toward Mary. "You see. Johnny's father was the reason your mother changed his name and tried so hard to make it appear he was her natural son."

Nate cupped his chin in his hand. "So this man was here when the murder was committed?"

"Here? Oh, yes, he was here. I was there, when he held Johnny in his arms and told your aunt what a beautiful life they would all have together." She shook her head in disgust. "But I wasn't fooled. I knew it would never happen. I just never imagined it would end so quickly."

"And five days later?" Nate led her on with the story.

"I found her Friday morning. Tucked in her bed, with her neck broken. I'd come by to check on the babies, but no one answered when I knocked. I could hear Johnny crying, so I tried the door. It was unlocked. There she was, and Johnny was all alone, who knows for how long."

Mary's heart was in her stomach. "My God. How horrible."

"Horrible. Yes." Irene's face was long and sullen and now seemed to show her age. "I took Johnny out of there and called your mother. That's when this message you found was written."

"And Johnny's father? What happened to him?"

"They searched for him. First the reservation police then the State Patrol. They looked for a good long time. Concerned most, I guess, with what he'd do with the baby."

Nate cocked his head. "Baby? You said you had Johnny."

"Not Johnny. The other one."

"Other one?" Mary asked.

"Your aunt gave birth to twins. Twin boys." Irene shook her head. "I had a bad feeling when the second baby was born. An omen of evil if ever I saw one."

"What evil?" Mary prompted, leaning nearer.

Irene glanced up. "Strangest thing I ever saw. I'm a midwife and I pride myself on keeping things sterile when I deliver babies. Can't be too careful about infections." She glanced down at the table. "You're going to think I'm lying to you, but when that second child came out of the womb, a black and white feather fell down out of nowhere and landed on his belly."

Nate's face went white as Irene's shirt. He twisted in his chair and cleared his throat. "A feather?" he asked in a low voice.

"As sure as I'm sitting here. It was an omen. No one will ever convince me otherwise."

"Whatever happened to the other baby?" Mary asked, aware her voice sounded strained.

"His father, that man with those evil eyes, took him. Killed the mother and left Johnny behind, but took the other child with him. Guess, I shouldn't have been surprised. It was the other baby that looked like his father—the eyes, I mean. The boys were identical twins, only the eyes were different."

"Twins? I'd have never guessed." Mary shook her head trying to comprehend. "The birth certificate said it was a single birth."

"That was wrong. I know better. I not only helped them into this world, I buried their umbilical cords myself up by Shiprock. I asked for a special blessing for those boys, because I knew they would need it."

Mary sat in half-dazed silence as the truth sunk in. "Now I understand why my mother had to keep this secret all these years."

Nate finished her sentence. "She never wanted Johnny to know his father killed his mother."

Irene's eyes were intense. "And she'd have done anything to keep his father from finding him. Don't blame her, Mary."

Nate cleared his throat. "Guess I'd have been willing to falsify a few documents under those circumstances, myself."

Mary looked over at him, then to Irene. Now there was an explanation for the way she was feeling about coming here. Her intuition was better than she'd ever imagined. She considered Nate. A deluge of thoughts pounded through her head. What else had she been right about recently?

Mary realized the pounding wasn't in her head, but was coming from outside as a hard driving rain pelted the exterior of the trailer. A crack of lightning lit up the front yard as thick black clouds darkened the late afternoon to an eerie twilight hue. A fitting setting for the tale of horror they'd been enthralled in for the last two hours.

Nate glanced at his watch. It was after four thirty.

Mary took note of his gesture. "It's time we headed back to Santa Fe."

He shrugged. "Whenever you're ready." He wasn't going to rush her and he could only imagine what must be going on in Mary's heart. It had been an emotionally draining afternoon even for an outsider like him. The discovery of the adoption papers and Irene's revelations had changed Mary's family history, as she knew it. That had to have affected her deeply.

Mary rose and stared out the window at the worrisome storm. "It would probably be best if we left now," she said.

"You're welcome to stay for a while." Irene rose and came around to the other side of the table. "These late summer thunderstorms can be fierce. They don't call this time of year the monsoon season for nothing."

Mary smiled and turned back toward Irene. "We've taken enough of your time. You've done a great deal for my family. I'm grateful."

Irene extended her hand and clasped Mary's. "I didn't do anything anyone else wouldn't have, if they'd been in my place."

Mary shook her head and gave Irene a hug. "Your kindness and caring are much appreciated, as is your honesty."

Nate rose to his feet and shook Irene's hand. "Mary is right. You're a good person, Ms. Choula. You've been a big help to us, too."

Irene nodded graciously. "Please be careful out there. This rain is coming down in sheets."

Nate pushed against the front door and a deluge of rain pounded his face. Mary ran out as the door opened. They both made a run for the Pathfinder, sloshing through spongy earth and dodging puddles.

Nate grabbed for Mary's door handle and she waved him on around the car. "Get in," she said above the sound of the pelting raindrops. Seconds later, they were both in the car with streams of rainwater pouring down their faces.

"I don't think I've ever seen it rain so hard," Nate sputtered.

Mary shook her head. "It doesn't happen often. We get heavy rains in the late summer, but this one's really coming down."

Nate started the car. "Well, we'll get out of here and leave it behind. We'll be back in Santa Fe in time for a late dinner."

Nate put the Pathfinder in reverse and backed onto the dirt road. The road was muddy and streams of reddish-brown water ran in the ditches along the sides. Turning on the lights, he headed back toward the main highway.

Torrents of rain pounded across the road making it difficult to see. The wipers squeaked back and forth across the windshield making a rhythmic sound, but couldn't keep up with the downpour.

Mary was silent as she watched the riling water cut deep furrows in the earth. The arroyo along the roadside he'd noted earlier, now looked more like a rising river than a dry ditch. The horses, no doubt, had long since found shelter from the drenching rain.

Periodic flashes of lightning sent fingers of electricity from sky to earth, lighting up the area in a weird and eerie way. Thunder rumbled loud enough to be heard above the engine and the roar of the driving rain. The bolts of lightning illuminated the ground all around them and reached down to the mountains in the distance. If not for its fearsome power, it would have been stunningly beautiful.

"We'll be out of this soon," Nate reassured Mary.

Mary glanced at him and attempted a smile. But her posture as she sat clinging to her damp purse and the water-spotted envelope told him she was concerned about the storm and lost in her own thoughts.

Driving captured his focus, but there were things on his mind after their meeting with Irene. "I know it was a rough afternoon for you," he said, forced to raise his voice above the sound of the storm hammering on the vehicle.

"Yes it was." Mary looked down at her lap. She tried to shake the moisture from her purse and wipe beads of water from her jeans. "I'm soaked to the skin."

"Me, too," Nate said, shaking his arm and seeing water droplets fly. "Are you going to be okay?"

She nodded. "I'll make peace with the truth in time. I have to."

"Good." Nate maneuvered in the seat trying to keep a clear view of the road. "There are some important things we need to talk about. When we get back tonight, I'm going to do some checking on Johnny's father. I have some ideas if I can come up with facts to back them up."

Mary's head jerked in his direction. "Really? I want to hear about it. Some thoughts came to my mind, too."

Another giant flash of light illuminated the sky, followed by a deafening rumble of thunder. Small bits of ice began to peck at the windshield, increasing the earsplitting sound. The bits quickly turned to full-fledged hailstones and peppered down like falling gravel creating a deafening roar in the car. Nate shrugged and made a hand sign to Mary. It was useless to try to talk above the noise.

The steering wheel pulled to the right as the tires slipped in the mud. He'd better pay close attention and keep to the center of the road. The water was washing deep ruts and overrunning the roadway. He damn sure didn't want to get stuck out here.

The hail passed after a few minutes, but the going was very slow. It was becoming more difficult to see as the rain seemed to come down harder the closer they got to the highway.

"I'm going on. We've got to run out of this storm soon."

Mary fidgeted in the seat.

Thankfully, there were few cars going in the opposite direction. It was nearly impossible to see the lines on the asphalt. Passing traffic threw torrents of water across the windshield. The road looked like a creek, with the running water broken only by huge drops that hammered down. They crept along. Nate kept his eye on the right side of the road, where occasionally he could see the white line.

Over an hour later, the faint outline of some buildings could be seen ahead. "We're almost to a town," Nate called to Mary.

Her head bobbed. "I think you're right."

The rain had let up slightly. A traffic light ahead flashed red.

"Must have been a lightning strike," Mary said.

"A nasty storm, this one," Nate replied. It was almost impossible to see. Water ran across the street two and three inches deep and nearly reached the tops of the curbs as it filled the gutters.

At the light, a policeman in an orange rain slicker was stopping cars. Nate rolled up next to him and put down the window a few inches. "Where you headed?" the officer asked Nate in a loud voice, trying to be heard above the pounding rain.

"Santa Fe," Nate yelled back.

"Sixty-Four East is washed out on the other side of Farmington. We've got equipment headed that way, but it'll be awhile."

"Any other way we can go?" Nate asked.

"You could go back thru Shiprock and take 666, either North through Cortez or South through Gallup, but I don't recommend it. There are reports of flooding in both directions. It's treacherous driving."

"Maybe we should wait it out here."

The officer wiped water from his face. "That's what I'd suggest. This storm isn't supposed to lift until after midnight. Best bet is probably to lay over here in Farmington until it passes."

"Thanks." Nate rolled up the window and when the officer flagged him through the intersection, he drove on. "What do you think?"

Mary rubbed her eyes. "Anything's got to be better than driving in this. Maybe he's right."

Nate pulled at his damp clothes. "It sure would be nice to get dried out a bit. This is miserable."

Mary leaned toward her window and looked at the sky. "This doesn't show any signs of lifting and it'll be dark before very long. We'd be crazy to try to take the long routes."

A tingle ran through Nate. Soaked to the skin and tired from driving in the storm, a bright light loomed at the end of the tunnel. "Maybe, we should get a room." He tried to appear nonchalant.

A crease ran through Mary's brow. "A room?"

"Yeah. I don't think we'll be going anywhere until morning unless this breaks." Nate's heartbeat sped up at the possibility.

A hint of a smile tugged at the corners of Mary's mouth. "I guess we could— It would be much safer. I mean we would each get a room."

"Yeah. Right. That's what I meant. We could each get one. Of course." Nate stumbled over the words, but his internal heat rose enough it could have dried his clothes on the spot. "See any motels around?"

CHAPTER TWENTY-TWO

"Sorry, that's all I have," the desk clerk explained. "With a major convention in town and the Connie Mack World Series coming up over the weekend, this storm put the icing on the cake. Everything in town is filled up. No one will be getting through on the highway tonight."

Mary shifted on her feet, suddenly feeling uncomfortable. She looked over at Nate. Maybe this wasn't such a good idea.

"You make the call on this one," Nate swung his head in her direction.

"It's the only room left in town. This storm has wreaked havoc on travel," the clerk added.

"I don't see that we have any choice," Mary conceded. "It's either this or wait it out in the car."

"We can at least hole up here and be comfortable until the storm passes." Nate's expression changed. Getting a motel room had been kind of funny when he first mentioned it in the car, momentarily, kind of a thrilling thought. Now that they would have to share a room, the chill in her bones moved directly to her feet.

"One room, two beds?" Mary asked hopefully.

"One queen." The woman shot them an odd look. Mary's hackles ruffled. Whatever the desk clerk was thinking about the two of them, it wasn't her business.

Nate caught Mary's look. He shrugged and passed the woman his credit card. "We'll need a couple of extra blankets and a pillow." Then he whispered to

Mary, "It's just till the storm lets up. Consider our other options. We'll be more comfortable here than hanging out in some coffee shop all night."

"The restaurant next door had to close because of the high water." The desk clerk said over her shoulder, apparently catching part of the conversation. "There's a vending machine around the corner and hot coffee in the lobby. We're trying to get some sandwiches brought in. Sorry, we don't have anything else. The town's pretty much shut down between the rain and the lightning strikes."

Great. Mary rubbed the back of her neck.

"Room 212." She slid the plastic card across the counter. "Here's your key. I'll have someone bring up the extra blankets and pillows. Enjoy your stay." Mary swore there was a smirk on the woman's face, but she turned away and ignored it. She followed Nate to the elevator, giving the woman a coy look. After all, she was the one going upstairs with a good-looking man.

Okay. She shouldn't have thought it and she shouldn't have done it, but it was the principle of the thing. She wasn't in the mood for a small town busybody.

The hallway and the room smelled of eucalyptus that came from numerous dried arrangements both in vases and on the walls. It refreshed Mary's senses after the smell of her wet hair and clothing. The place was either new or freshly remodeled. The smell of newness hung in the air. The wallpaper was a terra cotta color with Navajo patterns accenting the border. Teal, sandstone, rusty reds and blacks formed designs that reminded her of those she used in her rugs.

Nate ran his key card, opened the door and stepped aside. Hesitantly, Mary stepped into the room first. It had a cozy, homey feel. Two large soft beige chairs sat on either side of a small gas fireplace that looked like a mini hogan. The colors of the wallpaper border swirled through the bedspread on the queen bed, which was adorned with pillows in bright solid colors.

Mary took the bed in with a glance as she wondered how they would figure this one out. That was just long enough to imagine its soft comforting warmth and to remind her of how exhausted she was. The day had taken its toll on her. The four-hour drive home in this storm sounded less appealing by the minute. This would be a good place to take refuge until it passed.

The room's air conditioner was blasting. A chill ran through her. Goose bumps rose on cool bare arms and a shiver ran through her. The damp clothes suddenly felt like ice packs stuck to her skin.

Nate crossed the room and turned the small round knob on the unit tucked beneath the window. "I think we can do without that." He smiled at her and took a seat in one of the chairs. Though his smile was genuine, something hung behind his eyes she couldn't identify. He was polite and distant compared to his earlier mood.

Rubbing the chill from her arms, she perched on the edge of the chair across from him. She shot him a half smile, but said nothing. Her thoughts churned as she tried to remember the last time she was alone with a man in a motel room. She avoided his eyes, not wanting him to read her thoughts.

"You look chilled," Nate commented as he rose and hit the switch on the fireplace. "Just as well get comfortable. We're gonna be here awhile." He settled back in the chair as orange and blue flames licked at the artificial logs behind the glass.

Mary rubbed her hands together. "Thanks," she said. "The heat feels good."

"Cold and damp outside. The hail cooled things off pretty fast."

Mary nodded. Their eyes met. They had more important things to talk about than the weather, but they were both avoiding the subject. Nate's eyes showed his fatigue, too. It had been a very long day.

Quietly, they watched the fire. The peace and the silence were nice. A knock on the door interrupted the moment. Nate opened it and a young man stood in the hall holding two blankets and two fluffy pillows in fresh white cases. "Extra bedding," he said as he looked around Nate and shot Mary a smile.

"Thanks." Nate took the bedding. He reached in his pants pocket and pulled out a tip for the young man.

"Gracias, sir." The boy nodded toward Nate. "Let me know if you need anything else." His smiling face disappeared quickly into the hall.

Nate turned back toward the room. "I'll stretch out on the floor if I get tired. You can have the bed."

"Oh." The words escaped unexpectedly. "That will be fine." She looked at the fire. Why did she feel so uptight and uncomfortable? They'd been together all day. Another shiver ran through her and she pulled at the soggy shirt clinging to her skin.

Nate scratched the back of his head and pulled one of the blankets from the stack. "Why don't you get out of those wet clothes and wrap up in this? We can dry your things by the fire."

Her eyebrow shot upward as if of its own will. He was being forward to suggest she take off her clothes. If her eyebrow had a will of its own, then so did her mouth. The words seemed to tumble out without her censoring them at all. "That's not a bad idea. I think I'll take a hot shower while they dry."

He nodded and a twinkle sparked in his eyes.

"I'm just cold," she snapped.

He put up his hands. "I wasn't suggesting anything. I don't want you to get sick."

"Yeah, right," she whispered under her breath as she grabbed the blanket. She avoided his look, though she wanted to read what he was thinking. Cold to the bone, she quickly prioritized her concerns. Sit here miserable or risk him thinking she was coming on to him. She rationalized it in a flash. What he thought was beyond her control. Her own comfort wasn't.

"While you're doing that, I've got a couple of calls to make," he said as she left the room.

In the bathroom, she stripped down without the slightest hesitation and stepped under the hot soothing water of the showerhead. It was a welcome respite. The situation was unexpected and she needed a few minutes alone to get a hold of her emotions.

As the water warmed her body, her thoughts began to flow clearly. They had no choice, but to wait out the storm. It was okay for them to be here together. She reassured herself. Nate was being a perfect gentleman and that was a good thing. She wanted him at arm's length. It had to be that way.

Their relationship wasn't anywhere near ready for intimacy. Maybe it never would be. Maybe there wasn't a relationship at all. To be truthful with herself, she wasn't ready to let anyone get that close to her heart, even if it had been two years—two *long* years. The water poured over the ache she tried to ignore.

She didn't need a man to complicate things. She could do this. She could play it cool. The storm would pass and she could make it through the night with her head and her hormones in tact. She took a deep cleansing breath. They had business to discuss—and Johnny's future, shame on her for allowing her thoughts to stray.

Drying herself with a large white towel, she picked up her cold wet shirt and jeans and considered putting them back on. She couldn't bear the thought. Slipping back into her damp under things for proprieties sake, she ran her fingers through her clean hair and toweled it dry. She wrapped the blanket securely around herself and tucked it under her chin. With one hand protruding through the front, clutching her wet clothes, she prepared to waddle into the main room.

These clothes are going to have to dry. She couldn't stand to wear them now she was warm. As she stepped off the tile and onto the carpet, she heard Nate's voice.

"See what you can find out, Coyote. This guy murdered Johnny's mother fifteen years ago. I want to know if they ever found him and brought him to trial." He paused, listening to Coyote on the other end.

"Yeah. Lonewolf was his name. That's all I know."

The drapes were open and Nate stood with his back to her, looking out the window as he talked. The sky was nearly black as night, although waning daylight hung on by a thread. Raindrops beat hard against the glass and ran down in sheets as she quietly approached the fireplace, spread out her clothes to dry and listened to the sound of Nate's voice.

"How about the car? Did you get out there to print it?" He stopped and listened. His broad shoulders silhouetted against the window made Mary's insides warm. He was a handsome, well-built man. That was undeniable.

"Who'd they send?" His voice raised an octave. He listened. "Interesting. How the hell did he know about it?"

"Right. Well, we'll be here till this storm lifts. I've got my cell if you need me." He listened again. "Coyote, how's your dad?"

There was a longer silence. "Sorry to hear that. Don't hang around if you need to go, okay?"

Mary took note of the concern and the affection in his voice. She was beginning to realize that beneath the lawyer armor he wore with such ardor, there beat the heart of a good man. A *very* good man.

Nate hung up his cell phone and turned around. He smiled and ran his eyes across her blanketed form from head to floor. It didn't take a mind reader to know his mind had flashed on what was underneath.

"I didn't hear you come out," he said softly. "Feel better?" he asked as he walked to the chair. Obviously, his mind was more on his previous conversation than on what he was saying.

"Everything okay in Santa Fe?" she asked, maneuvering herself into the chair while keeping the blanket wrapped around her like a mummy.

"Coyote's going to see what he can find on Johnny's father."

"I heard that. What about the car?"

Nate's eyes darkened. "It appears the police sent an investigator to take some prints."

"Really? What brought that on? We didn't call them."

"Exactly. And the investigator was Gonzales."

Mary shook her head. "Gonzales? So he is in on this."

Nate ran a hand through his hair. "It's gone about far enough." He shook his head. A deep crease imbedded itself in his forehead and he was silent.

He motioned toward a table by the door. "I went and got some coffee for us. They had some ham sandwiches down in the lobby so I brought some up. Even threw in a complimentary bottle of wine for the inconvenience of having to share a room."

Mary rose, clutching the blanket around her, and walked over to the table. She removed the lid from a Styrofoam cup and took a sip of coffee. "It's Smith," she said as she opened a packet of sugar. "I know he's the one behind this."

"But why, Mary? That's the one thing I can't understand. What reason could be so compelling that he'd go to these lengths? It doesn't make sense to me." His eyes were hard and serious and frustration crept into his voice.

"It's simple. He wants you out of the way, because you're his biggest threat."

"Threat?" Nate's eyes were softer, but filled with questions.

"Smith knows you have the capability to get Johnny out of this mess. That makes you his target."

"You know, I can buy that he's hell bent to send Johnny to prison. But I've been defending kids for a long time and this isn't exactly a case he needs to fear losing. Not to the extent that he's taken it. Something isn't right here."

"There are a lot of things that happen in life that aren't right, Nate. Can't you accept I'm telling you the truth about Smith and leave it at that?"

He paused and looked into the fire. "No, Mary. I can't. And I'll level with you. I've asked around, I've done some research, but I still don't have answers I can live with. That's why I wanted to be taken off the case. But in the end I couldn't." His eyes went to her. "And I couldn't, because of you."

The softness in his eyes, combined with the look of frustration on his face, pained her. A twinge of guilt ran through her. What she was putting him through wasn't right or fair. Maybe she'd been wrong to try to keep so much from him.

She looked into the cup of coffee and sat it down. Picking up the bottle of wine, two plastic cups, and two of the sandwiches from the table, she walked back to the chair by the fire and slid downward until she was seated on the floor facing Nate.

"Why don't you open this?" she said, handing Nate the wine bottle. She pulled the blanket tight and extended her chilled feet toward the fireplace. "I don't think I've been totally fair to you." She passed him a sandwich and smiled. "Maybe, I can explain it to you over dinner."

Nate looked at the bottle and smiled. "Well, it's definitely not the best from their wine cellar. It's got a screw off cap."

Mary shrugged. "That's probably a good thing. We don't have a corkscrew."

They both laughed. Nate joined her on the floor by the fire and poured wine in each of the cups.

Mary swirled her finger around the rim of the cup. Where on earth should she start and what was she willing to share with him? It was difficult to know what he would think of her once the truth was laid out. One of Grandpa's sayings rang in her ears. "Once you open a can of worms, you can never put the worms back in the can." That was her only fear.

Nate took a sip of wine and waited expectantly. His eyes went serious. He stared into the fire. The firelight reflected on his chiseled jaw and high cheekbones. After a few minutes, he broke the silence. "Mary, I can't believe Smith would go this far because of a grudge. Because you had a love affair with his son fifteen years ago? In high school, for God's sake?"

Mary's heart jumped to her throat and a flush instantly rushed to her cheeks. "I don't know how you know about that, but you've only heard part of the story." She wet her lips and took a sip of the wine, hoping for a surge of courage. "You said something isn't right, and it's Smith that isn't. Maybe it isn't entirely his fault. I don't know."

"Look, I know Smith hurt you, and I've heard he's a prejudiced bastard, but don't you think if the man's trying to kill me, I'm entitled to know why?"

A flash of lightning lit up the sky and thunder rattled the windowpanes. The lights flickered and went out, leaving the room lit only by the firelight. Perhaps the dim light and the wine gave her the courage to face the ghosts of the past. Nate was right. She'd put him in danger and he deserved to know why. She sank her teeth into her lower lip. There was one secret she would take to her grave, but the rest of her life needed to be open to Nate. Otherwise, he was facing her enemy for unknown reasons.

The firelight reflected in Mary's eyes. With his gaze, Nate traced the outline of her nose and her moist full lips. His eyes ran down her neck toward her breasts, the crevice between them visible above her wrapping. He forced his look away. He couldn't be tough enough to get to the bottom of the issues unless he kept his mind off what was buried beneath the blanket. He was grateful when she went on.

"What happened fifteen years ago was only the beginning. I wanted to leave it behind and I did. I left Santa Fe and went away to college." Her lashes batted as she spoke and her chest moved up and down. Outward signs what she was revealing came from close to her heart.

It was at that moment he realized, his best role was to listen and try to understand. He nodded. "That's when Johnny came into the picture, while you were away?"

Mary's head bobbed. "Yes. I was completely focused on my own life when it happened. Otherwise, I might have been more aware."

"We all have times when we're preoccupied with our own worlds and don't see any wrong in what we've done until later." He had a few old wounds of his own.

"I went to school and earned my degree." Mary went on. "I worked on my art and went to graduate school. By the time I came back to Santa Fe nine years later, I'd earned a name as an artist. I don't know if I came back because it was the right thing to do, or to spite Smith and those who taunted me. I came back an educated Navajo woman and a well-known artist, with an ambition to open my own gallery in Santa Fe. My mission was to prove the stereotype Smith tried to create, only showed his ignorance."

"You're living proof he was wrong. You know that, don't you?"

She nodded. "Oh, I know, but full-filling my dream took six more years and a lot of heartache. It has been a long painful journey." She looked down at her cup. "When I came home, my father's health was failing. Within a year, my mother and he both had become gravely ill and they passed away within months of one another."

"That must have been difficult. I can see why it left little time for your own ambitions."

"Johnny was only ten years old at the time. Grandpa was left to care for him and I knew it was too much. So I did the right thing."

"You shouldered the responsibility of raising Johnny and caring for your grandfather." Nate ran his hand down his chin. "Mary, you're quite a woman."

She leaned toward him, pressed her fingers to his lips, then spoke softly. "Please, wait until I'm done to make your judgments. All of my choices haven't been sound or for noble causes."

He caught her hand and squeezed it in his, but she pulled away and refused to meet his gaze.

She shook her head. "Let me finish, then we'll talk."

Nate took a sip of wine and glanced down at her feet. They looked small and fragile in the firelight. But he knew there was nothing fragile about Mary. She moved her toes nervously. It was obvious. This was difficult for her. "Just tell me," he whispered, wanting somehow to make it easier for her.

"A year later I married a man I met here in Santa Fe."

"Angelo."

Surprise flared in her eyes. "How did you know about him?"

"It doesn't matter. Please go on," Nate said quickly, fearful his comment would negate her trust.

She moved her neck as if to release the tension and continued. "Angelo was half Navajo, too. He came here from Arizona." She shot him a wary glance. She tipped her head and rubbed her forehead. "Angelo called me one night and told me he'd been drinking at a bar in Santa Fe and asked me to come drive him home. Of course, I went into town and got him."

"Of course," Nate nodded.

"Angelo was very drunk. We were in the parking lot and I was trying to get him out of the driver's seat so I could drive. I saw Jim Smith get into a car across the street, but I never thought anything of it at the time. I was intent on getting Angelo home. Smith was the furthest thing from my mind that night."

"Understandable."

"When I finally got Angelo into the passenger seat, I headed back to Chimayo. Five miles out of town on a dark road, an oncoming car swerved into my lane and hit us head on. I tried to miss him, but there was nothing I could do."

Nate silently listened.

"Thankfully, Angelo and I were both okay. We got out and I ran to the other car to see if they were hurt." Her voice was shaky. "There was one man alone. I reached into the car to feel for a pulse—there wasn't one. I managed to get the door open and I couldn't believe my eyes. Ethan Smith was the driver of the other vehicle. I tried to give him CPR, but he'd died instantly."

"You tried to resuscitate him?"

She nodded. "It was no use. He was gone."

"What a horrible thing to have happen. Especially, when you knew Ethan as you did."

"Things went from bad to worse. The police arrived and smelled liquor on Angelo. They took us both to the police station to test our blood alcohol levels."

"I'm sure that was standard procedure."

"Smith got there shortly after. Naturally, he was beside himself with the news of Ethan's death, but he told the police he saw Angelo behind the wheel of the car in town. The police started to doubt I was the one driving. Smith kept screaming at us and calling us drunken Indians. It was a nightmare. Before the night was over, we were both in jail charged with vehicular homicide."

"Wow," Nate whispered. A sick feeling settled in the pit of his stomach.

"The case went to trial and I told the world the truth. Not only was I driving, but when I pulled Ethan from the car and started CPR, he wreaked of marijuana." She cleared her throat softly. "Smith was hell bent that Angelo was drunk and had been driving the car. Having me involved made it worse. After all, we didn't have the most pleasant history. In the end, the case was dismissed, but when the truth came out, Smith turned his hatred toward me. He blamed me for killing his son and for starting the investigation that uncovered Ethan's drug use problems. It became a two-edged sword that's perpetuated pain and chaos in his life and mine. Smith and his vendetta have haunted me and my family ever since."

Nate was silent as he thought of the implications. Seeing Smith as a grieving father on a mission to avenge his son's death put things in a new light. The depth of the emotion intertwined in this drama left him at a loss for solutions. The picture was clearer, but he still had questions for Mary. He watched her in the firelight. He sensed there was more on her mind. He wanted her to keep talking, to keep baring her soul.

The thunder rumbled outside and the rain pounded the window, an odd mirror image of the turbulence pouring from Mary's heart. The storm raged on. He had her all to himself tonight. At last, she'd opened the stony doors of her heart and offered him hope of one day reaching inside.

CHAPTER TWENTY-THREE

Exhaustion swept through Mary, but she had to go on. The entire story would be told before she would stop. "A few months later, Angelo was arrested outside of a liquor store in Santa Fe. He'd been drinking. The store had been held up and they charged Angelo with armed robbery."

The injustice boiled in her soul. "Angelo was a lot of things, but he was never a thief. The charge was ridiculous. Smith went after it with everything he had. Right or wrong he would stop at nothing to send Angelo to prison. Including bribing the public defender to throw the case."

Nate rubbed his ear. "Can you prove he bribed the guy?"

"If I could have proved it, I would have been able to prevent what happened. Angelo was found guilty and went to prison. I was working with a new attorney to get an appeal, when I got the call that he'd been killed."

Nate covered his face with his hands. "Mary, you've lived a nightmare. You've literally been through hell. I didn't understand you until now. I've behaved like an ass."

She shook her head and looked into the fire. "It wasn't your fault. But now you know why trust doesn't come easy for me."

"Nor for me." His hand slid over the top of hers. "I've been stumbling in the dark. Now that the fog has lifted on a lot of things, there may be a chance."

She met his eyes. "Really?"

"Yes." He leaned closer, his mouth inches from hers. He wet his lips. "Tomorrow," he whispered.

Warmth spread through her chest. She shook her head. "You can't leave it at that," she breathed. "You know I want to know what you're thinking." *Damn.* He was tempting her, hovering so close she could taste his lips. Did he want to kiss her, or did he want her to make the first move? She bit her lower lip.

"Is an answer *all* you want?"

She nodded, but she lied. It was far from all she wanted.

He pulled back a bit. "Why were you so afraid to tell me the truth?"

"Would you have believed me in the beginning? I think not. What would you have thought of me then?" She paused. "If you burn your hand on the stove, you're very cautious about touching it again."

"Is it the fear of burns that comes between us?"

Mary raised an eyebrow and threw him a quick glance. "I think we're talking about two different things." She leaned away from him. "Perhaps, we should try to get some rest so we can get an early start in the morning."

He nodded. "That's probably a good idea."

Her emotions were at a peak. Clearing the air had lifted a burden from her shoulders, but it had also threatened to open old wounds. The heat building between her and Nate was frightening. With such desire came thoughts and words she'd not allowed in for a long time. *Trust. Commitment. Need.*

She rose and walked to the bed. Throwing aside the extra pillows and the bedspread, she slipped beneath the covers and left the blanket at the bedside. Nate watched from the corner of his eye. She could feel his wanting gaze even in the dim light.

There was silence for a few minutes then he got to his feet and spread a blanket on the floor in front of the fire.

"It's noble of you be such a gentleman," Mary said. "I'm the one who should be sleeping on the floor. After all, you paid for the room."

He shrugged. "We should count ourselves lucky we aren't sleeping in the car. Let's get some rest."

The glow of firelight illuminated his form and she watched his silhouette as he removed his shirt. A tingle spread through her entire body. The shirt slid across his bronze muscular shoulders as he unbuttoned the cuffs and let it fall.

She told herself to look away, but her eyes and the heat in her flesh betrayed her. When he reached for the button on his jeans, the wanting within her could be contained no longer. He turned his head toward her. He'd wanted her kiss. Did he want her still? An ache began inside and oozed through every cell of her body.

It had been a long time since she'd wanted for the touch of a man who had such desire for her. Not a word had been spoken, his fevered fingers hadn't pressed against her skin, but the wanting was there, stronger than anything she'd ever known. She closed her eyes, and tried to swallow. The heat and stiffness in her throat made it a conscious effort.

Her heart beat harder, her breathing shallow. The attraction she'd denied for so long, the strength she'd called on every time she'd turned and walked away from him had created a fearsome need. Every inch of her body was alive with burning desire. God, she wanted this man. She wanted him tonight. The quiet was deafening. Surely, he could hear her heart hammering and the catch in her breath.

"Mary," he whispered. Nothing more needed to be said.

She rose from the bed in one quick motion and grasped the blanket half around her. With whispered sounds and shadowed souls they came together in the firelight.

He pulled her to him. "I came to Santa Fe to straighten out my life, not complicate it," he whispered as he ran his hands down her shoulders and upper arms.

His touch ignited the fire in a part of her that had only smoldered for a long, long time. Hungrily, she succumbed to her wanting and pressed her mouth to his. He pulled her lips into his kiss, slow and longingly, as if wanting to drink from her soul.

His lips moved down the side of her throat, as he buried his face in her hair and placed soft moist kisses at the base of her neck. His desire and his tenderness pierced her deeply, dangerously close to the inner woman she'd shielded from the outside world for far too long. Close to the pain that had wounded her soul years before. He was gentle, he was caring and ever so near to breaking through years of armor she'd constructed. If it fell away, would her heart be safe in his hands?

Desire surged through her, igniting a passion she wasn't sure she could temper if he continued. Her mind urged her to make an attempt to pull back, but her body refused. She released the blanket and it fell to the floor. She couldn't retreat to the cold dark place in her soul when the warmth and love of Nate's arms awaited her. To hell with the fear of tomorrow's regrets and yesterday's pain, tonight, she belonged to Nate and the love he was offering.

Lost in his kiss, bare flesh touched bare flesh as she leaned into his chest. "You're sure?" he whispered.

"Yes. Yes." Her lips parted and she drank of his soul. With trembling hands he maneuvered the hook on her bra and she quickly released herself from its confines. She buried her upper body in the softness of his chest. Breath came in short puffs as his kisses trailed down her neck and his mouth found its destination, her nipple responding to his caress without hesitation. His hand slid beneath the elastic of her white lace panties. A moan came from her lips. She pushed against him, aware of the urgency forming beneath his jeans. In the midst of another fevered kiss, she found the zipper and slid it down, then pulled his briefs away releasing his magnificent manhood from its captivity. Her hand ran the length of his erection, smooth and pulsing.

"Oh, God, Mary," he moaned. Falling to her knees, she assisted his jeans and briefs to the floor and he followed her. With gentle hands, he eased her panties over her thighs and with one finger, pulled them over her feet. Taking one long all encompassing look at her naked body in the firelight, his eyes flared, "You are so beautiful," he said under restricted breath.

Fevered kisses ran the length of her body, stopping and nibbling in all the right places. She squirmed with desire, kissing him too, and caressing his body with her hands. His body was magnificent. No Greek God was ever so solid and beautiful. No warrior any more perfectly formed. His fingers gently crept between her legs and stroked softly. Her body melted into the pleasure of his touch.

"It's been too long," she whispered, her head spinning with the intoxication of uncontrollable passion. "I've waited for you so long."

Her body was on fire. Warmth and moisture flooded her. Placing his mouth over hers, he drew in her lips as he straddled her and let himself deeply into her. Breathless pleasure filled her body. She moved with him. Sounds of intense pleasure came from deep in his throat as his eyes glazed with ecstasy.

"At last I've found you," he gasped beneath bated breath. "Again, you are mine." She heard his words, but they were a blur beneath the growing intensity in her body.

"You first," he whispered in her ear as he moved his hips more urgently, skyrocketing sensation through her entire body. It had been far too long. She could hold it back no longer. A few gentle strokes and lights flashed like fireworks behind her eyelids. Explosions of pleasure vibrated through her, sending ripples of contracting ecstasy beyond her imagination. Seconds later, he melted into her. Shivers of pleasure and groans of sated bliss came from him.

"Oh, God," he exclaimed. "I never dreamed." Their legs entangled, their bodies still joined, they clung to each other, filled to overflowing with joy and contented pleasure. In the warmth and glow of the firelight, he pressed her to him and kissed her sweetly.

Nate ran his hand across her raven hair splayed across his chest and arm. She was beautiful and amazing. His body still hummed with pleasure. The intensity of her passion made him forget all else. Tonight, he didn't care.

Her head was on his shoulder, her lightly heaving breasts pressed to his chest. The feel of her skin next to his was pure heaven. He ran his fingers across the smoothness of her body and buried his face in her neck for one more kiss, all the while remembering the flower on the mountain. She was a woman beyond his wildest dreams. There was a feeling of completeness in his heart that touched the depths of his soul, like nothing before.

His mind flashed on the pictures that ran through his mind when they were making love. The bronze face of a beautiful maiden, much like Mary, mingled with the images of a warrior, the face from the painting, flickering firelight illuminating the passion in their eyes. He remembered his words, and hers. *I've waited for you... Together, again...* The ultimate question hung in his mind.

In the throws of passion they'd both felt it, both spoke it aloud. It may have defied logic, but tonight it didn't matter. This day had been made of new beginnings, of letting the past die, of impossible barriers falling away, and of new dreams taking shape. The existence of a world long ago where two soul mates began a journey together, crossing the expanses of time, didn't seem far-fetched to him at this moment.

Was it the message his strange visions were trying to deliver? Had he become delusional first with passion and now in the afterglow? If he was, he didn't want to know. If he died at this moment, he'd want for nothing and regret even less.

Mary opened her eyes and smiled at him.

He kissed her forehead. "You okay?"

She nodded, her eyes soft and dancing with light. Her face was more relaxed than he'd ever seen it. The sadness in the depths of her eyes had faded.

He rubbed his finger on her cheek. "You're so beautiful."

"Warts and all?" she smiled. "Even after you know all about me, you can say that?"

"None of it changes how I feel about you. Why would you think that?"

"I was in jail for a time because of Ethan's death. I was married to a man who died in prison. I guess, I assumed those probably weren't on your list of qualifications for the woman of your dreams."

"Dreams aren't reality. Life happens to people and not everything is within our control and fairy tale perfect. If you've come to grips with your past, why wouldn't I be able to?"

"It's haunted me. It still does. I guess, I thought—"

"What? That you'd slept with Saint Nathan? Not exactly, honey. I've got a few skeletons in my closet, too. Being an attorney doesn't necessarily mean you've always walked the straight and narrow. In a city like San Francisco there are always prominent people with a lot of money, willing to pay whatever it takes to keep their crap from crawling out from under the carpet. There's a lot of money to be made dealing with those people. If you don't have a conscience, you can work a lot of deals and pad your pockets in the process."

Her lips tightened and she ran her fingertips over his bare chest. "Is that what you meant when you said you came here to straighten out your life?"

"Yeah. I guess I finally got a conscience. Now, I figure I owe something back to society. There are lots of kids out there who need my help. I spent enough time getting ones off that really needed a kick in the butt."

"How about women? Any of those lurking in the shadows I should be concerned about?"

Nate shook his head. "Never had time for many. I was too busy working on my career. Had to have the big bucks and the fast car. That kind of lifestyle doesn't draw in choice prospects. That's one closet that's free of skeletons and old baggage." He took her hand in his and kissed her fingertips. "Think you can teach an old dude about commitment?"

Her eyes met his with a coy look. "If his heart is in the right place, I'd consider it."

"What about your heart, Mary? Is it free to move on or does it still belong to the past?"

"You mean Angelo?"

Nate nodded.

"Time is a friend to broken dreams and broken hearts. The pain lessens over time. Time and distance also works wonders for your view of the truth." She wet her lips and looked at the ceiling as she spoke. "I won't deny I loved Angelo. He came into my life when I needed someone badly. But in the end, he was the one who needed me. Angelo was a bird with the broken wing, and I thought I could fix him. His soul was good, but he could never overcome his body's need for liquor. He wasn't a bad person and he never meant to hurt me with his drinking. It was just stronger than he was. The night of the accident was only one of many times I had to go and pick him up at a bar. It was a regular thing for him."

Nate listened, feeling the pain and the wisdom in her voice. "That's a tough deal. I know from personal experience trying to fix other people doesn't make a good foundation for a relationship."

"I guess he was the only one I'd ever met that was more broken than I was—" A shadow crossed her face, and she closed her eyes. "If Angelo had left the booze behind him, my life would have been different. He wouldn't have fallen into Smith's devious world."

More broken than she? The comment made Nate uneasy. Was there still something she hadn't shared? "Who knows," he said. "The situation didn't help, but something else could have happened."

A tear glistened in the corner of Mary's eye. "True. But it turned out to be the perfect set up."

Nate leaned and kissed her lips. "I didn't mean to make you relive this."

She brushed at her eye. "It's not you. I was fine until all of this happened with Johnny. I don't waste my time reliving the past, nor do I waste it crying. Don't think of me in that light."

"I never have. You're tough as nails, Mary. But life has certainly put you to the test." He squeezed her hand. "It's okay to let down the wall and feel those emotions. It isn't a sign of weakness. It just shows you're human."

She rubbed her hands across her face. "There'll be time for that when Johnny is out of this mess. You never told me what you have in mind."

Nate glanced toward the window. "We'll deal with that tomorrow. For now, we can get a few hours of sleep before the sun comes up. The storm seems to have lifted." He rolled onto his side. "You know. We could even try out the bed."

She laughed. "Come on. But if we're going to get any rest, you'll have to promise to stay on your side."

Nate threw aside the blanket. "What fun would that be?" He couldn't keep his eyes off her as she crossed the room and climbed into the bed. Tonight, he'd tasted paradise in their lovemaking. She'd bared her body and her soul to him and he'd walked with her through the pain of her past and offered her a hand of hope. A hand he prayed she'd accept, to step away from what had been and join him in building a new life.

They'd go back to Santa Fe in the morning where new possibilities were alive for Johnny. A dark cloud came over his heart. And he'd find a way to deal with Smith. The only thing still troubling him was a sigh and a shadow on Mary's face, that told him there were more secrets hiding in her heart. Whether or not it mattered, would play out, eventually.

Mary looked down at the speedometer and glanced at Nate. She'd been pushing the speed limit, but she wanted to get back to Santa Fe. A sense of urgency was with them both this morning. Nate moved in his seat and glanced down at his shirt pocket. He removed the bag of feathers he'd placed there, yesterday.

"Keeping them close? Is it doing any good?"

A curious expression crossed his face and he placed them back in his pocket. "So far, so good, I guess."

An odd silence hung in the air. A tremendous amount had happened in the last twenty-four hours. She shot a quick look in Nate's direction. His expression spoke of the same feelings that hung in her heart. More things were going to happen when they got back to Santa Fe. She could feel it in the tension building. Another shoe was bound to drop.

"What next?" she asked, after a few minutes.

"I don't know, yet. I'm waiting to hear from Coyote."

As if on cue, Nate's cell phone played a few notes. He threw her a half smile and answered.

"Hello," he said. "About ten miles from town. You okay? You sound funny." He raised an eyebrow and glanced at Mary. "All right, we'll see you there."

"Everything all right?" Mary asked.

Nate shrugged. "I think so. Coyote wants us to meet him at my office."

A knot formed in Mary's stomach and she pressed the accelerator a bit harder.

Nate turned his head toward her. "Easy girl. We've got a lot more to live for this morning." He gave her a wink. He was right. The world looked different to her today, too.

His adoring gaze brought a flash to her mind of the warrior from her painting, the same face she'd seen last night over and over in the throws of passion. Why that face haunted her, she didn't know. It was Nate's face, no doubt, but it always came to her as the bronzed warrior with his long black hair flowing on an ethereal breeze.

Her dream warrior, she'd called him. Now, the man who stirred her soul to its very depths sat in the seat next to her, and the peculiar question of that connection played in her mind, and in her heart. Then it struck her. Nate and his feathers. Another oddity. She always thought of her warrior with the eagle feathers around him. The feathers swirling about him, and sprouting from the tips of his fingers.

Nate's voice brought her from her thoughts. "Park in the back lot. I don't see anything out front."

"Sure." Mary pulled into a space near the door. Within seconds, they were in the hallway hurrying toward Nate's office.

Coyote sat at the desk in Nate's chair. Papers were spread in front of him.

"You look like hell," Nate said as they came through the door.

"Just tired. It was a long night." Coyote adjusted his hat and leaned back.

"Your dad?" Mary asked, fearful of the answer.

"Dad's actually holding his own. They tried a new procedure on his heart early this morning as a last ditch effort. There's a chance it might work."

"That's good news," Nate said, searching Coyote's face. "What else is on your mind? What I hear in your voice and I see in your eyes doesn't strike me as joy or relief."

Coyote's look was solemn. He rose and offered Mary a seat. She shook her head and leaned against the wall. "After I talked to you last night, I tried to remember where I'd seen the name, Lonewolf. I ran through Johnny's file. I read your notes from your initial questioning. The name Lonewolf jumped off the page at me."

Mary's heart caught in her throat. "Lonewolf," she whispered and shot Nate a look filled with questions.

Nate nodded. "Johnny mentioned the name when we talked the first time."

"Why didn't you tell me that yesterday?" she demanded. Her stunned response jumped to anger.

"I didn't know what it meant and I didn't want to upset you until I had a chance to check it out." Nate's eyes shone with pure honesty. Perhaps, he had been trying to protect her.

Mary put her hand on her forehead in frustration. "Oh God, he didn't somehow find out. What if he found the papers?"

"Easy boys and girls. I have the floor." Coyote raised his hand and managed a fatigued smile. "I went to the jail and met with Johnny. I asked him why he said his name was Lonewolf in that interview." Coyote paced behind the desk as he talked. "He told me some guy had grabbed hold of him in the park here in Santa Fe a week or so ago." Coyote's eyes blazed as he turned toward Nate. "He mistook Johnny for his son."

"And the bastard's name was Lonewolf," Nate's eyes flared as he finished the sentence for Coyote.

"You got it. Said the guy kept calling him Lonewolf from across the park. Johnny kept walking, but the guy chased him down and stopped him. When he got close, he acted funny and then said, he was sorry he'd mistaken Johnny for his son."

"And Johnny?" Mary stood aghast as she listened to the story.

Coyote shrugged. "Thought the name was cool and decided to use it for fun with the other kids. He was scared shitless when they arrested him, especially after what happened to Angelo, so the first name that came to mind, he gave to the police."

Mary's mind was racing. She turned toward Nate. "What does it mean?"

"I think it means Johnny's father was here in Santa Fe with Johnny's twin brother sometime in the last few weeks."

Mary gasped and her eyes widened. "Oh my gosh."

"I don't know if we can prove it, but this, along with Irene's story and the drawing from the Los Alamos police, might buy us time for an investigation and get Johnny's bond reduced enough we could get him out of jail."

"What about the DNA test?" Mary asked.

"DNA can be the same for identical twins. It's not guaranteed, but it could answer the question." Coyote interjected.

"But wouldn't we have to have the other boy to prove it?" Mary asked.

"That's the problem." Nate's troubled eyes went to Coyote who pushed his hat back on his head.

"I think we have enough right now to take to the DA and make a proposal." Coyote pressed the issue.

"Can you do that?" Mary's heart lifted.

"Damn right I can." Nate turned toward Coyote.

"Got a preliminary for you with Smith at three o'clock today." Coyote's face darkened. "But before we start celebrating I want you to sit down and listen." He pointed to Mary and indicated the side chair across from him.

The seriousness in his eyes sent a chill through Mary. Coyote was never like this. She glanced at Nate, who looked at Coyote and shrugged, then stepped around in front of the chair and sat.

"Part two of my night, last night, concerns our friend the DA." Strain showed in Coyote's face. Mary's heartbeat kicked up a notch as she listened. "Last night when I was with my dad, things looked pretty bleak. We both thought the end was close. Thinking he was on his deathbed, he confided something to me he's never told another living soul." Coyote lifted his hat and wiped the perspiration from his forehead. Replacing the hat, he leaned across the desk and looked Nate in the eye. "Dad swore me to secrecy, Nate, but if Smith is the one behind the beating and tampering with your car, you need to know what you're dealing with."

Nate cocked his head and listened.

"Nate knows it all," Mary interjected. "I told him about the accident and Angelo's conviction."

"Well, I know something even you don't, Mary." Coyote shook his head as if he couldn't believe what he was about to say. "The day of the robbery Angelo was accused of, Smith called my dad into his office." He glanced at Nate. "Smith was the DA then and dad was the head of investigations for the Santa Fe PD. Dad was a year away from retirement. He told my dad there was going to be a robbery that afternoon. That he was to show up at the liquor store at five o'clock and place Angelo under arrest."

"What?" Mary shook her head in disbelief. "What are you saying Coyote?"

"According to Dad, Angelo was very predictable, dangerously so, it seems. He stopped every day at that liquor store and picked up a six-pack and a pint of vodka on his way home from work. He sat in his truck and drank a beer then drove home to Chimayo. You could set your watch by his schedule."

"He always came home with five beers and a pint and finished it all before he went to bed," Mary said in a low voice.

Nate rubbed his eyes and shook his head. Mary knew it was her pain he was feeling this time. It had been one hell of a way to live.

Coyote went on. "So Smith devised a scheme. Seems the liquor storeowner had repeated offenses for selling booze to minors and was in danger of losing his license. Smith intervened in the legal system, as it seems he's become skilled at, and in exchange for *fixing* things for the store owner, he got the guy to agree to testify Angelo held up his store."

"And your dad?" Nate asked.

"He objected soundly. Until Smith threatened to pull strings and get him fired before his retirement date. He was Smith's insurance. Dad was Smith's undisputable, upstanding witness, who was to coincidentally be in the parking lot at the time and see Angelo run from the building with a gun."

"Angelo never owned a gun." Mary was so taken back by the story she could barely speak. She could hardly believe Smith was capable of such devious actions.

"Oh, that was part of Dad's job, too. Plant the gun and a paper bag full of cash in Angelo's truck. You know, just any old gun from confiscated weapons at the station would work." Coyote snorted. He looked at Mary whose hands were over her eyes at this point. "I'm having as much trouble believing this as you. But dammit, Mary, my dad told me this story when he thought he was dying."

"I know." She bit her lip and shot him a compassionate look. "It's okay, Coyote. I want to hear the rest."

Coyote's voice was strained and higher pitched than normal. "Then my father, the man I've spent my life respecting, took the witness stand and perjured himself before a judge and jury by testifying he saw Angelo run from the store with the money under his arm and the gun in his hand."

Coyote sat down in the chair and buried his face in his hands. Emotion choked his voice. "Mary, I don't know what to say to you. My old man said there were three inmates in Angelo's cellblock he could connect to Smith. Somebody killed Angelo in the prison exercise yard. Smith told my dad Angelo had to pay for Ethan's death. Smith said he wanted you to know the pain he'd felt. My dad believes Smith had him killed."

"Jesus," Nate whispered under his breath.

Mary drew in a deep breath, trying to compose herself from the torrent of anger and pain raging in her soul. "I knew. I knew Smith did this. I knew Angelo was wrongly accused. I just didn't know how far Smith had gone to accomplish it." Tears threatened, but she choked them back. *No more tears. Not for sadness and not for anger.*

She looked at Coyote and the devastation in his eyes. She slipped onto her knees and reached across the desk for Coyote. She grasped his arms. "Coyote, you cannot hate your father for this. You have to forgive him. He's dying. You can't let this come between you and him, between you and his memory. He did a bad thing, but Smith played on his desperation. Smith used his power to carry out his vendetta."

Nate's eyes were on her. "Desperation indeed." He scratched his chin and gazed out the window. "I wonder how far Gonzales is from retirement?"

"About two years. I checked." Coyote retorted. "I had to tell you, Nate, even though it broke a confidence with my father. Smith is a dangerous man. His grief for Ethan has driven him insane. I want you to be careful. He's capable of almost anything."

Nate patted Coyote's shoulder. "I appreciate the sacrifice you made for me." He looked at Mary. "For us. Why don't you go home and get some sleep. We'll take it from here."

Coyote nodded. "It's been a long morning after a long night. I sat here for hours trying to find the courage to tell Mary." He reached across the desk and picked up the kachina. "And talking it out with your bizarre little friend here. You know something about him kind of gives me the creeps."

Nate smiled and took the kachina from Coyote. "Go easy on him. He's a family heirloom." Turning it over slowly in his hands, he tipped it over and glanced at the bottom. Suddenly, his face froze, then went pale, his eyes fixed on something on the base of the kachina.

"What is it?" Mary asked.

"Feathers." Nate turned the bottom of the carved figure so she could see. A circle of painted feathers in assorted colors outlined the perimeter of the base.

Their eyes met. There was a long silence. Nate rubbed his hand across his shirt pocket as a crease formed in his brow. He put the kachina back in its place on the desk.

"What does it mean?" Mary searched his face.

"I don't know," Nate replied. "I truly don't know."

"Well, what now?" Coyote asked, seeming not to notice what had transpired between them.

Nate cleared his throat. "You're going to get some sleep, while Mary and I decide what's next."

Mary nodded. That statement could have any number of meanings at this moment.

CHAPTER TWENTY-FOUR

"I'm trying to figure out how this deal with Johnny fits in with Smith." Nate turned toward Mary as he tried to set aside his thoughts of the kachina and assemble what he'd learned the last two days in his mind.

"Smith's behind it somehow," Mary stormed. "We already know he's capable of anything. You heard Coyote's story."

"I did. But too many other things have come into play. And all the pieces don't make sense." He rubbed his jaw, shooting another wary glance at the painted figure on his desk.

"I've wondered if Smith planned the attack on Stellar. I think he's capable of it." Mary continued.

"But I don't think he did. I think he jumped on the bandwagon when fate played into his hands." Nate moved behind his desk and sat in his chair. "If Johnny didn't do it, and we have a perfect match on the DNA, then either the DNA test was wrong, or Johnny's twin brother is the real assailant. Proven by the murder in Los Alamos, and the fact that Johnny had contact with someone in the park named Lonewolf, who mistook him for his son."

"That worries me. Do you think this man Lonewolf might figure out who Johnny is and try to contact him again? After all, Johnny would be his son, too."

"I don't know. Maybe we should be grateful Johnny's in the lock up right now."

Mary rolled her eyes. "I see your point." She let out a heavy sigh. "So what do we do?"

"From a legal standpoint, we don't have jack crap we can prove. Let's concentrate on Johnny right now. We've got a hell of a lot to prove and a lot of circumstantial evidence we're building a case on. And we're lacking one major component. The real assailant. At this point, it's all conjecture."

"Now you sound like an attorney." She rubbed her eyes. "What you're saying is there's a lot left to do to get Johnny cleared."

"Yeah. And it's going to be about as easy as finding a fart in a wind storm," Nate muttered.

"What was that?"

"Never mind."

"The biggest problem is no one knows what happened in that alley. And Smith and his people will use it to hang us." Mary paced in front of his desk.

Nate raised an eyebrow and moved uncomfortably. There were some things he hadn't shared with Mary. One more can of worms was left unopened. "The easy solution isn't going to happen. The only person who knows the truth can't help us."

"Stellar." Mary shook her head. "You're right. And she knows Johnny so well, I know she'd be able to tell if it was him. Even someone who looked like him wouldn't fool her."

"Good friends, are they?"

"More than that. They grew up together. Johnny's had a crush on her since he was in fifth grade. She probably knows him better than I do."

"You think she couldn't be fooled?"

"When you care that much for someone, you can tell. She could identify Johnny, even in the dark." An odd look washed over her face and she stared at Nate.

Her words hit him like a spear. His mind flashed on the vision he'd had in Grandpa's hogan. Mary's reaction and something in her eyes made him wonder.

Had she experienced the same vision? Dare he risk asking? His mouth went dry.

Mary regained her composure, but seemed rattled. "I think she would know." She ran a finger across her lips.

Nate glanced at his watch and fingered the keys on his desk. "I think, I'll run home and change into some fresh clothes before I meet with our friend the DA."

"Smith," she snorted. "I have enough on him to put him where Johnny is. Behind bars."

"Gathering the evidence we'd need, Mary, is going to take time. All we have is Coyote's statement."

"That will never be known to anyone," she snapped and seared him with her eyes. "Unless Coyote decides to bring it to light, it will remain in sacred trust. I'm already faced with destroying one trust to save Johnny."

"I agree." Nate nodded. "I feel the same way. But all these *sacred trusts* are standing between us and justice being served, so what do we really have on Smith that we can prove?"

"Nothing. But, tell me, will what Coyote shared right the wrongs or bring back the dead? Of course not. What it will do is destroy the reputation of his father and cause Coyote to betray someone he loves dearly."

"Then the bottom line is Smith is still in control. And we're going to have to work with it."

"Maybe the only way to stop Smith is to confront him. I'm going with you this afternoon," Mary said firmly. "He needs to give Johnny a chance. And I want Johnny out of that jail cell."

Nate shook his head. "I don't want you to come. You've got too much to deal with and you're way too close to this emotionally. Too many things have come at you, too quickly. You need time to work through it."

"Are you telling me I can't, Mr. Nakai?" Her words stung and so did her look. She hadn't called him that for a while.

"Yes," he retorted. "You're not up to doing this, Mary. It would be a mistake."

Defiance flared in her eyes. Her gaze went from him to the desk. She rubbed her lips together and swallowed hard. "I've got to go home and check on Grandpa. I'll catch up with you later."

"Damn," he whispered as she stomped out the door. Usually, bringing the facts to light helped solve the problem. In this case, the more he was enlightened the more complicated things became. Now it was driving a wedge between them, when at last the truth had set them free. The irony of it rushed through him and settled in his gut.

He didn't want Mary to be angry with him, but she was so damn hardheaded he'd never get through to her. After the night they'd shared, things between them could never be the same. The smell of her skin still clung to him. The taste of her lips was still sweet upon his. The depth of his desire and the power of his attraction to her had the ability to skew his thoughts. But they were dealing with serious matters that couldn't be approached without a clear head. Neither his head, nor hers. And his better damn well be in the game today.

He looked at his watch again. There was one thing he wanted to do before he met with Smith. He knew he was hoping for a miracle or at least some incredible luck. A little favor from the gods sure wouldn't hurt. If he ever needed them in his corner, he did this afternoon.

An eerie feeling swept over him. Apprehension tightened his chest. The same feeling he'd had the night he left Mesa Verde. The message came again. *Danger.* He rubbed his temple. The picture of Stellar flashed through his mind. From his gut feeling, he didn't have much time to get where he was going.

"The car's at the body shop and you don't know what happened to him?" Smith roared into the phone.

"I checked the hospitals and even the morgue. No call ever came in at the station. I guess I'm not surprised."

"So you're telling me, he walked away. What the hell did he do? Say, 'oh well,' and go back home?"

"He's not there, either. Or at his office. The guy at the body shop said he left in a cab with a woman."

"You went to the body shop?"

"I pulled up in front when I saw the car. Some guy was crossing the parking lot and asked me if I was there to take the prints."

"And you, of course, said yes."

"I figured eventually Nakai was going to report it. Didn't think it would hurt. Gave it a good dusting. Now we can be sure Ernie didn't leave any trace behind. Especially, since I'd already been seen, thought it best if I played along."

"But you said he didn't file a police report, you dunderhead. How does that stupid move figure in?"

"Nobody will ever be the wiser. If it comes up, I can explain it real easy."

"Yeah, right." *What a moron.* Smith gritted his teeth. "And I'll lay odds the woman was Mary Begay. Why the hell was she with him?"

"The guy at the shop told me Nakai said something about going to Los Alamos."

"Los Alamos? Ah, shit."

"What's wrong? Lots of people go there. Maybe he took a day trip with the dame."

"Nothing, you idiot. Nothing," Smith roared. "Just keep your head down and your mouth shut for God's sake."

"Whatever you say."

Smith's hands trembled as he put down the phone. There was a knock on his office door.

"Yes," Smith barked. "What is it?"

His blond middle-aged receptionist popped her head through the door and asked, "Everything okay in here? I thought I heard loud voices."

Straining to sound normal, Smith replied, "Everything's fine Mrs. Abernathy. Thank you for your concern."

She smiled and nodded as she turned to walk away. "Mrs. Abernathy, how's my schedule this afternoon?" Smith called after her.

She turned back. "Open until three o'clock. Then you have an appointment with someone named Nakai from the Public Defender's office."

Smith's hackles raised. "Nakai, huh?"

"Yes, sir. That's it for today." She closed the door and left him to his own devices. Some days he was grateful for her lack of attention to details. It made his life a hell of a lot easier.

Obviously, another plan had failed. Gonzales was a blithering idiot. "I never should have trusted him with this," Smith muttered. Nakai had gone to Los Alamos and he'd bet his last dollar Mary was in tow. One of the two of them had read the flipping Sunday paper. He hit the desk with his fist. He loosened his collar as heat boiled up the back of his neck.

Putting his head in his hands, he leaned on the desk. He had to calm down and think this through, logically. If they did find something in Los Alamos, it would take time. They didn't have a leg to stand on, unless they could find the Los Alamos killer and pull together the evidence. It was such a long shot. What were the chances there was a connection between the two crimes anyway? But all Nakai had to do was prove a reasonable doubt to a jury. And this could be his ace in the hole.

The only way left to get rid of Nakai was to pull the trigger himself and that wasn't an option. He had to face the truth and the potential consequences. Nakai probably wasn't leaving the case, so what were his other choices?

His eye twitched. If luck would play into his hands one more time, he could have the Begay kid's destiny sewed up. They'd lock him up and throw away the key. And Smith could turn the knife in Mary Begay's back one more time. The thought made his breath short.

He fingered the dial on the phone. He could call Gonzales and check on the girl. But Gonzales was an idiot. *Never mind.* He'd handle things himself from here on out.

He picked up the phone and dialed the reception desk. "Mrs. Abernathy, I'll be out for a while."

"You'll be back for your three o'clock?"

"With bells on, my dear. With bells on."

Fifteen minutes later, Smith looked both ways down the corridor before he stepped quietly into the room. He crossed soundlessly and stood at the foot of the hospital bed. Hands folded in front of him he studied Stellar Sanchez. She seemed small and frail propped on the pile of white pillows.

Dark lashes fringed her closed eyes. Cheeks that had lost their healthy pink glow were now slack and hallowed. A clear plastic tube was inserted into her mouth. A machine controlled her breathing. Up and down, her chest moved along with the hissing sound of the machine.

No family was with her. But he knew her mother, a Hispanic woman alone with far too many mouths to feed and far too little money to do it with. She was always haggard-looking and cross. No wonder she wasn't here. One less mouth to feed, one less child to clothe and send to school. And there was no hope here, only a hospital bill that grew with each passing hour. He removed a white handkerchief from his pocket and used it to wipe the perspiration from his brow.

He let out a long deep sigh. The person who did this to her was an animal. A wicked, evil piece of existence.

That person didn't deserve to be alive and well. Smith chewed at his lip as the hatred swelled within him.

It was a sad, unjust world where some punk gang member could do something like this to an innocent girl. He gritted his teeth. Then land some fancy big city lawyer, paid for by the state. He clasped his hands behind him and paced back and forth at the foot of her bed. And get off with only a slap on the wrist.

Yes, it was the same lousy fricking world where two dirty drunken Indians could kill a man's son and never have to stand trial. Two cold-blooded killers. One was dead, and the other was going to pay, and pay, and pay. The other was going to know the agony of losing everything just the way he had.

He looked back at Stellar, lying in that bed, being kept alive by machines. *More alive than dead.* She was lifeless, helpless and from what Gonzales said, hopeless. He plunged his hands in his pockets and chewed harder on his lip.

How long could she hang on? How long before— He'd heard of people being kept alive by machines for years. Yes, it was a crappy, crappy world.

Walking to the window, he stared out at a clear blue sky and rubbed his chin. The second this became murder one, he could convince a judge to put Johnny Begay away forever. Creating an outrage that would speed the trial through the court system toot sweet would be a cakewalk. He ran a hand through his hair.

Casually, he stepped nearer the side of the bed, a frown embedded in his brow. His eyes followed the array of tubes from Stellar to assorted machines next to him. So this was what was keeping her alive. Which ones were essential?

His hands trembled as he reached out a finger and ran it across one of the tubes. He looked at the machine, wondering if an alarm would sound if the tube were blocked.

One little squeeze, or one small hole and—

What the hell are you doing? The voice screamed inside his head. A flood of horror washed through him. He looked down at the tubes. Pulling back as if they'd burned his hands, he stepped away.

Dear God, has it come to this? Tears choked at his throat. The thought had actually crossed his mind to take the life of someone else's child. He'd have inflicted the pain and grief on another that had almost killed him. No matter how near death she was, he didn't have it in him to go this far. No matter how bad he wanted revenge on Mary Begay, he couldn't do this.

What have you become? The voices hammered in his head. Whatever it was, it wasn't this. His hands suddenly felt dirty. *Filthy.* He had to find a place to wash. Skirting the bed, he headed for the door. He stopped short in front of a mirror above the washbasin near the door. Who was that wild-eyed crazy man in the mirror? He ran his hands down his face as his heart hammered. *Shit. It's me.* Oh God, when did this happen to him? He rushed from the room.

Nate rounded the corner into the hospital room and was knocked off balance as someone pushed past, someone running from the room. Caught off guard, it took a moment before he realized it was Jim Smith who had brushed by. What the hell was he doing here?

Nate's gut riled. The bastard. He turned and glared after Smith as he disappeared down the hall. He'd deal with Smith in a while. He couldn't allow Smith to rattle him. He had a far different agenda. He had to see Stellar one more time, and the more open his mind was, the better chance he'd have of getting through.

He walked into the room. Little had changed since the last time he was there. Perhaps she was a little thinner, a little paler, but she still looked like the sleeping child that she was. He was tough, he was jaded, but his heart wasn't stony enough to avoid the sadness of this young life that seemed to be slipping away.

Stepping to her bedside, he took her small hand in his. He ran his fingers over the back of it and tried to release all he held in his mind except for Stellar.

He wet his lips and spoke softly. "Stellar, I don't know if you can hear me, but somehow you communicated with me when this happened. Somehow, I was there with you the day when you were hurt." He brought her fingers to his lips and went on. "Please, Stellar, we need your help. We need you to be okay and we need you to come back to us so you can tell us what happened. No one will ever believe me if you aren't here with me."

Tears welled in his eyes as he went on. "I know you're hurting and it's going to be hard for you to leave that place you're in, where you've found peace and rest, but I don't think it's time for you to leave us. I think if God wanted to take you, he would have by now. I really believe that."

Swallowing a lump in his throat, he went on. He had to. "I know I'm asking a lot, but I also know you love Johnny. And if you don't come back to help him, I don't know if I can keep him out of prison. He needs you, Stellar. We all need you. You're the only one who can make this awful thing stop for Johnny."

Nate shifted his feet and pressed her fingers to his cheek. "I want Johnny to be able to go home and I want you to help me find the awful person who hurt you. I swear to you, I'll find him. That I promise you. He won't get away with this."

He paused to wipe a stream of tears he could no longer contain with his other hand. "Honey, if there isn't any way you can come back, please, please send me a message. I heard you before, I can hear you again. I'd never even seen you then, now I'm here. I'm right here. You see, you and I are connected in some crazy way I don't understand. I can walk in your head and see through your eyes. It happened before, I believe it can happen again."

"I need your help, Johnny needs your help and this incredible woman I've fallen in love with, needs your help, too. You know Mary, don't you? She's been hurt so badly and I want to make things right in her life for a change."

"What's happened to you isn't fair and what's happened to her isn't either. If you can just open your eyes and be okay, then maybe, I can make some things right for both of you."

If only she could hear him. He gently brushed a lock of her hair aside and leaned closer. "You see, honey, people here need you and you need to live so you can grow up and have beautiful babies of your own. There are people who love you and want you to have a better life, and I'll see that happens, too, if you'll come back."

He looked down at her small hand in his. Dear God, she was only a child. "I wish I could know you hear me. I wish I could be certain. If you hear me, please give me a sign. I don't want to leave here without knowing." He looked expectantly into her face. She'd opened her eyes the last time. He was certain of it. He watched. He waited. Nothing. All that was there was the peaceful up and down motion of her chest and the hum of the machines keeping her alive. The lump in his throat swelled again. Gently, he pulled his hand from hers. He looked down at his palm in disbelief. Nestled in his hand was a snow white feather. "Oh my God," he whispered.

"Nate." A voice came from the doorway. "That was beautiful." Mary stood behind him, tears streaming down her cheeks.

"I didn't hear you come in," Nate stuttered unable to take his eyes from the feather in his palm.

"I'm sorry. I walked in while you were talking." She rubbed her fingers over her eyes. "I had no idea, you'd been here to see Stellar. You spoke to her like she is close to you."

Nate's thoughts were scattered. "I know her in a way I can't explain, Mary. I— Look, Mary. She heard me." He held out the feather for Mary to see.

She looked at him incredulously. "Where did it come from?"

"She put it in my hand. I asked for a sign and somehow—she put it in my hand."

"Sit down, Nate. You look pale." Mary took his arm and guided him into a bedside chair. Her hand trembled on his arm.

He looked into Mary's questioning eyes. "The last day I was in San Francisco, before I came here, I stood on a pier and I had a vision of what happened to Stellar."

Mary's chin quivered and her hand trembled as she put it to her mouth. "You saw Stellar?"

"Mary, I didn't just see her, I saw what happened to her—through her eyes. I didn't understand until I came here weeks later. When I saw her lying in that bed, I knew. I don't understand it, but it happened."

Mary's eyes were wide and she tried to comprehend what he was saying. "You never said anything. You never told me."

"I didn't tell anyone. I didn't know how I could ever explain it."

Mary bit her lip. Her look was sullen. "Then you saw who did this to her?"

"Yes, Mary, I did."

"Is that the real reason you decided to resign from the case?"

Nate nodded.

"Oh my God." Mary whispered. "I don't know what to say. You saw Johnny, didn't you?"

"I saw his face. Yes. But I also saw the eyes from that drawing, and the hat, too." He reached into his shirt pocket and held up the plastic bag. "With this damn black and white feather hanging from the brim. That's what I saw, Mary. That's what I've been trying to make sense of these last weeks. How can I prove what's in my mind in a court of law." His hands trembled as he held the bag.

"You can't, but we can find the boy and the hat it came from. It's what we have to do."

Nate nodded. "But first, I have to meet with Smith." He placed the white feather in the bag with the others. "Maybe, this one will bring more answers when I do."

"I'm going with you." Mary stood her ground.

"No." Nate was adamant. "Now isn't the time for you to confront your ghosts or his. It isn't right."

"I won't argue with you any more," she said, refusing to meet his eyes. She reached into her purse and pulled out a small bag of dirt. "I came to bring this to Stellar." She tucked it gently beneath the girl's pillow.

"What is it?"

"Healing soil from the Sanctuario in Chimayo." She bowed her head and whispered a prayer.

Nate watched her silently, rising to his feet and bowing his head. He nodded. "We could use a miracle."

"I still believe in them," Mary said stoically. "And I believe joy can rise above pain, and in the healing power of love, for Stellar and for me. Who can say what is possible or impossible in the world of the spirit. You know it's there, and so do I. You have to trust in it, Nate."

She turned toward him and he bent and kissed her lips. "If you can believe after all you've been through, Mary. I can believe, too."

"You told her you loved me," Mary said softly. Nodding in Stellar's direction, she hovered close to his lips. "You've never told me."

"I do love you, Mary. I'm sorry, I didn't say it before."

"It's okay. You've said it in other ways. Keep the faith. Together, we're going to take this on and conquer it."

"Her help wouldn't hurt." Nate looked at Stellar.

"Indeed it wouldn't." She glanced at her watch. "It's two thirty. You have a meeting to get to."

"Yeah. I'll have to strap on my hard ass for that one." He said, under his breath, knowing he'd have to reach deep down for the strength to confront Smith.

"You're up to the task," she smiled and kissed him on the cheek. "What kind of maiden would send her man to slay the dragon without a kiss?"

He smiled. She was right. He'd done it before; he'd do it again. He turned away and walked toward the door. An asshole was waiting for him across town.

Mary watched him walk away. It was her dragon he was going to slay and she couldn't let him face it alone. No matter how angry he would be at her for showing up, she had to be there. In time, he'd have to understand.

"Don't worry, Stellar," Mary said to the unconscious girl. "I won't let anything happen to him. I can't. This is my battle he's fighting, and it's your battle, too. He's put himself in danger and I can't stand by and do nothing." She patted Stellar's hand and walked out into the hall.

CHAPTER TWENTY-FIVE

Smith wiped the sweat from his face. He looked at his trembling hands. What a hell of a time to have to meet with Nakai. Maybe he could cancel. He glanced at the clock on his desk. *Too late. Two fifty-eight.* At least, he had the presence of mind to send Mrs. Abernathy home early. She was the last thing he needed. Nosing around every time somebody raised his voice. Things could get ugly with Nakai. In fact, he was sure they would.

The minutes dragged by. It seemed an eternity between each change of the digital numbers. What the hell did Nakai want? And Nakai had seen him at the hospital.

Smith wet his lips and slipped into the chair behind his desk. He had to stay calm. He had to pull himself together. His body vibrated. Dammit, he couldn't afford to fall apart. The case, the whole situation, was dangerously close to slipping out of his control—and he *always* kept things in his control.

He should have never gone to see the girl. *Stupid.* His inner voices raged. It was too risky, in too many ways. Look at him. He glanced down at his shaking hands. He was a flipping wreck.

Nakai was a sharp attorney. Nakai didn't lose cases. That was the reason Nakai had to go. No matter what. Smith stuffed his hands in his armpits. It would take a miracle for him to hide the state he was in from that shark. He shivered. He'd realized this afternoon, he was walking a tight rope. His teeth sunk into his lower lip. What was going to happen if he fell? He'd never known fear. Today, he was afraid.

Shit. Breathe, for God's sake. Breathe. Pull yourself together or it's over. It's all over. Nakai will be here any second. You can't let him see you like this.

He thought of the many times he'd stood before a jury and put on a convincing performance. He was getting older, but he could pull it off one more time. The stakes were different this time, but the act required was the same.

The internal lecture seemed to help, the extra oxygen he'd managed to suck in calmed his nerves. He straightened his tie. What the hell had come over him? Was he losing his grip? Had all the years he'd lived in his private hell of unfathomable grief and anger finally taken their toll? He'd been close to snapping before, but never anything like this. Today he'd looked in the mirror and seen insanity staring back at him. It was a sobering experience. A terrifying tight rope to walk.

Inhaling deeply, he blew out a long breath. He could do this. He could handle whatever Nakai could dish out. He had to. Wetting his lips, he reached deep inside himself and pulled out the one thing that never let him down. His hatred for Mary Begay. The daily emotion had sustained him for almost three years— Since the day she'd killed his son.

He would keep going until the woman had paid for everything she'd done. Vengeance would be sweet and it would be his. But for now, she hadn't begun to suffer as he had. A sense of control swept through him.

It was Mary Begay's fault he'd gotten to this point. And it was her fault Nakai was in the middle of it. Smith nodded, controlling the quiver in his lower lip. He could deal with her and Nakai, both if need be. He ran his hand down the right side of his desk, stopping at the middle drawer. And they better not doubt he had the guts and the means to do so. Whatever he had to do. After all, it was his job to see justice served. A strange sense of calm came over him.

A twenty-minute car trip across town, in anticipation of meeting with the man who'd almost killed him the morning before, had moved Nate from one highly emotional state into another. He rubbed a hand across his mouth as he walked down the hallway. Trying to focus on the sound of his shoes on the tile, he was determined to hold his anger in check. Keeping his cool would be essential.

Smith was in control of Johnny's world and Johnny could be in danger, too. Gonzales had to be involved. But there was no rock solid evidence to prove what he knew was truth. Until that changed, all he could do was play the game. And playing it was getting harder by the moment.

Nate stepped into the eerie quiet that hung over the reception area. There was no one at the desk. Nate glanced around. *Where is the bastard?* Was Smith too big of a coward to face him?

The silent emptiness of the office made him uncomfortable. He didn't like it. He observed the half-closed door. Smith could be in there. It could be a trap. He mustered his poker face and swallowed the rage he knew he must keep hidden. Cautiously, he approached. Rapping on the door with his knuckles to give Smith fair warning, Nate pushed the door open.

"Thought maybe you weren't here," Nate said. "The place looks deserted."

Smith leaned back in his chair behind the desk and glowered at his visitor. "I never miss an appointment."

Nate made a quick scan of the room to be assured Smith was alone. Gingerly, he stepped across the threshold and into the office. As he neared, an uneasy feeling came over him. A grim expression was on

Smith's face. Thick eyelids veiled the distaste in his eyes, distanced by his heavy glasses. An ominous feeling hung in the air, emitted by the man across the desk.

Nate recognized hatred when he saw it. The feeling was becoming mutual. His gut tightened. Considering the bastard had tried twice to get rid of him without success, he must be seething under the surface. He'd arranged the perfect frame for Angelo and successfully kept it hidden for more than two years. But even the best had a chink somewhere in their armor.

Smith said nothing, his jaw tightened.

Feeling less concerned a knife was about to be stuck in his back, Nate walked over to the desk. "Let's get down to business."

"By all means," Smith snarled and motioned toward the chair across from him.

Nate shook his head. "This won't take that long." He slapped a manila folder on Smith's desk and assumed his stance. His shoulders were squared and his feet wide apart.

"I hope you have a good reason for taking my time," Smith hissed.

"Johnny Begay. I'm here to negotiate his bail."

Smith snorted. "You're right. This won't take long."

"I didn't come here, because I thought you'd agree. I came, because it's proper protocol."

"He'll never see the light of day as long as I'm DA."

Nate shot a quick look at Smith, all he could stand. Anger seethed and his ears burned. Smith still held the trump card. There was too much on the table to risk losing his temper. He swallowed hard and kept his breathing even.

Nate flipped open the file. He removed the composite drawing and laid it in front of Smith. "I obtained this from the Los Alamos police. It was created from the description of an eye witness to a murder there four days ago." He pushed it closer to Smith.

Smith's eyes bulged as he examined the picture. He tapped nervously on the desk and his face went pale.

Nate went on. "Based on the resemblance between this boy and Johnny, I'm requesting bond be set. I'm also requesting an extension for the trial to allow time for a thorough investigation of this new evidence." Nate's voice echoed in the room like a reading by a bad actor. To him, it was rehearsed, cold and emotionless. The way he had to keep it, or he'd lean over the desk and strangle the son of a bitch.

Smith slid the drawing back toward Nate. "I won't negotiate anything. You'll have to take it to a higher court and I'll fight you every step of the way. For all I care, the little butcher can die behind bars."

"Just like Angelo?" Mary's voice came from behind Nate.

"Mary, this is not the time." Nate whirled. "I told you not to come here."

"And I told you I couldn't stay away." She ignored him and went on. "My brother can die behind bars like my husband, then you'll finally be satisfied?"

Smith looked from Nate to Mary. He grasped the edge of his desk and started to bolt from his chair. Glancing down and to his right, his frantic expression changed abruptly. He stopped and sat down. His face grew paler and his hands visibly trembled. "What are you doing in my office?" Smith barked at Mary.

"That's enough. This meeting is finished." An explosive situation was brewing and it was up to Nate to stop it. "We'll let the legal system decide. I'm taking this evidence to the magistrate and as far as I have to go beyond."

Smith's eyes narrowed. He glared at Nate. Defiance distorted his face. His mouth puckered and he spit on the drawing as Nate slid it back toward the file folder.

Nate clenched his teeth and he went on. "You'll be notified of the time to appear. Unless, of course, you have a beating to arrange or a car to tamper with that conflicts with the scheduled court date."

A visible quiver went through Smith's entire body. His eyes darted intermittently between Nate and Mary.

Nate's head pounded. His hand formed a fist. This was what he didn't want to happen. Mary stood behind him and to his left, and back several feet. He could feel the anger and the tension coming from her.

"I will get my brother out of jail, Mr. Smith. I promise you I will."

"I forbid you to be here you—you—" Rage quivered in Smith's features.

"Bitch?" Mary flared. "Is that the word you're looking for? Yes, Mr. Smith, as long as you are a threat to the people I love, I will be a bitch beyond your wildest imagination."

Smith's lips vibrated. "Yes, *bitch*. Filth. Dirty drunken Indian whore. Shall I look for more adjectives?" Smith seethed under his breath.

"That's enough," Nate stormed. He glared at Smith. "I won't tolerate you talking to her that way."

Smith slammed his fist onto the desk, as he turned his fiery eyes on Mary. "How dare you speak of what I've done to *your* loved ones. You killed my son."

"Shut up, Smith," Nate stifled a shout. Heat surged through him and he resisted an urge to throw a punch at Smith. He twitched, forcing himself to remember. The man held Johnny's future, for now. He couldn't afford to lose it, or to let this go any further.

"Is she your girlfriend?" Smith raged at Nate. "The whore's been around enough. First my son, then the drunk she married."

"I'm going to pretend I didn't hear that." Nate pushed the words past the fury in his throat. He reached for the saliva-spotted picture. "You filthy pig," he muttered under his breath. Every muscle in his body was taut, like a spring ready to pop. His eyes darted between Mary and Smith. He could hear Mary's breath behind him, stifling angry puffs of air. Nate knew her emotions were too high to face Smith. They were at a fever pitch. She didn't belong here in this state of mind.

"What you've done in the past, you won't get away with any more," Mary vowed.

Nate sized up Smith. His face was red as an apple. He glared at Mary and pulled at his tie. His pulse visibly pounded in the bulging veins at his temple and in his neck.

"I think it's time we left," Nate said over his shoulder to Mary. He shoved the drawing back into the folder. His blood boiled at Smith's behavior. "This is a matter for the higher court. I should have known it couldn't be resolved here. And while I'm there Mr. Smith, there will be a few more matters addressed about the ethics of the current District Attorney. I'm calling for a full scale investigation."

Smith's eyes went to Mary. "She's the cause of all this. Get her out of my sight."

"She's leaving with me."

"Maybe, nobody's leaving." Smith squinted, then grumbled under his breath.

Nate started to turn toward Mary, but hesitated for a moment, observing a change in Smith's behavior. Suddenly, a strange calm came over him. His hand moved from the desktop to the arm of his chair then down. A sliding noise caught Nate's ear. The faint sound of metal rubbing on metal caused him to turn back toward Smith.

The tip of a gun barrel appeared over the edge of the desk. Nate took a step back and threw out his arm to protect Mary, prepared to shield her with his body.

"No," Mary said as she pushed Nate's arm aside. "This is my war."

"Quiet. Don't anybody move," Smith said in a low raspy voice.

"You're flipping nuts," Nate whispered.

"That could be true," Smith said. Rising stiffly from his chair, he moved in sideways steps to the door and pushed it silently shut.

Nate focused his thoughts on escape. His brain twisted in his skull from their intensity. They had to find a way out of this. What should he do? Smith was insane—and he had a gun. Nate surveyed the situation as Smith moved from the door and stepped in front of his desk. Smith faced them. Nate stood about three feet away. Two side chairs were between them. Mary was two feet behind him and to his left, nearer the door. Behind him was a conference table with four chairs, beyond that, a full wall bookcase filled with law books. Not many options if Smith fired.

"You don't want to do this," Nate said to Smith. He didn't know if he could talk Smith out of it, but he didn't feel that this was planned. Smith's actions were erratic. His hands trembled as he held the gun. Wild eyes darted from Nate to Mary, then appeared to consider what to do next.

"I guess this changes things," Smith said. His mouth trembled as he spoke. He wet his lips. His breathing was heavy. Beads of sweat visibly popped from his face. Beneath his thick glasses, his eyes had a wild look.

Nate bit his lip nervously. What was Smith thinking?

"I never wanted this," Smith muttered.

"You've made the choice," Nate said, trying to think of a way out. The gun vibrated. Smith nervously loosened his shirt collar.

Instinctively, Nate knew this wasn't part of Smith's plan, but rather an act of desperation. Did he think he wouldn't get caught? Smith seemed to disappear for a moment into his own dilemma. Now that he had them at gunpoint, what was he going to do?

Mary was silent, her arms folded as she observed Smith. An occasional ragged breath told Nate she was angry, but too terrified to push Smith. She finally spoke. "I never thought you'd take it this far."

"Shut up," Smith said, waving the gun wildly.

Nate saw his split second chance. The gun was pointed away from them for an eye blink. He jumped, pushing the chair in front of him into Smith. Smith met the chair with his foot and thrust it upward and into Nate with the strength of a frantic mule. The chair caught Nate a sharp blow under the chin and threw him backward. Off balance and semi-dazed, he lost his footing and fell. A sharp pain split through the back of his head as it struck the edge of the table behind him. Blackness engulfed him.

The crack of Nate's skull against the table sent fear jetting through Mary. With no regard to Smith and the gun, and without a second's hesitation, Mary fell to her knees next to Nate.

"Nate, are you all right? Nate." She patted his cheek.

Seeming stunned by the turn of events, Smith hovered over them fingering the gun. Anger overcame her. She wouldn't allow Smith to touch him. She would protect Nate, if she had to put her own life between them.

Mary jumped to her feet and whirled toward Smith. "You could have killed him. But isn't that what you've wanted?"

Smith grasped the gun. "No," he said loudly. "I wanted him off the case and away from you."

Mary's heart hammered. She kept her eye on Smith's hand and the gun. Her breathing was fast. "When does it stop, Mr. Smith? Where does this end?"

She stepped nearer and he stepped back. "He's hurt. He may need help," she demanded. Nate was here because of her. How could she forgive herself if anything happened to him? "Maybe you have no conscience, but I do."

Smith shook his head wildly. "No. He did it to himself. What he did was stupid." Smith nudged Nate's foot with his shoe.

"Don't touch him," Mary seethed and glared at Smith. "You aren't going to destroy him. For fifteen years you've haunted my life and destroyed my happiness. You will never again come between me and anyone I love."

"Don't blame me for your miserable existence. You were born to it."

"That's what you believe, isn't it? You believe because I'm Navajo, somehow I'm a lesser being than yourself. You want to stuff everyone of my ethnic background into your own private stereotype. You deprive us of our individual identity with your ignorance and prejudice. It's time you wake up and realize the color of my skin has little to do with who I am. The blood in my veins doesn't make me different or any less human than anyone else. It runs red, just like yours. And my heart beats, and loves, and breaks like everyone else's." She drew back and paced in front of Smith. "It's what started everything, as far back as high school. I loved your son. God only knows why, but I truly loved him."

"You weren't good enough to shine my son's shoes. My son had potential. He had a future. And, damn you, I stopped you once, but that wasn't enough. You came back and ended his life. You stole everything from me."

"You never really knew Ethan," she seethed. "I stole nothing from you. You want to talk about stealing, Mr. Smith? Let's talk about how you and your son stole my self-esteem and my self-respect. You stole years of my life, ruined my reputation, and turned this town into a place where I couldn't walk without heads turning. You never saw how you and your son turned the dreams of a young impressionable girl around and made me feel as if I wasn't good enough. It took me years to change that in my own mind."

"It was a high school crush. A love affair between two kids, until you interfered." She pointed at him accusingly. "You couldn't leave it alone. Ethan had to hide his feelings for me from *you*. *You* owned him. He wasn't your son. He was your possession. You taught him the most important thing was to please you. Nothing else mattered. He was who he was because of you. He turned to drugs because it was the only place he could go to escape your expectations. The only place where he didn't feel inadequate."

"You're a liar," Smith screamed.

"Your son was using drugs in high school. You have no idea of the things you drove him to do." She shuddered. "Ethan died in a tragic accident. He came around the curve that night in the middle of the road. I tried my best to avoid him. Three years hasn't changed the truth." She leaned closer to Smith. "I had no way of knowing Ethan was driving that car. It was simply a tragic twist of fate, and nothing more."

Smith's chin quivered with anger and emotion. "If it was an accident, and you cared for him as much as you say, why did you try to destroy him after he was gone? Why did you testify that he smelled of marijuana? Why did you destroy his image and his memory?"

"Do you think I did it by choice? It was no more my choice than killing him. I did it because the truth was the only thing that could be said. Angelo and I were both in danger of being charged with involuntary manslaughter. I know you never believed me, but I was the one behind the wheel of the car, not Angelo. Stone sober, and with all my faculties. If I hadn't been, there would have been three fatalities that night."

"You're right. I'll never believe that," Smith snorted.

"I never denied Angelo was drunk, but I was the one driving. You know what the court did was right. They had to drop the charges. In the end, it was my word against the evidence. And we know what the evidence showed. You should be grateful the findings weren't made public. That your friends in high places wanted to protect you as one of the community's upstanding public servants. What do you think they'd think of you now, Mr. Smith? What would they say if they knew what you've done out of revenge?"

"Shut up. Either way, my son is dead and it was your fault. You killed the only thing I had left in my life worth living for." Smith barked through trembling lips. "Who do you think they're going to believe? You and your attorney came into my office and threatened me. I shot you both in self-defense."

"The only thing you had to live for, indeed." Mary narrowed her eyes. "And when Ethan died you made your revenge the only thing worth getting up for in the morning. Your need to destroy me and my world became your new reason for living."

Smith's body shook with anger. His eyes grew wilder. "You don't know what it feels like to lose a child—you can't judge me for what I've done, for what you don't understand."

Mary's insides tied in a knot. How dare he say such a thing to her. "You have no idea what you're saying or what I've been through. Do you think you're the only person on earth capable of feeling loss? You arrogant son of a bitch." She pulled back her hand to slap him, but the gun in his trembling hand forced her to withdraw. "This has to stop, before any more tragedies happen."

She observed Smith as he hung his head and looked at the gun. His shaking grew noticeably worse.

She glanced over her shoulder at Nate who was still out cold on the floor. "You can't continue to destroy innocent lives to satisfy your sick revenge for me. If it will keep you from destroying Johnny and Nate, and who knows who else may come between us—I'll do anything. This vendetta is between us. You and me. Do what you must, but end it here—today. Before anyone else's life is destroyed because of it. Do what you have to do. Feel the pain you have to feel, but end this madness." Her body was trembling. "I can't do this anymore. You can't do this anymore."

She watched him intently, trying to calm herself as the two were locked in a standoff. She meant every word. Even if he shot her, no one else would be hurt. She swallowed hard and recited the Lord's Prayer under her breath. The piece of quivering insanity before her obviously considered his options. One thought hung in the back of her mind. If he was going to kill her, she wouldn't die without him knowing the real truth about the son he'd elevated to sainthood in his own mind.

Smith circled her as she kept her eyes on Nate. She couldn't enrage Smith to the point of pulling the trigger until Nate came to. If Smith shot her, she wanted Nate to at least have a fighting chance.

Periodically, she shifted her eyes to Smith, playing cat and mouse with the madman. He was capable of anything, but to her knowledge he'd never done the dirty work himself. He was always the mastermind of the vengeance, but never the person who acted it out. She needed to buy time.

"I've tried to imagine how you could have put this scheme together against Johnny, but I don't think you did—"

Smith's eyes narrowed and he mopped his sweaty brow. "I didn't set your brother up. He's in this by his own doing."

"Not by his doing—by someone else's. Johnny was just in the wrong place—"

"Believe what you will." He cut her off and stared at his shaking hand. Then he began to speak as if she weren't in the room. "I didn't plan what happened to Johnny. The opportunity was there, ripe for the picking. It was too good to be true." He turned his eyes toward her. "I don't buy he's not guilty. He's just another Indian kid. Another gang member looking for trouble."

"Johnny has never belonged to a gang. He's not like that. Only in your mind is every Navajo boy a gangster—every Indian a drunk—"

"Every Indian a murderer?" he hissed.

"You've taken your prejudice and grief and constructed your own reality. You've built a world where you twist people's lives into what you want them to be. Then you convince yourself what you are doing is justice being served. As long as there is a Navajo, or a Begay in the picture, you twist and manipulate the truth into whatever you want it to be, into whatever serves your purpose. Into whatever feeds the sickness in your soul and keeps your vendetta alive. You are a sick human being, Mr. Smith."

"Shut up," Smith barked. "Shut up."

Mary glanced from Smith to Nate. She thought she saw a tiny movement. *Wake up. Please wake up.* Silently, she prayed.

CHAPTER TWENTY-SIX

The world was an abyss of blackness. Pictures floated in Nate's mind. The face of the old chief with black zigzag stripes painted on his face, and feathers intertwined in his long black hair, gradually became clear.

The chief's face was close to his own, close enough to smell the rancid breath of rotting teeth. The old man was angry, his eyes ablaze with rage. The late afternoon sun that came through the kiva opening above them cast an eerie light on the chief's face.

"You defied me. You were told," the older man seethed. "I commanded Mourning Dove to become the mate of Black Hawk. You deliberately defied my orders to bring back the bear and prepare the breast plate for your brother."

"Prepare another elaborate ornament for your favored son?" Lone Eagle spat. "This time an ornament to celebrate his union with the woman I love. You've gone too far." Lone Eagle strained against the straps of leather binding his wrists behind his back.

"Instead, you attempted to run away with Mourning Dove," Crow Feather raged. "To steal the mate of your brother and leave the safety I've offered you." His shadow loomed on the stone wall behind him, made larger than life by the fire in the center of the kiva.

"You cannot command the direction of people's lives. You are chief of the clan, not a god. Mourning Dove does not want to be the mate of my brother."

"That is not what he tells me." The old man's eyes glinted and his lips curled. "Black Hawk says she came to him willingly."

Lone Eagle's ears burned and his body tightened with rage. "Only because he tricked her. Tricked us both. She believed he was me. She would never have come to him of her own free will." Eagle glanced up the ladder behind him, wondering where Mourning Dove was now. The thought that Black Hawk had his hands on her again, made his gut wrench.

Crow Feather threw back his head and bellowed out an evil laugh. The wicked glint in his eye told Eagle he knew where Eagle's thoughts had turned. "Your brother is cunning like a fox."

"Cunning like a rattler who slithers on his belly and attacks the unsuspecting." Lone Eagle snorted. "Deceitful and treacherous like his father. He is undoubtedly your flesh and blood."

"Unlike you." The old man glared. "He brings me pride. You only bring me disappointment and pain."

"If evil brings you joy, Black Hawk is capable of bringing you much." Lone Eagle returned his father's hard stare. "On the other hand, I'd prefer not to be like either of you."

"There is too much of your mother's people in you. You don't appreciate that I have given you safety from the marauding bands that raid and kill nightly on the mesa. You don't appreciate that I have let you live. Even now." Crow Feather paced, circling the fire pit.

"Allowing me to live. That is what you believe, isn't it? You are god over us all. We live and die at your whim."

The old chief reared back his shoulders and raised his head high. "It's true. I keep you here, and because I do, Raven's clan has let you live. This isn't a favor?"

"Life without freedom, life controlled and manipulated by the desires of a tyrant, is hardly life. It

is merely existence." Lone Eagle's lip curled as he spoke.

"And that existence for you is over. If freedom is what you wish, perhaps I should free you from the confines of your physical body," Crow Feather sneered as he fingered the flint knife tucked in the waistband of his loin cloth. "Although, I doubt the gods of sipapu will offer you welcome. Your stupidity and your arrogance have cost you, dearly."

"You would prefer to kill me in this way, rather than stand and fight me like a man. I shouldn't be surprised. Just as Black Hawk preferred to take the woman he loved by trickery, you prefer to kill your son like a sacrificial rabbit without standing to face him. There is too much at risk in facing your own fears."

The old one's face darkened as he considered Lone Eagle's words. "You believe I fear you?" His tone was mocking. "I fear no one. Least of all, a coward who would choose to run away rather than do as he is told." Anger flared in his eyes.

Pulling the knife from its sheath, he slashed the leather bindings on Lone Eagle's wrists. Stepping to the side of the kiva, he threw his son a spear. Firelight lit the older man's glowing eyes and the fearsome anger that consumed his features. "Then stand and fight me, if you dare."

Lone Eagle thrust the spear into Crow Feather's face. In one quick motion, Crow Feather cut the rawhide strap holding the point to the tip of the spear. It fell to the stone floor with a loud thud. Ducking low, Lone Eagle retrieved the spearhead and faced his father. Grasping the sharp stone point in his hand, Lone Eagle circled his father, dodging first left then right. The sharp knife blade whistled as it cut through the air.

"It should not come to this," Lone Eagle said. "No man, no boy, should have to fight his father to the death. It goes against nature."

"*It was you who asked for the opportunity.*" Crow Feather sneered. "*Perhaps, you are not man enough after all to kill even to save your own life.*"

"*We will soon see.*"

"*Let's make this more interesting.*" The chief bubbled with confidence. "*If you win this fight, the woman is yours. If you lose, she dies along with you.*"

His heart leapt to his throat. "*Mourning Dove? I thought she was the prize my brother wanted for his mate.*"

"*Let your brother fight his own battle. If she becomes yours, he will then have to kill you to win her back.*"

"*You have a bloody idea of what is sport, Father. Don't we have enough enemies around us not to seek them within our own clan?*"

"*Death and blood shed seem inevitable for us all. It's just a matter of time.*"

"*But what of the protection of your beloved brother?*" Lone Eagle mocked.

"*Even Raven is mortal. I'm not fool enough to believe we would be spared without his kinship in place. My brother lives a dangerous life. Raiding camps and killing is not a skill that carries with it the promise of longevity.*"

"*Then it appears none of us have anything left to lose. You can't guarantee your own safety.*"

"*We are safe as long as Raven lives.*"

"*And then?*"

"*We become the sacrificial rabbit.*"

Lone Eagle curled forward, and grasping the sharp spear point in his hand, circled Crow Feather. The gleam in the chief's eyes was like a big cat awaiting the final leap upon its prey. His lip curled in a confident smirk. It was obvious he'd already declared this his victory.

The long flint knife whistled through the air, as Crow Feather teased Lone Eagle with the sharp blade.

Beads of sweat popped out on the old man's forehead and he sneered, sure of his abilities.

Only the sound of heavy breathing and yucca sandals scraping on hard packed clay, filled the room. Smoke wafted from the fire pit and rose to meet the opening in the kiva roof. Like two mountain sheep, ready to fight to the death for dominance, they circled.

Crow Feather lunged, slashing at Lone Eagle's belly. Pulling back swiftly, Lone Eagle avoided the blade that grazed his bare stomach. The scratch stung. Beads of blood rose to the surface creating a solid red line.

The second time the old man lunged it was with full force. This time the knife blade pointed straight at Lone Eagle's heart. Lone Eagle stepped from his path. Crow Feather missed his mark. He staggered forward and grabbed Lone Eagle above the hips, trying to overpower him. To Crow Feather's surprise, Lone Eagle kept his balance and withstood the force of the blow.

With the spearhead clenched in his hand, Lone Eagle raised it, ready to drive it into the old man's back. He slowed but couldn't halt it. His stomach sickened as it pierced the skin. He stopped. Though his hesitation meant certain death, he could not kill his own flesh and blood. The evil would not claim him, too.

Crow Feather struggled with the weight of his son, finally throwing Lone Eagle off his back. A look of surprise was in his eyes. "Why did you stop? I would have killed you," Crow Feather yelled.

"Because you are my father," Lone Eagle screamed, rushing the old man and knocking him to the ground.

Now the sharp spear point was at Crow Feather's throat. The slightest movement and it would be over. The chief trembled both with fear and anger. "Still, you do not kill me? You are not a warrior. You will not defend your own life."

Lone Eagle's hand shook. Old hatreds boiled in his gut. Crow Feather pushed hard against him. Suddenly, Lone Eagle heard a voice—the voice from the stone. He

*looked deep into his father's eyes as a strange feeling
came over him. A voice came from his throat that was
not his own. "No man should raise his hand against
his father, nor brother kill brother. It is not part of the
natural way of things. The knives and spears, we drive
into the bodies of our brothers, will one day turn on us.
The evil must die and the peaceful ones be resurrected
or all who live will perish. Unless we stop the hatred
and the bloodshed among ourselves, no clan will
survive. A threat far greater will soon come from across
the great waters. The evil that walks this mesa will join
forces with their great numbers, if you do not stop it.
The horror has only begun."*

*"Lone Eagle. What is this voice that comes from
you?" Crow Feather's voice quavered.*

*"It is the voice of the ancestry you have denied me."
The words poured from Lone Eagle. His eyes felt
strange as they riveted into the old man's stare. He
placed his hand on the Crow Feather's forehead. "You
will not hurt me or the one I love again." The words
seemed to take on a life of their own. Their strange
power had an obvious affect on the chief. Crow Feather
stiffened beneath him and twitched. His face contorted
in pain. Lone Eagle rose, but the old man did not move.
His glazed eyes stared upward at the ceiling.*

"Go quickly," the voice in his head told him.

*Lone Eagle didn't know if his father was dead or
alive. If he was dead, it was at the hands of the
ancients. The action of some power Lone Eagle could
not control. His only thought was to climb from the
kiva.*

*"Now you will keep your promise," Lone Eagle
declared. "Mourning Dove and I are free."*

Mary watched Smith as he nervously fingered the
gun and ran his thumb across the hammer. His

breathing grew heavier. He looked toward Nate and wet his lips. He was debating on how to end this. His earlier threat weighed on her. He could indeed do what he said—kill them both and lie, saying they had come here to accost him. The evidence was in Nate's folder—and Smith knew it. Smith's eyes darted from Nate to the gun, then to her. An intense feeling of discomfort built in her mid-section.

Icy fingers of fear threatened to run the length of Mary's spine, wrestling with fifteen years of festering anger boiling from her core. She refused to succumb to her fear. It was essential she keep her wits sharp.

Smith considered his options. He was up against it. How could he let them walk out of here? Now that it had gone this far? He glanced at the gun in his hand. One thing was for certain, if he pulled the trigger, he'd be done with Mary Begay once and for all. He wasn't sure how it had gotten this crazy, how he'd come to this point, but Mary was right, he couldn't go on.

"I'll never forgive you for what you did to Ethan," he growled. "Never." He pushed the gun in her face.

The image of the old chief's face, contorted with pain, began to fade. Crow Feather's eyes were ablaze with hatred as he watched Lone Eagle climb the kiva ladder to freedom.

Crow Feather's words came through the haze. "I will follow you, and destroy you, no matter what it takes."

Lone Eagle glanced back one last time. The old man reached toward him and called after him. "My soul will not rest until it is so." The hatred in his words was fierce. This power he possessed had only brought more hatred. And Crow Feather was alive.

Voices and images swam in a haze in Nate's head, a blur of surreal pictures he struggled to comprehend. Pain throbbed in the back of his head as he struggled through a heavy fog. As the fog lifted, a storm of white whirled. At first he thought it was snow, then he realized they were feathers. Snow white feathers. He began to run. He had to get back. Had to get to Mary—

Fury boiled in Mary. "I've told you over and over it was an accident. If I could have prevented it from happening, I would have." The gun bobbed dangerously close to her face. Fear chilled her blood, but she fought it back.

"You don't have any idea what you put me through," Smith seethed.

"And you have no idea who your son really was."

"Ethan was my flesh and blood. You can't tell me anything I don't know about him."

She gritted her teeth. "Don't bet on it."

"Ethan was everything to me, my hopes, my dreams, my future. Because of you, I'll die a lonely old man with no one to carry on my name." He grabbed her arm and jerked her to him.

Her lower lip trembled as she looked down the barrel of the gun. "If you only knew what you're saying—"

"Because of you, I have nothing left. Other men my age spend their weekends with family, with their children and grandchildren. Because of you, I have neither," he hissed.

That was the final straw. "How dare you," she spat. "How dare you say such a thing to me." Her face flushed as emotion flooded her. She glanced at the gun. Suddenly, it didn't matter. *He doesn't know. He truly doesn't know.* If he was going to shoot her, she'd be damned if she'd die without revealing the truth.

"You don't know what he was capable of. You're ignorant. Ignorant of the truth. You've wasted years of your life hating me, conjuring up ways to get revenge. And your reason was because you have no grandchildren?"

She could barely speak the words. "You don't even know you're the cause of your own misery. Your hatred toward me, your expectations of who and what Ethan should have been, drove him to do the most horrible and ironic thing imaginable." Tears welled in her eyes. "You had a grandchild, Mr. Smith. A grandchild your son and a back street abortionist stole from my womb while I was drugged out of my mind. Drugged into a helpless state by Ethan and his friend. It was your son who took the life of the only grandchild you ever had."

Smith's face contorted. "You lie. Ethan would never do such a thing." Smith's hand shook uncontrollably. His voice was low.

"He did it for one reason." Her mouth curled in disgust. "Out of fear his father would find out he was still seeing me." Her body vibrated with anger. "You manipulative son of a bitch. All the years you blamed me. And all the years I blamed Ethan, and now I realize I was wrong. It was you who did this. You changed all of our lives."

Smith's face twisted into a grimace. "It can't be true," he whispered. "It can't be."

"Do you truly think I would make up such a story?" Mary asked. "Do you really believe something so heinous was a spur-of- the-moment fabrication?"

"You'd say anything to hurt me. My Ethan never did any of what you're saying." He pushed the gun closer to her face. "I should kill you for concocting such lies."

Mary's lips tightened and she glared into Smith's face and down the barrel of the pistol. "If you think I'm lying, go ahead and pull that trigger. You can kill me, Mr. Smith, but you can't change the truth. And I'm not going to my grave without you knowing how many lives you've destroyed with the poison in your soul, and that includes your own and everyone you've ever loved. If you can live with everything you've done and kill us both in cold blood, and justify it as grief, then you will one day join your son in hell."

He stared into her face, and his mouth quivered. His grip on her loosened as his eyes gradually reflected the horror of realization. The gun dropped to his side. "No," he said, softly. "I can't kill you." He raised the gun and looked at it as it lay in his hand. "I never knew," he whispered. "I never knew there was a child—"

A strange calm came over him. His eyes grew dark. In slow motion, his trembling hand brought the revolver to his temple. Strange nearly inaudible words began to roll from his lips.

Nate opened his eyes. In a semi-conscious state he'd heard voices. Mary's voice. Mary's words. He rubbed his head. The words of the old chief and Smith melted together in his brain. "But my soul will not rest until I destroy you, no matter what it takes."

A new realization sunk in. The pain in the back of his head made him flinch. His eyelids fluttered. Hazy images cleared. *The table. Smith's voice.* He tried to get his bearings. Adrenaline kicked in. He attempted to get to his feet. His body refused to move. He lifted his head.

Mary stood next to Smith. Their eyes locked in a standoff. Nate could only imagine what was going through her mind. He'd heard her painful story. His mind flashed on Mary touching the tiny cross in the churchyard in Chimayo. Now, he understood.

Smith had the gun pressed to his own head. If Smith pulled the trigger, she would be free of him at last. Nate couldn't blame her for the hatred in her heart. He bit his lip and strained to sit up. He had to get to them.

Smith pulled back the hammer on the handgun.

"No," Mary exclaimed loudly. In one swift move, she grabbed Smith's arm and pulled the gun away from his head. "This solves nothing."

"Leave me alone. My life is over." Smith struggled to remove her from his arm.

"You're a sick man. Sick in your mind. You need help, not this," she screamed at him.

"Stop," he cried. "Let go." The gun waved erratically. Smith wrestled with Mary. Smith held back the hammer. His finger struggled for the trigger.

The final rush of fear for Mary's life shot through Nate's veins and gave him strength. Staggering, he made his way to where the two struggled. Grabbing the revolver and forcing the barrel skyward, Nate stepped between them.

Mary whispered, "Nate. Thank God."

With his strength limited, Nate grappled with Smith. Mary ducked under his arm and tackled Smith, throwing him off balance and back onto the desk. Nate took advantage of the moment, using his weight to pin Smith down.

"Drop the gun," Nate yelled.

Smith's body went rigid.

"Let it go." Nate pushed harder and met the dark, disturbed eyes. They flared with hate. A strange feeling of recognition came over Nate.

Smith seemed to look into Nate's soul for a fleeting moment. A look of stunned amazement washed across his face. "You were once my son," he whispered. "That's where I knew you—"

An image flashed in Nate's mind, the face of a hateful old chief. "And your soul did not rest—" Nate breathed as the words connected in his mind.

Mary stood looking at the two of them. Silence filled the room. The gun dropped to the floor with a thud.

A voice cut through the quiet. It came from the outer office. "Smith. Smith. You in there?" Gonzales burst through the door, as his words tumbled out. "The girl woke up. Stellar's awake—" He stopped short at the sight of the three of them huddled over the desk. "What the hell's going on?"

Mary met Nate's eyes as she reacted to Gonzales announcement with a short gasp and whispered, "Thank God. She's going to be okay."

Smith pulled himself upright, as if it took every ounce of strength. "It's all right." He ran his shaky hand across his face. "It's over. It's all over—" His shadowed eyes narrowed and he confronted Gonzales.

A moment later, Smith shot Nate a troubled and disbelieving look. He slumped over on the desk and put his face in his hands. "I'm not sure what just happened. But I've lived this life of hatred before—" Streams of water ran from beneath his thick glasses. He wiped at them with his hand and laid the glasses on the desk. "I have to get help. I can't live with this pain anymore."

Gonzales stood frozen in disbelief. It was obvious he didn't know if he should run, or pretend he didn't know what Smith was talking about.

Mary looked at Nate then spoke for them both. "We'll see you get the help you need."

"At least we all came through it alive." A sob caught in Smith's voice. He gave Mary a sincere look and spoke in a slow strained voice. "I don't know why you stopped me, but I'd be dead if you hadn't."

For the first time, Nate saw compassion in Mary's eyes as she looked at Smith.

Nate touched the back of his head and winced, then reached for the phone and dialed 911. He hoped to God there was somebody in this town that wasn't entangled in Smith's web of deceit.

Two hours later, Mary stood next to Nate at the foot of Stellar's bed. Nate was obviously deeply moved. She'd seen him brush the moisture from his eyes when they'd entered the room and he first saw Stellar. Stellar was sleeping, no longer in a coma, and resting peacefully. The tubes were gone from her throat and the machines were silent. The nurse told them she had eaten her first meal since regaining consciousness.

"We've witnessed a miracle," Mary whispered. "The healing soil brought her out of this."

"Maybe more than one miracle." Nate whispered. He turned toward Mary and planted a kiss on her forehead. "I can't believe the courage you had to stand up to Smith and tell him to pull the trigger. Thank God you're safe. I've never met a woman quite like you."

Mary snuggled into his arms for a moment. "I don't know what came over me. I knew I couldn't let him kill you over the hatred that he had for me. Too much has happened, too many innocent people have already been hurt by his quest for revenge. I only knew that whatever happened today, this had to end."

"Well, it isn't quite over but at least Smith will finally get some help and be out of your life. And, hopefully, you can move on."

Mary smiled. "I'm ready to leave the past behind. Maybe this time around, I can share my love with someone who deserves it."

"That will be one lucky guy, when you find him."

She looked up at him coyly. "Who knows, maybe I already have."

Nate looked down at her and crushed her to his chest. The quills of the feathers in his pocket pressed into him as he did.

He reached into his shirt and pulled them out. "You know," he said. "I think these have finally begun to make some sense to me. Thanks to my encounter with Smith."

Mary stepped back and looked at the bag in his hand. "What was all that conversation between you and Smith about anyway? I think I followed some of it."

"Mary, I don't really know where to start, but if you're willing to listen, I think I can explain some of it now. I'll warn you, it's kind of out there."

Mary leaned closer. "I want to know what you think."

Nate removed the white feather and stroked it with his finger. "I'm beginning to believe that each one of these feathers represents someone in my visions. Someone from the past."

Mary nodded. "You've said the prayer and asked for answers. It seems since you placed them next to your heart several answers have come to you."

Nate nodded and pulled out the other feathers. "This may sound completely crazy, but what if each of these represented a soul that has come here from the past?" He wet his lips and studied her face for a response.

She raised an eyebrow, but seemed intent on what he was saying. "Go on. I'm listening."

"In my visions, I've seen faces from the past. Let's pretend these symbolize those souls, and that they came to me to bring some sort of message. You told me the feathers symbolize spirits of ancestry trying to reach us." He went on as she watched and listened carefully. He pulled a black feather from the bag. "One thing came through loud and clear in my visions. Crow Feather was the name of the chief who was my father in the past. I remember his name distinctly. What if this feather symbolizes him?"

Mary was filled with an overwhelming epiphany. She remembered Smith's words to Nate during the struggle. They suddenly made sense.

Nate continued to remove the feathers. "I think the others represent something. Like this soft gray dove feather. It could be you. Beautiful then, beautiful now." He shot her a gentle smile. "This blackish brown feather represents someone, too. The ranger said it came from a hawk."

Mary listened intently. *Black Hawk. Ethan.* The thought sprung to her mind instantaneously. In the past he'd tried to steal her love. In this life, he'd stolen her child. What if Nate's theory was right?

She cleared her throat. "There are those who doubt the power of such things. But some of us have seen it first hand. I, too, had a vision by the fire in Grandpa's hogan. I believe we shared that vision."

"I had a feeling we did."

"Then perhaps we also both have a feeling about who that feather represents." She fought back the emotion that choked at her voice. "Nate, you must learn to trust these feelings. In matters of the spirit, they sometimes prove more sound than our minds."

Nate sighed and nodded. "The last two have me stumped. They aren't part of my visions. But I saw this magpie feather in the premonition that came to me about Stellar's attack. And it came to me in a strange way. I think it means something significant." He examined the white one once again. "This is my mystery feather. The one Stellar somehow sent to me from wherever she was when she was in the coma. I don't know how she did it, but I knew the second it touched my hand, that all these feathers had come to me through some strange spiritual force. And I knew somehow Stellar and the boy who did this to her, fit into some ancient mystery."

"Don't forget the feather like that in the police report describing Star's killer," Mary whispered. "To me it seems like the feathers are part of some ancient message that you're picking up on. And I believe you may find the answers to the two mystery feathers when we find the real killer."

Nate shrugged and continued. "I have moments when I wonder if I've gone insane, then I look at you and I know it's more than some crazy dream. I am getting these messages, but I don't know what to do with them. Is my job right now just to listen?"

"I think it goes way beyond that," Mary said. "What about the circle of feathers on the base of the kachina in your office? Consider how closely they match some of these feathers. I wouldn't discount the meaning of that. Isn't the kachina some family heirloom?"

Nate's eyes looked deeply into hers. "I've been thinking about that and your Grandpa's talk about a circle of souls. And an eerie reference in a letter from my own grandfather—"

"Wow, that's a lot to get my head around." Mary sighed. "I'm having enough trouble dealing with the real world. There are so many things still unresolved. Johnny's trial has been postponed because of the new evidence, but what do we do from here?"

Nate shook his head. "We have to find the owner of this." He held up the magpie feather. "You're right. It damn sure isn't over."

Mary took a deep breath. "I know. Do you think Stellar can help us?"

"I sure hope so," Nate said.

At that moment, Stellar made a small sound, and their eyes turned in her direction. A smile came to her pale lips and she raised her hand, pointing in Nate's direction. "I know you," she said softly. "I saw you in my dreams. You came to help me. And there were all of those feathers."

Nate's heart fell to the pit of his stomach. "Welcome back, darlin'." He placed his hand on her blanket-covered foot and shot a glance at Mary. "This just keeps getting stranger."

Stellar nodded in his direction and closed her eyes again.

"I would like to take Stellar to Chimayo when she's ready to leave the hospital." Mary whispered. "It'll take time for her to get her strength back."

"Do you think her mother will let you?"

"I think her mother would be grateful."

Nate scratched the back of his head. "Well, with Stellar in need of special care and Johnny getting out of jail, maybe you could use some help out at your house."

Mary shot him a glance from the corner of her eye. "Only problem is, with all these people living there, I don't have a spare bed for you, Mr. Nakai."

"Well, I guess I'll have to share yours." He kissed her on the nose and pulled her to him.

Her love and warmth helped temper the chill that ran through his bones. There were many challenges ahead of them, and a lot of mysterious secrets and unanswered questions between here and whatever was to be their destiny.

The End

Please turn the page for a preview of
SPIRIT WHISPERS

PROLOGUE

800 years ago

"The wind smells of death today." The old man wrinkled his nose and tipped back his head, squinting as his keen eyes followed the canyon rim. "A stranger watches us." The words of her grandfather sent a stab of fear through Kaya's heart.

"You are old and imagine things." Her grandmother scolded and stirred the pot of corn gruel with a flourish.

"Heed my words, old woman. Watch yourself today. There are strangers near the canyon."

"No dog barks. No warrior on watch sees what you see. Your senses fail you." She hurried around her cooking pot and scooped mush into bowls.

Kaya sat quietly, listening, swallowing her fear ahead of her breakfast. Shooting a wary glance to the towering canyon walls, at her grandmother's nod, Kaya took pottery bowls and began to pass them, first to her grandfather then to her two older brothers.

Kaya looked down as she took another bowl from the weathered hands. Pretend as she might, the old woman hadn't taken her husband's warnings lightly either. Distracted by the conversation, her grandmother had stepped back from the coals of the fire with tiny wisps of smoke coming from her dry yucca sandal. As they exchanged a glance and the last of the breakfast bowls, Kaya saw the tired look in the old one's eyes.

Kaya was young, just seventeen but she, too, felt the exhaustion of constant fear and worry. Even her two broad-shouldered brothers across the fire ate in silence. They knew that it was only a matter of time before their grandfather's words became their own self-fulfilling prophecy.

Few villages remained, and in the end, no village would be spared. The truth was cold and brutal, but all knew it was their inevitable destiny.

Raven squatted on the canyon rim, watching the waking village below. The eyes of six warriors peered back at him from beneath full war paint, as they quietly dispersed themselves along the rocky ledge. He shook his head and raised his hand. Now was not the time to attack.

They would wait. If what he was searching for were here, he would know soon enough. If not, all would follow him, or be destroyed. Rolling back on his heels, he made himself more comfortable. A ripple of movement across the canyon rim told him the others followed suit.

The day was just beginning. The wait could be long. Timing was of the utmost importance when less than twenty warriors must do the work of a hundred.

As the moment of quiet overtook him, his thoughts wandered through the past months and their bloody reign of terror. The sickened feeling was fleeting. Like the emotions stirred by the smell of death and the sight of human blood on his hands, the remorse was short-lived. The more he killed, the more jaded he became to the horror and guilt that tried to remind him of who he used to be.

CHAPTER ONE

Present day

Archaeologist Alex Nakai stepped from his SUV and let his large Golden Retriever out of the backseat. Yellow Dog bounded from the vehicle, brushed against Alex in an affectionate gesture, and with his nose to the ground was off to explore. Opening the tailgate, Alex assembled his gear then tightened the straps of the heavy pack around his upper body and waist.

He took a deep breath of fresh air and surveyed the southwest Colorado landscape with its unique mixture of mesas and high desert that gave way to lofty peaks on the horizon. He winced as his thoughts pushed aside the peace of the moment and crushed it with the nagging unsettled feeling in his heart.

Things had happened so quickly in the past weeks, maybe too many things for him to get his head around. Just hours ago he'd been contemplating the prospect of starting a new life with the woman of his dreams, Jessica Sinclair, when a phone call had forced him to change direction. He just hoped Jessica could understand that this had nothing to do with her. The decision had been more about a voice from within, than the one on the telephone. And he was already feeling bad about dragging her along with him on this dig. He had to go, but the timing sucked.

He took a deep breath as he gave a final jerk to the straps. Up until now he thought people who heard voices in their heads were disturbed. Now the voices were inside his head and he didn't know how to deal with them. He only wished he were more confident, they weren't leading him astray. No wonder the lump in his stomach seemed to outweigh the load on his back.

The call had come from the University of New Mexico. They needed an expert in identifying the forensic evidence of cannibalism—cannibalism that had happened more than eight hundred years ago. True, his past work for the University had taken him places in South America and Mexico giving him the experience needed here. But what had been ritualistic in some cultures didn't fit with what he knew or felt in his heart about the Pueblo people, his own newly found ancestry.

Cannibalism. He'd encountered it before, but this time the word sent a chill down his spine. He couldn't explain it so he tried to ignore it. It was essential he get that feeling under control if he was to make an unbiased assessment. There was an eerie feeling to this place and he couldn't explain it.

He rummaged through the boxes in the back of the SUV searching for his flashlight and some archaeological journals that contained more information on the subject.

He sighed when the second box he opened contained the recent gift from his grandfather, and what had now become his questionable companion on this trip. He repeated the inscription carved into the family heirloom aloud. "Spirit Dancer—Chasing Star. What the hell does that mean anyway?"

He felt compelled to pull away the wrappings and hold the kachina in his hands one more time. As he did, an odd tingling sped through him. Something about the strange wooden figure sent shivers through his body. He closed his eyes and, just as it had the first time he held the statue, a blazing blue star flashed through his mind. But this time, an odd thing followed. The flash of the star illuminated the face of an old man, his wispy white hair blowing on an ethereal breeze. It was there for a second and then gone.

An eerie voice echoed in his ears. "The blood of ancient Pueblos flows in your veins. It is your destiny to free us from centuries of lies." Alex dropped the kachina onto the tailgate and stepped back. He swallowed hard as an uneasy feeling settled in his middle.

He placed the kachina back in its wrappings, looking into its face as he did and speaking directly to it. "Why me, huh? And why now?" He shook his head and glared at the faceless figure. Although he knew he'd get no answer, somehow he felt better having a place to lay the blame. One thing was for certain, since the kachina's arrival, things could go from business as usual to down right weird faster than the streak of Haley's comet. And they left him damn near as spell bound. He rolled his eyes, wondering how he could explain this one to Jessica, or should he even try?

He thought of his last email from his brother Nate. Nate was experiencing a rash of unexplainable things in his new life in Santa Fe, too. But Nate dealt with criminals and such. Bizarre was probably a daily word in Nate's vocabulary. Not so much for Alex, at least until not lately. And he had a sinking feeling things could get a lot more bizarre.

He shouldered his pack and called to Yellow Dog, grateful that he had a good long hike ahead of him to get his head screwed back on right. Jessica would be along shortly and he'd have some time to think things through.

ABOUT THE AUTHOR

Sharon Silva grew up in the mountains of Colorado and her heart does not journey far from there still. Her love for the outdoors and a "simpler way of life," are reflected in her writings. Her elementary school years were spent attending a one-room schoolhouse in a small mountain community. It was in those early years that Sharon fell in love with books and the magical world of story. She began writing stories and poems of her own at the age of nine.

Sharon's favorite stories then and now have always been romantic adventures that contain paranormal elements. Her fascination with ancient spiritual places and the possibilities of mystical realms intrigue her, fuel her imagination, and inspire her stories.

The blending of Native American cultures in her own bloodlines, having three great-grandmothers descended from three different tribes, has led Sharon on a journey of research, respect and strong spiritual connection to the world and people who existed long before America was "discovered" by explorers from across the ocean. That connection was the foundation for The Crystal Legacy series.

Sharon is an awarding-winning author of several romantic suspense novels and countless poems. She lives in Colorado with her own real life hero, her husband of more than thirty years. When she isn't writing or researching a new adventure, you'll find her drag racing with her husband, spending time with family or working in her garden.

Dear Readers,

Thank you so much for reading Eagle Dancer. I hope you enjoyed the adventure. I love feedback and I love to hear from readers. Authors love and need reader reviews to keep providing the very best books and achieve success. Please take time to stop over at Amazon and review this book. You, the reader, are the reason we authors spend hours honing the stories of our hearts into books for you to enjoy. For us, the reader is what it's all about so we want to connect with you.

Please visit my website at www.sharonsilva.com for some interesting tidbits about the series and my other works and to sign up for my newsletter. New releases will be announced there when they become available. Also keep up to date and get to know the author by connecting with me on any of the following:

Facebook: www.facebook.com/sharonsilva

Twitter: sharonsilva@sharonsilva

Spirit Dancer, the first book of The Crystal Legacy Series is now available for purchase at www.Amazon.com or at www.sharonsilva.com. Spirit Whispers, the third book of the series, will be available soon at these same sites. A sample chapter has been included for your enjoyment.

Thank you! I'll see you again soon in the pages of a new adventure.

www.ingramcontent.com/pod-product-compliance
Lightning Source LLC
Chambersburg PA
CBHW060345260626
47160CB00006B/2211